FOLLOW MY LEADER:

OR,

LIONEL WILFUL'S SCHOOLDAYS.

WITH NUMEROUS ILLUSTRATIONS

By "PHIZ,"

(HABLOT K. BROWNE.)

VOL. III.

Publishing Office:

HOGARTH HOUSE, 32, BOUVERIE STREET,

LONDON, E.C.

ILLUSTRATIONS.

VOL. I.

PART III.

CHAPTER I.

AFTER TWO YEARS.

THERE is a certain period in the existence of youth, during which an interval of two years exhibits a more marked change in physical development than a dozen at any previous or sequent epoch.

We allude, of course, to the time which intervenes between the years of fifteen or sixteen, and seventeen or eighteen. It is then that the boy attains manly stature with a startling and almost unpleasant rapidity, inasmuch as he finds that his legs and arms project much farther beyond the limits of his jackets and trousers than is consistent with a respectability of appearance—it is then that the incipient down upon his cheeks and upper lip darkens, and gives him a sort of toffee-eating appearance—and it is then that his voice "breaks," and causes him to speak in a pleasing mixture, compounded of a squeak and a growl. Two years have passed since the events recorded in the concluding chapter of the second part of this faithful history—let us see how our principal characters have been affected by the lapse of time.

In that somewhat dingy but highly aristocratic thoroughfare known as Bury-street, St. James's, and in the drawing-room of one of the houses thereof our old friend, Sam Scarecrow, was busily engaged in giving the finishing touches to the breakfast service already arranged on the table.

Time had effected but very little change in the long youth's personal appearance. He was a little longer perhaps, and even thinner, and the knobby portions of his frame had attained a further development, but his countenance had the same angular carved-out-of-wood appearance, and his squint was still as miraculously ugly as ever, and on his upper lip there was developed a reddish smear, which an ordinary observer would have attributed to the unremitting consumption of damp ginger-bread, but which Sam himself declared to be a moustache, and cherished accordingly.

He was surveying the result of his morning's work with an air of conscious pride, when the door was opened a little way, and a light, sandy-coloured head of hair made its appearance, attached to a pale thin face, the principal feature of which was a nose, resembling the blade of a carving-knife in shape, and apparently composed of putty.

The head of hair and the face belonged to Mr. Jarvie Johnson, valet to an Italian count, who occupied the second floor; and he, on the strength of his master's title, assumed a superiority over Sam, which the long youth very much resented.

"Party goin' on aperiently?" said Mr. Johnson, after an inquisitive look at the table, and the extra number of plates, cups, saucers, etcetera, which garnished the table.

"Hallo! you there again?" growled Sam.

"Yes, it's me," replied the inquisitive Mr. Johnson, "who's a comin' this morning?"

"Don't fret yourself," retorted Sam; "nayther you nor your guvnor's invited, so he can eat his frogs in his own two pair back, and you can pick the bones arterwards, if there's any left."

"Come now, don't cut up rusty, my good feller," said Mr. Johnson; "experience is everything, and I'm willing to do you a good turn if I can. That table ain't half laid as it ought to be."

"Wot's the matter with it?" said Sam, a little suspiciously; but he was very anxious to have everything in first-rate order, and he was aware that the count's valet had far more knowledge of the subject than himself.

"Everything," replied Mr. Johnson, rapidly changing the position of the articles upon the table, shifting the knives and forks, turning the cups upside down, and performing some kind of legerdemain with the cruet-stands, but all so swiftly and dexterously that Sam's squint followed his motions in vain.

"That don't look right," said Sam, doubtfully, as he saw the well-arranged table reduced to a jumbled chaos of china, glass, and cutlery.

"That's because you ain't used to the ways o' these young swells," replied Mr. Johnson. "Bless you, they'd scorn to have anythink like common people. You've got some of the haristokracy comin', ain't you?"

"I believe you," said Sam. "There's young Lord Vansittart, who'll be a hearl afore long, and Mister Drummond, who's studyin' for the harmy, and Mister Priggenham, the bishop's son, and a lot more, all gents o' the fust horder."

"It's lucky I came in then," continued Mr. Johnson, "or there'd have been a nice row. Now, I don't see none o' the sauces which these young swells likes. "Where's your regular ' Pick-me-up Relish,' and your ' Knock-me-down Sauce?'"

"Never heerd on 'em," said Sam, blushing a little at having thus to confess his ignorance of the existence of those delicacies.

"I thought not, but no young swell as knows what life is never thinks of taking his breakfast without 'em. Hullo! is that your guvnor's bell?"

"Yes."

"All right, you cut away and answer it, and while you're gone I'll put the right sauces in the cruets, out of the count's own bottles."

"Thankee," said Sam, "you ain't a bad feller arter all, and I'll stand a drop o' summat good arter breakfast."

And away the long youth hurried, while Mr. Johnson, with a curious grin upon his countenance, took the cruet-stand, and in a few minutes came back, just as Sam returned from his young master's dressing-room.

"Here you are, Mister Samuel," said Johnson. "This here's the ' Knock-me-down,' that's the ' Pick-me-up,' and this is some o' the new kind of ' Caper Sauce.'"

"Thankee," said Sam, much gratified, "I'll remember you for this."

"I think you will," muttered Mr. Johnson with a grin, as he left the room.

A moment after a loud rat-tat-tat summoned Sam to the street door, and there stood Charlie Drummond, looking rather pale, and a little heavy about the eyes, and with him were our other friends, young Vansittart, Thomas-ap-Pryce, and a new acquaintance, Heavitop Priggenham.

"Ah! Sam," said Charlie, heartily, "there you are then, as good-looking as ever. Is Mr. Lionel in?"

"Which he are, sir," replied Sam, literally grinning all over, from the topmost hair of his head, to the very toes of his boots, "and glad I am that you've come, for every blessed minit for the last two hours he've been ringing his bell to know if that warn't you a comin' up the street?"

Our hero heard the knock, and came out ready to receive his old chums almost as soon as Sam had opened the door, and then what a hearty greeting passed between the friends!

"Come in, Charlie. In with you, Van. I am glad to see you. I thought you were never coming. How are you, Priggenham? You look as happy as ever. Come along to my snuggery; and you, Sam, have breakfast on the table in five seconds, or I'll murder you."

And so, talking all together, laughing from sheer lightness and gaiety of heart, and shaking hands over and over again, Lionel hustled his chums into what he called his "snuggery," a small room, littered in almost every available inch of space with books, writing materials, papers, journals, sticks, canes, riding whips, fencing foils, boxing gloves, pipes, cigar boxes, photograph albums, and the thousand and one odds and ends with which a young bachelor, with plenty of time and money, thinks it necessary to surround himself.

"What a snug little den you have here, Li!" said Vansittart, as he looked vainly round for some place in which to deposit his hat. "Everything out of its place, and no room for anything. That's what I call comfort."

"No chaff now, Van," laughed our hero, "or I'll pay you back in your own coin when I come to see you. Only fancy, it's two years since we last met; but you don't seem to have altered a bit—neither do you, Charlie."

"I can't say the same of you then, Li, for you have been getting up the scaffolding for an elegant pair of whiskers."

"His chin new reaped shined like a stubble-field at harvest home," said Charlie, quoting from Hotspur's speech.

"Dry up, you fellows," replied Lionel, trying to repress a strong tendency to blush—a juvenile habit which he had not been able to rid himself of entirely. "Ah, here's Sam. Breakfast ready?"

"All ready, Master Lionel," replied that youth, squinting horribly with delight at seeing his young master's chums once again, and with satisfaction at the thought of the surprise he had prepared for them in the new-fashioned arrangement of the breakfast-table.

Vansittart was the first to enter, and as he looked at the table his countenance certainly did assume an expression of surprise, but there was none of the rapture that Sam expected to see.

"Why, old fellow," he said, "you've never had breakfast thus?"

"Had?"—began Lionel. Then he caught sight of the table, and frowned angrily.

"Why, what on earth, Sam?——"

Sam came up smiling, but when he saw the expression on his young master's face he almost dropped the dish of whiting he was carrying.

"What the devil's the meaning of this?" continued Lionel.

We are sorry to record that so strong an expression escaped our hero's lips, but it was his first attempt at entertaining his friends, and here at the very outset it was spoiled.

"I ask you," repeated Lionel, "what you mean by this? You say the breakfast is ready, and here are the cups in a pile in the middle of the table, the plates on the chairs, the cream jug in the sugar basin, the rolls on the floor, the preserves on the mantel-piece, the hot water in my hat-box, and the ham under the table, where that confounded cat has been licking it."

Sam tried hard to assume an off-hand tone when he replied to Lionel, but his voice faltered a little as he said—

"It's a kind of a sort of a new-fashioned way of laying of a breakfast."

"Then look here, Sam," continued our hero, who was quite at a loss to know the cause of his follower's strange behaviour, and was just then far too angry to inquire; "if you favour me with any more of this kind of a sort of a new-fashioned way of spoiling my breakfast, I'll oblige you with one of the regular old-fashioned kicks, which will make

it especially inconvenient for you to sit down for a month."

Sam answered not a word. He saw that Mr. Jarvie Johnson had made a fool of him, but he was too much ashamed to confess that he had allowed any one to "come over" him.

In ten minutes the breakfast was re-arranged in the "old-fashioned" way, and our hero and his chums seated, and ready, with the keen appetites of youth, to do justice to the meal.

By that time Lionel's anger had quite subsided. It was quite a novelty, indeed, for him to be out of temper with Sam, and all was going on well until, in an unlucky moment, Heavitop Priggenham asked for some sauce, and Sam, thinking that, on this point at least, he was safe, handed that gloomy young gentleman the bottle containing the celebrated "Knock-me-down Sauce."

The unsuspicious Priggenham poured some on his cutlet, then he put a bit of the cutlet in his mouth, then he put his knife and fork down in a hurry, covered his mouth with his hands, turned scarlet in the face, and then, before any one had time to inquire what was the matter, became dreadfully ill in the fireplace.

"What on earth is the matter?" exclaimed Lionel. "Did the cutlet disagree with you?"

"U-u-ugh! Oh, my," was all the reply that Priggenham could make verbally, but he pointed to the sauce bottle, and made a face so expressive of disgust and misery that a pantomime clown would have envied the possessor of it.

Lionel took up the bottle, smelt it, and looked at Sam in a very suspicious and significant manner.

"What's this, Sam?"

"Some o' the—the celebrated Knock-me-down Sauce, Master Lionel," replied Sam, who saw only too plainly that something else had gone wrong."

"Have you got any more of the same kind?" said our hero, very quietly, but there was a look about his eyes which made the lanky youth feel exceedingly uncomfortable.

"There—there's the Pick-me-up and the new kind o' Caper Sauce," said Sam, indicating the bottles which contained those delectable mixtures furnished by Mr. Johnson.

Lionel took out the stoppers, and had one sniff at the contents. That was quite sufficient. The next moment bottles and all were flung at the head of Sam as he dodged through the door, and bolted down the passage.

"I might ha' knowed it," muttered Sam, between his clenched teeth, as he wiped off the liberal supply of Pick-me-up and Caper Sauce which Lionel had bestowed upon him. "I orter ha' knowed that that Johnson chap was sellin' me. Dash him! Blow him! Jigger him! I'll have his life with the blackin' brush!"

And uttering that bloodthirsty threat Sam bounced down the kitchen stairs, and into the little cellar-like apartment, which was devoted to the purpose of boot-cleaning.

But Mr. Johnson was not there. He was still in attendance upon his master, the count, and the long youth had just made up his mind to seek him out wherever he might be, when the gentle tread of the perfidious valet was heard coming down the stairs.

"He cometh," murmured Sam. "Now for wengeance!"

And hastily but noiselessly he crouched down behind the long board, on which the boot-polishing process was performed.

Mr. Johnson had several pairs of very muddy boots in his hands, and, as ill-luck would have it, he pitched them over the board, and on top of Sam, who lay crouching like a tiger in his lair.

Sam uttered a howl, and sprang up, looking very much like a magnified edition of one of those toys which are at once the delight and terror of the infant mind—we mean a Jack-in-the-box.

Mr. Johnson started too, and turned a little paler; but Sam was already between him and the door.

"Why, Mr. Samuel," he said, "is that you? This is a hunexpected pleasure. You don't in a general way clean your guvnor's boots so airly."

"No, I don't," replied Sam, with a vengeful glance. "I've come to polish you off by way of a change."

"No larks now, Mister Samuel," said the perfidious valet, getting alarmed, for the aspect of Sam was truly terrifying.

"Sich is not my intentions," replied the lanky youth, who was now in the most deliberate manner taking off his coat, and rolling up his shirt sleeves.

Mr. Jarvie Johnson could not mistake the ominous character of these preparations, and he looked round him with a wild and frenzied eye for the means of escape.

But there were none. On his right was the boot-cleaning board, on his left the brick wall, behind him a ditto, with an advanced fortification of blacking bottles, and in front the bony Samuel, with wrath and a stern determination to fight depicted in every lineament of his expressive countenance.

The valet was a man grown, much older than the lanky youth, and presumably stronger, but he was an arrant coward, and was now in as great a funk as if Goliath of Gath had come to tackle him.

"Mr. Samuel," he said, in a very shaky voice, "my affection for you have been the sort o' thing a brother feels for his—for his uncle. You've no idea how fond I am of you."

"I know it," replied Sam. "You 'bliged me with a proof of your infection just now, and I've come to say how wery thankful I am for them there sauces. What was the names on 'em?"

"Now you mention it," said Mr. Johnson, eagerly, "I think as I made a little mistake, Mister Samuel, and give you the sauce out o' the wrong bottle. Your guv'nor ain't at breakfast yet, is he?"

"He are," replied Samuel, with a grim smile; "and what's more one of the gents have tasted that there sauce, 'the Knock-me-down,' and I've come to return it, as he find it don't agree with him."

And Sam, taking careful aim, smote Mr. Johnson full on the bridge of his nose, and knocked him among the blacking bottles, where he lay gasping and wriggling as the broken pieces unpleasantly reminded him that he was not "all among the roses."

"There were also another kind of sauce," continued Sam, looking upon his fallen foe with a complacent smile, "which you called the 'Pick-me-up,' and there were likewise another, the new kind of Caper Sauce, and in a sort of halligatorical way I'll give 'em back to you likewise."

So saying, Sam grasped the fallen valet by the collar, and dragged him up. Then, with a long-handled clothes brush, he dusted him most effectually until the brush broke short off, and with a final twist deposited him once more among the broken bottles.

"There, old feller," gasped Sam, breathless, but happy, "you gave me the Knock-me-down, the Pick-me-up, and the Caper Sauce, and I think I've paid you back. If you don't think so you know where to find me, and I'll be werry happy to give you the balance."

And Sam, resuming his coat, and wiping the perspiration from his brow, cast a final glance at his fallen foe, and hurried away, to make his peace with his young master.

CHAPTER II.

TOMMY—AND OTHER THINGS.

WHILE Sam was "having it out" with the playful Mr. Jarvie Johnson, our hero and his friends had resumed their breakfast, the injured Priggenham being promptly restored by a judiciously administered "nip" of brandy.

"Feel better?" inquired Lionel, who had given him the cordial.

"Yaas—think so," gasped Heavitop, "but it was deuced nasty, I do assure you."

"I believe you," replied Lionel; "the smell was enough for me, but pitch into the breakfast and take the taste out of your mouth. Poor Tommy, I wish he was here, it would have taken more than that to spoil *his* appetite."

"Haven't you heard anything of poor Codlings yet?" said Charlie.

"Not a whisper. You know that when his aunt died—the only relation he had in the world I believe —she left all her fortune to found an asylum for indigent cats, and our poor chum disappeared directly the will was read."

"It's my belief," said the gloomy Priggenham, "that he committed suicide."

"Not a bit of it," replied our hero; "Tommy wasn't the sort of fellow to do that."

"*I* would," added Heavitop, decisively.

"*You're* ass enough for anything," growled Charlie, in an undertone.

"Do you think that he has enlisted?" suggested Vansittart, "or shipped on board some merchantman?"

"That idea occurred to me," replied our hero; "and I've had a detective on the look-out for him at Charles-street, Westminster, and another at the docks. They each had a photograph of Tommy, besides a verbal description, so that if he had enlisted or shipped they would have nailed him."

"Yes, I s'pose they would," said Charlie, thoughtfully; "Tommy wasn't a chap that any one could mistake. He's sure to turn up somehow."

"I shall be glad when he does," added our hero; "I miss him tremendously, but I've no doubt that he's safe. After escaping that blow-up at Stiffback's he'd get over everything."

"I don't know, Li. A cat has nine lives, but they generally manage to use 'em all up somehow, and though Tommy is so lucky, he can't always expect to get off scot-free."

"We'll hope for the best, anyhow," answered Lionel; "I have a sort of presentiment that it won't be long before he makes one of our little party at Kramatome's."

"What! our new tutor?" laughed Vansittart, "the filler-up of empty heads with any kind of knowledge required, on the shortest notice and the most unreasonable terms."

"That's the party. By-the-bye, I suppose you've received an invite to breakfast with him?"

"I've got one," said Vansittart, "and I—and I," added the others.

"Next Thursday, at nine o'clock," continued Lionel; "that's the day after the fancy ball at Sillys's Rooms. What a bore! We shall feel too seedy to go."

"How do you like the idea of giving up your liberty again, Li?" asked Vansittart.

"I shall be only too glad to get rid of it," laughed our hero. "When I was at Styngy's and Stiffback's I used to long for the time when I should be my own master, but now I'm decidedly of opinion that too much liberty is worse than none at all. Where's the fun in lying in bed an hour late, or in stopping out all night, if there's nobody to call you to account for bad behaviour? I declare to you fellows, that I've been deucedly miserable this last four months, and I'll make it pretty lively for old Kramatome when I do go there."

"My sentiments to a hair," said Charlie, and young Lord Vansittart backed the opinion. As for Heavitop Priggenham, he expressed his conviction that everything was a "deuced bore," and that there was no such thing as happiness under the sun.

"We'll show you better than that, my boy," said Lionel. "Only wait till we get to Kramatome's, and you'll change your tune."

"He's better already," said Charlie, with a wink. "See how that sauce livened him up. I think that it's the first time in his life he was ever in a hurry."

"And it will be the last," said Heavitop Priggenham. "It's such a deuced bore to be in a hurry."

"You'll find yourself in that fix pretty often, old fellow," said Lionel, with a laugh, "if you keep our company. Poor Tommy was slow and sleepy, but we cured him."

"But that sort o' thing is so low, you know," said Priggenham, languidly. "No arist'cratic fellah's ever in a hurry."

"Ain't they, though?" replied Lionel. "Why, here's Van. You can't call him a commoner, and I'll engage that you'll see him in a hurry pretty often."

"'Specially if he ever has to tackle another pig-jobber," said Charlie.

"Ah, you remember that little mill, Drummond?"

"Rather; and so does Li, and the fifty pounds he won over it. By the way, Wilful, have you ever seen that pretty little girl you paid the money for the same day?"

But although the occurrence to which Charlie had referred had taken place nearly three years before, our hero was still sensitive on the point, and without replying to Charlie, turned the conversation in another direction, being aided therein by Sam, who made his appearance with one eye in a very promising state of inflammation, the result of his recent little turn-up with Mr. Jarvie Johnson. Lionel noticed it directly. Such a thing was hardly likely to escape his notice.

"What, Sam! have you been in the wars again?"

"I think he's been crying," said Charlie, "because you blew him up just now."

"Not me, Master Charlie," retorted Sam, indignantly. "Though I will go so far as for to admit that I were a bit upset. I've been a payin' the chap what give me that there sauce."

"Ah! and he's given you a receipt in full on that right eye of yours, Sam. I thought somebody had been playing you a trick, but I put you down for too sharp a fellow to be easily taken in."

"The best on us has our weak moments, Master Lionel," replied the long youth; "and I own as I was took in, but he won't do it never no more."

"You haven't settled him, I hope, Sam?"

"Not quite, Master Lionel. I think there's as much left on him as a furriner is likely to want."

"That'll do then, Sam. You can clear away, and for the future recollect that when I want any new kind of sauce I'll let you know myself. Don't try any more experiments, or I shall be under the necessity of ordering a coffin for you, and getting the corpse ready for it."

"Thankee, Master Lionel," said Sam, as gratefully as if he had been promised a diamond ring, instead of a sudden death.

"Now, what's the programme? as we used to say at Stiffback's. What do you think of a ride?"

"Deuced good," was Heavitop Priggenham's comment. "We'll go and show ourselves in the Park."

"Show ourselves at a penny a head," growled Charlie. When I'm seventy, and past galloping, I'll be content with a freezing canter in the Row, but not till then."

"Besides," added Vansittart, "what on earth can Priggenham want to show himself for? There are much prettier animals to be seen at the Zoo; only the people who go there have to pay their shillings."

It might be thought that this sarcasm was coarse enough for the densest intellect to perceive, but Priggenham was impervious. He only said, in his usual languid manner—

"Yaas, the Zoo's a deuced good place. Sundays go there myself."

"Don't go too often, old fellow," said Vansittart, gravely.

"Why not?"

"The blue-nosed baboon died last week, and the tailless Chimpanzee's very ill, and if anything happened to it, and you went before they had time to get another—why, don't you see, something unpleasant might happen. You're not the sort of fellow to feel happy in a cage, or to get full on nuts and apples."

"Stop it, Van," laughed Lionel. "A joke's wasted on Priggenham. You ought to know that by this time. But come along, we're losing time. We can get some first-rate cattle at Rackett's livery stables."

"Where shall we go?" said Charlie. "Priggenham votes for the Park, and the vote of the minority ought to be respected."

"Bother the minority," exclaimed Lionel, with a reckless disregard of political ethics. "If Priggenham likes to come he can, but I warn him that we're going to be in a hurry."

"Don't mind," said Priggenham, languidly, "that'll be the horse's affair, not mine."

"Bravo, Heavy," said Vansittart, "you came very nearly to saying a good thing."

While this little dialogue was progressing the dialogists, if we may be allowed to coin a word, were progressing also, and, attended by Sam, had reached Rackett's stables, who, knowing his customers, produced some cattle that were really good, as well as good-looking, fit for the Park, or equal to a dozen miles across a stiff country.

"Now, Li," said Charlie, when they were all mounted, "what is it to be? Follow-my-Leader, I suppose."

"Yes," laughed our hero, "the same old game."

And putting his horse to a canter he led the way, leaving chance or his horse's inclination to select the road.

So it happened that in the course of half an hour the novel spectacle of a party of well-dressed and well-mounted young gentlemen were presented to the wondering gaze of the inhabitants of the south side of Westminster Bridge, most of whom would have regarded the advent of a rhinoceros or alligator with rather less curiosity.

"Deuced queer place this you've brought us to, Wilful," said Heavitop Priggenham, whose knowledge of unfashionable London was extremely limited.

This remark of the languid one was called forth by the offence of some half-dozen or so of the "great unwashed," who, after the manner of their tribe, kept up a running fire of uncomplimentary remarks relative to the personal appearance of the equestrians.

"Some of Moses' blokes out for a holiday," suggested one critic.

"Not a bit on it—they're barber's clerks," yelled another—"I can smell the 'air-ile."

"Look at that cove with the curly wig," yelled a third—"they've run a tin-tack through him to keep him in the saddle."

This last playful allusion referred to Heavitop Priggenham, and as he was rather proud of his elegant seat in the saddle he became very wroth and indignant, and made a cut with his riding-whip at the nearest of his tormenters.

"What an ass you are!" exclaimed Lionel, sharply. "We shall be pelted for that."

And indeed there seemed every likelihood of that unpleasant consummation being arrived at, for a howl of execration arose from the great unwashed: handfuls of mud, pieces of orange peel, and stones were grubbed out of the gutter, and launched at the offender, with the result of filling up one of his eyes with a dab of unsavoury mud, and knocking his hat very much out of the perpendicular.

Lionel put his horse into a canter, and headed for the Old Kent-road, for they were now in a maze of narrow streets, bordered with houses in every style of dilapidation, and inhabited apparently by a population intimately acquainted with the interior of her Majesty's gaols.

"It's lucky we're on horseback," said Lionel, as he ducked to avoid a massive turnip, which an enthusiastic youth had purloined from a barrow to throw at the swells. But he suffered, for the costermonger who owned the barrow promptly followed him, and very nearly jerked his right ear off.

This incident created a diversion in favour of our hero, for the unlucky youth's mother was in the crowd, and instantly avenged the injury done to her offspring by clawing the costermonger.

Such a cheap and lively spectacle as a free fight or combat of two was not to be neglected by such a crowd, and in a few minutes our hero and his chums were forsaken by all, save one extremely ragged specimen of humanity, who kept pace with them, though on the opposite side of the way, but without showing any intention either to "chaff" or pelt the swells.

"What on earth is that chap after?" said Charlie, after they had given the ragged one a sharp run of a couple of miles. "Look at him, Li!"

"By George, he runs well, Charlie. Poor beggar, he thinks we want our horses held; but if he waits till we get down he'll have a longer run than he will like."

"He's come far enough already," added Charlie, getting a shilling out of his waistcoat pocket. "This will make him happy."

And, with a dexterous jerk, Drummond pitched the shilling on the pavement, just in front of the ragged runner.

It rang sharply on the stones, and bouncing up rolled for some distance. Everyone expected to see the lad pounce upon it like an albatross upon a flying fish; but, strange to say, he took not the slightest notice of the coin, but trotted along, as if he were running a match against time, and was bound to win.

Lionel, thinking that the first shilling had not been seen, threw another. This time it hit the tramp on the head, but it was treated with the same aggravating neglect; and a third, which Vansittart flung to him, shared the same fate.

"He's out of his mind!" said Charlie. "Fancy a ragged tramp like that refusing three shillings in succession."

"He's the king of the beggars, or else one of that royal family, and won't condescend to touch any metal other than gold," laughed Lionel. "But here we are, my boys, leaving smoky London behind us. Let's try a trot, we'll see what that fellow's made of."

The horses were not quite up to the American 2.40 standard—that is, they could not cover a mile of ground in the space of two minutes forty seconds; but they trotted fast enough to give any one but a professional runner the go-bye in ten minutes, but to the surprise of our hero and his chums the tramp kept them well in view, and when the fourth mile was covered still held his own.

"He's a wonder," said Vansittart, admiringly. "Pull up, you fellows, and let's speak to him."

But no sooner were the horses reined in than the mysterious tramp stopped too.

"Hoi!" shouted Vansittart. "Come here, my lad."

But my lad, instead of accepting the invitation, backed away, and showed such an unmistakeable intention not to approach that our hero and his friends were more than ever mystified.

"He's a rum un," said Lionel. "What the dickens is his little game?"

"Deuced sensible fellah," sneered Heavitop Priggenham. "He knows he's not fit society for gentlemen, and keeps distance 'cordingly.

"He might keep his distance, Priggenham, and yet have kept the money," said Charlie. "I can't make him out."

"Then don't try," said Lionel. "That confounded tramp will make us lose the best part of the day if we stay here wondering. He's an escaped lunatic: set him down at that—drive on."

Once again the horses were set going, and in the exhilarating motion the mysterious tramp was soon forgotten; and, when they drew rein at Toppelton, some twenty miles from their starting-place, and ordered a lunch that made the innkeeper start with surprise, they were far too hungry to think of anything but the vacuum behind their waistcoats, which peremptorily demanded to be filled without delay.

"I've seen some fairish feeders in my time," said the landlord to his wife, in the secure recesses of the bar parlour, "and the young gents themselves have pecked a goodish bit; but lor', that red-haired cove with the squint, he do astonish me. He've had a couple o' pound o' the cold meat—then he had a go at the cold biled, and spiled the look o' that—then he cleared out the greens and taters—and now he've made a hole in my double Gloucester big enow to put my hed in, to say nout o' bread and pickles; if he doan't hav' a fit of happleperplexity afore he gits hoam, call me a liar."

The red-haired chap with the squint, thus politely alluded to by the landlord, was, of course, none other than Sam, whose powers of gorging are already well known to our readers.

He had, in truth, made a meal, the sight of which would have been enough for a delicate appetite, and leaning back in his chair, he picked his teeth thoughtfully with a fork, and gazed, with an air of dreamy abstraction, born of a full stomach, out of the window of the little back parlour where he had taken his meal in solitary state.

Now Sam was apparently gazing at a pigeon-house on the top of a barn to his right—we say apparently, because, owing to the extraordinary squint he possessed, he happened to be intently regarding the left-hand corner of the inn yard, and while thus wrapt in "meditation fancy-free," he became aware of a figure stealthily observing him from behind the shelter of a pump.

Sam was a little sleepy—naturally so, perhaps, when the heavy nature of his lunch is taken into consideration, but after a time he began to fancy, in a drowsy manner, that the face was familiar to him.

He had surely seen those eyes before, and that nose, so like a button mushroom, and that mouth, so admirably constructed to take in enough for a meal at one try—surely they all belonged to some old acquaintance.

Sam thought for awhile, and suddenly, as he saw the figure leave the shelter of the pump, and glide across the yard, the light of recognition beamed upon his countenance, and he said, half aloud—

"Well, I'm dashed if that there ain't the ragged cove wot was follerin' us awhile ago, and if he ain't Master Codlings besides, I'll eat him."

For a moment or two Sam thought that he must be dreaming, and rubbing his eyes vigorously with his knuckles he looked again.

"It's him sure enough," he said, half aloud. "That there nose, them eyes, and that figger can't be mistook, unless Master Codlings have a twin somewhere about, and that can't be, very well, two sich as him wos never made. He's thinner certingly, and his bellows must be a sight better than they wos in the hold days, but it's him, and now for the capter."

Sam was perfectly convinced by Tommy's manner that he wished to escape notice, but the long youth was fully resolved to have him, for he knew how ardently Lionel desired to see his old chum again, and he himself was scarcely less anxious.

"Master Codlings always were a rum 'un though," thought Sam, as he stealthily made his way to the back door, "only fancy his comin' down to that ere condishun. Why his clothes is nothin but large holes with bits of rag round 'em."

By the time that Sam had concluded this un-favourable criticism upon Tommy's habiliments he had reached the back yard of the inn, and saw that young gentleman dodging with the sagacity of a Red Indian, and trying hard to obtain a view of the interior of the house through the back windows.

"He's trying to get a peep at Master Lionel," thought Sam, "but why on airth don't he go in the front door and axe for him in a manly way?"

Not being able to answer this question to his satisfaction, Sam adopted Tommy's tactics, and dodging with masterly caution succeeded in getting well in the rear of his intended capture.

"When he were at Stiffback's," said Sam to him-self, "I could hev give him ninety yards out of a hundred and lick him easy, but now he's a reg'lar Deerfoot. Want of grub have pulled him down."

Now it so chanced that the landlord himself had been made aware of the presence of, what he con-sidered, this very ragged and rascally-looking tramp prowling about his back yard, and very naturally came to the conclusion that the said tramp had come to steal something.

The landlord was a man of prompt action, and without waiting to put down the saucepan of steam-ing potatoes he had just taken from off the fire he beckoned to the ostler.

"See that there tramp, Jim." he whispered; "run round to the stable door and nab him if he tries to cut, while I tackle him this end."

Jim obeyed, and bolting through the front door reached his post just as Sam pounced upon his prey and enfolding Tommy in his long arms uttered a shout of triumph.

But his exultation was short-lived. The once fat short-winded Tommy was now as active as an eel. With one quick motion he wriggled clear of Sam, and with a second he lowered his head and butted the long youth into a horse trough which happened to be awkwardly convenient, and thus he would have made good his escape through the stable door but for the ostler, who with outstretched arms barred his exit.

Tommy did not hesitate a minute, but rushed at the foe with desperate determination, and in two seconds the ostler had swallowed two teeth, and began to feel anxious respecting the safety of his liver and other vital organs, when the landlord came to the rescue, and at once terminated the combat by extinguishing Tommy with the saucepan.

Now a saucepan is at no time—at least in our opinion—a comfortable kind of head-covering; but when it has been for an hour or so in company with a very hot fire, and is moreover half-filled with potatoes cooked to scalding point, the maddest maniac in "Bedlam" would hardly elect to have his head kept warm in such a fashion.

"I've got him!" roared the landlord. "Blarm his ragged carcase—I'll warm 'im!"

It was evident that poor Tommy's old ill-luck still clung to him with fond affection, though all the hap-pier circumstances of his boyhood had fled.

He could not express his agony by howling, for reasons which will be plain; but he spun around the yard like a teetotum, swinging his arms like the sails of a windmill, retaliating on the landlord by flinging him on a muck-heap, and finally tumbling over Sam, and going head first into the horse trough.

There was a loud hiss, and a cloud of steam arose as the saucepan plunged into the cold bath; and oh! how Tommy blessed the happy accident that saved him from being boiled alive—at least, so far as that most essential part of him—his head—was con-cerned!

But though Tommy had escaped from the sauce-pan, he was once again within the grasp of Sam,

and that long youth, with a view of making certain of his captive this time, not only secured him with his arms, but opening his mouth, which, as our readers know, was one of the largest size, he anchored himself to the back of Tommy's neck.

Sam had in doing this no cannibalistic intentions —he only intended to lay hold of his captive by the collar, but it unluckily happened that poor Tommy had no collar. His clothing began somewhere about the middle of his back, and so his skin paid the penalty.

The torture of the scalds and the bite combined was truly awful, and so were Tommy's yells, for they penetrated two thick brick walls, and reached the apartment where sat our hero and his chums.

"Hallo!" said Lionel, when the first agonised howl set his teeth on edge. "What on earth's that?"

"Only the old boy sticking a pig in the back yard," was Charlie's explanation.

"The devil a bit. The pig never wore a tail that owns a voice like that."

"Perhaps some Turks are having a game of Bul-garian atrocities out there," suggested Vansittart.

"Let's go and see," replied Lionel. "That's the best way of getting at the truth."

And in something less than a minute the whole party—except Priggenham, who was too dignified to hurry himself—were out in the back yard gazing at the quartette, which was at that moment aug-mented by the arrival of a rural constable, who, not to be outdone by his metropolitan brethren in the science of "running 'em in," fell over a stable-fork, and ran that in—to his regulation breeches, ripped up a good foot of cloth, and a corresponding portion of his own hide, which happened to be behind it.

"Sam," shouted Lionel, "where are you? and what the deuce is the meaning of all this?"

Our hero could not at first perceive his faithful follower, inasmuch as Tommy—much against his will, though—screened him from observation; but the long youth heard his young master's voice, and roared in exultation—

"Here, Master Lionel! This way! I've got him!"

"Got whom?" said Lionel, as he neared the horse-trough. "Why! What! Here, Charlie—Vansittart! Come here. I'm dashed if Sam hasn't found Tommy Codlings!"

CHAPTER III.

SAM ENLIGHTENS THE LANDLORD.

THE eye of affection is proverbially keen, and in Lionel's case it had need to be very keen indeed to enable him to recognise in that tattered tramp the once plump and rosy Tommy Codlings.

But he did it, and in a moment the indignant land-lord and his assistants beheld, with disgust and astonishment, the strange spectacle of his swell guests crowding around the tramp and vainly en-deavouring to shake hands with him all at once, and evincing the most unequivocal signs of being in a high state of delight.

"Well, I'm danged," gasped the landlord, "this bangs everythink! I'm as charytable as most men, but blow all tramps and sich, they're pison!"

The landlord had suffered much wrong in his time at the hands of those roving gentry. He had lost his eggs and his chickens, his pewter pots and cans, and once his pony and a set of harness, so that one can hardly wonder if he "came down" heavily upon the tramps when he had the chance.

With a sensation of unutterable disgust, which was shared by the ostler and the injured policeman. he now saw Tommy being half led, half dragged into the inn, and feeling that the line must be drawn somewhere, he entered a protest.

"Beg pardon, gen'lemen," he said, "but may I be so bold as to ax wot you're going to do with that—hat low wagabone?"

Lionel, Vansittart, and Charlie were by far too busy questioning Tommy to pay any heed to the landlord, and Sam, who had unfixed himself from the horse trough, took it upon himself to answer the question.

"Hush!" he said, in a mysterious whisper, "don't you know who that is?"

"He's precious like the chap wot stole the 'arf gallon cans and six pint pots a month ago, and if there's law to be had he'll get a twelvemonth on the mill."

"Nonsense!" replied Sam, lowering his voice still more. "D'ye think my guv'nor would take up with a tramp? That's young Lord Winklepin."

"Lord who?" gasped the landlord. "You don't gammon me with sich stuff as that. Lords don't go about with their shirt tails comin' through their breeches, and never a shoe to their feet."

"He's doin' of it for a wager, I tell you," continued Sam, drawing upon his vivid imagination for a possible excuse. "Five thousand pounds was the bet, and he've won it."

The landlord had heard in his youth sundry tales concerning the mad Marquis of Waterford, and being, like most Englishmen, a fervent worshipper of the aristocracy, he began to think it just possible that Sam's tale might be true.

"Well," he said, in a respectful whisper, "now I come to think of it there was somethink in his heye which looked harrystocratic like, and the way he bowled that hostler over showed that noble blood was in his harm."

"No mistake about that, old feller," added Sam. "His is the noblest of blood that's made—reg'lar blue, you know."

"I think I drawed a little from his nose with that saucepan," said the landlord, "and it seemed to me kind o' red."

"Change of hair does that," explained Sam, readily; "it's blue when it's inside."

"Oh, that's the way, is it?" said the landlord, perfectly satisfied with the explanation. "I hope them taters warn't too hot. If I'd known he was a lord, I'd have swallowed pot and all afore I'd have tipped 'em over him."

"It's done now and can't be helped," said Sam. "I don't s'pose he'll be werry 'ard on you. If you goes down on your knees, and pollergises, he'll kick you round the yard three or four times, and say no more about it."

"Will he do that? I say, that's a comin' it a little too strong, you know. A man o' my build don't kick light; but if he's a lord I s'pose he must have his own way, and they'll spend a good bit o' money afore they goes, and I can put the kicking down in the bill."

"That's the way to talk," said Sam, giving him a friendly slap on the back, which seemed to drive his backbone into a position not contemplated by Nature when she built him; "and now you go and put some more coals on the fire, for, if I knows anythink, there'll be a jollification over this affair."

Sam was right. He had hardly done speaking when the bell of the little parlour rang furiously, and the landlord, with an agility which did him great credit, considering his weight, bounded gaily along the passage, in the full hope of getting a princely order.

He got an order, a liberal one, but not precisely the kind of one he expected, for directly he entered, Lionel demanded the biggest tub in the house to be filled with hot water, and a liberal supply of the strongest yellow soap and scrubbing brushes to be got ready.

"It must be years since you smelt soap, old fellow," laughed Lionel, "and I strongly suspect that you'll have to be scraped, unless the scrubbing brushes are quite new, and—landlord."

"Yes, my lord."

"Is there a ready-made clothes shop near here?"

"Not nearer than London, your lordship."

"Don't 'my lord' me, there's a good fellow," said Lionel. "I'm not a lord."

"Beg your grace's gardon," returned the landlord, who was fully impressed with the idea that his guests were members of the peerage, and that if they were not "lords" they must be "dukes."

"Wrong again," laughed Lionel; "I'm not a duke either."

"Beg your r'yal 'ighnesses parding," said the landlord, with a bow which threatened to dislocate his spine.

"Let it go at that," said Vansittart. "You're elected to the rank of a prince of the blood royal, Li, without any herald's fee to pay. If you correct him again he'll make a crowned monarch of you."

"Have it your own way," said Lionel. "But what are we to do about a rig-out for Tommy?"

"If your r'yal 'ighness and noble lordships would accep' the hoffer, my boy, Bill, have a noo Sunday soot, which, if I may make so bold, is just about his noble lordship's figger."

"That'll do," said Lionel. "Fetch them out, and look sharp with the hot water and soap. Tommy must be dying for want of a wash. And when you've done that, get the best dinner ready that you ever heard of. I'll leave the details to you; charge what you like, but let it be good."

"I know how to treat a gent when I get him, your r'yal 'ighness," said the landlord. "In a couple of hours you shall have a feed as Buckingham Palace wouldn't turn up its nose at."

"Better rig Tommy out, and go back to the Langham to dine," suggested Charlie.

"No," said Lionel. "We found Tommy here, and where the happy meeting took place there will we celebrate the week. You've got some wine, landlord?"

"Which I have, your r'yal 'ighness. In p'int of hage, its ekal couldn't be found in Noah's Ark."

"All right, landlord," laughed Lionel; "but don't let the game be quite so old. I'm afraid that a brace of pheasants out of the ark would prove a little too tough for our taste."

"Or too high," added Vansittart. "But perhaps Tommy would prefer a blow out of tripe or cow-heel, or à la mode beef, and a pint of porter to wash it down with."

"What do you say, Tommy?" added Lionel. "Will you have any of these delicacies included in the bill of fare?"

But poor Tommy was as yet speechless. He sat in a corner of the room, looking about him with a dazed, bewildered air, and something very like a tear twinkling in either eye. And little wonder—he had been alone, friendless, penniless, for so long, that the warm greeting of his old chums, coming upon him so suddenly, had overpowered him.

Though every one, except perhaps the aristocratic and exclusive Heavitop Priggenham, was dying to hear the story of Tommy's adventures, they were too considerate to press him then. The first thing was to make Tommy feel at home, and to regard the miseries of the past two years as an ugly dream, for miserable that time must have been, as his ragged condition proved only too well.

So far as Tommy was concerned it seemed to him that he was in a dream now. With those familiar faces before him, and those well-remembered voices in his ears, it was easy to believe that the dear old schooldays were yet things of the present, and if Mr. Stiffback had walked in then and there, and ordered him a couple of dozen in the flogging machine, Tommy would have accepted the sentence with joy.

This he felt was friendship—true and sincere. His chums were rich, well dressed—above all, what the world calls "respectable"—yet there was no avoidance of him now that he was poor, ragged, and hungry. They did not turn their heads the other way, like the Pharisees and Levites of old, and walk on the other side. ut gave him a welcome as warm and hearty as if he had come to them blazing with diamonds, and the possessor of the wealth of the Rothschilds.

Tommy remained quiet, thinking of all this, until the tub of hot water was brought, and Lionel. Vansittart, and Charlie pulled off their coats and tucked up their shirt sleeves. Then he said, opening his little round eyes to their fullest extent—

"I say, Li, what are you going to do?"

"Help to wash you, of course," laughed our hero in reply. "Don't you remember how you washed the Bobbles family once? We'll do the same by you now, only a little more effectively."

"That be blowed!" returned Tommy. "You're up to some of your old larks, Li, and mean flaying me with that scrubbing-brush."

"We'll handle you as tenderly as if you were a new-born baby, Tommy, we will indeed. Now give him a shake, Charlie, and those rags will drop off."

And before Tommy had a chance to offer any resistance Charlie and Vansittart had seized him, and with a couple of vigorous pulls his clothes—the front of an old shirt, half a pair of trousers, and some string for braces—came off, and Tommy stood revealed in all his native beauty.

But not for long. He had scarcely time to utter remonstrance and aim a kick at Priggenham, who was handiest, when he was tripped up and shot into the hot water, and held there while Lionel scrubbed him.

It was a roaring bit of fun for the boys; and the landlord, who stood in the doorway gazing with respectful astonishment at the operation, thought it was all a part of the bet, and smiled in sympathy.

After the bath came the dressing, and then the dinner, and a merrier party, it would be safe to say, never handled knife and fork.

Every moment it became more and more like a dream to Tommy Codlings, and now and again he laid down his knife and fork and gazed around him with a startled air, as if he expected each moment to wake again and find himself the hungry tramp he had been but one brief hour ago.

Sam was almost beside himself with delight, and did such extraordinary things in the way of waiting that Lionel had to order him to stand in a corner by himself, or Tommy would certainly have been choked or poisoned.

They had some champagne after dinner, and Lionel, forgetting the effect that such wine would have upon Tommy after so long an abstinence from everything more intoxicating than "four half," filled his glass again and again; and in consequence, the long-lost one first grew very merry, then tearful, and finally—and with startling suddenness—went to sleep.

"You've done it now, Li," said Charlie. "You've made the poor old boy tight. I was thinking that the wine would upset him."

"Then why didn't you say so before?" returned Lionel, a little savagely. "What's the good of saying so when the thing's done?"

"Hush, boys. Don't row," said Vansittart. "I've got an idea."

"Better than Charlie's, then, I hope."

"You'll know when I tell it you," replied Vansittart. "What do you say, now, if we take Tommy back to London while he's asleep, tuck him up in bed, and when he wakes up in the morning persuade him that his poverty and tramping, and all that, was nothing but a dream. We can easily give the hotel people the tip, and if we're careful and keep our countenances he'll swallow it."

"A good idea that," said Lionel. "We can buy some clothes, a portmanteau, and so on, and mark 'em with his name, and write a few letters dated a year or two back, which will help the deception."

"You see," added Vansittart, "the past must have been a very painful and unhappy one to poor old Tommy, and it will be a real charity to make him think that it was only a dream, and not a reality."

The plan was adopted unanimously. A trap was hired, and Tommy, dead asleep with the combined effects of fatigue, champagne, and excitement, driven to Fleury's hotel in Jermyn-street; a stock of clothes and other necessaries purchased and marked, the hotel proprietor and waiters instructed, the letters written, creased, and rumpled to make them look old, and then, delighted with the ingenuity of their plan, the chums left Tommy to snore in peace, little thinking into what trouble they were leading the hapless Tommy by their well-meant kindness.

CHAPTER IV.

IN WHICH TOMMY CODLINGS IS SOMEWHAT BEWILDERED TO ACCOUNT FOR HIS SURROUNDINGS.

TOMMY awoke in the morning feeling very much as if some one had taken out his brains and boiled them, and then lit a fire in his interior, and dried up every available particle of moisture in his throat and mouth.

"Here's a go!" he gasped. "Oh, lor', I must be in a fever."

Poor Tommy gazed around him with a hazy look. His eyesight was not particularly clear that morning, but he thought there was something very much the matter with it, indeed, when, instead of the dingy, greasy, evil-smelling tramps' lodging house he had been accustomed to of late, he found himself in a handsomely, even luxuriously, furnished bedroom.

"I'm dreaming still," he thought; "I'll shut my eyes, and perhaps I'll wake up presently, but I think I'd like to dream a little more like this. Lor', how nice it is!"

Tommy closed his eyes and sank back upon the pillow in a delicious, dreamy langour, and by degrees there came back to him a dim recollection of his adventure of the preceding day, but it was as yet so dim that he could not decide whether it was a dream or a reality.

"The more I come to think of it," mused Tommy, "the more puzzled I am. I could swear that I remember running after Lionel and the others all down the Old Kent-road, and being washed in that dashed tub and having dinner, but where did I leave 'em, and how? Why is it I don't recollect that? And where the dickens am I now?"

Tommy thought a little more, and then resolved to clear up the latter part of the puzzling question he had set himself by getting out of bed, and testing in a practical way.

He began by catching one foot in the coverlet, and pitching head first against a mahogany wardrobe, which was certainly far too solid to have anything dreamy about it.

"Oh! my," ejaculated Tommy; "that's real, I'll swear, and so's the black eye I shall get. Blow it! why couldn't I get out of bed without tumbling down? Out of practise I suppose."

The noise of the fall was enough to bring a solemn-looking waiter to the door with a jug of hot water.

"Did you knock, sir?"

"*Did* I knock," growled Tommy. "I should rather think I did—look at my eye."

"Bit of raw beef, sir? Hoppydeldock, sir?" suggested the waiter.

"I'll have the beef, I think. But, I say, who are you, and who am I?"

"Beg your pardon, sir," said the waiter, with an air of the profoundest astonishment.

"Who am I, I say? and what is this place? and how the dickens did I come here?"

"You're pleased to be jokkylar this morning, sir," said the waiter, who had, of course, had his instructions from Lionel, and played his part with the ability of a born actor.

"Never mind whether I'm jocular or not," said

AS THE PAIR OPENED THE DOOR A GIGANTIC FIGURE APPEARED IN FRONT OF THEM, AND BECKONED THEM TO FOLLOW.

Tommy, putting on a very severe frown; "is my name Codlings?"

"Such have been my impression, sir, for the last six months," said the waiter.

"Six months!" gasped Tommy. "Have I been here six months?"

"Which your bills can prove it," replied the waiter; "you paid it yesterday, sir, if you remember, and give me something for myself, like the liberal gent you've always showed yourself."

"Eh! what?" said Tommy, "me pay a bill—me! Why I haven't had a copper to bless myself with for months."

The waiter smiled a smile of respectful incredulity, and glanced towards the dressing table, on which were a handsome gold watch and chain, several rings, a pocket-book, and quite a handful of gold and silver money.

Tommy followed the glance of the waiter's eyes, and stood bewildered at the wealth displayed.

"I say," he said, after a pause, "whose is that?"

"Yours, sir, to the best of my belief."

"But I say, that won't do you know, I must have been picking somebody's pockets in my sleep. I've got here in a mistake for somebody else. Are you sure, now—will you take your oath, waiter—that I am me—I mean that me am I? Oh! dash it, you know what I mean."

"Certainly, sir."

"Well, I s'pose it's all right," said Tommy, who was now in a helpless state of muddle, for on looking in the pocket-book he found a number of bills, all duly receipted, and addressed to "Thomas Codlings, Esq., Fleury's Hotel," besides several letters, some from Lionel, Charlie, Vansittart, and others from people whose names he had, to his recollection, never heard before in his life.

"Blow it! I can't make it out," murmured Tommy, turning round and round in a purposeless and bewildered manner. "Here's a letter from Li, dated months ago, reminding me of the jolly evening we spent at Lady Comeover's ball, and how tight I got at Evans's afterwards, and polished off two bobbies. Why, that was the very time that I was partners with Irish Mike in a whelk barrow just over London Bridge. When trade was bad he ate up all the stock, and chucked the vinegar and shells at me for my share. Dash it! I remember it quite well. I'm sure it happened."

"Ere's the beef for your heye, sir," said the waiter, reappearing with a slice of that luxury on a plate.

"Blow the beef!" retorted Tommy, wildly. "What's beef to whelks? Where's my barrow, and where's Irish Mike?"

"Whelks, I believe," said the waiter, in a tone of lofty scorn, "is a species of yaller winkle, and Irish is low parties as don't suit my taste, sir."

"If Mike was here," said Tommy, "he'd drop you one on the nose for that, and make you swallow every whelk on the barrow, and pay for 'em afterwards."

"It ain't for me to conterdick you, sir," replied the waiter; "but afore I'd let a coster—specially a Hirish one—make me swaller a whelk I'd swaller him—and without vinegar, too. But here's your friends a callin' up the stairs, Mr. Codlings. Will you see 'em?"

"Friends!" repeated Tommy. "I haven't got any friends since Biler Bill was taken up, and got six months for looking at a policeman."

"Who's that talking about policemen?" said the clear, ringing voice of Lionel in the doorway. "Ah, it's you—is it, Tommy? What a fellow you are for pitching into the bobbies! What have you done with the helmet?"

"The what?"

"The helmet—the policeman's helmet you bolted with last night after Priggenham's wine party. Don't you remember thrashing him in Air-street?"

"When?" gasped the bewildered Tommy.

"When? Why, last night, to be sure. Were you too tight to recollect it?"

"There's something the matter with me," said Tommy, "but I'm blest if I know what. Where am I? Who am I? Who are you? And what's become of Irish Mike and the whelk barrow?"

"You're in a bad way, Tommy," replied our hero, preserving his gravity with great difficulty. "Have you had any soda-water this morning?"

"No, I haven't, and I don't want any. You look like my old chum, Lionel, but you ain't him—you can't be. This is a dream, and I want to wake up."

"You want a bottle of soda-water and a plate of hot pickles—that's what's the matter with you. Waiter, go and get them, will you? and order breakfast at ten."

Tommy was powerless in the hands of his old chum, and allowed himself to be planted on the edge of the bed; and when the soda-water and pickles arrived, took his dose without a murmur, only from time to time murmuring faint inquiries after Irish Mike and the whelk barrow.

"You must have had an uncommonly strong dream last night, Tommy," said Lionel, when at length he had succeeded in persuading his bewildered chum to dress himself and accompany him to the breakfast-room. "Why, Charlie and Vansittart will chaff you out of your life if you go on like that."

"Are they here, then?"

"Here! Of course they are. Where else should they be? Don't you remember the fancy ball?"

"Eh!" said Tommy, with a bewildered stare.

"Oh, come now!" exclaimed Lionel, affecting annoyance at the plump youth's ignorance of his meaning. "Don't lay it on too thick, Tommy. You can't have forgotten the fancy ball."

"I remember," said Tommy, vaguely, "when Biler Bill and me went out with fancy air-balloons, and we went into a pub to get a pint of four-half to moisten our throats before we began to cry 'em, and some lanky chap stuck pins in 'em when we wasn't looking, and when we got into the street they were all like saveloy skins with the meat picked out."

"Bother you and your saveloys!" laughed Lionel. "There's something better than that for breakfast, anyhow. Pitch in, Tommy, and let us see if you have lost your appetite as well as your memory."

But Tommy soon showed that his eating powers were by no means lessened. Even the dissipation of the preceding night had only the effect of increasing his appetite instead of impairing it.

Our old friend, Sam Scarecrow, was as much or more delighted than any one at Tommy's recovery, and every now and then he exploded a perfect volley of chuckles, generally managing to drop a dish cover, or sometimes the dish itself, to conceal the breach of respect.

Lionel and his chums had, of course, agreed upon a plan to so purposely bewilder Tommy with regard to past events that he should come at last to doubt the evidence of his own memory; and before breakfast was over they had succeeded so well in mixing up fact and fiction that Tommy really fancied that the miseries of the past two years were nothing but a dream.

"But there never was such a dream for being real," said Tommy. "Now, there's my aunt—I had an idea that she was dead."

"Your idea is correct so far, then, Tommy," replied Drummond. "The poor old lady is as dead as a first-class funeral and permanent appointments in the family mausoleum can make her."

"So I didn't dream that, then," Tommy continued, doubtfully. "How about her money? Did I dream that she had left it all to that dashed institution?"

"Very nearly right again, but she had the grace to bequeath you two hundred a-year, Tommy."

"Oh, she did, did she?" said Tommy, brightening

up a little. "Well, that is not so bad. Two hundred a year to do what I like with, eh?"

"That's a good notion of yours, pretending to be ignorant of that, Tommy, when you've had the spending of it for the last two years—and overdrawn your account regularly every quarter."

"It's funny, though," mused Tommy. "You've no idea, Li, how poor I thought I had been all that time. Why, I assure you, I've almost worshipped a shilling, and could hardly bring myself to believe that there was such a coin as a real sovereign in the whole world."

"In your dreams that was, of course," remarked Lionel.

"Of course," said Tommy, simply, and a roar of laughter followed the confession, much to the surprise of the plump youth, who quite failed to see where the laugh came in.

For three days this neat little game of mystification was carried on unremittingly by Lionel and his chums. Tommy was taken to localities and into houses which seemed perfectly strange, but which, he was gravely assured, he had visited a hundred times before. People as unfamiliar to him as his ancestor Adam came up and shook hands in a mock-familiar way, and at last Tommy, with his usual easy temper, took it all for granted, and would have acknowledged Brigham Young to be his brother if that gentleman had set up any claim to the relationship.

At last came the day appointed for the fancy ball, and early in the morning appeared Mr. Moses Nathan, the great costumier, with the dresses.

"I s'pose," said Tommy, as Nathan bowed himself almost double into the room, "I've met this chap somewhere before, too?"

"Met him before!" said Lionel. "Why, of course you have. He'll remember you, if you don't remember him though, Tommy, especially at the end of the month."

"Why?"

"Why? Oh, you innocent! Nathan, here's Mr. Codlings trying to forget that little bit of paper you hold of his."

"Aha!" chuckled the costumier, taking the cue at once, "Mishter Codlings will have his leetle choke."

"Due at the end of the month — ain't it, Nathan?"

"Chust so, Mishter Wilful, but if de shentleman vant him renewt it can be done on de usual derms."

"There's liberality for you, Tommy," said Lionel. "Don't you hear Nathan say that he will renew your bill on the usual terms, instead of clapping on twenty per cent. for the accommodation?"

Poor Tommy, who had never seen a "bill" in his life, was perfectly innocent of having ever put his name to such a document; but he, of course, set it down as one of the many things he seemed to have forgotten so unaccountably; and if Nathan had then and there demanded a thousand pounds of him he would not have dared to refuse payment.

Tommy was to go in the costume of a clown, and of course to sing "Hot Codlings" in character. Lionel had chosen the undress uniform of a Life Guardsman. Vansittart made his first and only appearance as a Wild Indian of the Wilderness, Heavitop assumed the garb of a harlequin, and, as a capital joke, Sam was to assume the traditional garb of Apollo, which airy attire set off the symmetry of his person to immense advantage.

"By George!" laughed Lionel, when the little party had donned their respective costumes, "we shall create a sensation."

"Sam will be the lion of the evening," added Charlie. "If he gets away before the girls tear him in pieces I shall be astonished."

"They don't get up to any of them sort o' games—do they, Master Lionel?"

"They won't mean you any harm, Sam; only they

will be so taken with the elegance of your figure that each one will want you for herself, and try to get you too."

Sam glanced complacently down at his legs, and thought that if he could could only show himself to Mary in that dress the conquest of her obdurate heart would be assured.

But before he had time to do more than entertain that pleasing reflection, a knock came at the door, and a waiter entered, bearing on a tray two cards, which he handed to Lionel.

Our hero took them, glanced at the names, and then said, with an air of dismay—

"Here's a go, you fellows. Here's Kramatome and Priggenham's father, the bishop, come to see us."

"Oh! my eye," gasped Charlie, in dismay, "let's get these things off."

"That would take a good half hour, and Kramatome says that he can't wait five minutes."

"Let's go in as we are then," said Vansittart; "the bishop will be pleased with the sight of his darling son in such a costume."

"Where is Priggenham?"

"Over there, taking a private peep at himself in the glass."

"I say, Heavitop," Lionel called out.

"What's matter?" rejoined the languid youth.

"Come into the next room, there's a fine cheval glass there, where we can see ourselves at full length."

"All right," replied the conceited Heavitop, swallowing the bait at once, and, unsuspecting, he allowed himself to be led out of that room, across the passage, and so to a door, through which Lionel pushed him with a jerk, and the rest of the masqueraders following, found themselves in the awful and reverend presences of Mr. Kramatome and the bishop.

CHAPTER V.

IN WHICH IT IS CONCLUSIVELY PROVED THAT VIRTUOUS INDIGNATION IS A BETTER ARTICLE FOR SHOW THAN FOR WEAR.

BISHOPS' and priests' tutors are, we believe, mortals, like more ordinary kind of men, but their position so elevates them above the rest of humanity that it is really wonderful how any one should have ever dared to think of trifling with them.

Mr. Kramatome could only gasp and stare for the first few moments, and doubt the evidence of his eyes, while the bishop's full-gravity and port wine complexion grew mottled with pallor, for he at once jumped to the conclusion that they had landed by mistake in a private mad-house.

But if the bishop was in a funk, and Mr. Kramatome astounded, what were the feelings of Heavitop Priggenham when he found himself in a tight-fitting spangled harlequin's dress, launched into the presence of his parent, and that parent a bishop?

It was too, too dreadful, and, uttering a faint squeak, he reeled into a corner, and swooned away with terror.

There was something in the voice which both Mr. Kramatome and the bishop seemed to recognise, and, as the supposed maniacs were bowing and smiling felicitously, all except Tommy, who was indulging in the most hideous grimaces and contortions, they managed to pluck up courage sufficient to ask what the intruders wanted.

"You sent for us, I believe, sir," replied Lionel, politely.

"Why, what?" faltered the astounded tutor. "Who in the name of wonder are you?"

"My name is Wilful, sir," replied our hero, calmly. "This is Lord Vansittart, the other is Codlings, and this ——"

"Enough, sir, enough," exclaimed Mr. Kramatome, becoming in an instant scarlet as a poppy with indignation and anger. "This is most scandalous! most ——"

At this point wrath choked Mr. Kramatome's utterance, and he fixed a glare on Tommy, which, if it had possessed the fabled power of the basilisk, would have crippled him on the spot.

Meanwhile the bishop, not a whit less angry than his companion, had singled out the limp form of his hopeful son, as he leaned against the wall, and in a day-of-judgment kind of voice, he said—

"Heavitop, is it indeed you that I behold in that garb of iniquity?"

Heavitop, at the sound of that well-remembered and much-dreaded voice, opened one eye, shuddered, and closed it again, gave a feeble kick, but made no further attempt to move.

"I am afraid, my lord," said Lionel, "that Heavitop is a little overcome. The pleasure of seeing his father so unexpectedly has been too much for him. Allow me to assist him."

And before the bishop could accept or reject the offer, Lionel had lifted Heavitop under the arms, hauled him across the floor, and dropped him into his loving father's embrace.

Even a bishop knows how to temper mercy with justice, and to carry out the golden precepts of Solomon.

"My son," he said, in a voice broken by emotion, "the wise king has written—'spare the spoil and rod the child.' You have outraged your parent's sense of propriety, and you must suffer."

Thereupon he seized him gently by the back hair, and the tight harlequin's suit, lending itself conveniently for the purpose, he smacked him with his episcopal right hand, until poor Heavitop howled dismally, and three waiters and four chambermaids stood amazed in the doorway, looking on the novel spectacle of a real bishop condescending to spank his son like an ordinary mortal.

Mr. Kramatome gazed in wonder too, but as he had a great respect for the Church, and especially the higher dignitaries thereof, he did not dare to question the correctness of the bishop's conduct—he only contented himself with gently intimating that the operation would be more seemly if performed in private.

"True, my friend," replied Heavitop senior. "My son's disgraceful conduct moved me to wrath, which I regret, but we will resume this discussion upon our arrival at home. Will you accompany me as soon as your business with these—these young persons is concluded?"

"What I have to say now," added Mr. Kramatome, sternly, "is soon said. In the first place, Wilful, inform me why you have chosen to insult me by making your appearance in these digraceful costumes?"

"There was no intention to insult you, sir," replied our hero. "We were going to a masquerade ball to-night, and had just tried on the dresses when your cards were sent in. There was no time to change them for our own clothes, and we came as we were, rather than keep you waiting."

"A plausible excuse, Wilful," said Mr. Kramatome; "but rather too ingenious to be true. I distinctly forbid you to go to that sink of iniquity called a masquerade ball, and you will please to take up your residence at my house at once. Your farther leave of absence is stopped. I expect to be obeyed, and that implicitly."

And without another word the angry and indignant tutor drew his handkerchief from his pocket, blew his nose with a sharp ringing sound, like that of a trumpet, and stalked away, accompanied by the bishop and the suffering Heavitop, junior.

There was silence for a moment or two after the departure, and then Lionel burst into a hearty laugh.

"It's all very well to laugh," said Vansittart; "but there's no ball, old fellow, and our leave is stopped."

"Hullo! what's this?" said Charlie, picking up an oblong piece of enamelled pasteboard from the carpet. Kramatome must have dropped this when he pulled out his handkerchief. Look, Li, it's a ticket for the very masquerade ball we were going to."

"So it is, Charlie. The hypocritical old rascal! He means to go himself—to this very sink of iniquity."

"Then I'll tell you what," said Vansittart "we'll all go too, and if he is there we'll have such a lark with him that he won't forget it in a thousand years."

"I'm on," said Lionel. "Come on, you fellows, and let's plan the lark out. I shall enjoy it. I haven't had a good one for years."

CHAPTER VI.

FAREWELL TO LIBERTY.

"POOR PRIGGENHAM will get in for it," laughed Lionel. "Who would have thought that a bishop could have condescended to spank his son like an ordinary mortal?"

"Quite against the rules, I should say," added Vansittart. "He ought to have excommunicated Heavitop."

"I wonder what he'll larrup him with when he gets him home?" added Charlie. "Not with the episcopal crozier, I hope, or poor Heavitop will have sore bones to dance at the ball with."

"Let's get these things off first," said Lionel, "for all the servants in the hotel are grinning outside the door—and then we can settle matters."

There was indeed a crowd grinning outside the door, composed of not only the servants, but of several of the swell guests, who were gazing aghast.

An old Indian officer, indeed—invalided on full pay, a pension, and a liver complaint—called to his servant for his sword, and loudly declared his intention of cutting the liver out of the vile plebeians who had dared to invade the sanctity of the hotel.

"Now," said Lionel, as soon as they had got rid of their fancy dresses, and were once more wearing the ordinary costume of the nineteenth century; "now for our little plot. I take it for granted that old Kramatome will be there?"

"Certain," said Charlie, jumping to the conclusion with the easy agility which youth alone possesses; "and the bishop, too."

"Oh, come!" said Tommy, opening his little round eyes. "Don't fetch it too strong, Drum. A bishop couldn't go to a fancy ball. It's high treason, ain't it?"

"Gammon and spinach," retorted Charlie. "Why, you must remember our spotting the Archbishop of York at the Argyll Rooms last winter. What a jolly old cock he was—stood no end of oysters and champagne afterwards! Come, Tommy, you must remember that!"

Tommy did not, for the best of all reasons—the circumstance had never happened; but he set it down to his unaccountably bad memory, and tried to look as if he knew all about it.

"Of course Tommy does," added our hero. "He remembers how he bet the archbishop that he wouldn't walk round Regent Circus, through Tichborne-street, and down the Haymarket, in full dress—gaiters, big lawn sleeves, and all."

"And did he?" said Tommy.

"Did he? Of course he did. He jumped into a hansom cab, drove down to Lambeth, borrowed a suit at the Palace, and in one hour was walking down the Haymarket in full fig, and you had to fork over fifty pounds."

"Did I?" said Tommy, opening his eyes wider than ever.

"Of course you did. You had to borrow the tin from old Moses, and he's had you in his clutches ever since, and there you're likely to stop as long as you will insist upon playing guinea points at whist when you know no more of the game than a guinea-pig."

"Do I really bet 'em?" said Tommy, thoughtfully. "I never used to. Irish Mike used to toss me coppers sometimes, but he nearly always won—or if he didn't he said he did, and punched my head to convince me."

"A good way of arguing, that!" laughed Lionel. "But come, this isn't business. What are we going to do about this ball?"

"Let's all dress up as bishops," suggested Tommy, "and take the shine out of the real article."

"Wouldn't do," said Lionel. "That would be carrying the joke too far. We should be kicked out of the ball-room if we did that."

"And serve us right too," added Vansittart. "A lark's a lark, but we must draw the line somewhere. Religion's too sacred a thing to be made a jest of."

"But not a bishop," said Charlie, with a wink.

"That's quite a different thing," added our hero. "But after all, you fellows, I think we'd better leave it to chance. Let's go to the ball, and trust to luck for the fun to turn up."

"But I say, Li, how are we to find out Kramatome? He'll be in some fancy dress, and he's sure to wear a mask."

"We'll find him out fast enough, never fear," replied Lionel. "The thing is to keep him from finding us out."

"Shall we obey his orders, and go up to his house to-morrow?"

"Certainly. We'll pretend to be obedient, and very sorry for what we've done, and all that; and when he's started for the ball we'll follow."

"How about poor Heavitop?"

"Oh, we'll call and fetch him."

"He'll be too funky to come, Li."

"Not he; you've only got to tell him of all the swells who will be there, and promise to introduce him to a duke, or a prince of the blood royal, and he'd walk there on his head."

"Is he such a snob as all that?" laughed Vansittart; "if he is, by George, we'll astonish him. We'll present him to all the crowned heads of Europe, Asia, and Africa."

"Don't you think it will be best, boys," said Lionel, after a moment, "to go to old Kramatome's at once? We might get a chance of smelling out if he really is going—and, if so, what dress he's going to wear."

"Hear, hear," said Charlie; "I second that motion. Tell Sam to pack up, and we'll be off as soon as a cab can take us."

"You'd better not entrust Sam with your packing," said Lionel, "if ever you want to find your property again. He has the most ingenious way of putting things where nobody can ever find em, that you can imagine."

"Thanks for the tip, Li, I'll look after my own traps, then."

"You'd better, and you too Tommy, cut away—you're the slowest, and you'd better begin at once."

"Oh! am I?" said Tommy, in an injured tone. "Why when I lodged in Slum-alley, Seven Dials, along with Irish Mike, the house caught fire, and we were'nt two minutes in dressing, packing up, and getting the whelk-barrow and the stock out into the street."

"At that rubbish again about Irish Mike—are you?" replied Lionel. "What a fellow you are, Tommy! there's no such a person as Irish Mike. You dreamt it, you know."

"Oh, ah! so I did," said Tommy, doubtfully, "but you've no idea how real it all seems, Li. I fancy I can hear Mike swearing at the policeman, and I can smell the very whelks in the sack; they were a week old, you see, and rather strong."

"There, cut away," laughed our hero; "you'll smell something better than stale whelks by-and-bye. If Heavitop Priggenham were here, he'd cut

your company for alluding to such vulgar things in his aristocratic presence."

"Blow that Priggenham," grumbled Tommy, "I begin to hate him as much as I did those Bobbles, at Stiffback's—a conceited stuck-up muff."

"Take care he don't hear you say that, Tommy. Heavitop's sure to send you a challenge."

"I'll fight him—I'd like to fight him. I learned how to handle my fists a bit while I was with Irish Mike, and ——"

"There you go with your Irish Mike again," interrupted Lionel. "'Pon my word, Tommy, you won't be fit for decent society if you don't leave off making allusions to such vagabonds."

"It's the most extraordinary dream I ever heard of," said Tommy; "it gets mixed up with everything."

"It will mix you up with a lunatic asylum if you don't look out, Tommy," said Lionel, gravely. "You'd better have medical advice about it if you don't improve. Those deliriums are serious things if they're not checked in time."

And away Lionel went, leaving Tommy to get on with his packing in a rather gloomy state of mind, from which he was only roused by the reflection that he would soon meet the aristocratic Heavitop, and by punching his head relieve his own overburdened intellect.

Lionel and Vansittart proceeded to their own rooms, leaving Charlie and Tommy at the hotel where the cabs were ordered to be in readiness in an hour's time.

Before that period had elapsed our five friends—for our readers will allow us to reckon Sam amongst the number—were all ready, and looking so jovial and happy that no one would have guessed that they were relinquishing their liberty for the formal restraint of a private tutor's establishment.

Mr. Kramatome's establishment was situate in the classic regions of Bloomsbury, the mausoleum of departed greatness, the happy hunting-ground of poor gentility and unsuccessful art.

Mr. Kramatome's house in Queen-square was gloomy of course—a vermilion mansion, with gold railings, would look dull in *that* neighbourhood—but there was an air of primness and neatness about it which most of its neighbours wanted.

The windows were clean (a rare thing indeed in Bloomsbury—you never hear of a servant being spiked on the iron railings in that district)—the doorstep looked as if it had daily intercourse with a pen'orth of hearthstone, and the curtains were white, another rarity.

The bell-handles and door-plate, the latter with "Mr. Kramatome" in small Roman capitals upon it, were polished to a pitch of brightness that would have fitted them for a jeweller's window; and, altogether, there was full justification for Lionel's words, as the two cabs drew up to the door.

"My word, Charlie, old Kramatome keeps his slaveys up to the mark."

The door was opened almost before the echoes of the double knock had died away, and a scrupulously neat and well-brushed but worn-out looking footman conducted them down the passage, through green baize-covered folding-doors, and so into the sanctum of Mr. Kramatome.

He was seated at the table, writing with a sharp pen, which scratched and spluttered viciously, as if it were quarrelling with the paper.

He looked up as our heroes entered, and frowned like a July thunderstorm.

"What is this, young gentlemen?" he said in a severe voice. "I ordered you to return to-morrow."

"You did, sir," replied Lionel, politely, "but we were so ashamed of our late conduct, and so afraid of being led away into temptation again, if we were left alone, that we thought it best to put ourselves under your protection at once."

"Oh, you thundering humbug!" thought Charlie,

as he put his hand to his face and coughed, to choke down a strong tendency to laugh.

"Ahem! very good," said the tutor, after a pause. "Your reason is a praiseworthy one—if, as of course I cannot doubt, it is true. But remember this in future, that I insist upon punctuality, and that virtue consists as little in being too early as in being too late."

"Quite so, sir," said Lionel, who as usual took the lead. "We will endeavour to meet your wishes in future in every way."

"I hope so," replied the tutor. "I only receive pupils upon the full understanding that they render me implicit obedience, and that I have complete control of them—that I stand, in fact, *in loco parentis*. Unless this authority is delegated to me I decline to receive anyone."

"We quite understand you, sir," said Lionel, again.

"And I you," replied Mr. Kramatome. "I have made a special study of the mind and character of youth, and the boy does not live whom I cannot read as easily as I can what is written on that paper."

"Don't you be too clever, old boy," thought Lionel, "or we shall take you in yet. If I don't teach you a thing or two before we part, my name's not Wilful."

"You have brought your servant with you?" continued the tutor.

"I have, sir."

"Let me see—er—what do you call him?"

"Sam Scarecrow, sir."

"Decidedly descriptive," answered the tutor with a slight smile, "but that is only a nick-name, of course?"

"It is the only one he has," replied Lionel, "and I doubt if he would change it for the proudest patronymic in England."

"Very good; if he is satisfied I am," said Mr. Kramatome, as he rang the bell. "You can go now, young gentlemen. Joblot will show you your rooms, and you will dine with me this evening."

CHAPTER VII.

THE SAME OLD GAME.

"NOT a bad crib," said Lionel, after the bedrooms had undergone a critical survey, "but I wish they were arranged on the old school-dormitory plan—all together."

"Oh, that don't matter much," said Vansittart. "We can easily get together when we choose: our rooms are all in the same passage."

"How about the rules though?" said Charlie, pointing to a neatly written card, framed and hung up against the wall—"Rule V.: Any pupil detected leaving his own room or entering any other room, or holding conversation with another pupil or pupils during prohibited hours, shall be punished with solitary confinement, at the discretion of the principal."

"Cheerful, that," was Lionel's comment. "Reads like a slice of an Act of Parliament or a criminal indictment."

"And the others are all as bad," said Charlie— "the whole twenty-two of 'em."

"Everything seems to be forbidden, and nothing permitted," added Vansittart. "I say, Li, we've got into a clock-work shop this time."

"It is the sort of man," said Tommy, reflectively, "who would have invented the flogging-machine if Stiffback hadn't been beforehand."

"Perhaps he's bought the patent and improved on it, Tommy," said Lionel; "so look out, old boy. You're sure to break the rule that forbids snoring."

"Here, dash it, Li, there's no rule against that!"

"Isn't there though? Read that—'Rule XVI.: Any pupil guilty of riotous behaviour, or of causing an unseemly disturbance or noise in his bedroom, will be punished by deprivation of leave of absence at the discretion of the principal.' Now, Tommy, if your snoring isn't exactly 'riotous behaviour,' it's certainly an 'unseemly noise,' so you're in for it."

"This is tyranny, you know," said Tommy, who snored like a whole brass band. "I'm not going to put up with such a rule as that."

"You'll have to, old fellow. You're in for it now. But, there, you can tie a towel over your head, and get under the pillow, that will muffle the sound."

"Yes, and me too. I should be a ready-made article for a coffin in the morning."

"I say, what's your name?" said Lionel to the melancholy footman. "Is Mr. Kramatome very strict?"

"Strict ain't the word for it, sir," replied Joblot, after a careful glance around to see that there was no other servant within hearing, "the Pennytenshary's a perfeck Parydise to this here place."

"You don't look very happy I must say," laughed Lionel.

"You see, sir," continued Joblot, "I came here under a contrack. He ses to me when I came after the place, 'Joblot,' ses he, 'I don't want no referentials, I can see right through a man at a glance,' he ses, which was lucky, for I hadn't got a character o' my hown jest then, and I'd brought a friend's, which I thought might do as well. 'Werry well, sir,' I ses. Then he ses 'Wages is not partikler high, but there's lots o' perkesits from the young gents as come to study, and,' he ses, 'the wittles is onlimited.'"

"That was liberal anyhow."

"So I thought, sir," said Joblot, with a miserable expression of countenance. "But you see that was where I was took in. If the wittles was onlimited *the time to eat 'em in warn't*,"

"I see," laughed Lionel.

"In course you do, and so did I arter I'd put my name to the contrack. We has five minutes to breakfast, and ten minutes to dinner, and I put it to you, gents, how is a man, even when he's handy with his knife and fork, to get enough wittles into him in that time?"

"Unreasonable," said Lionel.

"There ain't no time to chaw, and so I tried bolting the wittles. The first week I choked five times, and had to be stood on my 'ed behind the scullery door to bring me round, and now I suffers from a hindychestun which'll bring me to a hearly grave."

"Let us hope not," said Charlie. "You're reserved for something better than that, Joblot. You'd make a fortune in the undertaking business."

"Thankee for the hint, sir. When this 'ere contrack's over I'll try it, but he's got me fast for three year, and one ain't gone yet. Oh, dear!"

"Poor Sam," thought Lionel; "if he comes under the same rule, and is fed by contract in that way he won't be so fat as his own shadow in a month."

"I say, Joblot," said Charlie, "does Mr. Kramatome feed himself in the same way?"

"He says he do," replied the melancholy footman, "but do he look like it?"

"He certainly does not," said Lionel, "but you mustn't judge by appearances. Look at my servant Sam. Now, you'd think that he was fed by contract as well as you?"

"He are this certingly, sir," said Joblot, "but there's a 'appy look about his heye, which seems to say that he has a hour for his dinner, and *spends the time well*."

"You're a judge, Joblot," laughed our hero. "There's something to buy a private leg of mutton with, go and spend it wisely and well. And now, you fellows, what's the next move?"

"Wait till something turns up."

"But that was old Micawber's plan, and see what became of him. Let's turn up something for ourselves," said Lionel. "Old Kramatome's safe in his study—let's hunt round the house and see if we can find out any fun."

Everbody jumped at the idea except Tommy.

"No, Li," he said, resolutely, "I made a vow when we were at Stiffback's, that if ever we met again, I'd keep clear of you when you mean't going in for a lark."

"But, why, Tommy? I'm sure you always enjoyed yourself."

"Did I? Oh! yes, I daresay. Come now," was Tommy's indignant reply, "wasn't I always the one pitched upon when that dashed flogging-machine wanted exercise? Wasn't it me as every blessed bobby and beadle and shopkeeper always dropped upon, while you got off scot-free? Come now, Li, tell the truth, don't sneak out of it."

"All your fancy, Tommy," said Lionel, coolly, "like that dream of yours about Irish Mike. But if you won't come, stop behind."

And away our hero started, followed by Drummond and Vansittart.

Tommy watched them until they turned the corner out of sight, and then he began to wonder what they would find out. Then the demon of curiosity prompting him he began to feel sorry that he hadn't gone with them, and from that to following them was a very short and easy step.

"I'll just creep up behind 'em," said Tommy, "and see what they're at, and when they come back if they try to cram me with any of their yarns I can be down upon them."

Tommy went on round the corner where his chums had disappeared, but there he found that the corridor branched off in opposite directions, and the puzzle was to know which way Lionel and the others had gone.

"Blow it, here's a nuisance," thought Tommy. "Now if I was an Indian I could put my nose down to the oil-cloth and smell at the war-trail, but I ain't. I know, I'll do as they do at blindman's buff, turn round three times and then go ahead."

Tommy closed his eyes firmly, turned round three times with a staggering, uncertain motion, like that of a tipsy teetotum, and then shot forward head first against the sacred waistcoat of Mr. Kramatome, just as that gentleman, with a lady on his arm, opened the door and stepped out into the corridor.

CHAPTER VIII.

TOMMY'S ADVENTURE.

THE sensation Mr. Kramatome experienced was like an earthquake, a flash of lightning, and a bad stomach-ache all rolled into one, for Tommy, being giddy with turning round, had, so to speak, rifled himself, and butted the tutor with horrible accuracy in the exact locality of the diaphragm.

The lady who was anchored to Mr. Kramatome fared scarcely better, for she was of a light, spare build, and the jerk with which she was detached from her partner whirled her round like a feather in a gale of wind, and finally landed her on Tommy, who was sitting on the floor feeling for his head, which he had some dim idea had been knocked off in the encounter.

"Oh, what is it?" shrieked the elderly lady. "Oh, save me! Is it serious? Is it fire?"

"I don't know," murmured Tommy, vaguely. "I think it was Irish Mike. I felt just like this once when he hit me on the head with a bushel of whelks in a sack."

By this time Mr. Kramatome had recovered his breath and his footing, and fairly boiling over with wrath he glared round and beheld Tommy in the fond embrace of the lady whose heart (and banking account) he fondly hoped one day to call his own.

Mr. Kramatome never doubted for an instant but that it was a carefully-conceived plot to assassinate him, and elope with his promised bride; and, without calling upon Tommy for any unnecessary explanations, he seized him by the hair with one hand, and began to "punch" his head most scientifically with the other.

"You audacious, double-dyed scoundrel!" roared the tutor. "I'll teach you to try your scoundrelly tricks on here. Take that—and that—and that!"

Now, it had never been a habit of Tommy's to take much of that kind of article without making a fair return, and—as my readers know—he was now in much better form than in the old days at Stiffback's. He closed manfully with Mr. Kramatome, and returned his blows with good interest.

But the tutor, like most University men, was an accomplished boxer and heavier than his opponent, besides which, Tommy's old ill-luck told against him, for fully half the blows intended for Mr. Kramatome were wasted on the air, or knocked the dust out of the carpet; while every one of his enemy's blows told with deadly effect.

The fight would have ended badly for Tommy but for the presence of mind of the lady, who, knowing the efficacy of cold water in fainting fits, thought it might possibly be equally good in cases of superabundant energy; so, seizing a jug that stood conveniently near, she emptied the contents with great impartiality over her lover and his supposed rival.

Of course, though, Tommy had the worst of it, even when there was the greatest desire on the part of the lady to dispense even-handed justice. Tommy's share went down his neck, and wetted him to the skin, while Mr. Kramatome's portion remained outside.

It brought them to, though. Cold water is a fine thing for bringing the thermometer of passion from fever heat down to zero. If during a riot the firemen were called out, instead of the military, and a few gallons of cold water pumped on the crowd, it would be far more effectual than lead, and not half so weakening.

But to resume. The combatants ceased to struggle, plunge, and lurch on the carpet. Each relinquished his hold, and scrambled to his feet, Tommy glaring out of his only available eye, and Mr. Kramatome squinting furiously down a nose which resembled nothing in the world so much as a ripe tomato.

"Who are you—and how dare you—you insolent blackguard?" panted the tutor, by way of commencement to a polite conversation.

"And how dare you, for the matter of that?" grumbled the injured Tommy. "I didn't agree to pay two hundred pounds a year to have my head punched the very first night. If you *begin* educating a chap that way, how do you leave off? Swallow him, I s'pose."

"Why," exclaimed Mr. Kramatome, aghast, "it's one of my new pupils, I declare."

"Of course it is," growled Tommy. "What do you want to go and knock a fellow's head off before you can find out whose it is?"

"Don't talk to me like that, sir. Where is the ruffian who knocked me down at first? That's all."

"I pushed against you in a gentle kind of way," said Tommy.

"Don't talk to me about pushes," said Mr. Kramatome, fiercely. "It takes more than a push to upset me. If it was not you who did it?"

"In a sort of a way I leaned up against you, a little hard perhaps, but I didn't see anybody else about," was Tommy's explanation.

"You are an idiot, sir!" thundered Mr. Kramatome, his nose getting redder than ever, which was exceedingly difficult, and very creditable to the nose.

"Go to your room, Codlings. I'll lean up against you presently, sir."

"I'll make him wish for a pair of wings and a gold

harp if he does," growled Tommy. "Blow it! how he has bunged my eyes up. The passage looks three miles long. I wonder where the first step is? I ——"

Tommy didn't finish that sentence for nearly a quarter of an hour, as, just at that moment, in consequence of his impaired vision, he missed the top step, and passed over the other forty-nine in such a way that he hadn't time to count them till he got to the bottom, and then he didn't feel any interest in the question.

Somebody else did though, and that was Joblot, the melancholy footman, who was passing with a trayful of Mr. Kramatome's best cut wine glasses, claret jugs, decanters, and such like ware.

As Tommy turned his last somersault his right foot caught Joblot in the middle of the back, and one loud crash rang out the knell of the whole ten pounds' worth.

The melancholy one looked at the wreck with an expression of the most utter misery.

"Oh, my!" he groaned. "You've done it now whoever you are. There's ten pounds at least gone to smash, and the guv'nor 'll call it twenty, and according to the terms of our contrack all broken harticles must be paid for or worked out. Twenty pound and five pound a year—that's another five year o' penal servitood."

"Hullo!" murmured Tommy, dreamily, as he recovered from the effects of the fall, and struggled into a sitting posture; "where's the balloon? What did they let the gas out like that for?"

"Why did you go and let drive your foot in the middle o' my back, sir?" demanded Joblot; "but there, it don't matter, if you hadn't done it somebody else would, and p'raps have spiled me as well as the glass."

"Where's Irish Mike?" gasped Tommy, wildly, still oblivious as to his precise whereabouts. "Let's have another round, he don't fight fair, he hit me with the eighty-one ton-gun."

"And swallowed the balls in mistake for Cockle's pills. Here, Mister Scarecrow," shouted Joblot, as he caught sight of the long youth at the end of the passage. "Here's one o' your young gents fancies he's the Woolwich Infant, and wants me to fire him off."

"Blow me if it ain't that young himidge of a Codlings," muttered Sam, as he came running up in obedience to the shout; "wot a chap he is for getting into a scrape to be sure. He get's more than his fair dose of pepper in *this* world. They ought to make a first-class hangel of him when they gets him in the other one, if a right balance is struck. Come up! What a weight he is to be sure! He's growed a couple o' stone since the day afore yesterday. That's about the only thing he's lucky in—his wittles does him good."

"And do you know why?" said the melancholy footman.

"Not pertikler," said Sam.

"It's becos he has a proper time to eat 'em in. Feed a man on winkles and turtle-soup, and saveloys and wenson, and give him only five minutes for his dinner, and they don't do him a bit o' good—the wittles turns to bile, and the man turns yaller, and falls away to skin and bone, like me."

"Look here, old feller," said Sam, "I don't think you're a bad sort, and as soon as we've got Mr. Codlings all right, and out of the way, we'll have a chat. I may be able to do you a good turn, and you may be able to do me one."

"You scratch my back and I'll scratch yourn!" replied Mr. Joblot, quoting a vulgar but expressive proverb. "Oh! Mister Scarecrow, if my fizzical powers wasn't so redoosed by want of time to eat my grub in, I could a tale unfold."

"Reel it orf, then," said Sam; "let's have arf-a-yard now, and I'll stand a quartern to ile the jints."

Sam stood the quartern, and then another, and another, until Mr. Joblot grew remarkably confidential, and imparted to Sam some information of an extremely valuable and interesting character, respecting that upright and moral character—Keziah Kramatome, M.A., of Oxford, fellow of several learned societies, and private tutor to our hero and his chums.

CHAPTER IX.
ON THE WAY TO THE BALL—FIRE!

ANY young gentleman at all worthy of the name would have scorned to appear in public with such a disfigured countenance as Tommy bore, but it would have taken a good deal more than a pair of black eyes and a headache to keep our plump friend from any amusement on which he had set his heart—as was the case with the fancy ball.

"Besides," he said to Lionel, "I shall have my face painted, and two dozen black eyes wouldn't show through such a coat of whiting as Sam will lay on."

"All right, Tommy, only if the whiting does come off, don't you go near Priggenham, or he'll faint."

"If I do go near him it'll be to serve him with a dose of black eyes for himself," replied Tommy. "Do you think that old Kramatome will go after all? I told you what a lovely nose I'd given him."

"He'll go, of course. He'll tie on a false nose, and wear a pair of pasteboard goggles to hide his black eye."

"Has he got a black eye, too?"

"Rather; Joblot told Sam that he was up all night putting vinegar and raw beef on it; but it's no good—it's as black as your boot this morning."

"Hooray!" said Tommy.

"It won't be hooray for you, my boy, when he's well again," said Lionel. "He's let you off to-day because he can't show himself in that state, but you look out for squalls next week."

"Blow next week!" said Tommy, defiantly. "This week is quite enough for me while it lasts. I say, old Kramatome won't put on his fancy dress here, will he?"

"Not likely—ha, ha! Fancy the sensation he would create in Bloomsbury if he did!"

But further speculation as to that problematical event was checked by the necessity for preparation. The dresses had to be looked over again to make sure that there was no fatal deficiency which would spoil matters at the last moment.

Mr. Kramatome had left early in the evening, with positive directions that no one should leave the house till his return.

To this Lionel and his chums returned an obedient "Yes, sir—certainly!" But to themselves they winked, and muttered "Walker!"

Joblot had been taken into the conspiracy, and with exceeding artfulness he managed to lure the old housekeeper away from the window, while our hero and his chums shot up the area steps dressed in their fancy dresses, over which flowed from head to heel the sheltering folds of their Ulsters.

"Jolly coats these," Vansittart said. "No one could guess whether a fellow was a pee or a policeman in such a rig."

"They're first-rate," replied Lionel; "and as its a chilly night suppose we walk to the ball."

"Done with you," said Vansittart and Drummond, but Sam, who was following a short distance behind, had an objection to offer—

"Beg your pardon, Master Lionel, but here's Master Codlings. His coat do 'ide his figger; but there's the chalk on his face. He do look that ghastly in the lamplight that it give me quite a turn just now when I looked at him."

"Oh, nobody'll notice him. Keep your hat well over your eyes, Tommy."

" All right, Li."

And so the little party went on, until at a crossing a respectable old lady, seeing some well-dressed young gentlemen, stopped to inquire the time, and pitched upon Tommy to satisfy her curiosity.

"Certainly, ma'am," replied the plump youth, with his accustomed politeness; but the instant he stepped into the light of the lamp to look at his watch, the old lady caught sight of his death-white face, and with a shriek that would have set the teeth of a marble statue on edge, she dropped her umbrella and fled.

"Con-found you, Tommy! There you are already. Hurry up, or we shall have the police after us. We had better take a couple of cabs, after all. That old party will have a fit, and if she goes off you'll be responsible," said Lionel.

"It was Sam's fault. He would lay the white on too thick," said Tommy, in excuse.

"Keep that tongue still, and that hat more over your eyes," said Lionel. "I—hullo! what's that?"

A deep lurid glare in the sky, pierced by tongues of brilliant yellow and scarlet flame—a dull hoarse roar as of an angry sea beating on a rock-bound coast—a dozen streams of men and women and children, all struggling, all eager to reach one point, the entrance to a narrow street, where a little band of stern-faced men in tunics and helmets withstand the rush—one glance at this and the boys knew that it was that familiar yet ever fascinating sight—a fire!

"This way, you fellows. It's Sillys's Rooms that are burning, and all the people are inside!" cried Vansittart. "Here comes an engine—catch it as the crowd opens, and run through with it; then we are all right. I know the chief, and he will pass us anywhere."

Almost breathless with excitement the boys waited for the engine, which came with a fierce onward rush like a dense squadron of cavalry charging a battery.

It was a dangerous feat that our heroes were about to attempt, and many a grown man of proven courage would have thought twice before attempting to "board" the engine, which, at the full speed of its two half-bred horses, came thundering on.

They did it, though—all but Tommy, who, mistaking a fireman's leg for one of the fixtures, and grabbing it firmly with both hands, dragged him off his perch, and reeled into the crowd, hugging him with a fond embrace, and knocking a dozen of the spectators down like skittle-pins.

The fireman was nearly mad with vexation, for he was a young hand, anxious to distinguish himself; and here, almost at his first fire, Tommy had baulked his hopes of promotion and a medal.

He was a strong man, and of a warm temper, as became his profession. Without wasting any time in useless explanations, he scrambled to his feet, glared around him, picked out an inoffensive old gentleman who had got wedged into the crowd much against his will, and staggered him with a tremendous blow right between the eyes.

There was a policeman close by, also anxious to distinguish himself, and he promptly took the fireman into custody.

"I've got you!" he growled; "and now I means to run you in."

"There's two parties to that question," said the fireman, now fairly maddened with the pain of his bruises and the loss of his place on the engine. Let go, will yer?"

"Come on!" said the constable, with a tremendous tug at the fireman's collar.

"I won't!"

"You'd better come quiet."

"I'll see you——"

The rest of the sentence—which we are inclined to think consisted of some very bad language—was fortunately lost in the uproar created by the cheers of the admiring crowd.

Our friend Tommy, with his usual good luck, had managed to exchange the frying-pan for the fire. True, the arrival of the police had diverted the polite attentions of the fireman, but it must be remembered that he was on the ground in the midst of an excited crowd, and he couldn't get up again.

In about ten minutes Tommy's unhappy carcass was intimately acquainted with every variety of boots and shoes worn by the populace of London.

Wellingtons, Bluchers, Napoleons, riding-boots, spring-side boots, lace-up boots, apologies for boots, kicked him, trod upon him, and gave him such an unmerciful bruising that if he had been run through a sausage-machine he could hardly have suffered more.

Tommy howled for mercy—for help—threatened vengeance against his tormentors, and even—we are sorry to add—swore.

But he might as well have whistled "God save the Queen" in the hope of stilling a West Indian hurricane. In desperation Tommy adopted extreme measures, and taking firm hold of a foot which happened just then to be planted on the pit of his stomach, he raised himself by a great effort, and took a juicy bit out of the calf.

The unfortunate possessor of the calf brought his leg up with a jerk which loosened three of Tommy's front teeth, and left him a specimen mouthful of Noses's far-famed four-and-ninepenny trousers.

The victim was a sort of giant in his way, six feet four inches in height and sixteen stone in weight. He felt sure that a dog had bitten him, and as he had a horror of hydrophobia he charged the crowd like a mad bull in his fear, and for a moment cleared a space just sufficient to allow Tommy to get upon his legs.

"I never was so thankful for anything in all my life," gasped Tommy. "Oh, my, ain't I sore! I'd give ten pounds to be out of this crowd."

But our old friend was not yet destined to achieve his wish. Goliath of Gath or Hercules would have been powerless to extricate himself from such a wedged-up mass of humanity.

There was another warning cry from the crowd, another engine dashed up with a rattling roar, and Tommy was jammed in more helplessly than ever.

In the meantime Lionel and the others had succeeded in gaining the inner circle, where the Captain of the Fire Brigade was stationed, directing the efforts of his little army against the might of the destroying flames.

He recognised Vansittart at once, and passed them on to a position where they could see the scene of destruction to full advantage.

The fire had begun in the basement, and so rapidly had it spread that before the alarm was sounded the dancers on the upper floor had their retreat cut off.

The windows of the third and fourth floors were crowded with dozens of figures, arranged in their quaint, grotesque, or handsome costumes, frantically gesticulating for help.

"By George," said Lionel, aghast. "What horrible danger they are in. Where are the escapes?"

"Coming, I suppose," said Charlie. "But they always manage to be a couple of hours behind the engines. That's why they're called fire-escapes, because they always manage to escape the fire by coming when it's out."

"Don't joke, Charlie," said Lionel. "This is awful. Look! the smoke is coming out of the windows where they are, and I fancy I can see the red glare of the fire behind."

"Here comes the fire-escape!" shouted Vansittart. "Hurrah!"

"And there's another coming up the other way," said Lionel, echoing the cheer, which was instantly taken up by the crowd, and drowned for a moment the noise of the engines, and the roar of the conflagration.

The escapes were got into position with marvellous rapidity, but not an instant too soon.

With the agility of cats the practised firemen ran up the ladders, broke in the window frames with their short hatchets, and then, by twos and even threes, lowered the terrified masqueraders.

Before the task was half completed the heat of the flames was so intense that one of the engines had to play over rescuers and rescued alike, to cool them, and beat down the blinding suffocating smoke.

"Some of them will suffer for this to-morrow," said Lionel. "Look, boys, there's old Kramatome, as I'm alive! I could swear to him. There again—ha. ha!—they pumped clean over him that time."

Lionel's keen eyes had not been mistaken. It was indeed Mr. Kramatome, attired in the tight and airy costume of a troubadour, blacked with smoke and soaked with water, as he slid, limp and helpless, down the sack of the escape.

"Come on, boys," said Vansittart, "they're all safe now—he's the last—let's go and give him a lift."

"It will only be polite to offer him our assistance, now that he's in trouble."

"Won't he be wild just?" laughed Charlie. "Keep your Ulsters well buttoned up. If he twigs our fancy dresses we shall be in for it."

"It won't matter—he will be in such a fuddled state that he won't know whether we're in full dress or stark naked."

By the time this little colloquy was over our heroes had made their way to the foot of the escape, where the miserable revellers were huddled together, Mr. Kramatome the wettest and most miserable of them all.

"Good evening, sir," said Lionel, bowing politely, "I hope you have had a pleasant time. Rather warm for dancing though, I think."

Mr. Kramatome opened his eyes, stared at the boys, and then, as he recognised them, he felt that the cup of his misery was full. He was lowered in the sight of his pupils, and could never hope to command more than outward respect, if he was lucky enough to get so much as that.

"May I offer you a little refreshment, sir?" added Vansittart, with grave politeness. "You must have found that fire-escape rather trying."

Mr. Kramatome's reply was not quite audible, but we think it had some reference to a place several degrees warmer than the burning house from which the tutor had just escaped.

He was by far too wet and uncomfortable to argue with the boys just then; but he swore a mental oath that he would be even with them before long, and whether he succeeded or not my readers will discover before many more chapters of this veracious narrative are written.

The messenger he had sent in search of a cab came back about this time, and Mr. Kramatome, without going through the useless formality of saying good-bye to our heroes, strode off, looking a more disconsolate scarecrow than ever any farmer put up in a field to frighten sparrows.

"We shall suffer for this, I bet," laughed Lionel. "Don't you feel funky, Tommy? Hullo! where is he?"

For the first time our hero noticed the absence of the unlucky youth, and with some small degree of alarm.

"I hope he hasn't got into any mess," said Vansittart, "and none of us near to help him out. Sam, have you seen Mr. Codlings anywhere?"

"Not arf a hinch of him, my lud," replied Sam, "since we ran on alonger the hingine."

"No more have I," added Charlie. "I saw him run at the engine when we did, and I made sure that he came through as we did."

"Then, knowing Tommy as well as you ought to, Charlie," said Lionel, "you might have guessed that he would tumble under the wheels, or some game of that sort."

"We'd better tip one of the police, and get him to find out," said Charlie.

"They're all too busy. There isn't half enough of 'em now to keep the crowd in order. We must hunt for poor Tommy ourselves; and the sooner we start the better. Kramatome's all right, and the fire's not worth looking at now. So come along, boys."

Willing as ever to follow such a Leader as Lionel, Vansittart, Charlie, and Sam closed in behind, and elbowed their way through the crowd towards the spot where Tommy had last been seen.

It was by the merest accident in the world that they came across the unhappy man, the calf of whose leg Tommy had "sampled," and who was recounting the history of his woes to as many of the crowd as would listen.

"That's Tommy's work for a hundred pounds," said Lionel. "That's just his way."

"Hang it, Li," said Charlie, "give Tommy his due—he always fought fair when he had a chance; he wasn't the sort of fellow to bite and scratch like a girl."

"Not when he had the chance, Charlie, as you say. But he must have been on the ground when he bit that chap's leg. Don't you see that?"

"Of course, I see now; but the man says it was a dog."

"Oh! he could say anything—it was Tommy as safe as you're born. Sam, keep your eyes open—with that squint of yours you can see half a dozen boys at once."

"Certingly, Mister Lionel," was Sam's reply, delighted at the compliment paid to his powers of vision.

But if Sam had been endued with the eyes of Argus he could not have seen Tommy, for the very excellent reason that the young gentleman in question was out of sight.

In fact, Tommy had met with an adventure which nearly paralysed him, and made him verily believe that he was qualified for a berth in "Bedlam."

It was just after the rush of the crowd had removed him to a safe distance from the gentleman whose calf he had taken liberties with, when Tommy heard a once familiar voice close behind him, and this was what the voice was saying—

"Be japers, Moses, it's meself that would give every blessed copper that's in me pocket to meet ould Tommy Codlings ag'in. Faith! it's the good chap he was entirely, the only bad dhrop in him was his bad luck, and faix ye couldn't go ag'in him for a misforten."

Tommy, by a mighty effort, managed to turn himself round, so as to get a view of the speaker, and there sure enough was Mike—the Mike of his dreams—carroty Mike, the owner of the whelk-barrow himself—none other.

"Why, it is Mike," spluttered Tommy; "it's him—and yet, how can that be. There isn't any such a chap; Li said so. I dreamed all about him."

Tommy stared so hard that before many words had gone by, Irish Mike returned the compliment with interest.

"Howly saints!" he gasped, "it's Tommy—it's his own blessed ugly self come back."

And without asking permission, Mike, still smelling very strongly of stale whelks, elbowed his way to Tommy, and catching him round the neck, hugged him in a fond embrace.

"Here I say, you know," said Tommy; "this won't do, I don't know you, you're dreaming, and so am I."

"Dhramin' is it, honey?" said Mike, enthusiastically; "dhrame away, Tommy, me bhoy, ye'll wake up and find it rale enough prisintly. Come along wid ye—Moses, clear the way."

Moses, apparently on the best of terms with Mike, was a truly good-tempered Israelite, of the "old clo'" persuasion—and clearing a way by the simple process of lowering his head, and butting all obstacles out of his path—soon piloted Tommy and his old friend clear of the crowd.

"Now, Tommy, alanna," said Mike, "I've found ye at last. Will ye shtand a drop o' the crathur?"

Tommy's appearance did not strike Mike as being altogether inconsistent with his old profession, for, as my readers will remember, Tommy had a considerable share of mud on him, and he had been so trampled upon that he was nearly as ragged as Mike himself. In truth there was nothing of the " swell" about our old friend except his nose, which was a good deal larger than Nature ever intended it to be.

"I tell you," said Tommy, "I don't know you. You're Irish Mike, are you?"

" It's that same I am as sure as you're Tommy Codlings."

"Of course," replied Tommy, with an air of the most profound conviction. " That's it—I don't know you, you know; and you don't know me. It's a dream. Lionel told me so."

"A dhrame? Bedad," said Irish Mike, waxing indignant, "I'll show ye the sort o' dhrame it was. Smell that Tommy; ye remember him, ye omadhaun."

Mike here clenched a very dirty fist and placed it just beneath Tommy's nose; so close, indeed, as to tickle it and make him sneeze.

"It smells the same," said Tommy, "and yet it can't be, you know. I'm a swell, you know, and swells don't associate with chaps who keep whelk barrows, and never wash themselves."

"Howly saints," said Mike, aghast, "ye're a pretty article to grumble bekase I don't use scented soap. Faith, wasn't it ye're ownself that I used to scrape down wid an oyster knife, and black me boots wid what came off o' ye?"

"That's a lie," retorted Tommy, hotly. "Why you know you took an extra twopence a week out of my share of the profits for soap, and twopence more because you said it aggravated you to see me so clean."

"There now, and faix he pretends he don't know me, while he remembers all that illigantly," said Mike, triumphantly. " I tell ye what, Tommy darlint, if ye don't come right away to the old sheebeen beyant, and stand some whisky I'll make ye ready for ye're wake."

More bewildered than ever Tommy allowed himself to be dragged along by Mike, without offering the least resistance, and in something less than five minutes he was seated in the little parlour of the public-house, drinking whiskey by the quartern, and wondering vaguely how long it would be before he woke up.

"I went to sleep about four or five years ago," said Tommy to himself, "and I haven't woke up yet. When I do I shall find myself at Stiffback's or Styngy's, or—— Blow it! perhaps all that was a dream too. It is awful."

Mike soon discovered that his old partner had plenty of money, and as his one failing was a love of the "potheen" of his native land he fairly revelled in whiskey punch—hot, strong, sweet, and plenty of it. Nor was Moses, his companion, far behind him, for that amiable young Israelite never missed an opportunity of enjoying himself when it could be done cheaply.

Tommy drank too, not because he liked it, but because, being in a dream, as he thought, the liquor could by no possibility do him any harm, so, taking glass for glass with his companions, Tommy became rapidly very drunk indeed.

It was just as Tommy had reached the lachrymose, or tearful, stage of intoxication, and was weeping bitterly over the fate of a certain greatuncle Joseph, who had died of an overdose of oysters when Tommy was six weeks old—it was just at that pathetic and interesting point that our hero and his chums, piloted by Sam, entered the

parlour in search of refreshment, and found what they had begun to look upon as lost for good, their old friend Tommy—but in what a condition!

CHAPTER IX.

TOMMY CODLINGS ENLISTS IN A VERY QUEER REGIMENT.

AS our hero and his friends entered Tommy was busily engaged in the attempt to carol the inspiring ditty of " Pour out the Rhine Wine," but, owing to a shortness of memory, or a surplus of whiskey, he mixed up the tune and the words in such a manner that the redoubtable Herr Richard Wagner's " Music of the Future" could hardly have equalled it for discord.

"What in the name of wonder is he at?" laughed Lionel.

"Getting tight as fast as possible," said Charlie. "But who are these chaps with him, Li? No good by the look of them."

"They've got Tommy into a lure evidently. They mean easing him of his watch and any other little trifles of that nature he may have about him, if they haven't done it already," said Vansittart. "I say, you fellows, what are you doing with that gentleman?"

"Gintleman," replied Irish Mike, "faith, it's that same he is. It's me ould friend, Tommy, come back to life again."

"So you are Irish Mike, are you? and do you mean to say that you know my friend?"

"Know him—is it? Bedad, I've slept wid him, got dhrunk wid him, and punched his blissed head a score o' times. So I think I ought to know him as well as I know the Cove o' Cork or Banthry Bay."

"I love him," murmured Tommy, thickly; "for he's the darling of my heart, and he lives in our alley."

"Just step this way a minute, will you?" said Lionel to the young Irishman.

"I will that same, for I like the looks o' ye;" and in a few minutes Lionel had explained the state of affairs to Mike, who, warm-hearted and generous as his countrymen usually are, declared that he would poison himself with whiskey sooner than stand for a moment in the way of Tommy's prospects.

"I'll swear it was all a dhrame of me own," said Mike.

"That won't do, though; Tommy's had too much in the dream line already, and he'll go fairly cracked if we try him any more."

"What a prize he'd be for a recruiting sergeant now," laughed Vansittart, as Tommy began to feebly wail forth the touching legend of the "Young Recruit," and concluded with a fervent declaration that he thirsted for the blood of two score of Russians.

"Will you go for a soldier, Tommy?" asked Lionel.

"Who're you?" mumbled Tommy, shutting up one eye very tightly and trying hard to look straight out of the other.

"There's too many of you for to count. 'Oh let me like a shoulder fall.'"

And Tommy, in the effort to rise and give due emphasis to the song, fell—not like a soldier, but after the manner of a very tipsy civilian.

"Pick him up, and get a bottle of soda-water," suggested Charlie. "We'd better get back, too, or old Kramatome will be down on us in the morning."

"He be bothered! He won't dare to say a word to us after to-night. If we were to split about the fancy ball it would ruin him. Let's have our spree out now we have started.

The soda-water had one good effect on Tommy. It made him uncommonly ill in the fireplace, and sobered him, but not much."

"Feel better, Tommy?"

THERE, CLEARLY DEFINED AGAINST THE MURKY BACKGROUND, LIONEL SAW A GHOSTLY IMAGE OF—HIMSELF.

"I'm aw ri'," was Tommy's indistinct and most mendacious reply. "I want go for shoulder."

"Soldier, you mean, Tommy."

"I shed shoulder, didn't I? Anybody gi' me shilling I'll list."

"What regiment, Tommy?"

"All 'shame t' me. I don't care."

"You feel bloodthirsty, Tommy."

"Awful! I shwims in gore. Len' me a knife."

"A knife wouldn't be any good in your state, Tommy. You want a sausage machine."

"If Tommy really wants to go into the army there's a fine chance for him. The recruiting-sergeant of the "Devil's Own" is in the bar, looking out for likely young sinners. Will you join, Tommy?"

"Courshe I will."

That was enough for Lionel and the rest. In less than five minutes they had borrowed from a slaughter-house next door some ox tails, and three or four sets of the largest and sharpest kind of horns. Then setting fire to a couple of pennyworth of sulphur, to give the proper flavour to the whole affair, Lionel, as the sergeant, marched in, and surveyed the new recruit with a properly ferocious aspect.

"So, young man, you wish to enter the service of His Satanic and Diabolic Majesty, King Beelzebub the First."

Tommy nodded—he was almost past speaking.

"What are your qualifications?"

"Dunno."

"Do you think you're wicked enough? Did you ever poison your grandmother?"

"Never—hic—had gran'mother."

"Would you poison her if you had one?"

"I wouldn' 'min'."

"Did you ever steal a penny out of a blind man's tray?"

"No; I'd—hic—scorn such a—hic—ack—."

"I'm afraid you're not half wicked enough for us," said the sergeant of the Devil's Own; "but you're young, and may learn better yet. Corporal, give the recruit his Majesty's shilling."

The coin—which had been made nearly red-hot in a shovel placed over the fire—was tipped into Tommy's hand; but it didn't stay there long, for with a marrow-freezing howl he sprang up, and with one back-handed hit floored Sam, who was standing behind with a tray and pewter-pot full of blazing methylated spirit.

Luckily the burning spirits fell into the fireplace, or our heroes would have witnessed two conflagrations that night. As it was, the blaze caused Sam to see a brilliant display of fireworks, which Mr. Brock, of the Crystal Palace, would have found it difficult to match for beauty.

The pain did more to sober Tommy than the soda-water; it rendered him more furious and bloodthirsty than the whiskey even, and before any one had time to interpose Tommy had clutched his old friend and companion, Irish Mike, by the hair of his head, and did his best to reduce his intellectual countenance to a state of pulp.

Tommy was strong with wrath and liquor, and, moreover, he had taken Mike at a disadvantage. He had got his head screwed down to the table, while his body was doubled up underneath.

"Let go, Tommy," said Lionel, who was himself so weakened by convulsions of laughter that he was quite unable to render the unfortunate Mike any assistance. "Do you want to kill him?"

"I want to kill everybody!" panted Tommy. "However, there's another one in the eye!"

It took all three of them, though, to drag Tommy away from his victim, and by this time poor Mike was very seriously damaged, and his lips resembled fresh boiled saveloys; his nose, which, in its normal condition, resembled a button mushroom, was now the shape and size of a Windsor pear, and his eyes excelled in brilliancy of colour the rainbow hues of a peacock's tail.

"Let me get at him, the murtherin' blayguard?" roared Mike. "He's spoiled my Sunday face, and I've promised to take Bridget to chapel to-morrer. Let me get at him, and I'll ate him widout salt."

"Sit down and have some more whiskey, Mike," said Lionel, who, with Vansittart, had to employ his utmost strength to hold Mike in. "You shall have a couple of sovereigns to buy Bridget a new bonnet with, and yourself a new bird's-eye fogle that will take all the shine out of that black eye."

The promise of the money, and the prospect of unlimited whiskey combined, could not be resisted.

Mike suffered himself to be tucked up in a chair by the side of his chum, Moses—who, with the calm philosophy so characteristic of the full-roed Israelite—had employed his time in putting away as much of the whiskey as he could hold—while the others were wasting their energies in fighting.

Tommy, indeed, had so far wasted his stock of energy that he had fallen asleep in his chair, and was snoring with as much power as if he had a four-poster mahogany bedstead to perform in.

"Tommy will remember this night, I bet," said Charlie. "My stars! what with the excitement, and the fighting, and the whiskey, he'll feel high-dried and ready for the snuff-mill."

"We'll persuade him that it was all part of his dream," said Lionel. "And you, Mike—if ever you meet him again, you'll keep to your bargain, and pretend not to know him, or even to have met him. You understand?"

"Faix, I do," replied Mike, pocketing the two sovereigns Lionel handed him. "I'd disown me ould grandmother on the same tarms."

"Better stick to your family, Mike; never disown them. And now, who'll get us a cab—a four-wheeler—for it's time we moved?"

Mike was off in an instant, and in a very little while returned with the information that the cab was at the door.

Then Tommy was lifted up, still snoring happily, then safely deposited in the vehicle, and our heroes rattled away in the direction of Bloomsbury.

CHAPTER X.

MYSTERIOUS.

"NOW the job is to get in without being heard," said Vansittart. "Old Kramatome will be full of venom for this night's work, and we shall be dropped upon."

"No fear. Besides, he knows we're out, and an hour or two won't make any difference."

"Sam has squared Joblot, the footman. They're fast friends already, and he'll get us in on the quiet."

"We'd better, if it's only for Tommy's sake. It wouldn't do for Kramatome to see him in this state. He'd expel him to a certainty."

"What, and lose Tommy's two hundred a year? Not he. The covetous old sinner would put up with no end of larks before he'd forfeit that."

"I hope he has made up his mind for that, as he will certainly have to go through a great deal before he says good-bye to Lionel, Vansittart, Drummond, and Co.," laughed our hero. "Hi, Sam! tell cabby to put us down at the corner. We'll carry Tommy to the door."

The order was obeyed—the cab pulled up—the man was paid—and Lionel and Charlie, with the help of Vansittart, lifted Tommy out, and carried him to the front door of Mr. Kramatome's commanding premises.

"Con-found the chap!—how heavy he's got already! He'll be fatter than ever in another month."

"How are we to get in, Sam?"

"You keep back a bit, Master Lionel, "and I'm a-goin' to whistle a toon through the keyhole."

"Is that the signal?"

"That's him, Master Lionel."

"Don't whistle too loud, Sam, or you'll give the office to the wrong party."

"Never fear, Master Lionel."

And Sam crept softly up the steps, and, placing his mouth to the keyhole, began to whistle that plaintive and pathetic ballad, "The Two Obadiahs."

Sam got through the first half dozen bars, and became so interested in his occupation that he never noticed that the door was being very slowly and softly opened from the inside.

Sam had shut his eyes as he reached the chorus, and was breathing the soul-inspiring strains with more energy than discretion, when the door was suddenly opened to its widest extent, and somebody shot a pail of water over him.

At such close quarters a pailful of water delivered by a muscular pair of arms has an unpleasantly powerful effect, and so Sam found it, as gasping and breathless he reeled backwards and fell, as a matter of course, full on the top of Tommy, who lay snoring snugly on the steps.

"I'll teach you, you vagabonds," roared the angry voice of Mr. Kramatome himself, "not to come here whistling your blackguard tunes through my keyhole at eleven o'clock at night. Police!"

"Hang the old fellow," said Lionel, "here's a pretty mess. Come on, Van, let him know who we are before he makes any more noise, or, by George, we shall spend the night in the station."

"Hi, Mr. Kramatome," said Charlie, "don't you know us, sir?"

Now the tutor had known perfectly well who it was all the time, and had, in fact, arranged this little plan on purpose to revenge himself for the boys' discovery of him at the fire, but, of course, he now affected the utmost surprise.

"Dear me, young gentlemen, is it really you? I hope I haven't made you very wet, but certainly I never expected that pupils of mine would disgrace themselves by whistling nigger songs through keyholes."

"Oh! no, sir, we're not wet at all; only my servant Sam, and perhaps Codlings, may be a little damp."

Tommy was indeed a "little damp"—the water was streaming from every pore, and that, and the shock of Sam's fall, had very effectually awakened him.

He was sitting on the bottom step, looking the very embodiment of damp and abject misery, wondering what on earth he was, and if this was only another phase of the strange dream which had so perplexed him lately.

"I've had the nightmare often and often when I was at school—the chaps said it was over-eating, but that was spite—I know it used to be like Old Nick sitting on my chest; but the worst of them was nothing to this."

"Get up, Tommy," said Lionel, "and come in; don't you see that you are keeping Mr. Kramatome out in the cold?"

"Who's he?—and who are you?—and where am I?" demanded Tommy, wildly. "I can't put up with any more of this."

"It's all right, Tommy. You only want to get those wet things off and tuck yourself comfortably in bed, and you'll be as right as Big Ben."

"I don't want to go to bed. I want Mike. Where is he? He wouldn't see me put upon like this."

"There you go, with your nonsense about Mike again," said Lionel, as he helped Tommy into the passage. "There's no such a man as Mike, or if there is you don't know him, and he don't know you."

"You had better get that young gentleman to bed at once, Wilful," said Mr. Kramatome, sternly. "It is my opinion that he is intoxicated, and the rest of you are little better. You are the most disorderly pupils I ever had the misfortune to receive under my roof. During the short time you have been here you have succeeded in utterly demoralising the whole establishment. We will have a serious conversation about this matter to-morrow."

And away stalked Mr. Kramatome, with all the dignity which a long-tailed dressing-gown and a black eye could confer upon him.

"We shall get it warm to-morrow, and no mistake," said Lionel, "and I think if Tommy had his dose now, it would do him good for he's shivering as if he had the ague. Sam, see if you can get some hot water, and nutmeg, and sugar—we'll give Tommy a tumblerful of port negus."

"Don't trouble for that," said Vansittart; "I've got a spirit lamp and kettle in my portmanteau, and a pack of cards. We'll tuck Tommy up, and then have a night of it."

"Against the rules, you know."

"Blow the rules. They were only made to be broken. I don't feel sleepy, and I'm not going to bed yet."

"But there are the other students in the next rooms to us. They'll report us."

"Let 'em—much good may it do them."

"Up you go, then," said Lionel. "You light the candle, and see Tommy safe in bed. I'll wait here a bit in the dark, in case old Kramatome comes sneaking about."

The others went, and Lionel remained, leaning quietly against the wall for ten minutes, but no stealthy footfall betrayed the presence of a spy.

"It's all right," thought our hero, "he's had enough watching for to-night, I'll be off."

He turned to ascend the broad, old-fashioned staircase; but while he was yet half-way up, he staggered suddenly—his heart seemed to cease its beating, and the blood to thicken in his veins—for there suddenly flashed out against the murky background a ghostly image of himself.

CHAPTER XI.

IN WHICH TOMMY TRIES TO SOLVE THE MYSTERY WHICH ENVELOPES HIM.

THE apparition, wraith, fetch, double—call it what you will—was visible to Lionel for no longer than the lightning occupies in tearing its furious pathway through the storm-black sky; but that instant was enough to impress that sight upon his memory for life.

Let us strive as we may—let hard-headed reason, cool science, lifelong experience even, argue against it, there is yet something in every human breast that will thrill at the touch of the spirit-hand of superstition.

That our hero was physically brave no one who has thus far perused this faithful history can doubt, but now he had to hold tightly to the balustrade with one hand, while the other wiped the cold dew from his forehead.

"What *was* it?" he thought, as he looked at the blank darkness above him. "It could be no delusion. I saw it. But what does it mean? Is it a warning? Is it a warning?"

There flashed back upon his memory then a weird old German legend, telling how a student had met his double in the quaint old streets of Leipsic, had followed it, seen it enter his own house, and, warned by the spectre, had turned back. When the light of morning came his courage returned, and he went home—to find that the ceiling had fallen in and would have crushed him but for the warning.

How long Lionel would have stood there rooted to the spot in meditation it is hard to say, but just then he heard Vansittart's voice softly calling to him from above—

"Li, where are you? What's up?"

"Nothing. I am coming," replied our hero, in a voice so strangely unlike his own that he started at it. "I am coming."

"What the dickens have you been up to?" Vansittart continued, as Lionel went in. "We've radressed Tommy, and put him to bed, and—— Hullo, something *is* the matter, Li. How pale you are!"

"It's a chill," replied Lionel, with a forced laugh. "I've caught cold to-night, I expect. I want some of that wine. That will bring me round."

"It's something more than that, old fellow. A dozen colds wouldn't put *that* look on your face. Let me ring up Sam, and send him for a doctor. By George! I believe you're going to be seriously ill."

"No—no! It is nothing, I tell you," said Lionel, impatiently.

Vansittart said no more then. He felt certain that something had happened, but what could it be to occur in that brief interval? He had no suspicion of the truth, and, holding to his first impression that some illness threatened to attack his chum, determined to watch him closely.

Both by habit and intention Lionel was abstemious, and it increased Vansittart's suspicion that his friend was ill when he saw our hero pour out a large glass of brandy from the spirit-case, and drink the powerful spirit as if it had been water.

It steadied his stricken nerves, brought back the colour to his cheeks, and made him look himself again—much to Vansittart's astonishment, for he knew that at ordinary times that quantity of spirit would have more than sufficed to intoxicate him.

"Better now, Li?" said Vansittart.

"Why, what's been the matter with him?" asked Charlie, who had been busily engaged in preparing the negus and sorting the cards at the other end of the room.

"Nothing, I tell you," said our hero. "Vansittart will make such a fuss about nothing. Sit down, and let us begin."

And with a hasty, impatient air, Lionel dragged a chair to the table, while Vansittart and Charlie, wondering at the strange conduct of their chum, seated themselves also.

"Now, what shall the game be?" said Charlie. "Whist?"

"We ought to have four," Vansittart said, "and there are only three of us."

Lionel sat facing the door, and as Vansittart spoke he moved his head to reply with some light jest, when there, before him, with its hand raised, as if in warning or menace, he saw, for the second time—his DOUBLE.

Both Vansittart and Charlie saw the startled, fixed look upon our hero's face, and glanced towards the door. But they could see nothing of the strange apparition, and again, and more forcibly, they felt the conviction that some illness threatened their chum, and that his wild looks were the premonitions of delirium.

Charlie telegraphed to Vansittart by a look the query "What can it be?" and Vansittart replied in the same manner, "I can't tell."

"Li," said the latter entreatingly, "what *is* the matter, old boy? There's something up, I know. Won't you tell us? Let me send for a doctor. Hundreds live about here."

"No, I tell you, Van," replied our hero, calmly enough, but he was very pale. "There is something the matter, but not with my health. I am perfectly well. As to what I——. There, I can say no more now. I will tell you, perhaps, in the morning."

"You're fagged out—that's what it is," said Vansittart. "Undress, and step into bed. I'll see you to your room, and tuck you up comfortably."

"I'm not going to bed to-night, Van—nor am I going to leave this room," was Lionel's strange reply.

"Well, we said we'd make a night of it," replied Vansittart, hesitatingly, "but don't you think you'd better turn in, old fellow?"

"Look here, Van, and you, Charlie," replied our hero, earnestly, "don't try to argue with me, or

dissuade me. Go to bed if you like—but I mean to sit up all night."

"Have your own way, Li," said Charlie, with a laugh; "but hang me if I can make you out at all. Any one would think that you had been filling yourself full of whiskey in company with Irish Mike, instead of Tommy."

"Never mind, Charlie. You turn in, and go to roost," was Lionel's reply. "If anything happens ——"

"Why, what should happen?" said Vansittart, as Lionel paused, for he had nearly unwittingly betrayed the motive for his strange conduct.

"Who can tell?" laughed Lionel, but the laugh was anything but natural in tone. "Another fire perhaps, or burglars, or one of you fellows might take a fancy to walk in your sleep, and so get into danger."

"That's all nonsense, and you know it, Li," said Charlie. "But, if you sit up, so do I."

"And I," added Vansittart. It's hardly fair to us, Li. You ought to have more confidence in your chums."

"It isn't want of confidence, Van. You know better than that. If it wasn't for fear of being laughed at I'd tell you now what it is. Forget all about it till morning, and then, before breakfast, I promise to let you into the secret."

"Agreed. Let vingt-et-un be the game. Cut for bank."

"Don't make too much of a row if you win, Charlie," suggested Vansittart. "You can lose like a gentleman, I know, but you're apt to get a little excited if luck goes your way."

"Hang that!" exclaimed Charlie, in an injured tone. "You're a nice fellow to talk about getting excited over winning, when, only a fortnight ago, you pitched your cue through a plate-glass window worth five pounds, because you won that game of billiards, and beat the sharper."

"That was an accident."

"Well, any way, you had to pay for the window. Besides, who's to hear us if we do kick up a row?"

"You forget Toddyboy's room is opposite. He's a student of natural history, and sleeps light, poor fellow."

"Why should he sleep light if he studies natural history?"

"Well, just now, Charlie, you see, he's writing a work on the manners and customs of the 'Norfolk Howard,' and in his enthusiastic pursuit of entomology he keeps a number of the dear little insects in his bed. That's why he sleeps light, Charlie."

"Here, you tell that tale to Tommy when he wakes up," growled Charlie, "and cut the cards if you're going to play."

Lionel's purpose may be easily guessed. He was confident that the strange vision, apparition, spectre —call it what you will—was meant as a warning, and he resolved to keep awake to see if anything would come of it. Yet he was so ashamed of the superstitious feeling that he had not the courage to confess to his most intimate chums.

An hour he had passed pleasantly enough, but towards three o'clock the fatigue and excitement of the previous evening began to tell upon both Charlie and Vansittart, and after a few ineffectual struggles to keep awake, both fell asleep, with their heads resting on the table.

But no touch of sleepy-fingered Somnus weighed down Lionel's eyelids. Like Othello, nor poppy, nor mandragora, nor all the drowsy syrups of the East could medicine him to that sweet sleep which he owned yesterday.

Alternately pacing the room, or fidgetting uneasily in the chair, Lionel waited until the dull dawn filtered suddenly through the window behind, and a glance at his watch showed him that it was six o'clock.

"I'm a fool," muttered Lionel, starting up, and overturning his chair with a crash which awoke

Vansittart and Drummond, "and I've promised to tell those fellows too. Dash it for a fit of indigestion or something like that! I've sat up all night, and nearly scared myself into a lunatic asylum."

"Hullo!" growled Charlie sleepily. "Why, where—oh my, how sore I am! I feel as if I had been playing a football match under Rugby rules."

"And I feel as if I'd had a turn-up with a pig-jobber and got the worst of the fight," added Vansittart. "You been to sleep, Li?"

"No," replied our hero, rather shortly, and certainly savagely.

"Well, what's the result of the night's watch? You promised to tell us."

"Don't hold me to my promise—there's a good fellow."

"Oh, but I will, though. What do you say, Charlie?"

"Rather," replied that young gentleman, whose countenance could not have been more expressive of discontent if he had been suffering from tic-douloureux and cholera in combination. "Out with it, Li."

"Not just yet. As I promised I suppose I must; but not till the last moment."

"Unfriendly beggar to keep his chums in suspense. After keeping us out of bed all night too."

Charlie was so disgusted that his feelings could not find vent in words alone, and taking the ewer he went to the bed where Tommy lay on his back, with his mouth wide open, and an interrupted succession of the most hideous snores proceeding from his snub nose.

"Disgusting little beast," growled Charlie, "I believe it was his snoring that made me so sore. I'll snore him!"

And tilting the ewer Charlie filled poor Tommy's mouth with the ice-cold fluid.

The snoring ceased immediately, and there was a deep and solemn silence for a few seconds, during which Tommy's interesting countenance changed rapidly from scarlet to crimson, then to purple, and then—he burst!

At least that was what it looked like to the other boys, for Tommy was quite hidden by the shower of spray he threw up, and Charlie, who was nearest, was as wet as if he had been out in a a heavy shower of rain.

Tommy all this time was trying hard to fetch a breath. His mouth was wide open; so were his eyes, and he looked something like a tenor singer at a concert doing his best to squeeze out a reluctant top-note.

It was a proceeding full of the deepest interest to the others, who patted him encouragingly on the back, until, with a gasp like that of a broken-winded bellows, he drew in his breath, and said—

"Oh, my!"

"Feel better, Tommy?"

"I dunno. What was it?" demanded Tommy, feebly.

"Nothing, Tommy. Only you've been dreaming again, I expect."

"Oh, dash it! *That* wasn't a dream. I can feel it now, you know. Did—did Irish Mike have anything to do with it?"

"There, that proves that you've been dreaming, Tommy," laughed Lionel. "Irish Mike again!"

Tommy assumed a meditative look, and began to scratch his head with a slow and thoughtful forefinger.

"Didn't I see him last night?" he said.

"Of course not."

"Didn't I get into a crowd near the fire? And didn't he and a Jew chap collar me, and make me pay for a lot of whiskey? And—and—— I'm not very clear about the rest."

"I shouldn't think you were, Tommy. Why don't you try and get that nonsense about Irish Mike out of your head?"

"It's a mystery," said Tommy, with a bewildered

air; "but of this I am resolved—I'll find it out. I'll go to Pollaky, and offer him any amount. But solve this mystery of my existence I will!"

"Bravo, Tommy!" applauded Lionel. "And now, if you want to solve the mystery of what there is for breakfast, you'd better make haste and dress. There goes the bell."

CHAPTER XII.
THE SOLUTION OF THE MYSTERY.

FEW things are more destructive of romance than the first chill hour, and the dim half light of a dull foggy morning, especially with the adjunct of a sleepless night, and so our hero found it, as he left Vansittart's room to seek his own, and make a hurried toilet.

"Confound it!" he muttered. "I shouldn't mind so much if I hadn't promised to tell those other fellows. Dash it! what an ass I was! Hullo! what the deuce are you getting in the way for?"

These last impolite words were addressed to somebody who was on all-fours in the corridor, and over whom Lionel had very nearly thrown a somersault.

The individual uttered a sharp howl of anguish, for the toe of Lionel's boot had "fetched" him under the left ear, and, scrambling to his feet, revealed the long, lean figure, and cadaverous face, and freckled sandy-thatched head of Mr. Toddyboy, the naturalist.

"Be careful," he said—"be careful, Mr. Wilful, I beseech you."

"One need be," growled Lionel, who was, as my readers know, in anything but a good temper, "when you take a fancy to crawl about this dark passage on all fours. Why the deuce don't you wear a signal lamp, so that one could steer clear of you?"

"It ain't a habit of mine. I assure you," said Mr. Toddyboy, who seemed to be labouring under strong excitement.

"I hope it isn't," retorted Lionel, "or we shall be likely to quarrel."

"Don't do that, Mr. Wilful, I beg of you. I was only going to ask you a few questions."

"Ask away then, Toddyboy, and let me go by. I want my breakfast."

"Have you seen such a thing as a cobra lying about anywhere?"

"A *what*?"

"A cobra—cobra-di-capello—a snake, you know?"

"Good gracious, no!"

"And there's a carpet snake too. I had 'em safe in my room last night, and now they're gone."

"What!" ejaculated Lionel. "Were they alive?"

"I should think they were," replied Toddyboy.

"Great Heavens!" exclaimed our hero. "Why, the bite of either of them would be certain death!"

"That's so," said Toddyboy. "I have experimented with them myself, and tried every known antidote, but the rabbits and dogs which I subjected to their bite always died, and in awful agony."

"We must alarm the house," said Lionel. "There is no telling into what hole or corner those snakes may have crept. Hang it, Toddyboy, if they do bite anybody I hope you'll be the first victim!"

"Thank'ee," replied Toddyboy; "but they might bite you, you know, and if they should how would you like to be treated? Shall I inject ammonia into the veins?"

"Inject your grandmother!" said Lionel, savagely, as he bestowed upon Toddyboy a push which sent him flat upon his back. "Here, Van—Charlie—come here! That confounded ass of a naturalist has let a couple of venomous snakes loose. 'Ware bites!"

Just as Vansittart and Drummond came hurrying out of their rooms in answer to Lionel's shout, a succession of piercing shrieks was heard, the door of Lionel's room was flung open, and a housemaid, with a pail in one hand and a face that was considerably paler, came flying out.

"By George! she's found the snakes," said our hero, as he caught the girl by the arm. "Where are they, Mary? Are you bitten?"

"Oh, in the bed! Oh, how could you sleep with such nasty things, Master Wilful? They're yards long, and when I—I turned down the bed-clothes they barked at me. Oh!"

"My good girl," said Toddyboy, the naturalist. "They couldn't have done that. Snakes can't bark."

"They can bite, though," retorted Lionel, angrily. "But you hear what the girl says, Toddyboy. You understand how to handle these reptiles, I suppose, if you're good for anything. Get your basket, or whatever it is you keep them in, and shut them up. Confound them, and you too!"

Toddyboy, only too happy to have a chance of regaining his pets, darted off, and soon reappeared with a couple of long, flat wicker baskets, lined with flannel, and, closely followed by our hero and his chums, but not by Mary, entered Lionel's bedroom.

There was some cause for the poor housemaid's screams, for on the bed, coiled, ready for a spring, and exhibiting every snake-like sign of anger, was a fine cobra-di-capello, fully four-and-a-half feet long, its head and neck vibrating, its diamond eyes glittering, and the "capello"—or hood from which it takes its name—fully expanded; and down beside it was the not less dangerous, though smaller, carpet snake, a tiny drop of whose venom, infused into the blood, will in a few minutes transform the strongest man into a loathsome corpse.

And now our hero and his chums had the mortification of seeing Toddyboy, the despised naturalist, perform a feat which any one of them would have shuddered to attempt.

They saw him approach the hideously-beautiful cobra, whistling a low monotonous dreamy tune, holding the while one of the wicker baskets, with the lid thrown back.

The cobra seemed as appreciative of music as any enthusiastic frequenter of the "Monday Pops," swinging his little neck from side to side in unison with the tune, and making no attempt to strike, although Toddyboy was well within reach of the deadly fangs.

The boys fairly shivered with apprehension when they saw the naturalist put out his hand, grasp the cobra by the neck, and tuck him into the basket with as little ceremony as if he had been a string of sausages.

The lid was closed, and fastened down, and then a similar ceremony was gone through with the carpet snake, and for the present all danger was over.

"I cannot help admiring your pluck, Toddyboy," said Lionel, "in doing what, I frankly own, I would not have dared to do myself; but I must insist, for the common safety of all of us, that you get rid of these snakes at once, or render them harmless by drawing their poison fangs."

After a good deal of hesitation and attempts to prove that there was no real danger, Toddyboy gave his word, and marched gloomily off to his own room.

"And now, boys," said Lionel, gravely, "I'll keep my promise, and tell you the reason of my strange behaviour yesterday, for to what I then saw I certainly owe my escape from certain death. If I had got into bed with those two horrible reptiles nothing could have saved me."

And then in a few brief but emphatic words our hero told of the strange apparition of his double, and of the mysterious sense of danger with which it had impressed him.

"By George, it's the strangest story I ever heard. I always laughed at that sort of superstition; but, hang it, Li, there must be something in it more than mere chance."

"I shall think so to the end of my life," said Lionel. "But come, boys, there's no time to lose. Dress and then breakfast. I shall enjoy it none the less when I think how near I have been to losing all earthly appetite for ever."

CHAPTER XIII.

SAM INITIATES THE FOOTMAN INTO THE DELIGHTS OF A "SPREE."

SAM had struck up a cordial friendship with Joblot, the footman, who, he found, was a "man arter his own 'art," and if it had not been for this little grievance, which he was rather too fond of ventilating, the long youth would have pronounced him to be perfect.

"It's no use grumblin' about it," he said, to Joblot one day, when that gentleman was particularly sore at having been called prematurely away from the consumption of a deliciously juicy leg of pork, crowned with the crispest of crackling, and redolent of the most fragrant stuffing; "why don't you do summat?"

"Wot can I do?" groaned Joblot; "I must obey horders, or I loses my wages as well as my dinner."

"You needn't do nayther one nor t'other. If the old 'un rings afore you've done, answer the bell, but take the rest of your grub with you, and eat it as you goes along."

"You're a genus, Mister Samuel," said Joblot, admiringly. "Why didn't I never think o' that afore? When that pork comes up ag'in, I'll have a bit o' paper ready, and pop my whack into it if I ain't got time to finish afore my bell rings."

So said—so done. Joblot's mouth fairly watered at the idea, and when pork was served up again at the kitchen table the hungry footman took one huge bite at the meat, and then, when the old cook's eye was off him, tilted the rest into a sheet of newspaper, and crammed it into his coat-tail pocket.

He had hardly swallowed his first mouthful, when the fateful bell rang.

"There's the bell," snapped the cook, who was remarkably vigilant in obeying these particular orders of Mr. Kramatome. "Be off now, Joblot, don't stop gormandising there."

"It's a blessed shame a man can't eat his meals in peace," growled Joblot. "There's a lot o' gravy and and a lovely tater I ain't touched yet."

"Why—here, I say," gasped the old cook, as she cast an eye at the footman's plate, and found all the meat gone, "what have you done with it?"

"With wot?"

"The pork. I put a good pound and a 'arf on your plate."

"Well, it was put there to eat, and I ate it," returned Joblot. "If the time is cut so precious short I has to make up for it somehow, and bolt my wittles 'stead of chewin of 'em."

"Well, I never," murmured the old cook, who, thinking that, as usual, Joblot would leave on his plate all that he had not time to eat, had cut three lovely slices, which she intended for her young man —Z 9945.

"You're a hostridge," she said, indignantly, "and ought to be fed for a month on old keys and rusty nails."

But the cook's malicious wish was lost upon the footman, who, with a light heart and heavy coat-tails, was on his way to answer the bell.

Mr. Kramatome had visitors to lunch with him that day. Three old widow ladies, each with a couple of the most cross-grained, snappish, snarlish, pet dogs, that ever died of over-feeding.

It so happened that the whole half-dozen had quite recently been under the hands of an experienced veterinary surgeon, whose treatment of pet dogs consisted in giving them nothing to eat for the first week, less the next, and a sound thrashing by way of exercise every morning.

This treatment was wonderfully effectual—it

made the dogs dreadfully thin, but their ill-temper vanished, and their appetites became tremendous.

The instant Joblot entered the room the dogs smelt the pork, and each one made up his mind, first to find out the source of that smell, and then to have that source or perish.

The sensation of a strange dog who comes behind you, and audibly sniffs at your calves, is one calculated to thrill even the bosom of a strong man with alarm. Multiply that sensation by six, and you will have the precise state of Joblot's feelings when he became the subject of these lap-dog's attentions.

"Innocent darlings!" murmured one fair spinster of fifty. "Not one atom of false pride about them, you see, Mr. Kramatome. In spite of his lowly station, they even condescend to notice your footman."

"Oh, blow it!" thought Joblot, in an agony of apprehension, as two of the "innocent darlings" stood on their hind legs, and began to scratch his stockings. "Oh, lor! I'd give a pound to let out a good kick behind. Ow—ow!"

Joblot could not avoid giving utterance to a couple of short howls, as a sharper set of claws went through his stockings and ploughed up the skin.

"Joblot," said Mr. Kramatome, "what are you making that noise for? Have you no sympathy with the innocent endearments of these intelligent domesticated specimens of the canine species, whose beauty is only equalled by their intelligence and—"

"Ow!" A shriek in a very high key from Joblot broke the thread of Mr. Kramatome's discourse.

"What's the matter now?" said the learned man, severely.

"Oh, if you please, sir, one of the bru—one of 'em has bit a piece out of my leg."

"I am astonished!" said one of the maiden ladies, with emphasis. "Your footman's education has been neglected, Mr. Kramatome, or he would not make such a fuss about a trifle. The darlings only meant it in play."

"Trifle!" growled the injured Joblot. "It was nigh on 'arf-a-pound, and the system of wittling in this ere establishment ain't good enough to allow of a man losin' all that at one bite."

"What are you saying there, Joblot?"

"Nothin', sir. Only if you'll allow me to go and have this 'ere leg o' mine tied up. It's bleedin' awful. My right shoe's full o' gore now."

Each of the six ladies set up a little scream.

"Which of my dear pets was it that bit you?" asked one in an anxious tone.

"That one, mum," replied Joblot, pointing to a vicious-looking black and tan terrier. "He's a worryin' of the limb now, but 'ard work and want of wittles have brought me that low that I daresay he finds it a bit tough."

"Oh! my poor dear innocent little 'Fido,'" screamed the owner of the black and tan, "he'll be poisoned."

"Don't you fear, mum," said Joblot, a little indignant; "if I ain't fat I'm wholesome."

"Silence, sir!" thundered Mr. Kramatome, "you have been drinking."

"I haven't been eatin'," retorted Joblot, "you takes good care o' that."

"You're insolent, you rascal. I have a good mind to discharge you."

"I wish to the lord you would," said Joblot, faintly; "I'd rayther be in penal servitood, you get's a little time for your wittles there."

"Leave the room," roared Mr. Kramatome, "and don't dare to enter my presence again till you are sober."

There was a look in the tutor's eyes as he said this which warned Joblot that further argument might be attended with some personal danger, and he prudently retired, consoling himself with the thought of the pound or so of cold pork in his coat-tail pocket."

The pantry was the only part of the house where Joblot reigned supreme. He was monarch of the electroplate, and kept the key, and thither he bent his steps, licking his lips in anticipation of the treat in store for him.

Sam was waiting for him, smoking a full-flavoured twopenny Cuba, with the rapturous air of one taking his first whiff after a good dinner.

"Wot luck, Mister J.?"

"Middlin'. I got the pork, but I lost nigh as much of my own meat in the parlour upstairs."

"How wos that?"

"There's a lot of ugly old women up there with the governor, and a parcel o' dawgs, and they smelled the pork in my coat-tail pockets, don't you see, and came hangin' around my carves, and I reckon a drop o' gravy had got on the stockin', and one of the brutes made a grab at it and fetched a lump clean out."

"Let's look, Jobby."

"Not here, come into the pantry. The cook's that modest—although she's sixty-five if she's a day—that she turned her 'ed away and tried to blush becos I came into the kitching the other day without my coat."

"That's drorin' it rayther fine," said Sam, as the well-matched couple reached the pantry. "Now let's have a look at that leg of yourn."

Joblot rolled down the stocking, and displayed a very skinny calf, in the thickest part of which were plainly perceptible the marks of a very sharp set of teeth.

"I say, that's a bad bite," said Sam. "You'll hev to touch that up with coarsestick."

"Wot's that?"

"Stuff as you gets at the chemist's to keep away hyderophoby."

"I ain't got no money—and wot's hyderophoby?"

"An awful complaint," replied Sam, "which comes on people arter they've bin bit by dorgs. In about a week hair comes out all over 'em, and they grows a tail, and then they begins to bark like a dorg, and goes reglar mad, and has to be smothered atween mattresses."

"I say, now, Samuel, no larks!" said Joblot, turning pale, while his hair slowly elevated itself with terror.

"It's troo, every word. There ain't a minit to be lost, and as we ain't got no coarsestick, a red-hot poker will do as well."

"Not too hot, Samuel," pleaded the terrified footman. "Won't lookwarm do?"

"No, it must be as hot as blazes. You stay here. I'll go and get it."

And away Sam hurried to the kitchen, leaving Joblot in a perfect fever of apprehension, between his dread of the awful malady, hydrophobia, and the impending red-hot poker.

Sam was back with it in no time—a huge bar of metal that would have done duty as an area railing —the end almost at a white heat, and throwing off a perfect shower of brilliant sparks.

"Oh, Samuel, be careful," moaned Joblot. "That would burn a hole through a brick wall."

"It's ayther this or hydrophoby," said Sam. "So make haste and choose."

"I s'pose I must, then," groaned Joblot, holding out his leg and shutting his eyes.

Sam took a firm hold of the leg, and brought the poker down upon the bitten part.

It stopped there for about the space of a flash of lightning.

Joblot uttered a hideous yell, accompanied by such a tremendous plunge, that Sam and the poker went flying through the door, and into the little passage beyond.

Sam picked himself up and then the poker, which was curled up at the end like a fishhook, and restoring that domestic implement to its proper place in the kitchen garden, he went back to his patient.

Joblot was hopping round the pantry on his sound

leg at the rate of ten miles an hour, uttering the most awful imprecations and blasphemies upon Sam, the poker, the dogs, the maiden ladies, Mr. Krama-tome, and, to be brief, everything in general.

"Take it easy, mate?" said Sam, soothingly.

"Easy ——"

But we hesitate, Joblot's language was too strong for any but the readers of the *Englishman*, our compositors would faint, and the reading boys grow prematurely aged if we ventured to reproduce the suffering footman's language.

"Stop that row, and don't jump about as if you'd swallowed a spring mattress," said Sam. "Come here, and let me put a little ile on."

"Ile!" gasped Joblot, and again the peculiar language to which we have already referred was repeated, only stronger; and not until the sufferer was so exhausted that he could hop no longer did he permit Sam to apply the soothing oil to his wound.

"Ile's a fine thing for outward complications," said Sam, "but there's summit a deal better for the innards."

"Pork?" said Joblot, with the light of interest dawning in his eye.

"Pork!" repeated Sam, contemptuously. "No, pork's all wery well in its way, but when the 'art's 'evy, or you've got the toothache, or anythink o' that kind, there's nothink like a good drop o' licker."

"I smelt the cork of a gin bottle once," murmured Joblot, "but that was a long time ago."

"Smelled a cork! that's a pretty way of enjoin' yrself," said Sam. "Get that there stockin' on, and find yer 'at 'nd I'll show you wot I mean."

"I don't go out without leave," said Joblot.

"Take some o' the French kind o' leave," replied Sam, that's good enough for him. Make haste. I knows a crib where the whiskey's strong enough to make a man's hair curl with the wery smell of it."

Such a temptation could not be withstood, and in something less than ten minutes the friends were rapidly leaving the dismal square behind them, and nearing the more cheerful, if less aristocratic, region of the Tottenham Court-road.

Sam's acquaintance with certain regions of London was perfect, and he had, besides, the born cockney's faculty of finding his way about the streets by instinct, so after sundry devious turnings and twist-ings, executed with a skill and precision that fairly startled Joblot, Sam halted opposite the bottle and jug department of a quiet, dreamy-looking, little public-house, so quaint and old-fashioned, that no one would have been surprised to have seen Rip Van Winkle walk out of it.

"Here we are," said Sam, giving Joblot a gentle push, which sent him staggering into the bar, "now we can go ahead, Jobley, my boy."

"I think," said Joblot, as he felt in his coat-tail pocket, "that I'll polish this orf first."

And he drew forth and held up for Sam's inspection the pork which had been the cause of so much suffering.

"Oh, blow it! you're as bad as Master Codlings," growled Sam: "and he's the heaviest cove on a peck as ever I see."

But Joblot was by this time impervious to sar-casm or insult. He had called for a loaf of bread, some mustard, and a plate, and was disposing of the meal with wonderful dexterity.

"There's one thing about him," said Sam, musingly, "he don't keep a feller waiting long."

And, indeed, almost before these reflections had time to pass through Sam's brain, the last morsel of stuffing had disappeared, Joblot had cleaned his knife by the simple and primitive process of licking it, and then pronounced himself ready for any-thing.

"Two quarterns of Irish 'ot—plenty of lemmon an' sugar, gov'nor," was Sam's first order.

The order was promptly obeyed, and the friends retired to the snug little parlour with their liquor.

Joblot took a sip which made him wink with delight.

"Prime, old feller, ain't it?"

"First chop!" said Joblot, taking a second sip, which nearly emptied the glass. "Is this whiskers?"

"Werry near right, old feller; but don't go too fast; you ain't used to it, you know."

"Which is the best way to get used to anysing?" said Joblot, already a little thick and hazy in his speech.

"Take plenty on it, of course," said Sam.

"Thatsh way. I'm goin' to get use to whiskers," replied Joblot. "Let's have another glash, Samuel. Lor', how you do put me in mind of my poor old grandmother."

"Me?" said Sam, a little staggered at this com-pliment.

"She was just 'bout your figger, Samuel, and her mustarch was just 'bout big's yourn, only 'twasn't—hic—carrotty."

"Here, I say, Joblot, you draw it a little milder," said Sam, indignantly. "Your grandmother was a very nice old party, I daresay, but don't you go to drorin' caparisons between us."

"I loved her," murmured Joblot, who was by this time deep in his second tumbler of whiskey, "she had only one eye, and no nose to spheak of, for her old man bit it orf one day in a family dishpute, and though they give him a domestic immediate——"

"A what?"

"A domestic."

"You means a cosmetic. To make him sick wasn't it?"

"Yes—and though it brought the end up ag'in, it warn't fit to look at, let alone bein' put on."

"They must have been nice parties to live with," said Sam. "Pretty lively about there sometimes."

"I shay," demanded Joblot, "where's my whiskers?"

"You drank it, leastways all as you didn't spill over your shirt front."

"You're a liar," retorted Joblot, furiously, and in one syllable.

"Hallo!" exclaimed Sam, aghast at the sudden and warlike turn affairs had taken, "that whisky have got into your 'ed quick; I told you to go slower."

Joblot fixed a strong glare upon Sam, and after sundry ineffectual attempts to rise from his seat, succeeded, and at once fell upon his friend, and clasping him in a tight embrace, they rolled upon the floor, bringing everything within reach to the ground with a bewildering smash.

The landlord had a prompt way of dealing with disorderly customers. Persuasion he knew was generally wasted, so he sent for the police directly he heard the smash, and before Sam had recovered from the first shock of his downfall he felt himself collared, roughly dragged from the grip of Joblot, and shaken until his teeth chattered.

CHAPTER XIV.

TOMMY CODLINGS TO THE RESCUE.

SAM'S indignation was tremendous, and quite naturally, if my readers will only consider how he had suffered—first in spending his money on an ungrateful friend, and then in being assaulted by him as a recompense.

"You let go o' me," he roared, indignantly, "wot hev I done?"

"You'll find that out soon enough when you gets to the station. You give 'em in charge, governor."

"Rather," replied the landlord, "I makes short work of sich scum of the airth as them. There's damage done to the tune of three pound, and I'll have it out of 'em. Run 'em in!"

"Come on," said the policeman who had Sam in custody.

"Git orf," gasped Sam, savagely, and letting out a blow at random, he fetched Joblot under the chin, and put him out of the fight.

The three other constables had it all their own way then, and by sheer weight Sam was forced down, and hauled out into the street, but not until he had set his mark upon some of his captors.

"This here's a six months' job," said one, who had a something on his left eyebrow which felt like Primrose Hill. "Lay it on thick, Wilkins, when you get into the box; swear till you're black in the face."

"I could do a bit o' that now," responded Wilkins, whose nose had been nearly flattened by one of Sam's round-handed hits.

"The landlord can swear to a little, and we'll do the rest," said Z 9945. "I knows one o' these chaps; he's footman at a place on my beat, and he split on me bein' found in the kitching once alonger the cook, and I'll make it uncommon warm for him now it's my turn."

"Better get a stretcher then," said another constable; "it looks better when we gets to the station. Besides, this chap's tough enough to give us a lot o' work, unless we straps him down."

As it is a much easier job to carry a refractory prisoner than leading him, this course was unanimously agreed upon. Two of the police went for the stretcher, while the others remained to discuss the case, and imbibe sundry liquors, which the landlord, with an eye to their giving a favourable opinion of his house to the magistrate, treated them to.

Joblot was almost helpless, for Sam's last blow, added to the surplus of whiskey, had nearly settled him outright, and Sam, to give himself a chance to think over the means of escape, pretended to be in an equally exhausted condition.

The two constables who had gone in search of the stretcher had a long way to go, and, of course, as they were in a hurry, several things occurred to delay them.

They came across a street fight, and as there were no other constables near, they had to move the crowd on—then an obstinate old woman would persist in getting herself run over, and she had to be sent off in a cab, and the driver of the van duly entered in the official note-book.

"I never see such luck," growled one. "Them other chaps will be full up to the eyes with licker afore we can get back."

"I vote we has a drop now," said the other; "I'm hawful dry."

In a weak and thirsty moment his mate assented. They were near a quiet-looking public-house, and stealthily stepping into a side bar found themselves face to face with their inspector, who immediately took down their names for being found drinking while on duty, and ordered them off at once.

"Of all the dashed luck," growled one.

"We'll take it out o' those chaps when we gets back," said the other. "Here we are, at the station. Pick out the wobbliest stretcher you can find, Bill."

Meanwhile, the constables who remained behind had not been slow to avail themselves of the landlord's hospitality, and had tasted samples of his liquors all round, beginning with half-and-half, and concluding with a few half-quarterns of old Jamaica rum—neat.

"I shay," murmured Z 9945, after he had deposited his last half-quartern of rum between the collar of his tunic and his neck, "d'you begin to feel lil' bit queer?"

"No' mush, I can shee four prishners though, an' there wasn't on'y two lil' while 'go."

"It's all ri'," said Z 9945, "we can shay vi'lence of prishners caushe injury to—hic—'ed, and conch-quenshe 'pediment speeshe."

"That'll do," said the other, making a frantic effort to drink his rum, and emptying the measure into his right eye, with consequences extremely painful and inflammatory to that organ.

"Blow it!" muttered the landlord, turning pale with affright as the constable set up a most unmelodious tipsy howl, "I shall have my license endorsed for this, and most likely refused renewal at the next meeting of the Middlesex Muffs. I must water my liquors a little more, they're too strong. Keep your mate quiet a bit, can't you?"

"Keep quiet your—hic—shelf," was Z 9945's furious reply, "or—hic—run you in."

"Who'd keep a public-house while there was a respectable crossing-sweepers' berth open, I'd like to know?" grunted the landlord. "Oh! bust it, why don't them other chaps come with the stretcher and clear this lot out. If this goes on much longer they'll want half a dozen stretchers and a police-van."

But for reasons already well known to our readers, the constables did not hurry themselves going back.

Knowing that they would infallibly be reported, when they had not committed any particular crime, they deemed that they might just as well deserve the inevitable punishment, and on their way back with the stretcher they paid about fourteen visits to various public-houses, with a result which may be better imagined than described.

Our old friend Sam watched the proceedings of his captors with an eager anxiety, for the more they drank the more hopeful he became of escape.

"The worst of it is," he thought, "that dashed donkey, Joblot, is so precious tight that he won't be able to move. Hi, Jobby!"

Sam called his friend in a hoarse whisper, and emphasised it by a "drive" in the ribs with a particularly sharp elbow.

But neither the whisper nor its accompanying "drive" had any more effect upon Joblot than they would have had upon the Woolwich Infant.

"I wouldn't care," said Sam, again, "only the poor cove 'll lose his place and his carakter besides, and he'll be sure to blame me for doin' of it."

Sam's sterling good nature rendered it impossible for him to leave a friend in the "lurch," whatever that may be. He might easily have got away himself—the policemen were too tipsy to have prevented him, and the landlord would have been only too glad to rid himself of the whole lot at any price.

It was at the very moment when Sam had arrived at a desperate resolution—to knock the two policemen on the head with a chair, and carry Joblot on his back to a place of safety—that, to his intense astonishment and delight, he saw the door of the parlour gently open, and the plump features of no less a personage than our old friend Tommy Codlings present themselves.

CHAPTER XV.

TOMMY MAKES THE BEST OF IT.

TOMMY'S appearance may be accounted for in a very few words. He had tried to take a short cut from the square to Lionel's old quarters in St. James's, as a matter of course he had lost his way, and had stepped into the public-house to ask for information.

"Would you be kind enough to tell me —" he began, when his astonished eyes caught sight of Sam.

"Here, I say—hullo! why, Sam, what's the matter?"

"Hush-h-h!" hissed Sam, in a whisper, that might have been heard a hundred yards away; but there was little necessity for caution, as both the policemen were partly asleep, and wholly drunk, and nothing short of an earthquake or a gunpowder explosion would have had any effect upon them.

Tommy, obedient to the beckoning motion of Sam's forefinger, advanced on tiptoe.

"What is the matter, Sam?" said Tommy, who seeing what appeared to be the corpse of Joblot lying in a corner, jumped to the conclusion that murder had been committed, and that Sam was the criminal.

"I'm in custody," said the long youth.

"What did you do it for?" gasped Tommy.

"I ain't done anything—it was him," replied Sam, pointing to Joblot.

"Oh! he did it himself then," said Tommy, much relieved. "Did he poison himself? They can't touch you for that you know."

"He ain't dead," said Sam, "leastways, only dead drunk; and now the policemen is werry nigh as bad there's a chance of getting Joblot away afore the others, as is gone for a stretcher, comes back. Would you mind callin' a cab, Mister Codlings; Joblot'll lose his berth for certing if he's took up."

Tommy's good nature would have started him in search of the Lord Mayor's state coach if it had been necessary. He nodded to Sam, went out of the parlour on tiptoe, and in a few minutes returned.

"Did you find one?"

"Yes," replied Tommy. "Make haste, for there's two more bobbies coming up the street, carrying something, but they won't be here for a few minutes yet, as they keep on falling down."

"Here's a lark," grinned Sam, "they're tight too, as well as the others; are you on for a game, Mister Codlings?"

"I don't mind," replied Tommy, a little doubtfully; "but you see, Sam, I generally get into such a mess when I try to enjoy myself."

"It's all right this time, Mister Codlings, I'll see you safe—it's the blue-bottles who'll get into a mess this time, and not you or me. Help me to put Joblot into the cab."

The landlord was at his door, in a state of dark and gloomy despair, but he brightened up a little when Sam and Tommy appeared, bearing the unconscious form of Joblot.

"Going to get him away on the quiet?" he said. "That's right. I was down heavy on you a while ago; but, dash me, if the police ain't ten times wuss. I hope you'll say a good word for me if I says one for you at the Court."

"I'll swear to any think," said Sam, fervently. "Let me give you a black heye, and say the bobbies did it, and then stole your liquor."

"I say," answered the landlord, as he helped to jerk the limp form of Joblot into the cab, "that'll be comin' it a little too strong—that's perjury."

"No, it ain't, if you kisses your thumb 'stead o' the bible, when you takes the hoath," said Sam. "But now, cabby, cut away—there's your fare, and and a bob over. When you gets to the house put this young man on the hairy steps, and ring the bell."

"Ain't you goin' too?" said the landlord.

"Not just yet. Me and this young gent is goin' to have a game with the policemen. My eye, ain't they precious tight—ha, ha! Blessed if they haven't dropped the stretcher down that hairy."

Even while Sam was speaking the policemen lurched heavily against some railings, and the stretcher fell with a crash below, breaking half a dozen panes of glass in the kitchen window, and flooring the proprietor, who was in the way.

The doubly injured man arose, swearing fearful oaths of vengeance, and, rushing up the steps, confronted the policemen, one of whom was knocking at the front door, while the other, having got hold of the area bell, was pulling away as if his life depended on his ringing it forty times in a minute.

"Leave off!" roared the infuriated owner. "Wot do you mean by it?"

"Where's our stretcher?" demanded the constable who had possession of the bell. "What do you go leavin' your hairy about for people to drop things into? You bring up that there stretcher or I'll run you in. We've got our hi' on you."

"Well, I'm blowed!" gasped the man. "Who's goin' to pay for my broken winders?"

"If you ses another word, and don't bring that stretcher in less than two minutes, I'll run you in for being drunk and disorderly, and constructin' a hofficer in the hexecushun of his dooty. Now then."

"Will yer?" retorted the angry and injured proprietor of the broken windows. "You're a pretty harticle to run anybody in, you are. As for runnin' me in—you try it on, that's all."

Of course a crowd had gathered, a crowd always does, be the cause little or great, and a couple of volunteers descended the area and brought up the stretcher, and also a few spoons and some knives and forks, to which they helped themselves through the broken window.

Having gained possession of the stretcher the constables once more put it on their shoulders, and paying not the slightest attention to the oaths and threats of the injured party, made their way across the road to the tavern, where Sam and Tommy awaited them, hopeful of the fun that was to come.

It was not long in coming, for the bearers of the stretcher scorning to take any notice of such a trifling barrier as a door, charged at it, so the front legs of the stretcher went through the ornamental plate glass, and the front policeman went on his ornamental nose and broke it.

The fall had one good effect, for the shock and the consequent bleeding sobered him considerably. He got upon his feet, opened the door in the legitimate way, and dragged in the stretcher.

"Come on," he growled savagely to his mate; "it's my belief that you're drunk."

It was also the belief of several of the crowd, for they expressed it very loudly in words, but at a safe distance.

"Now let's get this job over," said the constable who had damaged his nose. "we're safe to be reported, and I means to take it out of somebody. Hallo!" he added, as he entered the parlour, "blow me if the others haven't been going it worse than us."

They had. One was snoring like a trombone played by machinery, and the other was lying on his back, singing "The Same Old Game" in psalm tune, and in a very minor key.

"This is a nice game o' yourn," said the landlord, who was reduced to a state of despair at the prospect of losing his license, "have some soda water all round, and an hour's sleep, and let the chaps go."

"We daren't," replied the soberest of the policemen; "the inspector met us, and we had to tell him what we wanted the stretcher for. We must run somebody in."

At that moment Sam and Tommy, both looking as fresh as spring violets after a shower of rain, came up and bowed politely to the constables.

"You've kept us waiting a long time," said Sam, "which is hardly perlite, considerin' the wallyable nature of our time."

"More cheek," growled the constable; "but we'll soon take it out o' you. Dash you, it's all through you that we're reported."

"Never mind," retorted Sam, affably, "it brings you afore the public. I don't know what your name is, but it'll look oncommon well in a noose-paper, I've no doubt."

"And you'll look oncommon well in Newgate Gaol," said the constable. "Just get a pail o' cold water for my mates to put their 'eds into will you, landlord, and we'll make a move."

"Get it yourself if you want it," growled the landlord; "a pretty mess I'm in, through you. All my trade stopped, and a case for the marking of my license."

The policeman was in no mood for argument just then. He went behind the bar, filled a pail with water from the tap, and returned to the parlour, where Sam and Tommy, purple in the face with laughter, assisted them.

"Now, Joe, take your helmet orf and just shove

your head in that," said the pail bearer, "and you chaps stop grinning, will you?"

"Oh! lor'," gasped Sam, "I've been a many pantermines, but this is the biggest joke I ever came across. Four bobbies, and all drunk—my eye, what will the inspector say?"

But Z 9945 was busily engaged in the effort to persuade "Joe" to put his head into the water, by way of sobering him sufficiently to do his duty.

Joe had, however, the very strongest possible objection to water in any form, and Z 9945, in desperation, at last seized the pail and emptied the whole of the contents over his head.

But Joe was past the aid of cold water. It did not make him sober, but it made him, naturally, very wet—and savage, too, for he fell upon the man next to him, and, holding his helmet tight with one hand, punched his head with the other.

"I'm dashed if I know wot to do," groaned Z 9945. "I never see such a game. We shall be sacked for certing."

"Now, look here, you know, added Sam. "Where are you going to lock us up? We ain't used to be kep waiting like this ere."

"You shut up, will you?" said the constable, savagely. "You'll get locked up soon enough—never fear."

"It ain't perlite, any way," said Sam; "and if yer don't take us precious sharp, we'll go to the station and lock ourselves up."

"I've had enough o' your cheek, my lad. Only wait till I gets in the box to give evidence agin you, you'll want all your sauce then, and more too."

"P'raps I shall—*when* you get into the witness-box," laughed Sam. "But you ain't there yet, old feller!"

"And there's your mate, too. The chap as —— Why, hullo! That ain't him."

Z 9945, though far, very far, from sober, was still able to discern the difference between plump Tommy Codlings and the thin—not to say skinny —form of Joblot, the footman.

"Yes, it is," retorted Sam; "or if it ain't, who is it?"

"Why, he's twice as big."

"That's because you're tight, and see double," was Sam's retort. "Our cook would know him if she saw him."

This touched Z 9945 on a very sore point. Many a comfortable meal and many a bottle of beer had he obtained from that same old cook, and to think that he was in danger of losing her affections—and the consequent cold mutton—was truly maddening.

"Look here," he said, "I ain't spiteful naturally, but don't you make any more delusions to cook, or I won't answer for the consequences. I'll do you a good turn now—you can cut."

"Thankee for nothin'," said Sam. "If we'd had a mind to cut away, we could have done it an hour ago, but we want to be took, and you'll have to take us."

"That's the way to put it. It'll be a sort of novelty don't you see?" added Tommy.

"All right," said Z 9945, "have it your own way now. You see I'm nigh worried to death, but when I do get you in, I'll make you sweat for this."

"Make haste about it then," said Sam. "Look arter that mate o' yourn wot you give the cold bath to; it's cruelty to hanimals to leave him in that state."

The constable said little then, but he vowed a very strong oath to be revenged on his tormentor before long, and then, with the aid of the landlord, he set to work to sober his three companions.

"I say," said Tommy, "don't you think we'd better cut it, Sam? When these chaps do come round they'll be as mad as hungry tigers."

"I didn't think, Master Codlings," said Sam, reproachfully, "that you were a gent to go back on a lark when you'd once begun. Master Lionel never did."

"No more will I, Sam," said Tommy, hastily. "Only, you know, it might be dangerous."

"Mister Thomas," said Sam, impressively, "Peelers is p'ison to me. I hates the 'ole lot on 'em. They were down on me heavy when I was on the tramp alonger Bellars to Mend and Long Jim; and whenever I gets a chance I returns the compliment."

A very liberal supply of cold water, emptied upon the heads of the three superlatively tipsy constables, established in them some show of animation.

"Now for the lark," chuckled Sam. "Z 9945's got his mates up, and now he's getting the stretcher ready."

"I say," said Tommy, looking doubtfully at the uncomfortable-looking machine, "are they going to put us on that? Yes, of course. They'll lay us down side by side, and strap our arms and legs."

"I don't see any particular fun in that," remonstrated Tommy. "Where does the joke come in?"

"You'll find that out, Master Codlings. Here comes Z 9945. Pretend to be werry wiolent, and, if you don't mind, swear a bit."

"I'd rather not do that," replied Tommy, with a shake of the head. "Irish Mike used to swear awfully, and offered to teach me how. But I never could use bad language—it always makes me feel sick."

"You'd soon get used to it, Mister Codlings," said Sam, "if you was to turn author, and be late with your copy now and then. The langwidge the printer 'ud pelt you with would make Irish Mike's sound like poetry arterwards."

Tommy shook his head, as if he doubted the power of anything on earth to make Irish Mike's language poetical; but he had no time to express his opinion verbally, for Z 9945, having got his men upon their legs, at last came up and laid violent hands upon Sam's collar.

"Draw it mild, old feller," said Sam. "Choking ain't no part of the contrack."

"I've had enough o' your cheek," growled the irate official; "and now I'm going to take it out of you. Collar the other one, Joe, and strap 'em up."

Tommy, obedient to his instructions, called the constable a craven hound, and kicked him on the shin—a polite attention to which Joe promptly replied by catching Tommy and choking him until his eyes stood out like hat-pegs.

Tommy got really angry then, and fought with such valour and determination, that it was not until two other constables fell upon him and flattened him out, that he was vanquished.

"Now we've got you," said Z 9945, as he wiped the perspiration from his face, and glared at his captive lying strapped upon the stretcher, "you'll get shook a bit, on the road, my lads. Sea-sickness will be a perfect luxury to the jolting you'll get."

"I likes it," replied Sam; "it stimulates the nervous system, and hacks benefishally on the congestion."

"Up with the stretcher now," said Z 9945, taking hold of his end of the apparatus; "this end fust, never mind about standin' 'em on their 'eds, it'll do 'em good."

Joe and another accordingly raised their end, but their grasp was unsteady, and it fell with a jolt which loosened every tooth in Tommy's head.

"Oh, my!" yelled Tommy. "Why ain't you careful?"

"Keep quiet," whispered Sam; "if you let 'em know you're hurt they'll do it more and more. Sing a little. Let's do the 'Run 'em in' chorus."

"How can a fellow sing when he's upside down," retorted Tommy. "Oh, Lor'! there they go, at the other end now."

After so many unsuccessful trials that Tommy and Sam felt as if they had been in a couple o' dozen railway accidents, the four constables succeeded at length in getting their burden fairly on

LIONEL WILFUL AND VANSITTART INTRODUCE TOMMY CODLINGS TO HIS UNKNOWN BETTER HALF AND FAMILY.

their shoulders, and so into the street, where a considerable crowd was assembled, eager for the fun.

"Don't you find 'em heavy?" roared one, a good-humoured-looking brewer's drayman. "Better send for a balloon, hadn't ye?"

The weight of Tommy Codlings alone was quite as much as four ordinary men would have cared to carry for more than a hundred yards; and Sam, although he was thin, possessed a good deal of bone, and between the two the four policemen, even in a sober condition, would have had quite as much work as they cared for.

As it was, they were so much surprised with their load that they turned to the right instead of the left, and had gone wrong to the extent of fully half a mile before they found out their mistake.

"Turn round, Joe," gasped Z 9945. "Blowed if we ain't nigh a mile out of our road."

Joe, whose tongue was hanging nearly a foot out of his mouth with thirst and fatigue, groaned heavily, and dropped his end of the stretcher.

The sudden release of that portion threw all the other constables off their balance, and once more Sam and Tommy were ignominiously rolled into the mud.

The plump youth was, of course, the chief sufferer; his side was the heaviest, and that landed first upon the pavement with a thud like that of a pavior's rammer.

"Yah!" groaned the crowd.

"You're a set of scoundrels," shouted one old gentleman, a member of the Anti-Vivisection Society. "What are your numbers? I insist upon having your numbers instantly."

"Our numbers are very much like yours, guv'nor," retorted Z 9945. "Number one. And if you'll take our advice, clear out, and take care of it."

"You—you insolent, low-minded scoundrel!" gasped the old gentleman, as he felt for his pocket-book wherein to register the offending policeman's number. "I—I——"

"Pick up your end of the stretcher, Joe, and let's git on," said Z 4995, "or blowed if I don't draw my staff and do somebody a mischief."

It was a difficult task indeed for the unhappy constables to shoulder their burden again, and the process was by no means a pleasant one to Sam and Tommy, but the thought that the constables were in a worse plight still comforted them, and they bore the shaking patiently.

"I say," whispered Sam, after they had been carried about a hundred yards on the return journey, "how do you feel, Mister C.?"

"Awful," groaned Tommy.

"Do the straps cut you at all?"

"Dreadful, I'm pretty nearly sawn in half on this side."

"Then we'll return the compliment," said Sam, "and cut the straps. I can just reach my knife, I think."

A brief struggle, and Sam had gained his knife, cut through the straps, and he and Tommy were free.

"Oh, what a comfort that is! murmured the plump youth, as he flung out his arms, and nearly rolled off the stretcher.

"Hold on to the side, Mr. C.," said Sam, "or you'll get a fall that even your fat won't stand."

"Now, Sam," retorted Tommy, in an indignant tone, "don't you be personal."

"Beg parding, Mister Codlin's. No offence, only you air rayther plump, you know; and in a sort of way it forces itself on a party's mind, don't you see?"

"Oh, all right," said the easily-pacified Tommy. "Only, if a fellow *is* fat, he don't like to be always told of it, don't you know?"

"Wot do yer say, Mister Codlin's, to havin' a bit of a game with these here policemen?"

"I'd rather get off this confounded stretcher," was Tommy's reply.

"We'll do that," said Sam. "Lift your 'ed a bit, and try if you can see the hend of the street."

Tommy did, and at infinite risk succeeded.

"I see it."

"Well, when we get there, do you think you can manage to stand up?"

"I'm sure I couldn't, Sam. I should fall off, to a dead certainty."

"No you won't, if I get up first and help you."

"But what for?"

"There's a lot of narrer streets and courts down that hend," said Sam, in explanation, "and if we jumps off we can bolt and get safe away afore they can touch us. I've been carried quite far enough to satisfy my gentility and stimulate my happetite."

"I shan't have any appetite for a week to come," groaned Tommy. "Be careful, Sam."

Sam had managed to get upon his knees, and now with much difficulty hauled Tommy up.

It was no easy job, for the stretcher wobbled fearfully from side to side, but at length they managed to get upon their feet, and just then the enlivening strains of a barrel organ playing a hornpipe reached their ears.

"Go it, Master Codlin's," said Sam, "we'll shake 'em up a bit. Give 'em a reg'lar good breakdown. Hoop-la!"

Tommy fell in with the idea at once, and brought his light fantastic toes down with a succession of jerks, which made the stretcher creak again.

"Walk a bit steadier, Joe," growled Z 9945. "wot are you jerkin' the thing about like that for?"

"Tisn't me," gasped Joe, "it's Wilkins, he's shovin' it all this way."

"You're a liar!" retorted Wilkins, with more force than politeness, "it's the chaps behind. Oh! my shoulder's broke."

"Hooray," roared the crowd. "Go it, chuck your hats about."

This polite invitation to continue the performance was wasted, however, for just then Z 9945 happened to look up, and the sight that met his astonished gaze made him gasp for breath.

He stopped suddenly, but the others went on, and as a natural consequence his end of the stretcher tilted over, and Sam and Tommy made an involuntary and unexpected jump to the ground.

For a wonder Tommy fell upon his feet, and before he had an opportunity of carrying out his intentions of expostulating with the policemen upon their carelessness, Sam had caught him by the arm and dragged him down a narrow court, long before their pursuers had recovered from their astonishment.

CHAPTER XVI.

MR. KRAMATOME IS TREATED GRATIS TO A LITTLE MUSIC.

MR. KRAMATOME was an ardent lover of music, but not of such music, you understand, as charms the vulgar ear. Verdi, Rossini, Offenbach, Lecoq, were names abhorrent to him; and only Wagner and a few of the great German colossi of the past were, in his idea, to be called musicians at all.

An organ-grinder—or, in fact, an itinerant musician of any kind—was classed with the more noxious reptiles of the earth, and so vigorous had been his prosecution of any unhappy minstrel who found himself in the neighbourhood that the square was shunned like a plague by all whose "beats," or "pitches," were made in that direction.

The faintest sound of any musical instrument was enough to draw Mr. Kramatome from the region of his study, and sternly order the performer off; and as soon as this little peculiarity became known to Lionel the spirit of mischief prompted him to action.

"This is the dullest old crib that ever was," said Lionel to Charlie, "and we'll wake it up, old boy."

" It'll have to be something very startling to wake this sleepy old den up, Li."

" I mean it to be."

" What's your idea?"

" What do you think?"

" A gunpowder explosion?"

" No."

" A Tichborne meeting, with Kenealy for president, and Whalley for vice?"

" Not that even."

" Well, I give it up. If it's anything livelier than that it must be a good notion."

" You know how fond the old boy is of music?"

" Yes, of what he calls music—the music of the future—with Wagner for a prophet."

" I was speaking sarcastically, Charlie."

" Then don't do it, Li—it don't suit you a bit."

" I don't call you a judge of sarcasm, Charlie."

" I'm as good a judge of that, as old Kramatome is of music, anyhow."

" That isn't saying much."

" But to the point, Li. What's your plan?" said Charlie.

" We want to make the place lively, don't we?"

" That's certain."

" Well, suppose we hire an organ-grinder by the day, and get him to play just under our window."

" Only one?"

" We can have two."

" Why not half a dozen?"

" And why not every blessed street musician in London, while you are about it?" said Vansittart; "nothing like doing the thing well while you are at it, Li."

" Hang it, Van, the square wouldn't hold 'em all."

" The more the merrier," said Vansittart; "that's a good old proverb, which you will find it difficult to better, Li."

" Right you are, Van," said Charlie; " I vote for the lot."

" It'll cost no end of tin."

" Hang that," said Vansittart; "a good hearty laugh is worth any money. I'd offer to pay for the lot, only I know you'd feel offended."

" I certainly should," replied our hero, "halves in the fun, halves in the cost. By George, won't old Kramatome be riled?"

And the three friends indulged in an anticipatory roar of laughter, which made the very windows echo their merriment.

" But how to carry out our plan," said Lionel.

" Ah! how is it to be done? Who knows most about the manners and customs of the wandering minstrel?"

" I know that in the classic region of Hatton Garden they most do congregate," said Charlie.

" Then the best thing we can do is to go there and find them out."

" But how?"

" By the smell of course," laughed Charlie. " An ordinary nose can scent an organ-grinder, or a performer on the hurdy-gurdy at the distance of a quarter of a mile."

" On a fine day and with the wind in my favour I'd undertake to sniff one at half a mile."

" It's all right. You know the Italians are an ancient race, and they're bound to smell a little stronger than the nations of a younger growth."

" Hang that," said Vansittart. " If scent goes by age what would a Chinaman smell like?"

" Ask Bret Harte, or any of the denizens of Sacramento, Silver City, or Nevada," replied Lionel. " They hold the neck of a bottle near a Chinaman for five minutes, then cork it up, and when they want to kill anybody they have only to let the smell out and that party is ready for the undertaker."

" That story is as strong as the Chinaman," said Vansittart, "and a little of it will go a very long way indeed."

" Is it agreed about the little music, then?"

" Of course."

" Consider it done."

" There's a good deal to be gone through before we can say that. Agreement is one thing, but doing is another. There was a man once who agreed to eat the moon if any one would prove that it was made of green cheese, but the agreement hasn't been fulfilled yet."

" Nor likely to be."

" You never can tell," was Vansittart's reply; " but we'll do our best to bring the organ-grinders' compact about."

" By the way," said Charlie, " it would be an improvement to have a few of the German bands, and a nigger troupe or two."

" Don't go in too heavy," said our hero. " If we make it too musical Kramatome might enjoy the tune, and we should have had all our trouble for nothing."

" Never fear. If he can enjoy the tune we provide for him he must be a fitting inmate for Colney Hatch. As it is I mean to lay in a stock of cotton wool, and I'd advise you fellows to do the same."

" Which will be the best day?"

" Thursday. It's his day for getting up the examination papers. Toddyboy and two of the other 'saps' are going to pass the college soon, and Kramatome is 'working the oracle.'"

So the plot was cast, and on that very day our hero and his chums set to work to carry it out.

For three days they worked hard, and at the end of that time they had engaged the services of ninety-seven organ-grinders, twenty-three hurdy-gurdy men, ten performers on the cornet, three full (German) bands, and two sets of Christy minstrels, all of whom were bound by contract to appear in the square at 11 a.m. on Thursday.

CHAPTER XVII.

TOMMY PAYS A VISIT TO A GROCER—AS USUAL HE HAS THE WORST OF IT, AND IS RESCUED BY HIS FRIENDS—A "LITTLE JOKE," AND ITS RESULTS.

BUT Thursday was two days distant, and naturally something must be done in the meantime to keep the pot boiling. When four such young gentlemen as Lionel and his friends, with plenty of money in their pockets, are let loose on society, of course society suffers, and with the commendable resolve to have a lark at any price and by any means, our young friends left the roof of their highly respectable tutor, Mr. Kramatome.

It was getting late, and already the street lamps were glimmering and blinking like sleepy children at dusk.

Sam Scarecrow was one of the party, and the long youth, maintaining a respectful distance, amused himself by depositing innumerable boys' caps into shops, down areas, and other places, where most likely the searchers for their rightful property would be afflicted sore by wrathful tradesmen, or servants disturbed from a quiet tête-à-tête with certain male cousins from the country.

Not content with this performance Sam leered hideously at every pretty girl; and Lionel, turning round, beheld his faithful follower standing gracefully on one leg, and blowing kisses at a matronly lady seated reading at a window.

" Sam," said Lionel, severely.

" Yes, sir," Sam replied, as his face vied with the colour of his hair, and the elevated leg came with a crash into its proper position.

" Have the goodness not to make an idiot of yourself."

" Wery good, sir," Sam replied, and was the picture of innocence and virtue in an instant.

" Li," said Lord Vansittart, " I rely on you to provide the programme for the evening. What is to be the first thing?"

" Oh, anything that starts up," returned Lionel.

" this is a foraging expedition for larks—eh, Charlie ?"

" That is so," said the youth addressed.

Tommy would have spoken, but, passing at that moment a grocer's shop, the words were taken out of his lips, and he found himself floating down three steps in a style far from graceful.

A yell of agony arose as the plump youth, reeling against the counter, sent a dish laden with butter on the floor, and Tommy bounding up fell over a barrel, and thrust his head into a bag of chestnuts.

The proprietor, a sallow, disagreeable-looking man, like an animated candle, rushed out of the back parlour, and shouting for his assistant, literally fell upon Tommy. and finding that his arms were not of sufficient length to encompass the rotund form, clutched at a certain fleshy part, and pinched it with all his might.

"Oh, I say," Tommy screamed, as he rose to the surface of the chestnuts, "what are you doing, you unmanly wretch ? Let go your hold, will you ? Yah-h-h-h, I shall never be able to sit down again with comfort."

"That's no business of mine," gasped the grocer, and to his shopman he said, "William, run for a policeman. I've been watching the young thief a long time, and now I have him."

"It's a lie," Tommy roared, furiously, "I'm not a thief. I was pushed down, that is, fell down your confounded steps."

The shopman, a greasy looking youth, with the combined odours of soap, tallow, sugar, tea, coffee, and Spanish onions clinging to his garments, bounded up the steps, grinning with delight, but his career was cut short by Lionel, who seizing him by the collar shook him until his teeth rattled.

"What's the matter?" Lionel roared. "How dare you rush into the street, and tread on my toes ?"

"I beg pardon," the assistant spluttered, "I didn't see you. Master have caught a thief, and I'm going for a policeman."

"A thief!" Lionel cried, indignantly. "How dare you utter such words before my face ? That unfortunate young gentleman is my friend. Here, Sam, hold this fellow while we settle this little matter. Come on, Van and Charlie."

"You've done it now," Sam cried, squinting awfully at the affrighted shopman. as he collared him by the shoulders and jammed him into a doorway—"You've been and gone and done it now, and no mistake."

"What have I done ?" howled the embryo grocer.

"You've heerd of the Dook of Hedinburgh," Sam said in a thrilling whisper. "Well, that's him as handed you over to me, his equilerry. It's sudden death to the man as put his beetle crushers on his Rile Highnesses's patents."

"How should I know it were the dook ?" the assistant exclaimed, turning ghastly pale.

"Well, p'raps he'll let you orf with your life if you go down on your marrow bones and beg his parding, but he's in a hawful rage 'cause your master called Lord Winklepin a thief."

Whilst Sam was terrifying the unhappy grocer's assistant into a state of imbecility, Lionel, Van, and Charlie were arguing the point with the grocer himself, who evinced great reluctance to part with Tommy on any terms.

"I've suffered awful," he said. "Boys is pi'son to me, and I'm down on 'em. It was only last night that a dozen or more of 'em come and stood all of a row agin my winder, so that nobody could see into the shop, and when William rushed out with a pail of water they stood him on hend—that is, upside down, and dipped his 'ed in it."

"All this has nothing to do with our friend," Vansittart said. "Come, don't be obstinate, man, or we shall have to take the law into our own hands. You've made a mistake, and the best thing you can do is to own it with a good grace."

"I shall hold him until William comes back with the perliceman," the grocer declared.

"Your hair will turn grey before that happens," Lionel replied. "Your assistant is safe in my servant's hands."

"Then I will hold him till a perliceman passes."

The words were scarcely breathed when Lord Vansittart shot the speaker over the counter, and in less time than it takes to record the fact Tommy found himself gasping and panting in the street.

"Come on, Sam," Lionel shouted. "We have no time to lose. The bobbies will be down on us presently."

"Ain't I to hev a round with this chap ?" Sam pleaded.

"No, let him go," Lionel returned, impatiently.

"Not even a kick, sir?"

"If you linger another instant I will discharge you," Lionel roared.

As this awful threat was pronounced Sam released his prisoner, and, thrusting his hat firmly on the back of his head, folded his arms and trotted like a melancholy mute after his master.

"It's much too bad," Tommy Codlings groaned, rubbing the afflicted part, still indented with the grocer's finger nails. "There never was such an unlucky chap as I am. What did you push me into the shop for, Van ?"

"I really could not help it," Van replied, laughing; "you looked so tempting that I could not resist it. Besides, you know, if the fellow had any eye for business he would have offered a long price for you."

"What for ?" demanded Tommy, puzzled.

"Why to boil down for soap to be sure," Van said. "Let us go back to the shop."

"Not if I know it," Tommy said, backing; "that fellow has nails like a tiger, and knows how to use them."

"I knowed a man once," Sam Scarecrow chimed in dismally, "as had a wife as never cut her nails only once a year, and that was on Heaster Monday."

"Why did she perform the operation on that day ?" Lionel, demanded, regarding the lanky youth with a suspicious eye.

"Why, you see, sir," Sam went on, "he were a poor man, and couldn't afford a houting in a wan more than once a year, so his missus was that kind that she refrained from decoratin' his face on them occasions, for fear people should think he had somethin' catchin' about his wisage, and wouldn't ride in the some vehicle."

"That will do, Sam," Lionel said; "the next time I wish for one of your novel anecdotes I will let you knew."

"Which, sir, you will allus find me ready to command," Sam replied, and fell once more gloomily into the rear.

"I say, Li," said Vansittart, "what do you say ? Shall we get up a crowd?"

"How is it to be managed ?" Lionel demanded.

"I know," Tommy groaned; "Van means to pick a quarrel with a dustman or a coster. I remember one night when I was out with Irish Mike ——"

"Dreaming again," Lionel interrupted, laughing merrily. "Oh, Tommy, I fear you are too far gone to get that stupid idea out of your head."

"Well," Tommy returned, rubbing that perplexed cranium, thoughtfully, "if it was a dream it was—dash it all! I won't think of it."

"That is right," Van said. "Now then, here is a crowded thoroughfare. Sam, I rely on you."

"What to do ?" the lean youth said, smiling to such an extent that he looked like an ancient nutcracker.

"Not to make a fool of yourself," Van returned.

"I won't if I can help it," Sam replied. "I'm game for any think, wot's the programmy ?"

"Go down on your hands and knees, and pretend to be looking for something," Van replied, striking a match, and waving it to and fro. "Now, gentlemen, if you please, gaze thoughtfully on the pavement and on the roadway, and we shall have some fun."

"I don't exactly see this," Tommy said. "Where's the good of staring about? What is the little game?"

"I have lost something," Van replied, gazing earnestly about, and poking up the mud with his walking cane, "and I want to find it."

In less than a minute a crowd collected. Errand boys, clerks from the City, apple women, portly old gentlemen, pretty milliners, and a host of others stopped, and stared with wide open eyes and gaping mouths at the searchers.

Sam rushed to and fro, grunting like an obstinate locomotive, and nearly wore the knees out of his inexpressibles in the frantic endeavour to find the missing article.

Suddenly a murmur ran through the crowd, and a policeman shouldering his way, in a style only known to the fraternity and men of the fire brigade, exclaimed—

"Hullo, what is the matter here?"

"I'm looking for a five-pound note," Van replied, clutching at his hair, and knocking Tommy's hat off in his agony. "What shall I do?"

"Stand back there!" roared the constable, sending half a dozen small boys flying into the road.

The search was resumed, strangers took up the cause, lights were procured from shops, and the wildest excitement prevailed, and continued for some twenty minutes, when the policeman, hot and perspiring, said—

"Really, sir, I don't think you could have dropped it here. You must be mistaken."

"No, I am not," Vansittart said, holding the constable by a button and looking him calmly in the face. "My friend, did I say that I had lost a five-pound note?"

"You said you were looking for one," the constable gasped.

"And so I was," Vansittart replied, "and I regret that I have not found it, because I am very much in want of one at the present moment."

"Well, I'm dashed!" the constable said, completely staggered, and catching sight of Sam Scarecrow, who was not yet in the secret, bestowed such a hearty kick under the coat-tails that the lean youth flew out full length, and, clutching at the legs of a corpulent gentleman, brought him heavily to the ground.

"Wot's that for?" Sam yelled, as he rose and assisted the companion of his misfortune to his feet. "P'raps you'll be as good as to give a hexplanation o' this houtrage."

"I'll run you in, if I have any of your cheek," the constable cried, wrathfully.

"Yah-h-h! Coward!" the crowd cried. "Why don't you leave the poor fellow alone, you villain?"

"I ain't a goin' to be called a willain for doing my dooty," the officer roared, red in the face as a boiled lobster, and made a dash into the midst of the throng.

"Come along," Vansittart whispered to his companions. "Let them fight it out."

Slipping quietly away they beheld the valiant officer in the hands of the Philistines. Small boys attacked his shins, and men and women—with that desire to assert their rights and set at defiance the myrmidon of a tyrannical Government—fell upon him, and would have used him badly but for the appearance of other members of the force, when "Take care of Number One" was the motto of the day, and ere an arrest could be made the excited people had vanished like so many will-o'-the-wisps.

———

CHAPTER XVIII.

WHICH TREATS OF MUSIC—AND OTHER THINGS.

ON the fateful morning Mr. Kramatome rose two hours earlier than usual, and in a temper fifty per cent. worse than his normal condition of mind.

This, though, is little to be wondered at, when you reflect that he had before him the difficult task of "cramming" into the heads of three of his pupils twice as much information as Nature had provided room for, and that, when it was "crammed" in, the chances were that it would stop there, instead of letting itself out before the examiners.

He was not satisfied with simply ringing the bell that morning, but held on, and brought it out with about a fathom of wire hanging to the handle.

Joblot answered the summons with wonderful rapidity, but he opened the door with equally wonderful caution, only allowing the tip of his nose and one eye to peep round the corner.

"Come in!" roared Mr. Kramatome. "What do you mean by entering the room in that—that—poaching manner?"

"I thought it were fire," explained Joblot, "and I ain't insured."

"Take that," was Mr. Kramatome's reply, "and if my breakfast isn't on the table in five minutes you go without yours for a week."

He pitched the bell handle with a dexterous jerk at Joblot, the wire coiled itself around his neck, and two minutes out of the five was consumed in getting it off again.

"Of all the spiteful parties as ever kept a nigger slave, and called him a footman, he is the spitefullest," muttered Joblot.

When Joblot reached the kitchen, the cook was in a bad temper, for she had her suspicions that Z 9945 flirted with a housemaid on the other side of the square, and the five minutes were multiplied by six before the breakfast was ready.

"You vagabond!" said Mr. Kramatome, glaring ferociously at his footman, "how dare you waste my time in this way?"

"I can't help it," groaned Joblot, mournfully; "I ain't cook and footman too, sir. I happened to give her a lift with the toast, and then she gave me one with the toastin' fork, and if you don't believe me, Mr. Kramatome, sir, look here."

And Joblot turned round to display the rent in his garments made by the vengeful cook, but he had scarcely lifted up his coat-tails, when the toe of Mr. Kramatome's right boot lifted him into a corner of the room, and there he crouched on his hands and knees, opening and shutting his mouth in mute but expressive agony.

"Get up," gasped Mr. Kramatome.

"I can't," moaned Joblot, "I'm broke in 'arf."

He looked so limp that Mr. Kramatome thought for the moment that some injury might have been done to his spine, and in his agitation poured a little hot tea down his neck to refresh him.

It did refresh him, a little too much, perhaps, for he gave such a vigorous jump that Mr. Kramatome was knocked violently backwards against the table, and jammed his head so firmly into a large tin of Australian beef that it fitted him like a new hat.

Self-possession is an admirable quality, but Mr. Kramatome had very little of it that morning.

He got up and glared round him for a neat and handy weapon of destruction—a crowbar or a pick-axe, or a double-barrelled breech-loading blunderbuss would have suited his frame of mind just then—but, luckily for Joblot, all the furniture was of a peaceful description, and he was obliged to have recourse to the old familiar boot, which he used to such effect that the unhappy footman was kicked right along the passage, down two flights of stairs, and into the area before the sole came off, and Mr. Kramatome began to feel a little tired.

The cook was the only witness of the latter portion of the performance, but she, instead of screaming, as every right-minded female deems it proper to do in such circumstances, smiled approval, and as soon as Mr. Kramatome had gone, fetched a bucket of water, and threw it over Joblot in a fit of humanity which was of a very doubtful kind.

Joblot was sitting with his back to the coal-cellar door, gasping and breathless with pain, when the cook's polite attention "fetched" him with full force in the face, knocked him through the cellar door, and down the steps on to a friendly knob of coal which mercifully stunned him.

"There," murmured the cook. "Drat the fellow! I'll jest bolt the door, and keep him there for a hour or two. I'll teach him to go sneaking and pryin' about whenever Jim (this was Z 9945), poor feller, comes after a little bit of supper."

Red both with anger and exertion, Mr. Kramatome returned to the breakfast-room, ordered a fresh meal to be made ready, and applied himself once more to the analysis of the examination papers.

This was an exceedingly difficult task—one which required a cool head and unruffled nerve.

Mr. Kramatome had neither just then, and he chewed at his nails, and pulled his hair, until he looked about as happy and peaceful as a grey old tomcat on the war-path.

"Let me be calm," muttered the tutor, as he gulped down the half of a cupful of scalding tea, and brought the tears into his eyes with the exquisite agony it caused him. "Let me be calm," he repeated, and set the cup down with a violence that cracked the saucer in a dozen pieces, "or I shall never be able to understand these papers myself, to say nothing of forcing their contents into the thick heads of Toddyboy and the others."

The tutor drank about a quart of strong tea, judiciously spiced with a little old cognac, then retired to his bedroom, where he soused his head vigorously with cold water, and finally, calmed and composed, sat down in his study for a few hours' steady close work.

"How fortunate!" he murmured, "that this neighbourhood is so quiet and peaceful. No braying German idiots, with more brass in their constitutions than in their cornets. No repulsive Italians with a box full of stomach-aches—miscalled an organ—no still more loathsome vagabonds of home-growth pollute the atmosphere, and fright the slumbering echoes. All is in harmonious repose, and but for Joblot and the tax-collector I might indeed be happy."

It was a quarter to eleven when Mr. Kramatome concluded this affecting soliloquy, and if our hero and his friends could have listened they might have been touched by it, and thereby diverted from their purpose. As it was they were all a great deal more anxious for the success of their plot than to secure any one's peace and quiet.

"I hope those chaps will be punctual," said Lionel. "If they don't all come together the fun will be spoiled."

"They'll come fast enough," replied Charlie. "Each one of 'em thinks that he has a good job in hand, and will be wanted to perform again."

"But, by George!" added Vansittart, with a laugh, "won't they be surprised when they see so many of the same kidney in the square? They'll be jealous, and get up a fight, perhaps."

"If they do, there are the police."

"What's the good of Z 9945 among so many?" said Vansittart. "Poor fellow! Why, the very fleas those fellows carry about with them would eat him alive."

"Let's see, how many are there altogether. There are ninety-seven grinders, and twenty-three hurdy-gurdies—that's a hundred and twenty; then the German bands muster seven or eight players each—that's twenty; and with the cornets and the niggers we shall have a hundred and sixty or seventy of 'em."

"That's a good lot," said Tommy, approvingly. "But I say, Li, if you could only have got Irish Mike here with his tin whistle he would make more noise than all the others put together. He——"

"Now, Tommy, how many more times are we to warn you against dragging Irish Mike into the conversation? We don't want Irish Mike. We don't believe in him, and if you continue to be so obstinate we shall have to cut your company."

"Or pitch him out of the window amongst the savage denizens of Saffron-hill who now approach. Hurrah! I can hear the first one."

"The first forty, you mean," said Lionel, starting up, and putting nearly two-thirds of himself out of the window. "By George! Van, there must be twice as many as we ordered—the square's alive with 'em."

There were four entrances to the square, three streets and a court; and as the clock of a neighbouring church chimed the hour of eleven the thoroughfares were fairly choked with the itinerant minstrels, all eager to be first in the field.

The organ-grinders began to play directly they got into the square, and Mr. Kramatome was in the midst of an awfully complicated problem in dynamics when the strains of some forty organs, all playing different tunes, thundered upon him in one tremendous blast.

His hair slowly elevated itself, and he turned pallid with alarm.

"Good Heavens!" he gasped. "What was that?"

Before he had time to arrive at anything like a satisfactory solution of the problem the brass bands got into position at the corner, and commenced, then the balance of the organ-grinders struck up, and the hurdy-gurdy boys, finding that street space was limited, got down the areas, and ground away, determined to earn their money or perish.

The noise was awful, indescribable, revolting. There are no adjectives in the English language capable of approaching within a hundred miles of the necessary atrocity requisite to picture it with the faintest approach to accuracy.

Mr. Kramatome turned the colour of every one of Judson's single dyes for the people—we do not exaggerate—and swore every oath that occurred to him at the moment, then he rushed to the window and flung it open with a crash that shattered some panes of glass, and "starred" the rest.

At ordinary times the crash of the falling glass could have been heard all over the square, but now the falling of a pin would have had an equal chance of attracting attention.

"Gracious powers!" gasped the tutor, as he gazed upon the sea of heads and organs, "this is a mutiny, a revolution. The foreigners have risen in a body, and are about to massacre us, and these fellows are sent on ahead to unsettle our nerves with their uproar, while their more bloodthirsty companions are advancing in the rear."

"It's first-rate fun," said Lionel to himself, for it was of no use trying to make his voice heard by any of his companions, "but it's an awful din. A little of this will go a long way even with me."

By cautiously craning his neck out of the window he could just catch a glimpse of the tutor, his eyes starting out of his head, his hands pressed closely over his ears, and his lips giving utterance to something which Lionel guessed to be a command to the performers to go away.

"Keep the game alive," roared Lionel. "My eye, Van, just come and take a peep at the old boy."

"Let's get some hot coppers and fling 'em out of the window," roared Charlie, and by dint of putting his mouth close to Lionel's ear he just managed to make him comprehend his meaning.

There was a fire in the room, and among them they had a good stock of pence and halfpence, which in a few minutes were made nearly red-hot, and then pitched amongst the crowd.

The greedy ones suffered, and, yelling at the pain of their burnt fingers, flung the torturing coppers back at the givers; but they only succeeded in breaking two or three more windows, and nearly choking Tommy, who happened to have his mouth open when a penny passed that way; but he managed to swallow it after a good deal of trouble.

One of the victims was a monkey, who, with the peculiar dexterity of its tribe, caught one of the red-hot pennies flying, and immediately making up his mind that Mr. Kramatome was the culprit, sprang on to the railings, and grinned and chattered with awful vehemence.

The tutor not unnaturally mistook the monkey for a diminutive organ-grinder (there is really a strong family likeness), and, shaking his fist at him, he roared—

"The audacity of the scoundrel, to climb up my area railings and swear at me! Go away, you low foreigner."

And reaching over, he so far forgot his natural dignity as to slap the "low foreigner."

The little gentleman in the red breeches instantly retaliated by seizing upon the tutor's hand, and fixing a set of very sharp and white teeth into it. Mr. Kramatome uttered a yell which, really, for a brief instant, was heard above the din of the combined musicians, and then he jerked his arm up with such force that the poor little " foreign gentleman " was hurled into the air like a cricket ball, and fell into the bell of an ophecleide on the other side of the square, and got jammed in so tight that it took the strongest man in the band half an hour to blow him out again.

Hastily binding his handkerchief about his wounded hand, Mr. Kramatome dashed down the window, thereby breaking the few panes of glass that were left, and rushed out into the passage.

"Joblot—Joblot!" he roared, in a voice that made the hall lamp swing like a pendulum.

But no Joblot appeared, and for a very good reason, as my readers know—he was locked up in the cellar.

The cook, though, was in the hall, looking through the side window, in the hope of seeing Z 9945 come and annihilate the foe, and Mr. Kramatome addressed himself to her.

"Where's that villain, Joblot?"

"I'm sure I don't know, sir," replied the cook, which was not strictly true, inasmuch as she had locked the unhappy young man in the cellar.

"Then just run out and see if you can find a policeman," roared Mr. Kramatome, " or two, if you can find them. Confound the lazy rascals! they're always to be met when they're not wanted."

"Begging your pardon, sir, but no respectable woman who deserves the name of such, would trust herself in the street with such a parcel of dirty foreigners. I should be ate up alive, or worse, perhaps."

"You'll drive me mad between you!" gasped the ferocious tutor. "Where are those boys?"

He rushed into the dining-room, red-hot and furious, to find Lionel and the others with the front window down, and they all looking serene and happy, and apparently engaged in study.

"Great powers, young gentlemen!" gasped the tutor, "don't you—don't you *hear* anything?"

"We thought we did, sir," replied Lionel, quietly.

"*Thought* you did! Merciful Heaven! you must be stone deaf."

"We found it rather soothing, in fact," added Charlie; "all except Toddyboy, and I believe you'll find him under some mattresses in the bedroom. But he never had any ear for high-class music worth mentioning."

"High-class *music*!—high ——" gasped the tutor. "Oh, I say!"

"Besides," continued Lionel, "if we had any objection, we shouldn't have liked to interfere with **your** private amusements."

"*My* amusements!" said Mr. Kramatome. "Do you suppose that *I* ordered these—these unspeakable vagabonds here?"

"Did you not, sir?" inquired Lionel, innocently. "We thought you did, and that they were playing Wagner. It's very like Wagner."

"Especially ' Der Ring des Niebelungen,' " added Vansittart. " I went to the Festival at Bayreuth, and this is the very thing."

This insult to the great prophet of the music of the future, added to what he had already undergone was more than Mr. Kramatome could bear. He withered them with a look of scorn (that is, he tried the withering business, but it very seldom succeeds), and dashed out of the room as hastily as he had entered it, determined to sally forth and scatter the enemy with his own hands.

CHAPTER XIX.

FIRE!

FOR the space of half an hour or so Joblot remained in a happy state of insensibility, and then he awoke, in a very misty state indeed as to things in general.

At first, being in the dark, he thought that he was in bed, but, though his couch was not of the downiest, he had never found it so nubbly as this, and by degrees he came to the conclusion that he was not in bed.

Then he became conscious that there was an awful, unearthly, appalling kind of sound around him—neither groaning, nor whistling, nor shrieking, nor squeaking—but a compound of all, and other noises of which he had no previous notion; and this, and the fact that he was very stiff and cold, induced him to believe at length that he was dead, and that the awful noise was the general break-up of the world on the last day.

This idea made the miserable footman colder than ever, and he shivered until he brought a hundred-weight or so of coal rattling down about him.

"That's it," he gasped. "I'm dead sure enough, and—sniff—I smell as if I'd been dead a good long time, too. Oh, loramussy on me, wot a hawful noise!"

Joblot waited in fear and trembling for his turn to come to go up, but as his eyes became a little more accustomed to the darkness, and his senses recovered from the effects of the fall, he began to realise that he was not in a grave, but in a coal-hole, and that he was not dead, but at the very least three-parts alive.

"Well, ain't I glad!" exclaimed Joblot. "I haven't got much to live for in a general way, but I don't know as I should be any better orf if I was dead."

With which remark, full of a subtle philosophy, Joblot arose, and groped around for the door.

Now, to find the door, or any other part of a room, when the said room is in nearly perfect darkness, is as hopeless as the search of Diogenes for an honest man.

Joblot felt nearly every piece of coal in the cellar before his fingers succeeded in touching the hasp of the door, and then he found it—securely fastened.

All this time the peculiar noise, which had at first alarmed Joblot, continued, and though he was now convinced that it was not due to the final Resurrection, yet he felt that it must be something very uncommon, and he wanted to get out and see what it was.

The more he wanted, the more he couldn't, though. The door was strong, old-fashioned, and iron-plated, and he might as well have kicked at the Great Pyramid, in the hope of battering the side in.

He listened again. The noise was worse than ever, and he could now hear the trampling of many feet on the pavement above the cellar.

" It's a fire, that's wot it is," gasped Joblo
►The house is a-fire!"

Then another horrible thought occurred to him.

" And by-and-bye the walls will tumble down, and I shall be smothered to death afore I can get out."

That idea added to the terrors of his situation, and the footman kicked at the door with such energy that he nearly deprived himself of all right to the name by kicking his very feet off.

At last, in the depth of despair, a bright, a brilliant, a dazzling idea occurred to him. If he set fire to the door people could not fail to take notice of the smoke ascending through the area, then he could shout for help, the firemen would lower a ladder, he would climb up, and all would be joy.

There was plenty of material for igniting a fire, for wood was kept in the cellar as well as coal, and Joblot soon had a goodly pile ranged against the door.

He had always a plentiful supply of fusees and matches in his pocket, as he was very tender-hearted, and when he went for a walk was certain to lay out one half of his small stock of pocket-money in that way.

They were rather damp, though, now, for a good deal of water had found its way into his pockets; but Joblot picked out a few of the driest, and after hatching them a little while, he struck the bunch and applied it to the pile of wood and coal.

It was fairly dry, and soon kindled into a brilliant blaze, which was very pleasant, for it lit up the gloom, and warmed Joblot too.

But when the coal took fire, and the smoke began to eddy round the cellar, Joblot began to cough, and in a little while he began to choke.

" I—wish—they'd make haste," gasped Joblot, as he gazed in dismay at the flaming mass of coal, which reached nearly to the top of the door. " I can—hardly—breathe, and—oh, ain't it—gettin'—'ot !"

It was getting hot, and no wonder if my readers will consider the effect of a couple of hundredweight of coal burning in a close cellar.

The trampling immediately over head had ceased now, but Joblot could still hear strange noises surging about him, and, lifting up his voice, he shouted—" Fire !"

He might as well have called " Milk," or " Water cresses," or " Mackerel," for any chance he had of being heard; but he shouted for all that—on the same principle which induces a drowning man to clutch at a straw : not because he thinks it will save him, but because there is nothing else handy.

Mr. Kramatome had taken up his hat with the full intention of charging the mob of musicians and scattering them in the fulness of his wrath, but when he got on the doorstep it seemed to him that the scattering would not be an easy job.

He was not a heavy man himself, and the other lot weighed a good deal—especially if you took the organs into consideration—and he stopped awhile to think about it.

Now, " stopping to think " usually ends in a man going back again, especially if there is anything unpleasant ahead, and this is the course which Mr. Kramatome pursued. He went back as far as the front door, and roared for the police with all his might.

In the dim distance he thought he saw the helmet of a policeman bobbing up and down like a cork in a gutter on a rainy day, and he waved his right hand frantically towards it.

" By George, this *is* fun !" said Lionel, who, with his chums, was in an enthusiastic condition of delight. Don't those chaps stick to their work, Charlie?"

" Well, ye-e-s," answered Charlie, doubtfully. " But I begin to wish, Li, that they were a trifle less conscientious about earning their money."

" We shall have the military out soon if this goes on much longer," laughed Vansittart. " The

authorities will think it's a riot. By Jove, what fun it would be to see a regiment of Life Guards charge this lot !"

" Not so much fun as you think, Van. Especially when it came to paying for the damaged organs, etcetera."

" No fear of that. All the men were paid separately, and by different people. There's little chance of our being caught. Besides, what matter if we were ?"

" Well, I don't know that it would matter much, except to Tommy."

" Oh!—ah, now, I like that. What have I got to do with it, when you kept me out of the joke on purpose ?"

" I know we did, old boy, out of consideration for you, as we have done many times before; but it's never any use, you know—you always get into a scrape just the same."

Tommy was about to make some defiant reply to this proposition, when Charlie spoke suddenly in an altered tone.

" I say, you fellows, where is the smoke coming from ?"

He pointed out of the window, and certainly there, in the region of the area, was a quantity of thin bluish smoke, but whence it came was difficult to say.

" Some of the organs on fire through over grinding," suggested Vansittart.

" Or a case of spontaneous combustion on the part of the organ-grinders—their clothes are greasy enough."

" It comes from somewhere," Charlie muttered.

" That's a wise remark."

" Hold your row, Li. Fire's no joke. Hullo ! There, I saw it then. It's the coal-cellar on fire—I saw the glare of the flame."

It did seem to be the coal-cellar, for the smoke had much increased in volume in that direction, and thin filmy streaks were oozing through the coal-plate on the pavement.

Charlie put his head out of the window as far as he could, and shouted fire with such energy that Mr. Kramatome tumbled backwards into the passage.

The word acted like magic. The cry was taken up and echoed along the streets, the organs ceased to play, the German bands made themselves as scarce as genuine German sausages, and in five minutes the engine from the station in the next street rattled up, scattering the lingering remnant of the grinders like dry leaves.

Lionel and his chums had not lost a moment in reaching the area, though just then they had no idea that any one was in the burning cellar.

" Let's break the door in," suggested Charlie, " I'll get the kitchen poker, that's heavy enough for anything."

" I wonder how it caught fire ?" said Lionel.

" Spontaneous combust ——"

" Bother your spontaneous combustion ! You're as big a nuisance with that as with Irish Mike. You think that anything will catch fire, even the Thames, if you tried to set it alight."

" I say, somebody called out," said Charlie, suddenly—" somebody in the cellar."

Just then a faint choking sort of wail was perceptible above the crackling of the fire inside. The boys looked at each other, and then, without thinking of the consequences, took a short run and dashed at the door.

It was nearly burnt to a cinder, and they went through it as if it had been a sheet of paper, scattering the fire right and left.

Joblot, who would no doubt have been as pale as snow if he had not been scorched a lively pink, was collared and dragged out before he had time to move an inch of his own free will.

It was time, for poor Joblot was very nearly done through. If there had only been somebody there to baste him he would have been a nice brown. As it was he felt like one of those indiarubber air-balls, and any of the boys would have shuddered at the idea of pricking him anywhere with a pin.

Tommy was one of the most zealous attackers of the door, and though he had not hurt himself much there was a red-hot coal somewhere about him which tickled him a good deal, because he couldn't find it.

He stopped behind in the cellar to look for it, because he did not like the idea of carrying dangerous combustibles into the house with him; and just as he thought he had his hand on it, the fireman above pulled the coal-plate up, and let the hose down.

Tommy was well acquainted with the sensation of a shower-bath in chilly weather, but he had never got used even to that. But this! It was awful. It took him fairly off his legs, dashed him into a corner, and kept him there. The steam choked him, the spray blinded him, and any one who knows the particularly agreeable smell produced by pouring water on a lively fire will feel sure that Tommy's nose was not very pleasantly tickled.

After a while one of the firemen came down, and found that the fire was out—and Tommy very nearly so.

Thoughts of distinction, of medals, of promotion rapid and profitable, filled him as he dragged Tommy forth; but when he learned that he had only pumped on him, and nearly rendered himself liable to a charge of manslaughter, he was extremely vexed.

So was Tommy, as that evening he lay upon his bed surrounded by his sympathising friends—sympathetic, no doubt, but yet there was more laughter about their sympathy than usually attends the genuine article.

CHAPTER XX.

IN WHICH OUR FRIENDS ARE ENTERTAINED AND EDIFIED AT TWO SHILLINGS A HEAD—SAM SCARECROW'S UNANNOUNCED APPEARANCE ON THE STAGE.

"THAT was not so bad a lark," said Charlie, referring to the five-pound-note episode, a few days after that memorable escapade. "Van, you are a genius."

"You flatter me," Van said, bowing with mock politeness, "but don't do it again, dear boy—it unnerves me."

"I think we have been getting on pretty well," Lionel said. "What is your opinion about the matter, Tommy?"

"That you fellows get all the fun, and I get all the kicks," Master Codlings replied. "Ah, it is all very well to laugh, but if you felt as sore behind as I do, you would smile on the other side of your face."

"There never was such a boy to grumble," Charlie chimed in. "I declare it amounts to ingratitude. Why, Tommy, you ought to feel much obliged to us for allowing you to see life in its various phases."

"If being kicked, cuffed, and pinched are the advantages of seeing life, the less I view of it the better," Tommy said. "But, lor, I ought to be used to it. When I was ——"

"Oh, yes, we know all about it," Charlie interrupted. "Now then, dear boys, time is on the wing, and we must make the best of it. What do you say? Shall we spend an hour at the Moon and Stars Music-hall?"

"I have no fancy for that kind of entertainment," Lionel observed. "I am very fond of music, but I confess that I have the profoundest contempt for a man who howls out questionable songs, wrapped in but a thin veil of decency, for a living."

"Hear, hear!" Van cried; "those are my sentiments. Sam, did you ever go to a music-hall?"

"I hev, my lud," Sam replied, "and warn't it jolly too? There was a chap in a yaller wesket, white hat, a blue coat, and boots that shined like mirrors, as sung a song about the time he went a courtin', and the people larfed to that hextent as made the building hecho."

"Don't mistake me," Charlie said, taking up the discussion, "I don't care a dump for the entertainment—only I thought we might get some fun out of it."

"As you like," Lionel said; "lead the way to this hall of revels and delight."

The Moon and Stars Music-hall stood in a locality exactly suited for the purpose. There was any number of squalid slums running from the main street, and poor people were as plentiful as field mice at harvest time.

A magnificent assortment of cabbage stalks, whelk, and winkle shells betrayed the fact that a street market was held there occasionally, and this was verified by two or three stalls doing a thriving trade in cold fried fish and bread.

As the amorous madman in Nicholas Nickleby would have observed, all was "gas and gaiters" at the Moon and Stars. There were men in livery strutting about, scowling authoritatively at the shoe-blacks as they clattered up the gallery stairs, and smiling blandly as the more wealthy gave up their checks and entered the stalls. There was sufficient gas to have illuminated a small town, and such glass as might have made even Messrs. Spiers and Pond envious.

Lord Vansittart approached the paying place, and observing that Sam was contemplating a modest sixpence with a hole in it, for the purpose of obtaining a seat in the gallery, he bade that angular youth put his money up, and follow him into the stalls.

"But it ain't the thing, my lud," Sam argued. "Suppose any of the Rile family was to twig you in my company it would ruin your pressidge for ever."

"Don't talk nonsense, Sam," Van said. "Royalty does not patronise this sort of thing, unless," hesitating, and winking at Li, "it is privately. Li, you are Sam's master, and I leave him in your hands."

"If he dares to open his mouth again," Lionel said, glaring at Sam until that youth's eyes were nearly straight with fright, "I'll kick him all the way home and back again."

Sam bestowed a smile of admiration on his master, and like the good faithful fellow he was followed him into the interior of the hall without another word.

"What do you say?" Charlie said, as they took their seats; "shall we have some champagne?"

"Bitter beer for me," Van said; "and I advise you to try the same tap. Messrs. Goosebery and Rhubarb may do a flourishing business, but they are no friends of mine."

"Then bitter beer let it be," Charlie said, ordering three tankards of a polite waiter. "What is yours to be, Sam?"

"If there's a licker as I prefers to any other as bein' light and refreshin' it's 'arf-and-'arf, sir," Sam replied, passing his hand across his mouth.

"We don't serve 'arf-and-'arf in the stalls, young man," the waiter observed, eyeing Sam with much disfavour. "It bein' a beverage as only the wulgar indulges in."

"I knowed you was a gentleman as soon as I seed your shirt front," Sam said, with much irony. "I'll hev a pint o' stout, and hev the goodness not to put your thumb in it."

The waiter, bestowing a most ferocious glare on the squinting youth, vanished, shrieking "three bitters and one stout," and presently reappeared with the foaming tankards.

"Who is that fellow on the stage now?" Charlie asked of him, as he tendered half a sovereign in payment.

"Fellow!" the waiter cried, aghast. "Why, sir, that's the celebrated Adolphus Caddy, as is making a thousand a year, and doing only three turns a night for the money."

"I'd make him turn something if I had my way," Van growled, under his breath. "The fellow's ignorance is only equalled by his cheek. I say, Li," he continued, turning to our hero, "how many men of brains would be glad of a fifth of that ape's income?"

Lionel nodded, and stared the singer almost out of countenance.

The song went on with a little explanatory dialogue between the verses, and it so happened that a young man, with carroty hair, and an odious squint was alluded to as the rival of the hero of the song. Charlie burst into a laugh, and instantly the attention of the house was fixed on the stalls, and as soon as Sam's personal beauties were observed the merriment became uproarious.

The singer, innocent of the sensation he had caused, stared about him like a man in a dream, and fancying that he had made some mistake looked at the conductor of the band for an explanation; but that gentleman, being in the joke, was shrieking himself into an epileptic fit, and in answer to every query rolled about in the agonies of mirth, and laughed the more.

Sam sat still for a moment, with indignant scorn flashing out of his resplendent orbs; but as peal after peal of irrepressible merriment arose from all parts of the crowded house he suddenly leapt to his feet, and before anybody could prevent him had bounded on the stage, and before Mr. Adolphus Caddy could open his mouth Sam's fist was against it with a force which put singing for a night or two out of the question.

"There," cried Sam, wrathfully, as he danced round the petrified vocalist. "There! that's for your imperence. Here's another for your wit, and here's——"

But luckily for Adolphus Caddy the blow was stopped by a carpenter, who, rushing on the stage, folded Sam in his arms.

"Why, you bloodthirsty willian!" the man gasped, staggering to and fro as his captive lunged, kicked, and struck out violently. "Wot d'ye mean by it?"

"I'll show you in a minute," cried the perspiring youth. "Take yer knuckles out o' my ribs, will yer?"

"Not till I see you handcuffed or in a straight weskit," the carpenter roared. "Hi, why don't somebody fetch the perlice? He's like a heel, and I can't hold him much longer."

The carpenter was right.

He did not hold Sam another instant, for that youth, suddenly bending his lanky form, with a jerk worthy of a finely-tempered steel spring, shot the carpenter into the orchestra.

He fell bodily on the conductor, whose mirthful accents were instantly changed to discordant yells of agony, and the only pity is that Wagner was not there to have retained the fiend-like howls in his memory.

A cheer followed this unexpected feat; the tide of public opinion was turned in Sam's favour, and the suffering Adolphus Caddy, perceiving it, fled from the stage, and was seen no more that night.

"Ladies and gentlemen," Sam said, slipping up to the footlights, and placing his hand on his heart in the most approved fashion. "I've licked two on 'em, and I'm ready for as many as likes to come, purwidin' it's one down and t'other come on."

"Brayvo! horray!" shouted the youths in the gallery, but the triumph of the plaudits received a chill when a small boy asked Sam to tell him the time by the clock round the corner.

"If you'll come down 'ere I will tell you, my lad," Sam said, viciously, and once more the long youth was about to address the audience when a couple of policemen put in an appearance.

"Li," Van said, hurriedly, "we must cover Sam's retreat."

"Oh, certainly," Lionel and Charlie cried in a breath.

"Come down," Lionel shouted to his servant. "Tommy, wedge yourself in between the stalls. No mortal bobby that ever wore a helmet could pass you."

"I shall be pounded to a jelly," Tommy Codlings said. "But never mind—here goes. But don't be longer getting him out than you can help."

"You may rely on that," Lionel said, casting a hasty glance at the approaching officers. "Now, Sam, jump over the seats. The people will make a lane for you."

"All right, sir," Sam replied. "I can skip like a kangaroo, and I pity the man as comes in the way of my boots."

"I call on you to assist me in the capture of this man," the foremost policeman roared. "Now, then young Orton, get out of the way," to Tommy. "Hi, there! Stop that lanky cove. He's given me a lot o' trouble afore."

"Oh, lor!" Tommy gasped, perspiring to a frightful degree. "It's Z 9945. Here's a go. Van, Charlie, anybody—help me! I'm fixed, and can't get out."

But nobody heeded him.

Sam was the focus of all eyes, and that youth's flying form was a sight such as is the lot of but few mortals to witness.

Bounding over chairs, forms, and benches, he rushed at the folding-doors, and meeting the fireman connected with the establishment so completely floored him that his brass helmet, striking the wall, hid his manly features from view.

Tears of anguish streamed from his eyes, besprinkling the floor, and smothered metallic groans came from under the headgear which had but a few minutes since been sufficiently imposing to awe a raging fire into an iceberg.

Sam stayed not, but rushed into the street, and Lionel, extricating Tommy from his rather perilous position, led the way for the open air.

Z 9945 and his companion brother of the truncheon did not know what to do.

Sam alone had created a disturbance, and yet it was hard to have so important a charge slip through their fingers. Matters were coming to a crisis.

Showers of nuts and oranges rained from the gallery, and so thickly were these favours bestowed by a generous public on the blue-coated preservers of the peace that they were glad to beat a retreat.

"I'll keep a heye on you gents," Z 9945 observed maliciously, as Lionel and his friends left the hall. "I knows yer and where yer live."

"Sorry I have forgotten my card-case," Vansittart said. "But never mind, old fellow. Come and have a drink."

Z 9945 and his friend exchanged glances.

"There ain't no harm in that," the former said. "It's been hot work, to say nothink of a horange as caught me a whack in the heye."

Adjourning to the bar the constables moistened their parched throats with beer, and finished up with a drop of something short to rectify the effect of the malt.

"I ain't a malicious man," Z 9945 said, with emotion almost amounting to tears; "but when I see that long cove all the wenom in my nater comes up to the sufface, and I feel nigh upon bustin'. Why, dash it all—here he is again!"

Yes, it was indeed Sam, but without his hat, and a great rent up his coat.

"Come here, Sam," Lionel said, sternly. "Come here directly, and give an account of your extraordinary conduct."

"I ain't done nothink to be ashamed on, sir," Sam declared. "Wot right had that feller to set the whole 'ouse larfing? Am I responsible for my 'air and heyes?"

"This is wot I calls delicious," Z 9945 exclaimed, smacking his lips, and feeling in his pockets for his handcuffs. "I little thought as 'ow 'he would tumble so beautiful into my hands."

"Put those things away," Lionel said, carelessly. "Van, lend me a pencil. Thank you. Now, officers, you may do as you like about locking my servant up, but if you do I shall be compelled to report you for drinking whilst on duty."

"Well, I'm dashed!" Z 9945 gasped, glaring at his brother officer. "Jem, wot's to be done?"

"I think we had better sheer out o' this," Jem wisely counselled. "That ere stretcher job nearly got us the sack. This 'er fat un was in that job, and he'd give hevidence agin us with as much pleasure as he'd sit down to a batter puddin'."

"Well," said Z 9945, gazing at Sam with the air of a man who had accidentally swallowed a fish bone, "you've escaped us this time by a fluke, my young feller, but I warns you that I'm down on yer anywheres and at all times."

"Much obliged, I'm sure," Sam replied, smiling as he alone could smile; "it ain't everybody as takes sich an interest in me. Won't you take something more to drink?"

"I've been sold," Z 9945 moaned, as he handed his glass to the barmaid—"I've been sold by a parcel o' young swells and a feller with a squint, but sich is life—sugar, yes, miss, if you please, a little bit o' leming, and not too much water. Thankee that's jist the flavour as soots my constitution."

The constables were again asked to replenish their glasses, and once more they partook of that beverage which cheers and inebriates, leaving fond tokens of memory in the form of red eyes, headaches, and bad tempers.

"We may leave them now," Van said. "Let us slip away now; they are safe here now till closing time."

And leaving another shilling for the constables' benefit with the barmaid they left quietly, and bent their footsteps for home, laughing gaily over the events of the evening.

It was a beautiful night, the moon riding high and shining like a plate of burnished silver in the cloudless sky.

"How beautiful!" Van said, looking up. "No painter ever produced a scene like this, poor and meagre as the surroundings are."

"Give me the country for a night like this," Lionel said. "The calmly flowing river, the peaceful meadows flooded with the glorious light, the old-fashioned farm-houses standing like bright visions of the past. I could walk about all such a night as this, and being alone not feel lonely."

And Sam, ogling the moon, was muttering to himself—

"'Ere's a night for 'Ampstead 'Eath with Mary on my arm, and we a talkin' lovin' like—oh," and the long youth clasped his hands in transport at the bare thought, "it would be 'eavenly."

The beauty of the night did not seem to affect the general public.

Men and women hurried by, homeward bound from the theatres, sportive youths adorned with cutaway hats and most gorgeous neckties made the night hideous by popular (?) songs at the top of their voices; every public-house was crammed to excess, and all London was reeking with its joys, sorrows, triumphs, and iniquities.

Our friends' attention was called to a vast crowd at the corner of a street. Shrill cries of "Go it, Slogger!" "Let him have it, Docker!" "Shut up his peepers!" "Good again—hooray!"

"There's a fight on," Van said, quickening his pace. "Come on, lads, we must see it out."

"I say," Tommy pleaded, hanging back a little, "don't get me into another mess to-night, for what with being jammed up between those stalls I feel like a red-hot jelly."

"Like cures like," Lionel replied. "Don't funk, Tommy. You have nothing to fear. We will take care of you."

A street fight is no uncommon thing in London, especially in those localities where poverty, drink, and ignorance go hand-in-hand, and as Lionel and his companions came up they perceived two men of the lowest type pommelling each other in a style rather brutal—even if British. The crowd looked on with delighted eyes and watering mouths, and when one of the combatants caught his adversary an unlucky blow, or reeled with him crashing on the stones, a cry of ecstasy rent the air.

"What is the matter here?" demanded a little ostler of Tommy, who was standing on tiptoe, endeavouring in vain to get a view of the conflict.

"A fight," Master Codlings replied; "but how it is going on I haven't the slightest idea."

The little ostler ran about in all the agonies of disappointment, springing up like a "jack-in-the-box," falling on his hands and knees in the hope of seeing through the spectators' legs, but failing all ways the excited little man became extremely savage, and, approaching the peaceful Tommy, said—

"I must hev a go at somebody. You're about my size—come on."

Before Tommy could reply or decline this pressing invitation to come on, he was favoured with a stinging blow between the eyes which sent him reeling back on Sam's toes, and that youth leaping up with a yell of agony, brought his fist down on the crown of a fat man's hat.

In an instant all was confusion.

Tommy and the ostler fired away merrily; Sam and his fat victim locked in each other's arms, rolled about like wrestlers in an exhibition match; Lionel, Van, and Charlie, with the instinct of the sons of old Ireland, hit every head that came within arm's reach, and in less than two minutes one of the prettiest little faction fights ever seen was raging, and continued until hoarse cries announced the arrival of the police.

"I think we have had enough for one night," Van said, as he rescued Tommy, and dragged him along, with his heels grating on the stones. "Sam, leave that stout party alone. You have done sufficient to him. Cab! four-wheeler. Jump in, Li and Charlie—there's no time to lose. Now, Sam, jump on the box."

And so they reached Mr. Kramatome's—Lionel, Van, and Charlie, laughing; Tommy out of wind, and groaning; the irrepressible Sam performing marvels with his legs on the box, and singing the chorus of the "Rollicking Rams" in a voice to which the chorus of the feline night-prowlers was harmony.

CHAPTER XXI.

IN WHICH TOMMY MAKES HIS FIRST APPEARANCE AS A HUSBAND AND THE FATHER OF A FAMILY—READY-MADE.

"I told you so, Tommy," said Lionel, as the friends were discussing the probable consequences of their musical lark, and the merits and demerits of the fireman's performance. "I said you were sure to get into a mess, no matter how much we tried to keep you out of it."

"I'll tell you what it is," retorted Tommy. "I'll cut the company of you fellows for a time, and see what that'll do. I'll go in for study, and keep myself shut up indoors."

"It'll be of no use, old fellow, if you do. You'll most likely get into a bigger mess than ever."

"I'll bet you five pounds I don't."

"Within a month?"

"Within a week."

"Done," said Tommy.

"Done," replied Lionel.

THE GUARDSMAN GOES THROUGH HIS DRILL, AND THE DRILL GOES THROUGH TOMMY'S TROUSERS.

There was a strong spice of resolution in the nature of our old friend Tommy, when he considered himself fully justified in taking any particular course of action, and his last little adventure convinced him that it was quite time to turn over the proverbial " new leaf."

He was laid up for a short time, but after recovering he had a very new and very strong bolt put on his door, laid in a stock of books, half a ream of blue foolscap, a gross of quill pens, and a gallon of the best ink.

"Lionel's a fine chap," he mused. " Perhaps the best that ever lived, and the others are worthy of him; but, dash me if I am good enough for their company!` Only look at the other day. It's a mercy that the house wasn't burnt down and the lot of us roasted alive. Then yesterday and to-day, those beastly organ-grinders and hurdy-gurdy men came lurking about the place, grinning up at the windows, and one of 'em had the cheek to knock at the door and ask if it was likely he'd be wanted again this week. My eye! didn't old Kramatome roar out when he caught sight of him."

Considering what the victim had gone through on that memorable day it is little to be wondered at if he did "roar out." In our opinion he would have been justified in committing manslaughter.

"Li is really too bad," continued Tommy, as he oiled the catches of the new bolt to make it work noiselessly. "He hasn't a bit of respect or consideration for anybody. He's not a bit better than Irish Mike used——"

Here, at the mention of that once familiar but now mysterious name, Tommy involuntarily paused.

"There now," he resumed, after a while; " there's another queer affair. If I never knew Irish Mike, how did I come to know his name and all about him? That's what beats me. I can't have had such a long dream as all that—dash it!"

But as far as Tommy was concerned, "that way madness lies," and to avoid the subject he grasped his Euclid and plunged into the mysteries of the Pons Asinorum—a bridge which he had never yet succeeded in crossing, and in all probability never would.

But Lionel and his chums, whether unscrupulous as Tommy declared them to be or the reverse, thoroughly enjoyed the joke they had so successfully played upon their tutor; and, although the consequences threatened to become serious, the fun was none the less relished on that account.

"That," said Lionel, craning his neck out of the study window, " that's the twenty-fourth organ-grinder who's come into the square to-day to pay his compliments. How pleased old Kram must feel!"

" What at ?"

" Why, at the compliment paid him by the musicians, of course," replied Lionel. "Gratitude is such a rare quality."

" In you!" retorted Charlie. " Where's your gratitude for the care and trouble exhibited by your pastor and master?"

"Gone where last year's snow went," replied Lionel; "and that's a vague address. Hullo, here's the old boy himself!"

Almost before Lionel had ceased speaking Mr. Kramatome entered the room, red-hot with rage, and trembling with the same complaint.

"Good morning, sir," was our hero's polite greeting as he offered the tutor a chair. I don't think we are quite perfect in our Political Economy yet."

"Political Economy!" gasped Mr. Kramatome. "You're quite ready with your private cheek, it seems. How dare you, eh ?"

"Really, sir," replied Lionel, "I must say that I do not quite understand you."

"What!" exclaimed the wrathful tutor, as he strode to the window, and waved the bulk of his body through it. "Look here, sir. Do you see those impudent blackguards?"

There were three or four of the burliest and most unsavoury organ-grinders bowing and kissing their dirty fingers to their patrons.

As Mr. Kramatome flung up the window one of the organ-grinders heard the sound, and, turning, kissed his hand, and bowed with a smile intended to be fascinating, but which was, on the contrary, productive of the keenest kind of aggravation.

We regret to record that Mr. Kramatome, far from being charmed by this act of courtesy, thrust his head out of the window as far as he could, and gave utterance to a most profane and blood-curdling oath.

Fortunately, the Italian's knowledge of English sacred or profane, was very slight. He took the oath for a compliment, kissed his hand again, unslung his organ, and began to grind the "Conspirators' Chorus " from the "Fille de Madame Angot."

"GO AWAY !" roared Mr. Kramatome, in tones which the largest capitals in our printing-office would fail to represent.

"He'll burst a blood-vessel if he does that again," said Lionel.

"He'll burst the organ-grinder if he comes near enough," was Vansittart's comment. "Who has any coppers ?"

"I have," said Charlie. " What for ?"

"To shy at the grinder, of course."

"You daren't do that while Kram's in such a rage. Look at him now, shaking his fist at the poor beggar."

"And look at the grinder. He takes it all for a compliment, and nods and grins back, while he grinds away harder than ever."

"There'll be a case of manslaughter in to-morrow's paper," laughed Charlie. "It's lucky that the American fashion of carrying revolvers isn't popular here, or that organ-grinder would go home in a coffin."

"I think he stands a very fair chance of going that way now," said Lionel. "Old Kram will take the poker to him presently, and that's a good deal more deadly than any revolver when it comes to close quarters."

"Not when you've got to tackle a nigger, though," said Vansittart. "I've seen a heavy poker bent double over a buck nigger's head in Cuba, and the beggar only laughed, and said it tickled him."

But here the conversation was prematurely stopped, for the tutor, finding that neither mild nor full-flavoured language had any effect upon the grinder, drew his head in, and requested one of the boys to ring the bell.

"Fetch a policeman," he said, when Joblot appeared, with his hand tied up and a crutch under his right arm. "Go out the back way, so that that blackguard can't see you."

"He's going away, sir," said Charlie. "Hadn't we better give him a few pence to stop and continue playing until the policeman can be fetched ?"

"Thank you for the suggestion," said the tutor. "It will be torture to endure another five minutes of that rascal's villainous noise, but I will suffer anything rather than he should escape."

Charlie knew well enough what he was doing when he made this suggestion. The custom of the genus " grinder " is to fly to other climes the instant he has received anything in the shape of current coin, and so it was the instant that Charlie chucked out his twopence.

"That was a good move of yours," whispered Lionel. "It wouldn't have done to have had the beggar in here. He might have spotted us."

"And then 'Exeunt omnes,'" laughed Vansittart. "Kramatome's fond of money, but he would certainly turn us out neck and crop if he thought that we had anything to do with the organ-grinder joke. It has turned his hair grey."

"Nonsense. It's been grey for years. He's only forgotten the dye this last day or two."

" Do you think he dyes his hair ?"

" I'm certain of it," replied Lionel. " I used to think he wore a wig until lately, but wigs don't change colour in that way."

" He changes colour enough for forty wigs," said Charlie; " but I say, Li, if he dyes his hair, and we can only get hold of the bottle, we might astound him a little."

" How do you mean ?" said Vansittart.

" Turn his hair blue or pink, or——"

" Oh, no ! None of that for me," said Vansittart. " I was in a hair-dyeing lark once when I was quite a youngster at school in Paris. I nearly died myself."

" How was that ?"

" Well, you see, there was the son of a French count, who was cultivating a little down in hopes of rivalling the Emperor's moustache, and what with ' Dubois' hair-producer ' and other preparations, warranted to torture and scarify the skin if they could do nothing else, had succeeded tolerably well.

" Like Mrs. Glass, having caught his hair he proceeded to dress it according to his idea of the correct thing, and as we chaffed him awfully about the colour, which was of a much more vivid red than Sam Scarecrow's, he conceived the brilliant idea of dyeing his hair."

" Did he apply to Alexander Ross, or resort to the more homely aid of lamp-black ?" said Charlie.

" No, he asked me to recommend him something."

" I see."

" I got him some nitrate of silver, and, as you know, a little will go a very long way. I told him to lay it on thick, and that afternoon his mamma, the Countess of Mountrochelle called on her darling Alphonse, to drive him on a round of fashionable visits.

" Well, Alphonse got himself up regardless of expense, and at the last moment put some finishing touches on his splendidly pointed moustache and incipient imperial.

" It was a lovely summer's day, and Alphonse looked the picture of self-content as the open carriage drove off.

" Their first visit was paid, I heard afterwards, to his darling grandmamma's, and though he fancied that he detected one of the servants grinning at him, he re-entered the carriage for a drive down the Bois de Boulogne.

" His nitrate-of-silvered moustache had now been exposed to a powerful sun for more than an hour, and had first turned a delicate green, and then a very deep—no mistake about it—Oxford blue.

" The Countess de Mountrochelle had an extensive bowing acquaintance, and it required all the well-known politeness of the French nation to keep their features under command as they passed the countess's carriage.

" ' My dear,' said the Duchess de Noware to her eldest daughter, ' that odious countess has got a blue baboon with her.'

" Some thought the countess had a fresh arrival with her, and wondered ' *Who* is it?' Others, again, who failed to see anything human in the gorgeously-appareled blue-moustached Alphonse, wondered ' *What* is it ?'

" Young demoiselles smiled and turned their heads, professors of natural history craned their necks to obtain a better view of the monstrosity, and old dowagers said sweet things under their breath.

" Meanwhile the hirsute ornament shone in the sun like a painted fly on the surface of a lake, and Alphonse, sublimely indifferent to all around him, reclined gracefully by the side of his darling mamma.

" Unfortunately the duchess was overheard. The countess turned her head, shrieked, and fell back petrified with amazement and indignation into the innermost recesses of her carriage.

" ' Alphonse!' she shrieked, ' is it thus you insult your mother, and expose her to the scorn of her friends ? Drive me home immediately!' she cried to the coachman.

" In vain Alphonse implored his mamma to listen to his account of the trick the perfidious English boy, your humble servant, had played on him.

" She would listen to nothing, but sent him back to Monsieur Darque's, minus the little draft on the Bank of France which his darling mamma always left as a souvenir of her visits.

" And he *did* come back, too, I tell you. All the suppressed wrath that had been smouldering in the bosom of his père, the Count de Mountrochelle, since the time he saw his splendid regiment of chasseurs, which he had headed on the morning of that fatal 18th of June, mowed down on the field of Hougoumont, burst out.

" Nothing but an assault-at-arms could check the fury of his wrath—nothing but my blood would soothe his wounded honour; and within a few hours I was visited by a certain Jean Montford, a toady of the count, with an intimation that rapiers for two and coffee for one would be served up in the morning, with a slight addendum that pistols would be substituted for swords if I preferred them.

" Now this was a serious thing, as at that time I knew very little indeed about the use of the foils, and had not had much practice in the pistol galleries; while I knew very well that my would-be assailant—besides the natural advantage of being some three years older, and about six inches taller than I—had received lessons in fencing from the celebrated Captain Tiercey, and was a reputed dead-shot at the ace.

" I said to myself, ' I must go and see this blood-thirsty Alphonse de Mountrochelle, and argue with him.'

" I carried this idea out at once. He seemed surprised to see me, and I thought for the moment that he was going to submit our quarrel to the arbitration of ' de box.'

" But there was no such luck. Alphonse might have been very brave with three feet of steel separating him from his adversary, but as he stood empty-handed, his little blue moustache almost bristling (only it wasn't strong enough) with rage, he did not quite take my eye as cut in the lines of Tom Cribb or Tom Sayers.

" There was a snake-like glitter in his eye which boded mischief though.

" I thought, perhaps, that a little bullying might be used with advantage, and when he said—

" ' You have accepted the challenge I sent by Montford?' I answered—

" ' I have.'

" ' Which weapons—rapier or duelling pistol?'

" ' I leave that to you.'

" ' You are confident,' Alphonse sneered.

" ' I am certain," I replied.

" ' Will you name the place ?'

" ' No, I leave that to you. I have one stipulation to make—that I name the time. To-morrow morning is not convenient.'

" ' Well, be it so,' said Alphonse.

" ' I name this day fortnight.'

" Had I fired a pistol in his face I do not think it would have startled him so much as this announcement of the date that would suit my convenience.

" ' This day fortnight!' he exclaimed. ' Such a thing was never heard of before. What are your reasons for such an arrangement?'

" ' I will tell you, monsieur. As you are probably aware, I am an Englishman, and we English have a habit of looking upon a duellist as a being considerably beneath the common hangman, for our Jack Ketch only obeys the law when he hangs a murderer.

" ' You would take my life to satisfy your own pride. You are a master of fence, and a dead shot. I am bound to confess that I have taken my lessons in the art of self-defence from Nat Langham, and only know how to hold a foil decently. I *have* shot a pheasant, and I once missed a hare (here he winced), but I fear my nerves are not sufficiently steeled to point a deadly tube at a fellow-being.

"'For all that I accept your challenge, though you must acknowledge that it is an unequal match. Don't you think, though, that you are going to have all the revenge to yourself. I shall take a fortnight for mine.'

"'What do you mean?' exclaimed Alphonse, first reddening, and then turning pale.

"'This is what I mean. I have consented to fight you in your own fashion, but before we meet in a manner which will probably put an abrupt stop to a life which, in spite of some slight drawbacks, I have found a very pleasant one, you must first fight me my way.'

"'Upon my honour I fail to comprehend you.'

"'Do you? Let me explain. I mean to thrash you as soundly as Bendigo thrashed Jem Hurst.' [Here I put myself in the most approved position.] 'And I mean to repeat the dose every morning for the fortnight, and at the end of that time, if you have nerve enough left to wink at a cat, you can murder me wherever you please.'

"By George! I frightened the young fire-eater. He was profuse in his apologies. I was his benefactor—his friend for ever. I had rather improved his appearance than otherwise by changing the colour of his moustache, and a lot of the same gag."

"If we serve old Kramatome in the same way there's no fear of his calling us out," said Charlie.

"No, but he's very likely to turn us out," said Lionel. 'I've got another little game on foot, though. One thing at a time is a good motto, especially in practical joking."

"That's so, Li. But what's your 'little game'?"

"I'll tell you when it's ready to come off, Charlie."

"*That* won't do. No secrets among us, Li."

"Well, then, prepare yourself for an alarming disclosure."

"I am ready," replied Charlie, in deep and tragic tones. "Say on."

"You know Tommy?"

"Which Tommy?"

"Why, our Tommy—Tommy Codlings, of course. There is but one Tommy, and Lionel is his prophet."

"Of course I know him."

"Well, do you know that he's married?"

"Married!"

"Married is the word, and married a good deal if the size of his wife is to be taken into consideration."

"You're joking with me now, Li."

"I'm not though," replied Lionel, with an expression of the most perfect gravity. "She told me so herself."

"*She*—what, Tommy's wife?"

"Yes, and as I looked up into her ingenuous countenance I couldn't doubt the truth of what she said."

"Looked *up*, Li!"

"Yes, she's six feet four if she's an inch," replied our hero.

"My stars—what a whopper! What will she be like when she grows up?"

"Grows up! She is past growing, or at least she ought to be. She's fifty if she's a day."

"What! And married to Tommy?"

"So she told me, and the children confirmed it."

"The what?"

"The children."

"Why, do you mean to say that Tommy has any children?"

"I didn't say that they were Tommy's exactly—only by right of purchase, as it were. The lady was a widow when Tommy conferred the honour of his name upon her."

Lionel spoke with such perfect gravity and com-

mand of feature that Charlie and the others were staggered for the moment, but the preposterous nature of the statement soon sent them off into a burst of incredulous laughter.

"You seem to doubt my word," continued Lionel, pulling out his watch. "It is now three. In a few minutes you will have incontrovertible evidence of the fact."

And Lionel, without the ghost of a smile upon his face, left the room.

"Do you know anything about this, Van?" said Charlie.

"Only what Li has just told us."

"But it can't be true, you know."

"It don't seem likely, but we had better wait and see. Hullo, there's a knock at the front door."

"Tommy's wife, for a pound," said Charlie, as he ran to the window. "And the family—two, four, six, eight of 'em. By George, Van, it's true!"

"It certainly does begin to look suspicious," laughed Vansittart. "But wait and see. Tommy is a little soft, I own, but he never could have been such an ass as to marry an elderly widow with eight of 'em."

Just then Lionel marched in, grave and composed, as if he were just going to be hanged—or to hang somebody. The sensations, to our fancy, are equally unpleasant.

Behind him was a tall, gaunt female, with a severity of expression which would have made an Old Bailey barrister or a bronze statue tremble; and behind her, in single file, walked the eight, ranging apparently from thirteen to three years.

"Mrs. Thomas Codlings, gentlemen," said Lionel, "and family."

"Delighted to make the acquaintance of Mrs. Codlings," replied Vansittart, with exquisite politeness of manner. "Come on a visit to your brother, I presume?"

"I've come," replied the gaunt female, with much emphasis, "to see my 'usband."

"Indeed," replied Vansittart, who began now to be deceived by the combined earnestness and gravity of Lionel and the supposed Mrs. C. "Rather young for that sort of thing."

"He's not too young for me," was the reply, delivered with an energy which struck terror to the hearts of her hearers.

"I was alluding to you, madam," replied Vansittart, remembering that a soft answer turneth away wrath. "I was astonished that you, in the prime of your youth and beauty, should have thrown yourself away."

"Don't *you* fret yerself," was the gaunt female's reply. "I knows wot I'm about, and now if someone 'll have the goodness to fetch my 'usband I'll be obliged to 'em. If not, I'll fetch him myself."

"Take a seat, Mrs. Codlings," said Lionel, with grave courtesy. "You shall not be kept waiting long."

But Mrs. Codlings refused. Indeed, she looked so gaunt and stiff that it seemed doubtful if there was any joint in her body which would enable her to assume a sitting posture.

Vansittart hurried out after Lionel, and taking him by the arm said in a whisper—

"I say, Li, what is this? It must be a joke, but you carry it off so well that I'm half deceived myself."

Lionel looked up, with the same grave unconcerned face he had hitherto worn, but the sight of Vansittart's anxious face was too much for him, and he burst into a hearty laugh.

"Of course it's a sell, Van; but I didn't mean to tell you of it till the last moment."

"But who is the woman?"

"The laundress who used to wash for me when I had diggings in St. James's. She's mad for another husband, and I've persuaded her that if she only frightens Tommy enough he'll marry her."

"Over again?"

"Yes. But of course we won't let it go as far as that."

"Don't be too sure, Li. If you set a woman's mouth watering for a husband it's a hundred to one but she gets him."

"Hush! Here we are at Tommy's door. Keep a solemn mug on, Van."

"Solemn as a cemetery."

Lionel tried the handle of the door, but it did not yield.

"Something new. Tommy's locked himself in. Hullo, Tommy!"

And Lionel began a vigorous tattoo upon the panels of the door.

"Go away," replied Tommy, from the interior of the sanctum. "I'm studying, and won't be disturbed by anybody."

"You be hanged! Come out, Tommy. You're wanted very particularly."

"I dare say I am. No, Li. I made up my mind to avoid larking and go in for study, and mean to keep my word."

"This is no lark, Tommy, I tell you," said Lionel, beginning to feel a little alarmed lest the plump youth's obstinacy should spoil the joke. "It's business——"

"Who wants me? Kramatome?"

"No. A lady."

"What lady?"

"She says she'll tell you when she sees you."

"Oh, ah! I daresay. That won't do now, Li. You can't take me in in that way."

"It's true. If you won't believe me, ask Van. He's here, and he'll tell you."

"Likely that. You're both in it, and I'm not to be done, Li."

"Very well, Tommy. Only recollect that if you don't come down to the lady she'll come up and fetch you. She said so."

"She be blowed!" was Tommy's ungallant reply. "Who is she?"

"Your wife."

"Eh!"

"Your wife."

There was a crash in the room as if a stool or a table had been suddenly upset, and then the bolt was swiftly drawn, and Tommy came out, looking pale and anxious.

"*What* did you say, Li? Who's waiting for me?"

"Your wife, Tommy. What a sly beggar you were to keep that from us!"

"I congratulate you on your taste, Tommy," said Vansittart. "She's a fine woman."

But Tommy, overcome by the startling nature of the information, had lost his balance, and sat down suddenly on the floor, his mouth wide open, and his eyes standing out like hat-pegs.

"Come along, Tommy," said Lionel, as he dragged his plump chum to his feet. You must be most anxious to see her again, to say nothing of the children."

"What!" gasped Tommy, and once again he became limp and helpless, and had to be supported by the strong arms of Lionel.

"One of the finest families I ever saw," said Vansittart. "The girls run to bone a trifle, perhaps, but they'll fill out in time."

"It isn't many young men at your age, Tommy, who can boast of possessing such a fine-looking family."

The remarks which Tommy made at this moment regarding families in general and his own in particular could not here be printed with due regard to that propriety which has hitherto distinguished this journal. Let it suffice to say that they were very strong indeed.

"Steady, Tommy, steady," said Lionel. "You surely wouldn't wish to meet your long-lost wife in such a state as this."

Here again we regret that Tommy's profanity

renders it impossible to print his remarks. We pass on to the time when the door was reached, and Lionel, flinging it open, introduced Tommy the bewildered to the presence of his loving if not lovely spouse.

CHAPTER XXII.

TOMMY'S INTERVIEW WITH HIS WIFE AND FAMILY.

TOMMY stood in the doorway, white as death, gazing at the gaunt female and her youthful family, when Lionel touched him lightly on the arm, and said—

"Why don't you speak to her? You see she is bursting to fold you in her arms."

"That be blowed!" Tommy Codlings gasped. "What does the woman want?"

"Hush!" Lionel said, in a whisper. "You forget yourself. Remember the oath you took at the altar."

"I'll take any number in any court of law that I don't know her, and have never seen her before," Tommy cried, damp with perspiration. Confound it! you fellows will drive me mad."

The lady, fixing her eyes on Tommy's plump form, smacked her lips, and made a step forward, with every one of the eight children clinging to her gown.

"Stand off," Tommy yelled. "Go away, you hideous old woman!"

"I am positively ashamed of you," Lionel said. "Van, did you ever see such an example of base ingratitude?"

"Never," Lord Vansittart replied; "but don't you think we had better leave them to make matters right? For my part I don't care about interfering between man and wife."

"I agree with you," Lionel said, gravely. "Mrs. Codlings?"

"Yes, sur."

"I suppose you would like to have a conversation with your husband alone."

"That is what I came for," said the lady. "I'll soon bring him to his senses."

"I won't be left with the hag," Tommy yelled, backing towards the door. "Lionel, this is some awful conspiracy, and if you don't protect me I'll hang myself, or do something."

"What can I do?" Lionel said, in well-assumed perplexity. "Why don't you confess that you have been humbugging us all along, and then I should know how to advise you? And, look here, Tommy," dropping his voice, "you can allow her so much per year for herself and your children."

"My children!" Tommy howled. "Why, I'll swear I never so much as——"

"Dear, dear, this is very dreadful," Lionel said. "Come along, Van—we can do nothing here."

As he spoke he thrust Tommy into the arms of his better half, who caught him and held him tight.

Lionel and Van slipped out of the door, and poor Tommy, more dead than alive, howled with terror as he heard the door locked from the outside.

"Let me go," he yelled, struggling and kicking furiously. "You're drunk, and smell of gin, you nasty old beast."

The lady took this compliment so much to heart that she boxed Tommy's ears soundly, and then, lifting him up with surprising ease, flopped him on the floor, where he sat like a refractory child, gasping, panting, and tearing his hair in sheer despair.

"Get up when I tell you to," said the gaunt female, threateningly. "Isn't it enough that you should desert me and the children, you unmanly scamp? I'm your wife, and I'll have my rights."

"This is another dream," Tommy murmured, faintly; "but I never felt one so real before. Dash it, how my ears tingle!"

"I'll make 'em tingle," said his lovely wife, "I'll

pull 'em off if you ain't very civil, and come home with me at once."

Tommy stared vaguely at the children, and began to hum—

"Father, dear father, come home with me now," when his spouse put a sudden stop to the performance by thumping him in the small of the back.

"Dash, it!—leave off!" Tommy roared. "You'll smash my backbone."

"Then why don't you listen to me, you vagabond?" cried the lady, bursting into tears. "How can you pretend not to know your lawful wife?"

The eight children began to howl most dismally, and the eldest boy, fully twelve years of age, ran forward, and evinced an inclination to devour Tommy on the spot, by setting a double row of extremely sharp teeth into the calf of his leg.

"Hang it!" Tommy roared, leaping to his feet, and facing his spouse; "this is too much. Take this little vampire off."

"Thomas," cried the youth's mamma, "come here directly. You must not hurt your papa."

"She says that I am his papa," Tommy said, faintly, as he fell back into his original position. "This is no dream. The woman's mad—the kids are all mad, and I'm a raving lunatic."

"You're not so mad that you don't how to ill-treat a poor lone woman," the female cried, piteously. "Ah, Tommy, deary, give me a kiss, and we'll make it all up."

"I won't," Tommy cried, desperately. "I'm not your husband. Where did I marry you?"

"At Scotland."

"That proves you are wrong. Tommy said, brightening up, "for I was never there in my life."

"If you contradict me," cried the loving woman, fiercely, "I'll precious soon make you remember it. Right or wrong I mean to take you home with me, so you may make up your mind to it."

"Oh, Lor', this is awful!" Tommy groaned. "I never heard of such a thing, but I won't be led like a lamb to the slaughter. I'll call for the police."

"A lot of good that would do," Mrs Codlings observed, with a fiendish chuckle. "You'll be taken afore a magistrate and sent to prison, as you deserve to be. Don't think that I was such a fool as to destroy my marriage certificate."

"Your what?" Tommy shrieked.

"My marriage certificate," she returned, flourishing an ominous-looking slip of blue paper; "you see I have the law on my side."

"Let me look at it," said Tommy, holding out his hand.

"Not if I know it," said the partner of his bosom. "You shall see it when we get home, but not before. So come along, and don't let me have any more trouble with you."

"And this is an end to all my hopes," gasped Tommy. "I looked forward with pleasure to leading a quiet sort of country life. I began to think that Irish Mike was only a part of a dream, but, dash it, what is the meaning of this?"

"The meaning is," said his loving wife, "that if you don't come home with me, your lawful wife, and these your lawful children, I'll pound you into a jelly, and carry you under my arm."

"I suppose you will let me say good-bye to Li and Van?" Tommy pleaded, "they are the best friends I have in the world, and, oh! it's hard to part with them."

"I don't object to that," Mrs. Codlings replied, graciously. "Tell them that they may come in; but no tricks, no trying to run away, for I shall be behind you."

The last hope died out of Tommy's heart.

He had intended to bolt as soon as the door was opened, but the gaunt figure of his wife hovered over him like a thunder-cloud, and, with his knees knocking violently against each other, he applied his mouth to the keyhole, and breathed the names of his old schoolfellows.

Lionel and Lord Vansittart entered the room, looking very grave.

"Well, Tommy," Lionel said, "have you and your wife come to a proper understanding?"

"I don't know about that," the fat youth replied dismally, "but she persists in saying that I am her husband. I shall call both of you to prove to the contrary."

"What will be the use of that?" said Lord Vansittart. "How should we know anything about it, and by-the-bye I must now tell you that I once heard you talking in your sleep about your wife."

"That settles it," Tommy exclaimed, "I married her in a dream, and she's turned up in reality. Come on, I don't care—I'm ready for anything. Ha, ha, ha! Good-bye, you fellows! Come along, missus."

Tommy was raving in earnest now, and Lionel, really alarmed, caught him in his arms as he fell in a half-fainting condition.

"Van," Lionel said, "take him upstairs, and put him to bed. Leave me to settle with the woman."

Lord Vansittart relieved Lionel of his burden, and ran lightly up the stairs with it dangling from his shoulders, and in less time than it takes to write it the door had closed upon the eight children, the amorous lady, and two sovereigns, at which she looked again and again in rapturous silence.

CHAPTER XXIII.

TOMMY IS VERY NEARLY INTRODUCED TO HER MAJESTY, BUT IS STOPPED BY AN OLD FRIEND—HE IS ASKED TO AWAKE, AND WAKES TO FIND THAT HE IS WALLOWING IN A SEA OF DREAMS.

"WE have carried this a little too far," Lionel said, as he stood looking at Tommy, now fast asleep. "I thought at one time he would have seen through the joke."

"There is nothing to fear," Lord Vansittart said. "He will wake as refreshed and jolly as ever. It will only be another dream, and Tommy is getting quite used to them by this time. Hush! he is moving."

Tommy sneezed, and, opening his eyes, stared wonderingly about him.

"Hullo!" he cried, "what is the matter?"

"That is just what we have been asking each other," Lionel said. "We found you on your back in the study."

"Found me where?" Tommy cried, sitting bolt upright.

"We found you on your back in the study," Lionel repeated, "and thinking that you were not well we put you to bed."

"I must have got in there out of her way," Tommy ruminated, screwing up his mouth and scratching his head. "I say, is she still waiting for me?"

"She!" Lionel said, looking at Van, "who are you talking about, Tommy?"

"Just as if you didn't know," the fat youth gasped. "Why, my wife to be sure."

"My eye!" Lionel cried, bursting into a roar of laughter. "Van, do you hear that? Tommy has had another dream."

"I tell you what it is," Tommy cried, struggling to get out of bed, "you fellows are making a fool of me, and I won't put up with it. What do you think I am made of?"

"Precious little muscle and plenty of fat," Lionel said. "But seriously, Tommy, what have you got into your head now?"

"Where's my wife?" Codlings gasped. "She said she had the marriage certificate, so I must be her husband. Where is she? Where are my eight children? They're mine by law, and I'll have 'em."

"Van," Lionel said, "run downstairs for Mr. Kramatome. I fear Tommy is in a raging fever. A doctor must be sent for at once."

Lord Vansittart had reached the doorway when Tommy called him back.

"I don't want old Kramatome, and I don't want a doctor," he cried. Here, sit down by my side, and tell me where that confounded woman is."

"I have told you before that you are labouring under a delusion." Lionel said. "Now, do try and go to sleep, and forget all about it. You have been studying a trifle too much."

"I believe," Tommy said, with an emphasis on every word, "that I am the most wonderful dreamer in the whole world."

"You are that." said Lionel; "yet everybody dreams, but perhaps not quite so vividly."

"Vividly!" Tommy echoed; "that is a very poor word for it. I not only see but feel, and the feeling sometimes lasts for hours after I wake. Do you know, Li, I begin to have a little faith in the old stories about witchcraft?"

"There you go," said Lionel. "I never heard a fellow talk such bosh."

"Didn't you?"

"No."

"Then you'll hear it till I die," Tommy said, firmly; "but you never will convince me that these visions are the result of indigestion or heavy suppers."

"Well, we have had enough of this nonsense," Lionel said. "By the way, I have had a letter from Lord Taddlepool. You remember him, Tommy."

"Lord Taddlepool," Tommy mused, "I can't say that I do."

"Why," Vansittart chimed in, "don't you recollect how, the night before the morning we found you at the hotel in Jermyn-street, you had been out with his lordship, and had no end of larks in the Haymarket?"

"I remember waking up in the hotel," Tommy replied, in a dazed manner, "but how on earth I got there I never knew. I dreamt that you fellows washed me, and gave me lots of champagne; but go on—of course you are right. What about this Lord Taddlepool?"

"He has written to me for your address," Lionel said.

"What on earth for?" Tommy gasped. "I suppose I must have met him by accident, for I have not the slightest idea of what he is like."

"But he knows you," Lionel said, calmly, "and he has taken quite a fancy to you."

"He must be a good fellow to take so much trouble about me." Tommy said. "Have you let him know where I am?"

"Of course," said Lionel; "and told him that you would ride down in your carriage, and meet him at the Palace at a quarter to three."

"My carriage—meet him at a quarter to three!" Tommy cried, starting up. "Oh, yes, I know, but you don't make a fool of me."

"Lionel made no verbal reply, but took from his pocket a double-milled superior extra creamed envelope, containing a missive, the contents of which made Tommy start like a Jack-in-the-box.

"You do not doubt me now, I suppose," Lionel queried. "Of course you can reply, declining the honour."

But Tommy was silent, and did nothing but stare at the letter quivering like a leaf in his trembling hands.

"It will be the greatest event of the season," Lord Vansittart said. "Only fancy Tommy Codlings presented at Court. Old Kramatome will go mad with rage and envy."

"But, hang it all!" Tommy gasped, as he dropped the missive on the counterpane, "why should Lord Taddlepool be so sweet on me?"

"As if you didn't know already," said Lionel; "his lordship would have been locked up but for you."

"How is that?"

"Why, the row at Barney's ended with the interference of the police," said Lionel, "and you hammered away with an empty champagne bottle to that extent that the bobbies ran before you like chaff before the wind. Lord Taddlepool called you a plucky fellow, and said that, if locked up, he would be ruined, and he promised to do you a good turn."

"Wonders will never cease," said the credulous Tommy Codlings. "I don't remember anything about it. But, I say, Li, how could you say that I would meet him in my carriage, when you know I haven't got one."

"That can be easily arranged, Lord Vansittart said.

"And is already," Lionel returned. "I have ordered a slap-up turn out, and if Tommy will only walk with me as far as Joses and Sons he can be supplied with a Court costume such as will make all the other swells blink with envy."

"But, I say," Tommy exclaimed, "I shall make a pretty mess of it."

"Not you," said Lord Vansittart. "The whole thing is in a nut-shell. You squeeze up to the door of the reception chamber, and, if possible, tip one of the flunkies to get you in first. Your name is announced; you enter; her Majesty places her hand on the back of yours, and you touch her dainty fingers with your lips, and bow yourself out."

"It certainly would be a great honour," Tommy said, with a fat smile.

"At any rate, you must meet Lord Taddlepool," Lionel observed, "or I would not be answerable for the consequences. He is an awful swell, and if you kept away he would vent his anger on me."

"I would'nt have him do that for the world," Tommy said, considerately. "I'll go; and, I say, it will be worth all the trouble and bother if only to talk about it afterwards."

"Of course," said Lionel. "Now then, jump up."

Tommy rose and donned his clothes with such extreme haste that he mistook his coat for his inexpressibles, and tried to thrust his fat legs into the sleeves, and, failing in this, did his level best to get his head through the baggy part of his inexpressibles.

Lionel and Lord Vansittart came to the rescue, and Tommy having been made presentable to the public gaze, set out in high glee, little thinking what was in store for him.

Messrs. Joses and Sons were equal to the occasion.

The head partner—a man with a decidedly Jewish cut of countenance—smirked as he informed his customers that "thousands of gentlemids cabe to hib for the very sabe thing," and Tommy was presently staring at himself in a mirror, his rotund form arrayed in all the magnificence of coat, vest, hat, frill, silk stockings, and low silver-buckled shoes.

"There, now, Tommy," said Li, "what do you think of yourself now?"

"Upon my soul, I feel quite at home," Tommy replied. "I believe that I was cut out for something."

"Of course you were," Lionel said, turning his head away, "but don't strut up and down before the glass quite so much. I don't mind, but there's a fellow behind the counter grinning, and I think he's grinning at you."

Tommy pulled up with startling suddenness, and, re-entering the dressing-room, resumed his every-day clothes, and went home with Lionel, but not before he had left word with Messrs. Joses to send the Court suit early on the following morning, and to be very careful not to crease them.

"Of course, after you are presented," Lionel said, as they wended their way along the busy streets, "you will be able to do me a good turn, and present me."

"It will give me the greatest pleasure," Tommy said, with a touch of conscious pride in his voice, "and, you know, I might be able to give you some good appointment where there is little to do and plenty to get. There are lots of such situations under Government."

"That would be awfully jolly. I shouldn't mind being Viceroy of India, or something after that style."

"I'm afraid that would be a little too strong at first," Tommy said, dubiously, "but it would all come in time."

And Tommy, good-natured, credulous, easily gulled lad that he was, fully believed it. He built tremendous castles in the air; but, alas, how soon they were to crumble at his feet and leave not even gilded dust behind!

"There's Sam," Tommy said. "Of course he would have to remain with you, but that is no reason why he should not be appointed something or other."

"Clothes-brusher to the prince," Lionel observed with a passive face; "I believe there is about fifteen hundred a year hanging to that noble appointment."

"Lor!" said Tommy, "I should not have thought it."

"Bless you, that's nothing," Lionel went on, as grave as a judge; "there are lots of people in the world who get well paid for keeping their mouths shut and their eyes closed."

"That's an easy way of getting a living," said the innocent Tommy. "Here comes Sam, I wonder what he is laughing at."

"It is only one of his smiles," Lionel said.

"Then I wish he wouldn't smile when he meets me," Tommy replied. "He contorts his features hideously, and makes me nervous."

"I'll speak to him about it," Lionel returned. "Well, Sam, what news?"

"The carriage and greys will be ready by three," Sam Scarecrow said, "and wot's more I seed the 'orses and the flunkies, the last bein' catiwatin', I do assure you. P'raps Mister Codlings would like to walk round and look at 'em."

"What for?" demanded Tommy.

"Well, sir, you see some people is partic'lar as to calves," said Sam, "and I thought as 'ow you would like to have heverythink tip-top."

"I have left it all to your master," Tommy said, not a little loftily.

"And you couldn't do better, sir," Sam said, squinting horribly at Lionel in the excess of his admiration. "There is calves and calves. I knowed a fine young chap as died with a broken 'art through a wearin' of silk stockings."

The thought struck Tommy that his legs would be similarly arrayed on the morrow, and he inquired how it happened.

"His name was Jinks," Sam said, with emotion, "and a finer speciment of a footman as ever walked behind a lady to church never lived. Well, sir, Jinks was well-nigh perfect, but he had one defect, and that was his legs, which were that thin as to bring him inter ridicool. So he took to paddin', and all went well, and it was rumoured that a hairess had winked at him from a carriage, when one day Jinks was hangin' on behind his missus's broom—"

"Brougham," corrected Lionel.

"I said broom, sir," Sam said, nothing abashed. "A boy with malice in his 'art ran up behind and stuck a penknife inter Jinks's legs. He didn't feel, poor young feller, but presently seein' the people larfin' he looked down and seed the sawdust pourin' out of his legs like winken'. The man as made the pads had swindled him inter the belief that they was made o' wool. Jinks fell orf the carriage in a faintin' fit, and they took him to the 'orsepital, but he never surwived the shock, and died as I said afore of a broken 'art, stimulated by the bustin' of his calves."

"Is that true?" Tommy said, looking at the youth.

"True, sir?" echoed Sam, "in course it is. I knowed another chap as ——"

"One of your stories is quite sufficient at a time, Sam," Lionel said. "Have the goodness to reserve your anecdotes for another and more suitable time."

"Yes, sir."

"And when you meet one or any of my friends in the street," Lionel went on, trying to look severe, "do your best to control your features."

"I will, sir," Sam replied, fervently. "It's the right heye as does all the mischief."

This brought them to Mr. Kramatome's, where Charlie and Van were waiting anxiously for their return.

"Have you succeeded in getting a suit?" Lord Vansittart demanded.

"How does Tommy look?" Charlie asked.

"One at a time," said Lionel, dropping into an easy chair. "Now, you fellows, let this suffice. All is arranged, and Tommy looks every inch of a gentleman in his Court dress. Hullo, there's a knock. I expect it is Joses and Son's man."

Tommy, anxious to see, rushed out of the room, and as soon as he was out of ear-shot Lionel said, "Now not another word about to-morrow, or we may go too far and spoil the joke."

"But you do not intend that he should really go to the palace?"

"Of course not."

"How will you prevent it?"

"I have arranged that, too," Lionel said. "He will be stopped, but how and by whom I don't mean to tell you until to-morrow; but one thing I will tell you, all Tommy's dreams will be eclipsed by the one in store for him."

"I beg to think he has dreamt sufficiently to last him a lifetime," Van said, laughing; "we must put a stopper on it soon. It's awful fun, but Tommy will smell a rat and bowl us out, if we are not careful."

"Of course it cannot last for ever," Lionel said, "but we can keep it up by varying the amusement. Hush! here comes Tommy as pleased as Punch."

Tommy bounced into the room hugging a huge parcel, from which he refused to part on any terms.

"No," he cried. "I know you fellows, and you will be playing some lark with my things!" and before they could stop him he had rushed off to his bedroom, where he locked up the treasured garments in a chest and kept watch over it until supper time.

The next day came, and Tommy, who was up long before the lark, jumped out of bed, and thrusting his head out of the window, looked up at the clear and cloudless sky, and then up and down the desolate, silent street.

Tommy closed the window softly, took a peep at the magnificent attire in which he was to appear, and then got in between the sheets again.

But he could not sleep.

Visions of fair ladies struggling for the honour of being his wife rose up before him and checked his very breath; honours were showered upon him like leaves at autumn time, and Tommy found himself speculating on how he should spend the fortune awarded to him by a grateful monarch for some great service.

Tommy awoke from his day-dream, and, scrambling out of bed, quickly dressed himself and ran downstairs.

He met Sam, who said, "Beg pardon, sir, but Lord Taddlepool left his card yesterday."

"Why did you not give it to me?" Tommy said, staring at the piece of pasteboard. "I would have given anything to have seen his lordship."

"He said he should see you to-day," Sam said.

"Yes, yes, I know," Tommy replied; "but really I should like to see what he is like."

"He's as handsome a young chap as ever wore boots," Sam declared, "and as to his mustachers, I never seed such beauties to curl."

Tommy sat down at the table, and pressing his hand to his brow, began to think.

"My loss of memory is something dreadful," he muttered, "and amounts almost to an affliction. I could swear to some things which everbody says never happened, and what everybody declares to have occurred I have no more recollection of than a post. I won't say anything to Li, but, hang me, if this goes on much longer I will consult an experienced medical man."

The opening of the door put an end to Tommy's soliloquy, and Lionel, Lord Vansittart, and Charlie rushed into the room and shook hands with the fat boy until he roared for mercy.

"I say," he cried, "leave off, Li, you are crushing my fingers."

"Couldn't help it, dear boy," said Lionel; "I am so awfully glad to see you looking so well. I thought perhaps you would be a little pale with thinking of the great coming event, but, upon my soul, you look as fresh as a daisy."

"There is quite a peach-like bloom on his cheeks," said Lord Vansittart.

"His eyes glisten like diamonds," Charlie added.

"By the way," said Lionel, "Lord Taddlepool called yesterday while we were out."

"Sam has told me so," Tommy said. "I have his lordship's card."

"Well, I fancy Kramatome smells a rat," Lionel went on, "and perhaps he might put a stop to the proceedings; so, if I were you, Tommy, I should slip away with the things in a cab, and dress at the livery stables."

"Dress where?" Tommy gasped.

"At the livery stables," Lionel repeated. "I have told Slasher the circumstances, and he will have a room ready for your reception."

"It's awfully good of you to take so much trouble about me," Tommy said, gratefully.

"Never mind that," Lionel returned; "you get away as soon as possible. I will make some excuse for your absence."

Tommy followed this advice, and, sneaking down stairs with the parcel behind him, he rushed into the street, and hailing a passing hansom drove to Mr. Slasher's.

The aristocratic job-master received him with many bows, and ushered him into a comfortably-furnished room, where Tommy was left to himself.

It took him at least two hours to dress, and no sooner was he ready than the carriage drew up.

"Well," Tommy said, as he leaned back among the cushions, "I little thought it would ever come to this. Dash it! perhaps, after all, it's only a dream."

Through crowded streets and silent thoroughfares the carriage rolled, and at last stopped at the entrance of St. James's Palace.

Tommy expected to see a gaping throng, horse soldiers, noble equipages, but there was nothing going on out of the common.

There were plenty of nursemaids, loiterers, and flunkies, and the truth broke upon Tommy that he had been sold.

Where was the mysterious Lord Taddlepool?

He looked about him in vain, but presently he turned colour, and halted, gazing at the figure of a man approaching him with open arms, and a huge grin on his face.

"Och, shure, 'tis the darlint once more."

The voice of Irish Mike as he greeted his old friend seemed to Tommy like some half-remembered dream of long ago.

"Why—what—eh—no—yes. It can't be—and yet it is," Tommy gasped, warding off the Irishman with a frantic motion of his hands.

"It's as much me as ivir there was," said Irish Mike, "and it's sthrange that I should meet you here. Bedad, come and have a dhrop of the crathur that I may faste me eyes on ye."

"Hush, for Heaven's sake!" Tommy whispered.

"Don't you see that I can't talk to you now. I'm going to Court Get away! Oh, Lor', haven't you any manners?"

"Manners, is it?" quoth Irish Mike. "I'd like to see the man who'd tache me how to behave. Bedad, so if it's the Court ye are goin' to so am I, and we'll go arm-in-arm, like two ginuine sons of ould Oireland."

"It's impossible," Tommy gasped. "Oh, Lor', I wonder where Lord Taddlepool is?"

"Shure, now don't take on and discard an old frind," said Mike. "It's come with me ye will whither ye loike it or not. Jist one glass, and thin I will lave ye to yer swills and gintry."

Tommy gave an awful groan, which seemed to rise from the depths of his stomach.

"I suppose I must," he argued with himself. "The fellow is as bold as brass, and will follow me anywhere. Dash it all! I thought Irish Mike was a dream, and yet here he is. I can't make it out. No, Mike, you cannot take hold of my arm. If I were seen with you my position in society would be ruined for ever."

"It's proud, ye are," Irish Mike said, drawing back. "Shure now, Tommy, ingratitoode is a bad thing. Didn't I pick ye up when ye hadn't a shoe t'yer foot? Bedad, I'll let the people know."

"Don't do that," Tommy cried, frantically. "Mike, I'm very sorry. I'll go with you anywhere, only don't create a disturbance."

So saying, Tommy rushed up St. James's-street, across Piccadilly, and dived into a quiet street closely followed by Irish Mike.

"There now, honey," said the latter, dragging the fat and panting youth into the bar of a secluded public-house, "we can sit down here and enjoy ourselves."

"Oh, what misery is this!" Tommy moaned. "I must be mad. Mike, am I awake or asleep? Pinch me if you please. Oh, lor! not so hard—that will do—ya-h-h-h."

Tommy's howl brought the landlord out of the little back parlour, and Mike ordered whiskey for himself and companion.

"You remimber Judy Callighan?" Mike said.

"Judy Callighan," Tommy repeated, scratching his head. "What! the old woman who always got locked up from the Saturday to Monday?"

"It's the self-same," said Irish Mike. "Bedad, she's gone and left all the good things behind her, and this very night it's a wake that will be held at her house."

"Oh! so she's dead then," Tommy said, evasively. "Poor old soul!"

"And it's you that will go with me to that self-same wake," Irish Mike continued; "and it's a merry time we'll have, what with the keeners and whiskey!"

"I'm very much obliged," Tommy said, gulping down half the contents of his glass of liquor, "but I am otherwise engaged, and cannot possibly get away."

"Bedad, you won't get away from me honey," Irish Mike replied, grinning hugely. "Shure and it will be a thrate to have a rale gintleman at the wake. I've seen ye dance, Tommy, and ye shall give us a jig to-night."

Tommy did not appear to understand the speaker. His eyes were fixed and glazed, and his head fell with startling suddenness on his breast.

Irish Mike ran to the door and gave a shrill whistle, and three youthful figures appeared and hustled Tommy into a cab and drove away.

Mike stood jingling something in his hand, and staring hard at the retreating cab.

"Bedad," he said, musingly, "it's soon he went to slape. Howly Moses, he'll rist well to-night."

As the cab rattled along Tommy's three guardians chatted and laughed.

"You are sure the mixture will do him no harm?" Vansittart said.

"I will answer for that," Lionel replied. "I took good care not to give Irish Mike too much for fear he might make a mistake."

It was morning when Tommy, with a feeling as if his head had been filled with molten lead, opened his eyes.

"I tell you, Mike, that you'll be sorry for this," he said. "How dare you follow me about? Why, what's this? Where am I?"

Tommy started up in bed and glared at the familiar objects in his room, and just then Sam knocked at the door, saying that the bell had rung for breakfast.

"Sam, Sam," Tommy cried out, "come in, I want to speak to you."

Sam dutifully obeyed, and stood at the bed-side, looking the picture of innocence.

"What time did I come home last night?" Tommy asked.

"I can't swear as how you went out," said Sam. "You complained of a bad headache and went to bed airly."

"Went to bed early!" Tommy cried aghast. "Why—why—where are the things I had from Joses and Sons?"

"Wot things?"

"Why those I ought to have gone to Court in," Tommy gasped.

"Master Tommy," Sam said, trying to look stern, and failing dismally in the attempt, "I didn't like to mention it, but you was that tight last night that it took four on us to carry you upstairs. Mister Lionel found two empty whiskey-bottles under your table, and naterally he thinks you went in for it rayther heavy."

"Can this be true?" poor Tommy gasped. "Merciful powers! I cannot be in my right mind."

"It ain't for me as knows my place to say nothink to a gentleman and a friend of Master Lionel's," Sam went on. "But if you'll take my adwice, sir, you'll moderate your transports when liquor is in the way. Lor, sir, how you did swear at Mister Kramatome!"

"Did what!" Tommy almost shrieked. "Sam, Sam, don't trifle with me—there's a good fellow! Are you sure I used bad language?"

"Bad langwidge!" Sam echoed. "That ain't strong enough to conwey the hawful mouthfuls of Billingsgate you got rid of. But that ain't the wust of it."

"What else did I do?" Tommy moaned, faintly.

"Why, sir, I think Mr. Kramatome could have stood the swearin'," Sam replied, "but when you dropped him a buster in the weskit you went a little too far."

Tommy wriggled and curled himself up in bed like a collared eel.

"I'll get up at once," he said. "Sam, help me to dress. I feel awfully shaky. I must apologise to Mr. Kramatome at once."

"I wouldn't do that until I saw Master Lionel," Sam said. "I heerd him say to Lord Vansittart that he thought he could make it square for you."

"Li is the best fellow in the world," Tommy said. "But, dash it! where are the things I went to the palace in? I'll swear it was no dream."

"Werry good, sir," said Sam. "I won't contradict you; but if you went to the pallidge I'm the Hemperor of Chaney. Look at your heyes, sir. They'll tell you wot you were up to last night."

"They certainly are very fishy," Tommy said; "and my temples throb dreadfully, but——"

"Hullo, you reprobate!" Lionel cried, rushing into the room, and slapping Tommy heartily on the back. "I say, Tommy, you must really draw a line somewhere."

"I shall draw it in a madhouse before long," Tommy groaned. "Li, how can I face old Kramatome?"

"I have made that right," Lionel replied. "Of course he could see the state you were in, and he

sent me up to say that you were to make no mention of the occurrence."

"You are a brick, Li," Tommy said, giving his friend's hand a grateful squeeze; "and what I should do without you I don't know. Did Lord Taddlepool call yesterday?"

"Lord who?" Lionel replied, opening his eyes wide in astonishment.

"Why, you know—the fellow who was to have introduced me at court," Tommy replied.

"To the best of my belief there is no such person in the world," Lionel returned. "Tommy, I am afraid you have been dreaming again."

"Why, Sam gave me his card!" Tommy cried, aghast.

"Wot, I, sir!" Sam exclaimed.

"Yes, you!" Tommy roared, furiously, "and I have it in my waistcoat pocket."

"Perdooce it, sir, and you'll conwince me," Sam said. "I'm open to argyment; but if I gave you a card may I—— But wot's the use o' talking? It ain't you, sir, as is sayin' all these things—it's the whisky."

"Stop a minute," Tommy said, fumbling in all his pockets. "I'll soon settle this. Why, dash it! where can the card have got to?"

"Of course you never had it," Lionel said, triumphantly. "Come, now, let us have no more of this nonsense. Breakfast is ready, and if you only eat something it will do you a world of good."

"I've swallowed what I can't digest now," Tommy returned, wringing his hands. "But I'll fathom this mystery. I'll advertise for Lord Taddlepool in the agony columns of all the papers. I'll call on Jones and Sons. I'll call on Slasher. I'll—— dash it! I'll go all round the world barefooted to know the truth. Perhaps all my life is a dream, and I shall wake up presently and find that I am somebody else."

CHAPTER XXIV.

TOMMY IS MORE PERPLEXED THAN EVER, AND DETERMINES TO MAKE A SACRIFICE—THE DRILL AND THE DRILLED.

MR. SLASHER stood outside his office, nibbling a piece of hay thoughtfully as Tommy came up with his three companions.

"Now, why will you make a fool of yourself?" Vansittart said. "Lionel, we really have no right to allow him to make himself so ridiculous."

"Oh, let him have his own way!" Lionel replied. "I suppose he will be satisfied after hearing what Slasher has to say."

"I shall be satisfied," Tommy said, "when I know that I am in my right senses, but not before. Good morning, Mr Slasher."

"Good morning," said the job-master. "What can I do for you?"

"I want to see those men who took me down to the palace yesterday afternoon. A blackguard interfered with me, and I intend to prosecute him," Tommy replied.

"There's some mistake here," Mr. Slasher said. "You've come to the wrong place, sir."

"No, no!" Tommy urged. "You remember—I dressed in that room."

"May I never see a bit of horseflesh again if you did," the job-master replied. "Gentlemen don't come here to dress, sir."

"Why don't you hold your tongue?" Lionel whispered in the perplexed youth's ear. "Don't you see what a fool you are making of yourself? Come away."

"I won't!" Tommy roared. "This is a vile conspiracy, and if I don't settle it I'll settle some of you. Let me see inside that room. I could swear to every bit of furniture in the place."

"Come in, sir," Mr. Slasher said, heartily. "This is one of the most extraordinary things I ever heard of."

Tommy rushed into the room, out of which he presently came, pale and trembling.

"Well," said Charlie Drummond. "Have you solved the mystery?"

"I am more in a fog than ever," Tommy replied, clutching at his hair. "There's nothing in the room I can recognise. Take me to a doctor."

"I have a jolly good mind to take you to a police court," Mr. Slasher observed. "Why, what do you mean you lump of—why, hang it, how should I know what your little game is? Perhaps you wouldn't mind turning out your pockets?"

"What for?" Tommy cried, aghast. "Do you take me for a thief?"

"There's more rogue than fool about you," said Mr. Slasher, seizing Tommy and shaking him rather roughly.

"There is no need for violence," Lionel said. "Our friend is a perfect gentleman, but unhappily labours under sad delusions, the result of extraordinary dreams."

"Oh! that's it," said the job-master, releasing Tommy. "Well, dreams are curious things, so I have no more to say in the matter, but don't let him come here bothering me again."

"I will be answerable for his conduct," Lionel said. "Now, Tommy, I hope you *are* satisfied."

Tommy mumbled out something to the effect that as far as Mr. Slasher was concerned he would like to make the liver complaint an impossibility, and then suffered himself to be led away by his friends.

"Well, now, I think we may return," Vansittart said. "I am really tired of such a wild-goose chase."

"You may do as you like," Tommy said, savagely; "but I intend to make one more effort."

"In which direction?"

"I am going," Tommy replied, slowly, "to Messrs. Joses and Sons who lent me the suit, and if I fail I shall come to the conclusion that I am either cranky, or the victim of some mesmerism or spiritualism."

"Why, I never thought of that," Lionel exclaimed "perhaps this is all old Kramatome's doing. I have noticed that he looks strangely at you sometimes, especially during dinner."

"So have I," Charlie chimed in, "and I heard him muttering something under his breath. He may be weaving a spell around you. I suppose you never smell brimstone in your sleep, Tommy?"

"No."

"Or hear strange sounds as you sink into slumber?" Vansittart said.

"There is a singing in my ears at times," Tommy replied, "and often I wake up with a start."

"Mercy on us!" Lionel cried, "this is very dreadful, and yet I had my suspicions."

"If I thought that such was the case," Tommy gasped, "I'd—I'd ——"

"Be very careful of what you say," Charlie said, pretending to shudder, "these mediums have an extraordinary knack of knowing what we say and what we think. Prospero tortured Caliban with cramps, pains, and itches, and old Kramatome may take it into his head to pile the dreams on thicker than ever."

Tommy's face turned ghastly pale as he listened, and then became flushed and heated.

"I have heard of such things," he gasped, planting his back against a wall, "but, dash it all, why should he worry me?"

"Of course he may not do so at all," Lionel said, "but if he does he has some deep motive, you may depend."

"Well, let the matter rest for the present," Charlie said. "We will keep an eye on Kramatome, and do our best to thwart him. I suppose you will give up your visit to Messrs. Joses and Sons—at least for the present."

"No," said Tommy, determinedly, "I am going there at once."

"Why do you try to hinder him?" Lionel exclaimed. "Let him have his own way. We will, however, return, or he may think we have something to do with this tomfoolery."

"Good bye, Tommy," Lord Vansittart said, waving his hand. "Mind you don't have another dream on your way."

"Don't stop to look at the time at the public-houses," Charlie cried.

"Beware of the cup that cheers but to despond," said Lionel, with a warning shake of his forefinger. "Make haste, and bring back a good appetite with you."

"Well," Tommy gasped, pushing his hat on the back of his head, and gazing pensively after his companions' retreating forms, "they may be right, but it is a most awful mystery. The Tichborne case was nothing to it. Arthur Orton lives in a state of paradise compared to the life I lead, but I'll put an end to this one way or the other. I was happy when I was hard up, but now——"

We must omit the remainder of Tommy's soliloquy, and bring him up to the imposing front of Messrs. Joses and Sons' establishment.

Tommy entered, and to his great joy beheld the same gentleman who had attended to him on the previous day.

"Good morning," Tommy said, smiling blandly. "My friends have been having a lark with me—in short they have endeavoured to convince me that you did not supply me with a court dress yesterday."

"I beg your bardig," said the gentleman of the Hebrew persuasion—"a court dress did you say, sir?"

"Yes," Tommy said, with a sinking heart, for he saw doubt and mistrust in the shopman's eye. "Of course you remember me."

"To the best of my dnolwich I dever saw you in my life," the gentleman with the aquiline nose replied, displaying a set of wondrously white teeth, "but we shall hab buch bleasure to wait upod you at any tibe."

"Do you mean to tell me?" Tommy exclaimed, staring blankly at the man—"do you mean to tell me that you did not see me yesterday afternoon; because if you say so you lie?"

"Jones," the shopman cried, "hab the goodness to show this gentlemad out, and see him into a cab. He's intoxicadid."

"I am not," Tommy cried, struggling in the brawny arms of Jones.

"Now, you must come out o' this," the porter said, "and why not do it quietly? If you are a gentleman you will not create a scene."

Tommy heeded not these words of wholesome advice, but struck out manfully, and kicked like five, but Jones was equal to the occasion, and Tommy presently found himself rushing madly across the street, with a horrible numbing sensation under his coat tails.

"This will end in murder," the fat youth gasped, as he ran foul of a four-wheeled cab, "or suicide. Dash it! I know what I'll do. I'll enlist, and go abroad. Cabby, drive me to Charles-street, Westminster."

"Wait till I see wot damage is done," the cabman growled, struggling out of the apron and half a dozen horse cloths. "Wot a buster you did come agin me, sir. I thought you had smashed the panels."

"I have hurt myself more than I have your confounded cab!" Tommy groaned, rubbing his knees and elbows. "Drive on."

"Where did you say I was to go to, sir?" asked the cabman.

"Oh, go to the devil!" Tommy roared, as he sat on a knobby part of the cushion, and remembered Jones's parting kick.

"Very good, sir," the cabman returned; "you knows the vay, and I'll drive; vich is the fust turning?"

"AND NOW," SAID THE SERGEANT, "DRINK THE HEALTH OF HIS MAJESTY FROM THE STEAMING TANKARD."

"I told you to take me to Charles-street, Westminster," Tommy roared.

And to Charles-street, Westminster, the dutiful cabman took our fat friend.

Tommy had plenty of opportunities to carry out his threat.

There were any number of recruiting sergeants on the look-out, and quantities of shabby fellows loafing about London—men out of work, yokels from the country, short-haired gentlemen who had just completed Government contracts in the wind-grinding and oakum-picking lines, wretched-looking lads biting their finger-nails—all casting furtive glances at the stalwart fellows in uniform.

Most of these loafers had been rejected for some reason or other, and the others were making up their minds when Tommy—burning with injury and smarting with pain—selected a stalwart grenadier, and accosted him with the boldness of despair.

"I wish to go into the army," the fat one said. "I stand five feet seven, and——"

"Never mind what height you stand," said the military man. "The question is, what are you going to stand?"

"Oh, anything you like!" Tommy replied, glad to have met such a convivial fellow. "Where shall we go?"

"Follow me," said the grenadier, "and I will soon make matters right for you. What regiment would you like to join?"

"I'm not at all particular," Tommy said; "only I should like a nice smart uniform."

"And your figger would set it off splendidly," the soldier said, leading the way into a private bar. "Humph—ah! Now, what shall I have?"

"Don't be afraid—I have plenty of money," Tommy exclaimed. "What do you say to a bottle of champagne?"

"No, thank you," the military man returned. "A drop of brandy will suit me better."

Tommy took a little whisky, and as the spirit went down so his own rose.

"I think I should do well in the army," he said. "I feel just in the mind for action. Give me a sword, and I'd fight my way through an army."

"You are made of the proper stuff," the grenadier cried, slapping Tommy so heartily on the back that the whisky nearly made its reappearance. "You shall join our regiment, sir."

"Am I tall enough?" Tommy asked, dubiously.

"That can be managed," the soldier said, dropping his voice. "There is a friend of mine who can do the trick for you."

"Take me to him," Tommy cried. "The sooner the better!"

"He's on duty now in Pall-mall," said the military man: "but I think, if it would answer your purpose to spring half-a-sov., I could manage it. You see I'm on the look-out for a recruit, as fine a young feller—barring yourself—as ever I set eyes on. Well, don't you see, if I'm out of the way, it's just a hundred to one that he will be snapped up while I'm away, and so, sir——"

"Of course, I understand," said the ever-credulous Tommy, opening his purse. It is a matter of business. We had better have a cab. But, stop. You are a recruiting-sergeant. Why can't you enlist me at once?"

"Why, it's just this," said the grenadier. "My friend has lots of influence, and can put any little matter as to height square, but I couldn't do that."

"Oh!" said Tommy. "You know best. Hansom!"

The brave warriors were soon on the spot, and it so happened that the guard was being changed, with the usual accompaniment of boys and nursery girls, in the midst of whom Tommy found himself struggling. and growling loudly against the illegal use of wicker baskets—when applied to the ribs—and perambulator wheels.

Somebody pushed him in the small of the back,

and the next instant he was waltzing with a big-headed soldier, who, in the act of presenting arms, received a bash on the nose with his rifle.

"Why, confound your great clumsy limbs!" gasped the man, tripping Tommy up. and sticking his bayonet through his inexpressibles. "You've done my drill, and now I'll drill you."

And with the utmost ease he shouldered the rifle, with Tommy impaled as securely as ever Servian was by Turk, and resumed the even tenour of his way.

"I say—oh!—dash it!" Tommy yelled. "Confound it, I shall fall and dash my brains out!"

Luckily for Tommy, a humane lady appeared on the scene, and the grenadier allowed Tommy to slide gently off the bayonet on to the pavement, where he lay gasping and floundering like a landed fish.

"Oh, you wretch!" Tommy gasped, placing his hands on the baggy part of his inexpressibles. "Confound and dash it, you shall suffer for this."

This threat had scarcely passed his lips when somebody rushed madly round the corner, and in such haste that he did not perceive the fat youth.

The collision was awful. Tommy howled, and rolled himself up like a hedgehog, while the other party shot out like a Chinese kite of fantastic shape, and having floated gracefully in the air for some seconds came a most awful cropper.

A grunt, a growl, and a naughty word, commencing with the letter D, caused Tommy to sit up and stare at the stranger.

It was Sam Scarecrow.

CHAPTER XXV.

SAM'S CONFIDENCE AND HOW HE LOST IT AMONG OTHER THINGS—TOMMY HAS AN INTERVIEW WITH MR. KRAMATOME.

YES. it was Sam Scarecrow, and every hair of his sandy moustache working like the bristles on the back of an angry cat. A freak of birth had adorned him with a squint in both eyes. but now the order of things was reversed, for his resplendent orbs looked perfectly natural, while every other feature was out of place.

Sam looked for all the world as if he had taken a packet of hair-pins and was doing his best to swallow them.

"It's Master Thomas," Sam said, as he picked himself up, with many groans plentifully besprinkled with questionable adjectives. "I never did see sich a chap—I mean a gentleman—to get in the way."

"How dare you fall over me, you unmanly brute?" Tommy yelled, pressing his hands to his waist-coat. "Your confounded feet are always doing something."

"Well, sir," said Sam, as he stooped to raise Tommy up, "it certainly were unfortinit, but I've hurt myself a jolly sight more than I hurt you; so, I think, the less said about the matter the better. Lor', sir, what is the matter with you? Bust it, you've been skewered like a penn'orth of cats' meat."

"It's that dashed soldier!" Tommy howled, pointing out the passing guardsman. "There were two in it, but the other has vanished. I'll have this one's life!"

Sam flung his arms round Tommy, and restrained him.

"No, you don't," Sam cried. "You keep still, or I'll borrer the bagenet and carry you home on it. Mister Lionel sent me to look for you, and a nice mess I've made of it."

"What have you done?" Tommy demanded, flattening his back against the wall, as he saw some ladies approaching.

"Done," Sam echoed. "I've been done like a dinner. I've been and gone and lost every farden, and every bit of joolry I had in the world."

"What?" Tommy cried, "have you been robbed?"

"That ain't the name on it," Sam replied, as he led Tommy away. "There was two of 'em. One was a chap as looked as if he came from the country, t'other was a genteel looking man with piles of sov'rins, and about a barrer load of bank notes stowed about him."

"I wish you'd be a little more lucid," Tommy said. "How did you lose your property."

"I'm comin' to that," Sam replied. "I met these two coves in a public-house as is in the Haymarket, and I overhears their conversation. The genteel chap said as 'ow he had come into a fortin', and didn't know what to do with it, 'so,' ses he, 'if you've any confidence you can earn fifty pounds in five minutes.'"

"And did he get it?" Tommy asked.

"He did," said Sam; "and that is the most hextra-ordinary part of it. 'Ow am I to make the money?' ses the cove from the country. 'Easy enough,' ses the t'other; 'you've only to lend me your watch and chain for five minutes while I go out, and when I come back the money is yours.'"

A light dawned on Tommy, and he looked up at Sam, and smiled grimly.

"Ah," said he, "I begin to see it all, and, I suppose, in the end, you parted with your valuables."

"Hear me out," Sam exclaimed, crushing his hat down on his forehead, "and you'll hear it all, and it may be a warning to you. The country chap seemed to hesitate, and then him with the coin ses, 'Here is a young chap as looks honest. He shall hold the coin,' and so I did, and in a few minutes back comes the dapper little feller, and gives up the watch and chain, and horders me to hand up the bank notes to the countryman, which I did."

"And then?" said Tommy.

"I was perwailed on to part with my ticker, ring, two pun ten in gold, nine bobs in silver, and thrippence in copper."

"Which, of course, you never saw again," said Tommy.

"I never did, and I never shall," Sam replied, with tears in his eyes. "The genteel chap went out fust, and as he was gone sich a long time the other went to look for him, and neither of 'em came back."

"It is a serious loss to you," Tommy said; "but I have no doubt your master will make it up to you in some way."

"It ain't the loss," Sam declared; "for the watch it never would go 'cept when I carried it, and the money can soon be made up again, but it's hard to be had, and that's where I feels it."

"Well," said Tommy, "it is no use of crying over spilt milk. So your master sent you out to look for me."

"Yes, sir," Sam replied, "but I don't think I should have seen you if I hadn't fallen over you, for I was bilin' over with rage. My horders, sir, was that you was to go home with me, and if you wouldn't walk I was to carry you."

"Sam," Tommy said, earnestly, "you are a very good fellow, and I have the greatest respect for you."

"Thankee, sir," said Sam; "it does my 'art good to hear you say so."

"And," Tommy went on, "I should like to do you some service, but you will have to do something for me in return."

"What is it?" Sam asked. "If it's anybody as wants pitchin' into give him a name, and I'll settle him."

"I want nothing in that way," Tommy replied smiling. "Look here, Sam, I feel convinced that tricks are being played on me—these supposed dreams of mine, you know—and I am in a very unhappy state of mind."

"And in my opinion, sir, you will continue so," Sam said, gravely, "so long as you take any notice of 'em, sir. Who's afeared of a dream? Cheer up, sir, and forget all about 'em."

"Then there is no gammon going on?" Tommy queried, dismally.

"The only gammon as I knows on," Sam said, "is wot you make yourself. Lor', sir, your dreams ain't nothing to some peoples."

"No!" Tommy cried, in astonishment. "I, at least, never heard of the like."

"Bless your innercent 'art," said Sam, "did I never tell yer one as my harnt once had?"

"Your what?" Tommy demanded.

"My harnt."

"Oh, yes, your aunt. Go on, Sam, I understand."

"Her husband was a sailor," Sam resumed, "and they did say that he did a little in the tobacco line on his own hook, but that's neither here nor there. Well, one night my harnt dreamt that her old man had gone to the bottom of the sea, and nothin' could convince her to the contrary. She went inter widders weeds, and in doo time there comes a chap ogling my harnt, and as she hadn't heerd nor seen anythink of her husband for five years she returned them ogles, and it was arranged that they should be married on Easter Monday. The day came round, and she got to church, and would have been spliced, but suddenly there was a row in the church, and my harnt looks round, and fainted in the parson's arms."

"What had happened?" Tommy asked, much interested.

"Why," said Sam, "my harnt's old man had just landed, arter going through all sorts of dangers amongst savages, and seeing the church door open thought he'd just step in, and see what was going on."

"Wonderful!" Tommy gasped. "How lucky."

"'Twas," Sam said. "Up the church he comes, knocks the beadle's head agin the font, and then rushes at the bridegroom, and gives him an awful oner in the wind."

"It must have been a spree," Tommy said, forgetting his own woes in the excitement of the moment. "What was the end of it?"

"That's soon told," Sam said. "The parson seeing how matters stood dropped my harnt, and bolted inter the westry. My harnt opened her eyes, and give one scream, and jumped inter her old man's arms, and then they went home."

"And I trust lived happily to make up for the long separation."

"Well, sir," said Sam, "I believe there was a few argeyments as had to be settled by a madgistrate, but I think, taking all things, they got on pretty well."

The conclusion of this interesting narrative brought them up to Mr. Kramatome's house, where Tommy was greeted affectionately by his three companions.

"Where on earth have you been?" Lionel said. "We have been looking and hunting for you everywhere, and, by the way, Mr. Kramatome wants to see you at once."

"Wants to see me?" Tommy gasped.

"Yes," Charlie said, "and he is in a frightful rage, striding up and down his study, and swearing in the most dreadful manner."

"Go to him at once," Lionel said. "If you keep him waiting much longer he will have a fit. Brace up your nerves, Tommy, and give him as good as he sends."

"If he says too much to me I'll pitch an inkstand at him," Tommy cried, desperately.

"Bravo!" Vansittart exclaimed, "don't stand his cheek."

"I won't," Tommy declared, and waddled away.

In good faith Mr. Kramatome's rage was frightful to behold.

He sat at his table, littered with books and papers, staring at times at the latter, with his hands in his hair, and his eyes gleaming with the fury of a basilisk's.

"Oh, you have come back at last," he cried, jumping up as Tommy entered the room.

"Yes, I have come back," Tommy said, "and I hear that you wanted to speak to me."

"And have you the confounded impudence to stand there and say you don't know what I want you for?" Mr. Kramatome spluttered.

"I didn't say so, but I don't know," Tommy replied hotly, and puffing out his cheeks.

The learned examiner took two furious turns round the table, and checking himself suddenly roared in a tone such as no speaking trumpet ever produced—

"Who the devil is Irish Mike?"

Tommy started, and sat down plump into a chair.

"Who the devil is Irish Mike?" Mr. Kramatome repeated in a wild shriek.

"A dream in the whelk line," Tommy explained, opening his mouth like an expiring cod-fish.

"Don't trifle with me, sir," Mr. Kramatome roared, shaking his fist under Tommy's nose. "I would have you know, sir, that—that—— Damme, it would give me the greatest pleasure to thrash you to a stand-still."

"Why don't you try it on?" Tommy yelled, leaping up, and swinging his arms round like mill sails. "Come on, you dried up old duffer. What's Irish Mike to you?"

"Nothing," Mr. Kramatome literally howled. "See here, sir. Look at your papers, and you will find that you have described him as the first man who undertook a voyage to the North Pole."

"And what if I have?" Tommy returned, savagely. "You know as well as I do that I cannot get Irish Mike out of my head, although he never lived."

"I know!" Mr. Kramatome gasped, skipping behind a chair.

"Yes, you know," said Tommy. "Ah, you needn't look at me like that. I can stand it now, and you won't send me off again in a hurry."

"Merciful Heaven!" Mr. Kramatome cried, turning as white as a sheet. I ought to have known it. My poor boy, you are not well. Let me see you to your room, and I will send for a medical man."

"Don't come near me," Tommy cried, brandishing a heavy ruler. "Move another inch and I'll knock your skull in."

Mr. Kramatome rushed to the window, and his mouth was opened to shriek for the police, when Lionel, Charlie, and Vansittart dashed into the room.

"What is the matter?" Lionel cried. "Tommy, put down that ruler, or I'll put you down in a style which you will find the reverse of agreeable. Mr. Kramatome, be calm, I implore."

"Calm," said the learned gentleman, faintly. "Calm! Take that fat wretch away—he is out of his mind."

"Fat wretch!" Tommy roared. "I won't stand that. I shall be called a pig next. Here, stand out of the way, you fellows, and let me get at him."

But the "fellows" did not stand out of the way, and for the time Tommy's bloodthirsty design was frustrated.

"There is nothing to fear, sir," Lionel said. "Codlings has overtaxed his brain of late. Vansittart and Charlie, have the goodness to see him upstairs. I will join you presently."

Drummond and Vansittart, shaking with laughter, bore down on their luckless victim, and carried him out of the room, Tommy expostulating, pleading, threatening, and declaring that Mr. Kramatome was a wicked magician, and knew more about the black art than Old Nick."

CHAPTER XXVI.

SAM GETS INTO FURTHER TROUBLE, TAKES A SERIOUS DISLIKE TO ALL WITH AFRICAN BLOOD IN THEIR VEINS, AND GETS MIXED UP WITH AN AREA AND SOME CABBAGES—MR. KRAMATOME DISDAINS TO USE THE KNOCKER, AND YET KNOCKS AT HIS DOOR IN A REMARKABLE MANNER.

AT times it was Sam's delight to wander about the streets of the mighty metropolis alone, especially when, having received his quarter's salary, he could flourish a handful of gold and silver, and do the heavy in remote regions where his station of life was unknown.

Then it was that Sam, in a most overpowering hat and a suit of shining black broadcloth, showed himself in the fashionable neighbourhoods, patronising the bars of gorgeous public-houses, and squinting out of countenance the fair damsels who tended to the wants of thirsty souls.

Sam had just received his money, with leave of absence for the day, and the lean youth, brimful of joy, dived below to polish his boots and brush his clothes, preparatory to presenting himself before an enlightened and grateful people, for Sam argued that a well-dressed man was a blessing to society, and a thing to be thankful for.

"These 'ere boots," Sam said, holding them at arm's length, and gazing at them with intense admiration, "is enough to warm the cockles of the 'art of any man. It's the foot as gives the boot a shape."

In this case the remark was positively true, for Sam's boots were extremely knobbly about the toes, but they were as black as jet, and shone with the brilliancy of Japanese tea-trays, so that their appearance made up for the trifling disparagement in form.

"Some chaps have no taste," Sam murmured, as he tied a blue and pink necktie under a collar of enormous dimensions. "There now, I think that will fetch the gals, and I'd wager that if Mary was here she'd relent."

Sam shook his head dismally as he put his coat and waistcoat on, smoothing the wrinkles carefully, and then placing a consumptive-looking watch in his pocket, and a dropsical ring on his little finger, he sallied out.

A short cut through the squares brought Sam into Regent-street, that inspiring thoroughfare lined with splendid establishments, and thronged with humanity of every degree.

It was the height of the London season, and the roadway was blocked with handsome equipages, the pavements teemed with the fashionable world of both sexes, the female portion being busily engaged in that pleasing occupation known as shopping, while the male—we, with some amount of reluctance, record—lounged about with a languid air, smoked perfumed cigarettes, and ogled the fair charmers.

Sam in his suit of shiny black was as proud as any nobleman in the land, and lounged about in a damp, limp style, which he presumed to be "the thing," and barring that he asked an elderly old colonel "where he was a shovin' to," his deportment proved a credit to him.

True he squinted most horribly when anything demanded his special attention, and called forth the indignant remarks of a jeweller, into whose window he was staring, the proprietor being under the impression that Sam was making faces at him.

Sam felt very much inclined to step behind and have a satisfactory argument with the jeweller, but he remembered that a gentleman is always dignified even under the most trying circumstances, and turning up his nose until it seemed to curl, he turned his back upon the plebeian tradesman, and once more mixed with the giddy throng.

There was a concert at St. James's Hall, and Sam presently found himself mixed up with a crowd of footmen and police, who hustled him off the pavement with such violence that his hat fell into the gutter.

An Englishman has his heart in his hat. You may break his nose, black his eyes, distress his ribs, and he will forgive you, but knock his hat off and his blood boils.

Sam picked up what was left of his hat (the wheel of a brougham had passed over it), and motioning the people back with his arms as if about to perform some acrobatic feat he rushed upon a fat and perspiring policeman, and smote him heavily on the nose.

The man reeled against a dignified footman, who, cannoning gracefully against a commissionaire, shot him through one of the glass doors into a heap of hired shrubbery.

In an instant all was commotion.

The public roared "stop thief," the police ran hither and thither, footmen howled, cabmen swore, but none were so much astonished as Sam, who felt himself being dragged forcibly along Air-street, across Glasshouse-street, and into Golden-square.

"There," said a familiar voice, "it's open to argyment, but I think I've got you out of a nice mess."

Sam, panting for breath, stemmed the torrent from his nose, occasioned by an unlucky collision with a lamp-post, and gasped—

"Why, it's Long Jem."

"Yes, and it's lucky it is me," the acrobat said; "but don't stop here jabberin', or the slops will be down on us, and Bellers is busting to see you."

"Where is he?" Sam asked, squinting dubiously at his rescuer, and wondering if he, like Tommy Codlings, were dreaming.

"We are stayin' at a crib in Silver-street," Long Jem replied, "and Bellers is there—mind, it's open to argyment, but there I left him."

"Well," said Sam, taking the showman's hand, "I am awfully glad to see you; it was wery kind o' you to resky me, but you might ha' been a little more careful. Look at my coat."

"It's open to argyment," Long Jem replied, glancing critically at the torn garment, "whether any borned tailor can mend it."

"And here's a 'at," Sam gasped, "it looks more like a concertina without any vorks. Dash it! I'm wus nor Mister Thomas for getting into a mess."

"You may be right," Long Jem mused, with a grim smile lingering about his lips, "but that's open to argyment," and then, in an exasperated tone, "Why don't you come along? Can't you hear the peelers a hollerin' like a pack of hounds? You'll be nabbed directly, and sarve you right."

"Let me fetch my wind," Sam gasped, opening and shutting his mouth like a mechanical pantomime demon. "Now I'm ready."

A very few minutes brought them to the salubrious locality of Silver-street.

Vegetarians and naturalists might have rejoiced at the formidable array of cabbage stalks and winkle shells which lay strewn about from one end of the thoroughfare to the other, persons of a pugilistic turn of mind might have shed tears of joy at the sight of half a dozen journeymen tailors hammering each other with a delightful indiscrimination of friend or foe, and Mr. Bradlaugh might have found ample material for another pamphlet in the legion of dirty, uncared-for children, yelling, fighting, and playing heaven only knows what kind of games.

"Here we are," said Long Jem, opening the door of a house, the doorposts of which were furnished with as many bell handles as there are buttons on a page's jacket. "Mind how you go; the stairs air a trifle dark, and that woman on the fourth floor will leave her pattens about."

The warning came too late.

Sam, eager to fold Bellers-to-Mend once more in a fond embrace, fell headlong over a tin pail, and

with a howl of mortal agony plunged into a cupboard on the landing, and kicked frantically amongst the cinders, cobwebs, discarded housecloths, and other articles of no further use.

Long Jem seized Sam's legs, and hauled them with the suffering body out from the débris.

"What did you go and do it for?" Long Jem, exclaimed, wrathfully.

"Oh, my shins," Sam howled, dismally, tucking up his trousers and stripping off two long pieces of skin. "Oh, lor', this is hawful."

"Didn't I tell you to be careful," said Long Jem; "but it's open to argyment whether the mention o' pattens inclooded tin pails and sich like. There's a hold gentleman on the next floor as have a habit of leaving his leg about."

"Leaving his what about?" Sam gasped.

"His leg—a wooden one," Long Jem replied, "though it's open to argyment whether his nateral one wouldn't be more favourable to strangers. You see this hold chap comes home drunk reglar, and when he's had a hextra dose he generally takes orf his leg and chucks it downstairs when he hears anybody comin' up."

"Wot do he do it for? Sam asked, nursing his injured legs.

"He thinks it's his wife," Long Jem whispered. "Come on, and don't talk too loud, he may be at home now."

With a fearful dread of pattens, pails, and wooden legs, Sam cautiously ascended another flight of stairs, and was wondering how much nearer the roof the strollers lived when a little door opened, and before Sam had time to speak, think, or act, he found himself waltzing in the arms of Bellers-to-mend.

"My bo-o-o-oy, the pride of my 'art, how fares it with you?" the showman cried.

"Don't," Sam roared, "you're bustin' my ribs, and I'm standin' on the hedge of the stairs."

"I can't help it," Bellers replied, giving Sam another hug, that brought forth a grunt like an expostulating pig. Come in, come in, my cherub."

"I feels more like a red hot jelly," Sam groaned, as he staggered into the room, and sat down on a three-legged stool. "I say, have you any stickin' plaister handy?"

"You know we always keep it," Long Jem observed, opening a drawer in the table, "but it's open to argyment ——"

"Bust your argyments," Bellers roared. "Now, Sam, you must tell us wot you have been doin' with yourself all this time, and how you're gettin' on."

Sam soon complied, and after a bottle of whiskey, with hot water, lemons, and sugar had been placed on the table, the trio became very merry indeed.

"And, now, wot's your little game?" Sam asked, as he concluded his own narrative, and mixed himself another glass of grog. "This 'ere don't look as if you've made your fortuns."

Bellers-to-mend shook his head rather dismally.

"No," said he, "the days for strollin' are dyin' out. Wot with cheap excursions and trains a'most everywhere people flock to London and gorge themselves with enough sights in a week to last them the whole year. But we ain't got no cause to grumble, Sam. Long Jem does the tater business."

"The wot bisiness?" Sam demanded.

"The tater," Bellers replied; "chucks 'arf a pound tater thirty feet in the air and catches it on his for'ead, you know."

"I once seed it done," Sam said, casting a sympathising glance at the acrobat, "and I never want to see it again."

"W'y?" Long Jem demanded, turning pale.

"It were in Albermarle-street, Picadilly," Sam said, slowly, "and there was two of 'em, one as did the tater trick, t'other stood on his 'ead and sang comic songs or drank glasses o' beer. Both these 'ere chaps was that drunk that they couldn't scarcely see each other, and all of a sudden the chap instead o' chuckin' the tater up sent it flyin' into a nobbleman's carridge."

"Wot was the damage?" Long Jem asked.

"The damidge weren't nothink to speak of," Sam replied, "but the tater bust on the nobbleman's heye, and the two chaps got a month each. Go on, Bellers, I see you've got somethin' more to say."

"Jem didn't take kindly to the line at first," Bellers-to-Mend resumed, "but after a few whacks he got used to it, and now there ain't a man as can stand agin him. At night we has a tent on Wandsworth Common as does the talkin' head."

"Wot!—a himitation o' Stodare's Spinks," Sam cried. "That's as hold as the ills."

"You're wrong my lad," Bellers-to-Mend returned; "we've beaten that holler. Will yer come down to-morrer night, and give us a look up."

"I shall be perroud to do so," Sam returned, "and I've only got to mention it to Mr. Lionel, and I'll lay a guinea to a goosebery that he and his friends will be there too."

"That will be fust-rate," Long Jem, said solemnly; "but it's open to argyment whether the gentlemen will care to know them, as——"

The acrobat ceased speaking, for Sam had risen and was standing in a threatening and extremely unpleasant attitude.

"You shut up," Sam exclaimed, "or there'll be sich a dashed fight here as never was. Mister Lionel is a gentleman, and when I say that I've said heverythink."

Long Jem spluttered out an apology, and Sam, sitting down, mixed himself another stiff glass of grog, and immediately flavoured it with a copious flow of tears.

"There ain't a nobler young chap in all the world," he cried.

"Who said there was?" Long Jem demanded, with a heaving chest, and emotion in every word he uttered. "I only said it was open to argyment whether he would care to mix with such as us, and everything is open to argyment, you know."

"There's one think as ain't," Sam declared, surveying Long Jem out of one eye.

"Wot's that?"

"Why, everybody knows that you are a born fool," Sam cried, bringing his fist down on the table, thus making the glasses jump and ring.

Long Jem rose, and proceeded slowly—very slowly indeed—to roll up his coat sleeves, when Bellers-to-Mend threw himself upon him.

"No, you don't," he roared. "You're both drunk, and don't know wot you are sayin' or doin'. Shake hands, and say good-bye till to-morrer."

"I'm willin'," said Long Jem, lurching forward.

"And so am I," Sam declared, supporting himself against the table. "Jem, if there had been any malice in my 'art I should ha' killed you at that moment. Fare thee well."

Sam was glad to get out of the room into the open air, for every object had been going round at a fearful speed, including Long Jem and Bellers-to-Mend, who, to the lanky youth's imagination, spun like teetotums.

"Wot's the matter with my legs?" Sam growled, as he rasped his nose against a brick wall. "Bust it! where are you comin' to?"

These last words were addressed to a gigantic negro, walking quietly down the street with a huge basket of cabbages on his head.

"Golly, it am you dat run agin me," the negro roared, clutching at his burden to save it from falling.

Sam drew himself up to his full height, and, squinting hideously at the dark-skinned son of Africa, said—

"I hate niggers, a lot o' lazy warmints, fit for nothin' but to be whacked. Go home, you dirty son of a blackin' bottle, and I'll—I'll—I'll send a misshingnary out to you."

"What for you interfere with me?" the nigger gasped, keeping a wary eye on Sam's movements. "Jes' you git out ob my way, or I gib you one dat —Oh, golly!—yah!"

Sam had rushed forward, and planted the nigger a blow under the chin, causing his teeth to rattle in a really marvellous style.

The basket of cabbages fell into the street, and the nigger, turning red under his dark skin, bore down on Sam, who, having lost sight of his foe, was sparring blindly at a post.

Two blows from brawny arms, swung round like millsails in a gale, settled the question, and Sam disappeared down an open area with lightning-like rapidity.

For a time all was a blank, and then he became conscious of voices.

Opening one eye with extreme caution he saw a dirty old man standing over him.

"What's the matter?" the long youth demanded, faintly. "How did I get here?"

"That's more than I can tell," the old man replied. "But come you did, with about a dozen cabbages rolling after you."

"Cabbages!" Sam exclaimed. "Oh—ah! I remember now. I was standin' lookin' into a shop winder, when a great cowardly nigger give me a buster, and sent me flyin'. I'll go now, and thankee for your kindness."

"There's a pavin' stone as will have to be paid for," the old man said, rubbing his hands. "Your head must be a hard one to crack a flag."

"And did I do that?" Sam cried, proudly, feeling for the counter result on the back of his head. "Wot's the price, old feller?"

"Five shillings."

Sam put his hands in his pocket, but only a sixpence remained.

"I've been robbed agin!" he howled. "Old man, give me my money, or I'll have your witals."

"Help! help!—murder! perlice!" the old man screamed, and Sam, not feeling inclined to further adventures, darted up the steps, and rushed homewards, with the remnants of his tattered garments flying in the wind.

Poor Sam soon became faint and out of breath, and stopping at a public-house he called for and drank sixpennyworth of brandy neat, and then, with uncertain footsteps, tottered to Mr. Kramatome's door, and sank down on the step as his hand touched the bell handle.

An instant after Mr. Kramatome came flying round the corner.

He had been in search of an experienced medical man learned in the causes and cure of lunacy, for he deemed Tommy Codlings to be mad.

The doctor had promised to be at the house in half an hour, and Mr. Kramatome was in a hurry to ascertain how the patient was getting on.

He drew out his latch-key from his waistcoat pocket, but he did not use it. A stumble, an oath, a loud crash, and the sound of Mr. Kramatome's head colliding with the door woke Sam Scarecrow.

CHAPTER XXVII.

MR. KRAMATOME COMES TO A CONCLUSION—DITTO DR. WISENUT—A PRESCRIPTION FOR TOMMY— STRICT MEASURES AND STRAIGHT JACKETS— LIONEL TO THE RESCUE—THE FAIR ON WANDSWORTH COMMON—TOMMY IS INTRODUCED INTO STRANGE SOCIETY—HOT WORDS AND HOTTER IRONS—DISREPUTABLE CONDITION OF THE TALKING HEAD.

MR. KRAMATOME sat on his doorstep, and propping his back against the area railings glared at Sam with all the fury of a basilisk; but the long youth's condition was such that no amount of indignation expressed by feature could affect him in the least.

Mr. Kramatome had bumped all power of speech

out of his head, but at last he found his breath and tongue, and—well, to put it as mild as possible, swore so roundly at Sam that he opened his glazed and stupefied eyes in surprise.

"What are you doing here, you drunken hound," Mr. Kramatome howled, as a violent pain shot through his cranium. "You miserable cross-eyed specimen of humanity, what do you mean by throwing me down? You—you—— Oh, dear, my head! It will burst, I'm sure."

"It's all ri', sir," Sam said, smiling sweetly. "Lend me a tanner, and I'll stand two threes o' whiskey."

"I thought as much," Mr. Kramatome groaned. "The disgusting wretch is intoxicated."

"I ain't," Sam said. "I'm only a little helevated. Don't be perroud, sir. Here's my hand—it's a honest and a friendly one. Let's be jolly."

We dare not record what Mr. Kramatome said, but his rage—or, rather, fury—was a sight to behold. White one instant—scarlet the next; now purple, with his eyes the size and colour of pyramid balls; then a kind of sickly green. He presently sprang to his feet, and throwing open the door, kicked Sam inch by inch into the hall.

The lamp had not been lit, and the enraged gentleman, missing Sam in one instance, smote the umbrella-stand with the full force of his leg, and a wail of unbearable anguish burst from his lips, which, floating like the howl of a banshee up the staircase, brought Lionel on to the landing.

"Who's there?" Lionel shouted. "Is that you, Sam?"

"D—— Sam!" Mr. Kramatome shrieked. "Bring a light. I have broken my leg."

Lionel presently appeared with a lamp, but stopped half-way, and stared in wonderment at the spectacle before him.

Sam was lying on his back, squinting blandly at the ceiling, his long legs elevated in the air, and forming a huge capital V, his clothes in tatters and besmeared with his own gore, brought to light by the combined efforts of the nigger's fists and his fall down the area; while Mr. Kramatome, with every feature twisted and contorted out of its proper place, hopped about like a wounded sparrow, using such adjectives as, we are glad to say, cannot be found in any grammar published for instruction.

"Dear me," said Lionel, recovering from his surprise, and running quickly down the remainder of the stairs. "This is very annoying."

"Annoying——"

Again Mr. Kramatome in his agony forgot himself, and that his pupil was present.

"Take that beast away!" he roared, almost foaming at the mouth, "or I shall take his life. Where's Joblot? Curse that fellow, he is always out of the way when he is wanted!"

But it so happened that Mr. Joblot, now sufficiently recovered from his fiery ordeal to dispense with sticks, crutches, or other artificial means of support, was close at hand—in fact, peeping round the corner, and enjoying the scene immensely.

"Here I am, sir," he said, meekly coming forward in the most natural way possible. "What can I do, sir?"

"Drag that swilling brute downstairs, and put him under the pump," Mr. Kramatome gasped. "Wilful, this blackguard shall not remain in my house another hour."

"You will at least hear what he has to say in his defence," Lionel replied, putting Sam into Joblot's arms. "It is my belief that the poor fellow has been drugged."

"I wish they had given him an extra dose," Mr. Kramatome hissed venomously. "I could do it myself with the greatest of pleasure. Confound it, that is Doctor Wisenut's ring. Joblot, you villain, get downstairs with that fellow, or I'll murder you on the spot."

"He's hawful 'eavy," Joblot groaned, as he tugged at Sam.

"Wilful," Mr. Kramatome exclaimed in a kind of shriek, "if you have any respect left for me lend a hand here, or I shall go mad. D —— that knocker, there it is again."

Lionel, choking himself with suppressed laughter, opened the door leading to the kitchen, and shot Joblot and his burden down the stairs just as Doctor Wisenut's footman played the devil's tattoo with the knocker for the third time.

Mr. Kramatome answered the door himself, apologising for the delay as the doctor, a portly man, entered with a slow and ponderous step.

"My house is in confusion from top to bottom," Mr. Kramatome said, with tears of anguish in his eyes. "This poor unhappy boy ——"

"HIF HEVER I CEASE TO LOVE," in vocal capitals from the lower regions, and in Sam's voice.

"Dear me," said Doctor Wisenut, "what is that?"

"Oh, nothing," Mr. Kramatome gasped, hurriedly. "Will you be kind enough to walk upstairs, sir?"

"May I be biled in a lobster pot hif hever I cease for to love," in a series of horrible yells from the kitchen.

Lionel leaned against the balustrade, and the lamp shook in his hand until the flame leapt up and cracked the glass.

"The patient is downstairs, I presume," Doctor Wisenut said, hesitating. "Had I not better see him at once. We can talk the case over afterwards."

"No, no," Mr. Kramatome groaned, clutching at his scanty locks of hair, "the poor lad is upstairs."

"I'm a Chickaleary bloke with my one, two, and three," more melody from the kitchen, with Joblot joining in chorus.

"The fact is," Mr. Kramatome stammered, turning whiter than the ceiling, "one of our male servants has been out for a holiday and has just arrived home in a most disgraceful state. Pray, walk upstairs."

There followed the sounds of a struggle, the overturning of a table, the crash of fire irons, and then Sam's voice was heard.

"Bust all doctors," he roared, in a husky voice. "Come down 'ere, and bring old Kramatome with you, and I'll spile both o' you in two minutes."

Lionel gave Mr. Kramatome the lamp, and before Doctor Wisenut could make any remark with respect to the extraordinary and unexpected challenge he had received, he felt himself being half-dragged up the staircase, and found himself standing before Tommy's bedside, and Lionel, having bumped Sam's head against Joblot's to his heart's content, entered the room.

"I would not go too near him at first," Mr. Kramatome whispered to the medical man; "he might bite you."

Poor Tommy did not look much like biting, for, thoroughly exhausted and tired out, he was dozing peacefully, watched by Drummond and Vansittart.

"Have no fear for me," said Doctor Wisenut, "I know how to deal with these cases."

As he spoke he approached Tommy, and touched him lightly on the eyelids.

Tommy looked at him for a moment, and then in no amiable tone demanded what he wanted.

"There," said Doctor Wisenut, turning to the lookers-on in assumed triumph, "I told you that he would be glad to see me."

"Am I?" Tommy growled. "Perhaps you will tell me what business you have in my room, before I get out of bed and kick you out."

"You must be calm," said the medical man, backing towards the door. "Pray do not disturb yourself on my account, I shall leave you directly."

"The sooner the better," Tommy returned, in far from the sweetest of tones. "If you are not another of these confounded dreams, you are a confounded ass."

The doctor rubbed his forehead thoughtfully on the delivery of this doubtful compliment, and shook his head sadly at Mr. Kramatome.

"I am afraid this is a bad case," he murmured, drawing the examiner away from the bedside. "I must send him a sleeping draught, and while it is acting we must blister the back of his neck and bleed him a little."

Poor Tommy, if he could only have heard this prescription and what followed.

"Having done this," Doctor Wisenut went on, "it will be as well to apply mustard leaves to his chest and soles of his feet."

"But he will never keep them on," Mr. Kramatome cried, aghast.

"Oh yes, he will," Doctor Wisenut returned, in a confident tone, "for I will send my servant round with a straight-jacket, which will keep him still against his will."

"And this," said Mr. Kramatome, again clutching at his rumpled hair, "is the end of all my hopes of peace and quietude. I feel very much like wanting a straight-jacket myself. I suppose you keep a stock on hand in case of emergency."

"No, sir, I do not," the doctor replied warmly; "and you will pardon me for saying that such a remark is, considering the circumstances, a little out of place."

Mr. Kramatome found that he had gone a little too far, and tendered an apology, at which the portly doctor smiled, and frankly offered his hand.

"I suppose we may safely leave the patient with his present attendants?" Doctor Wisenut remarked.

"Certainly." Mr. Kramatome replied. "They are his eldest and best friends, and can do much more with him than you or I."

"He must not be left alone to-night," the doctor said.

"He shall not," Mr. Kramatome exclaimed emphatically, "even if—if—if I have to sit up with him myself."

"That is well," Doctor Wisenut observed; "and now, sir, I will write the prescription, and send the straight-jacket. If I am wanted in the night I will rise at any hour, for I tell you that I am interested in this case."

The door closed upon the worthy pair, and Tommy leapt up in bed.

"I say, Li," he cried, "what on earth is the meaning of this?"

"Hush," said Lionel, gravely. "You heard what the doctor said—you really must be calm."

"Oh, that be dashed," Tommy did not say dashed, but no matter. "I tell you what it is, you'll make me ill between you, and then you'll be sorry for it afterwards."

"My dear boy," Vansittart said, "who has looked after you for years?"

"Lionel and all three of you," Tommy replied, "and I don't believe that you would let those beggars hurt me. What did they talk about? What are they going to do to me?"

"Nothing," said Lionel; "if you will only keep a still tongue in your head and obey orders. Don't you see that Kramatome wants to get the doctor's evidence on his side in case of an accident?"

"Accident!" Tommy echoed, turning the colour of the pillow-case—"accident, I—I don't exactly understand you."

"Well, let me put it in another way," Lionel went on. "Presuming that your suspicions are right about his power of mesmerism."

"My suspicions!" Tommy exclaimed. "Who put that into my head?"

"There you go, flying into a rage as usual," Lionel said. "I have a good mind not to talk to you at all. Presuming that the suspicions are correct it might be convenient for him to call in a medical man at the inquest, in case he sent you into so deep a sleep that he could not rouse you."

"I think I will get up," Tommy said, thrusting one leg out of bed. "I would much rather walk about the streets than stay here."

"Then I leave you to your fate," Lionel said.

"So do I," Drummond exclaimed. "Tommy, I am ashamed of you. I gave you credit at least for a little gratitude, but I am deceived."

"And I," Vansittart chimed in. "I must follow the same course and abandon you."

"Here, I say," poor Tommy pleaded, "you don't mean to say that—dash it! if I have said anything to hurt your feelings I am sorry for it. Forgive me. Whom should I have confidence in if not in you?"

Genuine tears stood in Tommy's eyes, and, the hearts of his companions melting immediately, matters were soon made right.

Tommy was to trust himself to their wisdom to bring him out of his present dilemma, and how they accomplished it will be presently seen.

Tommy had again fallen into a gentle sleep when Mr. Kramatome opened the door and beckoned to Lionel.

Our hero went out, and saw that the examiner held in his hand a queer-looking thing like a flat saddle, furnished with a number of straps and buckles.

"How is the poor boy?" Mr. Kramatome asked.

"Not quite so well," Lionel whispered back. "He has been raving about you, and if you will take my advice you will keep out of the way."

"I will," Mr. Kramatome said nervously. "But it will tire you all out to watch him all night."

"I will venture to do it myself, on one condition," said Lionel.

"And that?"

"A very simple boon I ask, and soon granted," Lionel returned; "Sam will wake in the morning sore and repentant. Leave me to deal with him."

"Well," Mr. Kramatome said, after a moment's thought, "I consent, but I must have no more of these unseemly disturbances."

"I will take care that you do not from him." Lionel returned. "Oh, that is the sleeping draught. Thank you, I will administer it at once."

"Of course you will require some little refreshment," Mr. Kramatome said. "I will send Joblot up with a bottle of wine and some sandwiches."

Mr. Kramatome hurried away, delighted beyond measure that Lionel and his chums had volunteered to watch Tommy, and the lads were only too pleased to be left alone.

Joblot brought a bottle of rare old port, and a little persuasion from Lionel, backed up by a coin of the realm known as half-a-crown, induced him to produce a second; and then, if Mr. Kramatome could have seen the patient and his nurses, all ideas of madness would have vanished from his mind.

The straight jacket was thrown under the bed, the sleeping draught into the fireplace, and the blister and mustard leaves, having been applied for an instant, were doomed to a watery grave in the wash-basin.

"I call this jolly," Tommy said, sucking down about half a pint of port negus. "If this sort of thing could be managed twice a week I shouldn't mind."

"What if Kramatome should be peeping through the keyhole?" Drummond said, looking dubiously at the door.

"His eye would fly out of his head like a bullet," Vansittart returned. "If we have only the sense to keep quiet, I will bet an Englishman's word to a Russian's oath that he does not leave his room before daylight."

For their own sakes and Tommy's they were very quiet, and at last dropped off one by one to sleep till dawn, Tommy curled up snugly in his bed, and the others occupying the easy chairs

Lionel was a light sleeper, and jumped up on hearing an approaching footstep.

Thinking that Mr. Kramatome intended an early visit he roused Drummond and Vansittart, and pinching Tommy in a tender part caused that youth to howl most melodiously.

"Keep it up," Lionel said; "howl away, or he will come into the room and find out how we have sold him."

Tommy roared like a bull, but still the footsteps came on, and presently the door opened, admitting not Mr. Kramatome, but the delinquent Sam Scarecrow.

"Oh, it's you, is it?" Lionel cried. "Now, perhaps, you can give some explanation of your disgraceful behaviour last night."

"I sartinly laid sufficient in to scald a pig," Sam replied, pressing his hand to his forehead, "but there air times, sir, when it can't be helped. It was all along o' Long Jem and Bellers-to-Mend."

"What!" Lionel exclaimed, in delighted surprise, "have you seen those two dear fellows? Where did you find them, Sam? Where are they, and what are they doing?"

Sam answered all these questions satisfactorily, and it was forthwith arranged that all should go to Wandsworth that very night.

"But what about me?" Tommy groaned, dismally. "I shall be left behind with that old beast, Kramatome."

"Not if you behave yourself like a good boy," Lionel said, coaxingly, "I will manage all that."

And he was as good as his word.

A representation to Mr. Kramatome that Tommy would be the better for a little air and exercise obtained the required permission, and in high delight the three worthies, with Sam bringing up the rear, sallied out on their wild career.

It happened to be Easter time—a season when people are bent upon holiday making, spending money, and drinking huge quantities of beer, and Wandsworth-common presented a gay scene.

Gongs, big drums, trumpets, barrel organs, and the firing of guns, blended in one hideous sound, made the air rock. There were the flaring, glaring circus, with its acres of painted canvas, the legitimate drama, with a stage full of strutting actors all roaring that the play was about to begin, the modest peep-show, with its energetic proprietor blowing away at a wheezy instrument, a menagerie, and a waxwork establishment, outside of which a suspiciously red-faced woman declared that "Daniel in the lion's den, and Job sittin' with Patience on a monument" might be seen for one penny.

There were learned pigs, ponies that did everything but talk, fish from remote parts of the world, lambs with a surplus number of tails, sheep with more legs than they could possibly find use for, lions, tigers, elephants, and mischievous monkeys by the hundred.

As the madman in "Nicholas Nickleby" observed, all was gas and gaiters on the common, and all required for thorough enjoyment was plenty of money and a good temper to stand the crushing.

The show belonging to Mr. Bellers-to-Mend stood next to the menagerie, and, failing to find the stroller or his companion, Long Jem, within its canvas portals (the performance having not yet commenced) Lionel suggested that they should view the wild beasts, and the rest assenting they paid for admittance.

Tommy seemed to have an instinctive dread that something would happen to him, and hung back a little.

"There's a splendid monkey for you," Lionel exclaimed, pointing out one great shaggy brute disporting with a number of its companions. "I should not like to meet that beast alone and unarmed in a forest."

"That 'ere monkey is as quiet as a lamb," said a voice behind him, "and so air the rest."

Lionel turned and beheld a man, who by his style of dress and general appearance was evidently the proprietor of the exhibition.

"Is it, indeed?" Lionel replied, "now I should have thought just the contrary."

The man approached the cage and called the ape to him, and as it shook hands with him he looked round with a confident smile.

"You see, gentlemen," said the showman, "there ain't no wenom in his 'art. Would any of you—un-locking the barred gate—like to go inside and have a little chat with him?"

As the cage opened Tommy felt himself raised from the ground, and the next instant to his unspeakable terror he found his neck clasped in the embrace of two long hairy arms.

"Hurrah!" roared the crowd, and one gentleman roared immoderately, his wife and daughter joining in chorus.

"Here, I say," Tommy yelled, faint with fear, "dash it all, you know! This is no joke—let me out. Bust the monkey, he is showing his teeth at me!"

"There's a group," Drummond said, admiringly. "I declare that Tommy looks quite natural in his present situation."

"Beautiful!" Vansittart exclaimed. "It's a pity that Tommy was not brought up with a happy family. How do you feel, old boy?"

"Awful," Tommy groaned. "I say, this will be a swinging job for some of you if you don't let me out. The brute is showing its teeth."

"It's only his fun, sir," said the proprietor; "there never was sich a monkey to smile as that ere. Don't get angry with him, sir—he wants to kiss yer."

"Yah!" Tommy gasped, turning pale and sick at heart with terror and disgust. "I call this a beastly shame. Why don't some of you, you grinning idiots, get me out of this? Li, you ought to be ashamed of yourself, and as for you, Vansittart, you may be a lord, but, dash me, if I ever met such a heartless scoundrel! Oh, lor', what is the beast up to now?"

The playful creature, with one arm encircled round Tommy's neck, searched with the disengaged paw for what it is almost needless to say was not to be found on the plump youth, and at last, disappointed, the ape gave Tommy a pat in the face which sent him sprawling on his back.

This was too much for even Tommy to bear. In an instant he was on his feet, and lunging out with his left caught the monkey between the eyes, and sent it whack up against the bars, and Lionel, seeing that matters were coming to a crisis, seized the protruding tail, and held on with might and main.

But all was not yet over.

The ape had long arms, and before Tommy exactly knew what was the matter he felt both his ears clutched and pulled in a most painful style.

"Here, I say—oh, dash it!" yelled the unfortunate youth, kicking and striking out at random. "Oh, bust it! Mur-der!"

"He brought it on himself," the proprietor said, calmly, "and now I won't be answerable for the consequences. Who shoved him into the cage?"

"That is a matter of no moment now," Vansittart said. "He is in, and the question is how are we to get him out?"

"Ah," said the showman, "that's the question. I wouldn't face that ere monkey now he's riled for a fifty pun' note."

"Help, help, help!" Tommy screamed. "Oh, dash it! my head is coming off!"

"Something must be done," Vansittart said, in an alarmed tone. "Sam, get into the cage, and beat the brute off."

But Sam's practised eye had caught sight of a formidable weapon.

In the open stove, planted in the centre of the menagerie, were some hot irons, placed there in case of urgent need, and the lean youth, selecting the longest and hottest, charged through the crowd, scattering men, women, and children, like chaff before the wind.

"Here, I say," gasped a fat farmer, grasping the baggy part of his inexpressibles, and performing an agonised dance, "why don't you look where you are coming to? Darn it, I'm on fire!"

"Then, why didn't you get out of the way?" Sam roared, flashing the red-hot bar to the damage of a swell's hat. Clear away there; this is no time for argyment, but I shall be glad to settle with any genelman as ain't satisfied as soon as I've tickled this wampire."

So saying Sam leapt up, and, holding on by the bars, applied the hot iron to the avenging paws, which at once released Tommy's suffering face.

"Now then, Mister Thomas," Sam cried, holding the enraged monkey at bay, "now's your time. Make a rush, and jump clear of the ropes."

Tommy did the first, but neglected the second, for his ankles caught the ropes, and shooting out with the agility if not the grace of a trapeze performer, he knocked down half a dozen of the audience like dominoes, and finally pitched head foremost into the pit of the proprietor's stomach.

"Oh!" roared the unhappy man, curling up, and squirming like a worm on a fish-hook, "Oh, Lord! Oh, my 'art and innards! Take your head out o' my wind, will yer?"

Vansittart and Drummond hauled Tommy to his feet, and before the injured exhibitor of wild beasts could recover breath and strength Mr. Kramatome's pupils were in the open air, Sam covering the retreat with the bar of iron which was still smoking hot.

"Take me somewhere, and let me sit down," Tommy gasped, "I feel awful bad. I say, are my ears much longer?"

"They are very red," Lionel replied. "I never saw such a colour, and if you could only transfer it to your cheeks you would look beautiful."

"Confound you and your cheek," Tommy growled. "Here let me get away from you, or I shall get into another mess."

"There," Lionel exclaimed, "that is always the way with you. We bring you out to enjoy yourself, and this is what we get for our pains. No, Tommy, you shall not leave us, for I am your guardian, and I have promised Mr. Kramatome that I will not lose sight of you for an instant."

"You will lose sight of me altogether one of these times," Tommy said. "Why was I born to such misery? I am the most unlucky chap in the world."

"That's open to argeyment," observed a voice in the rear, and Lionel turning beheld Long Jem and Mr. Bellers-to-Mend smiling and rubbing their hands.

"My bo-o-o-o-oy," Mr. Bellers-to-Mend blubbered as he shook both Lionel's hands, "this is a meeting I've looked forrard to since the moment we parted. Jem, ain't he growed?"

"It's open to argeyment," Long Jem murmured, surveying our hero with a critical eye, "but I think he have."

"And handsome," Mr. Bellers-to-Mend cried, enthusiastically.

"That likewise is open to argeyment," Long Jem said, solemnly, "but, I must say that takin' Sam as a speciment o' hooman natur that Mister Wilful is a Kooanor dimond alongside of him."

"That's personal," Sam said, wrathfully; "you leave my looks alone and attend to your own wisage, which is hopen to improvement."

"Enough of this," Lionel said, laughing; "never mind our looks. Here is my hand, Jem, and I am heartily glad to see you."

"That ain't open to argeyment," Mr. Bellers-to-Mend said, gravely, "and if you say it is, Jem, I'll knock you down."

Long Jem shook hands with Lionel, Drummond, Vansittart, and Tommy, in a melancholy sort of way, Sam looking on with clasped hands and moist eyes.

"I think we had better adjourn," Lionel said, "for you see, Mr. Bellers-to-Mend, that the crowd is beginning to take an interest in these joyful proceedings. At what time do you give your first performance?"

"There is no hurry," the showman replied. "As you have come down we shall do only one turn to-night, and arterwards—here he bent down and whispered in Lionel's ear—I knows a house where we can have a quiet chat and a nip of the finest whiskey to be had for money."

"I am agreeable," Lionel said, "and I can speak for my friends, but we may as well commemorate this occasion with something now."

Mr. Bellers-to-Mend smiled, Long Jem smacked his lips, and led the way to a roadside inn, within which was a cosy parlour, hung with sporting pictures and portraits of renowned professionals.

The showmen and Sam were in favour of whiskey, the rest taking wine, save Tommy, who would take nothing stronger than ginger-beer.

"No," he said, in reply to many arguments, especially Long Jem's, "I will not touch anything else. The last two or three doses of whiskey made me dream so horribly that I am determined never to touch it again."

"It ain't for me to say anything agin your resolution," Long Jem said, solemnly, "but it's open to argeyment whether you ain't doin' wrong. I knowed a cove who took a hoath that he would touch nothin' stronger than soda-water, and well I remember his hawful fate."

"What became of him?" Tommy asked.

"Ah, what indeed?" Long Jem returned. "He went inter the bizness, so that he might have plenty of his favourite beverage, and one hot summer's day he got through four dozen, and was commencin' of the fifth when a horder come in from the country and he had to drive orf immediate. Just afore he starts he ses to his missus 'I feel that light and corky that I don't know what to do with myself, I seem to be walkin' on hair instead of on the hearth.' 'It's the gas,' she ses, 'and if you go on swiggin' the beastly stuff you'll blow yourself up one o' these times, and leave me and the children widders.' 'If I do,' ses he, smilin' like a marter, 'the teetotallers will raise a subscription for you and put up a monyment to my memory.'"

"What became of him?" Tommy demanded, deeply interested.

"I'm coming to it," Long Jem said, finishing his grog and mixing a second glass. "Well, this chap gets into his cart, and then the hextraordinary part o' the story begins. He could'nt keep his seat no how, and as he draws round a corner the wind caught him, and he floated bang out, and nearly busted hisself agin a lamp-post."

"Can this be true?" Tommy gasped, setting down his ginger-beer untouched.

"Oh! it is perfectly reasonable," Vansittart said, with his hand before his mouth. "You see the gas had not only driven the air out of him, but inflated his body like a balloon. Go on, Jem, I am anxious to hear the end. Lionel, lend me your pencil, I wish to make notes of this case."

"A p'liceman picked him up," Long Jem went on, after another long and earnest communion with his glass; "but he could not hold him, for this chap was for all the world like a injer rubber ball, and bounced about to that degree when he was touched that the hossifer gave went to a frightful 'owl and backed."

"I can scarcely believe my ears," Tommy gasped.

"And no wonder," Long Jem said; "and if I hadn't seen his remains I shouldn't ha' credit it myself.

"His remains!" Tommy exclaimed, pushing his glass off the table, and smashing it into a thousand pieces.

"Ah, remains—ribbons if you like, for that was all as was left of him," Long Jem went on, a little hazily, being now deeply interested in his fifth glass. "But let me tell the story in my own way. Well, this chap, arter a deal o' difficulty gets inter the cart agin, and drives orf, hodin' on to the dashboard like grim death with his feet, but he hadn't got far when a storm bust, and as he opened his mouth to breathe there come sich a flash o' lightning as no mortal eyes ever seed, and jest afore the thunder there was a crack like a squib explodin', and then the pony trotted on alone with the reins on his back."

"And the man!" Tommy almost groaned, "what of him?"

"Sponshaneous convulsions." Long Jem replied, speaking with difficulty, and glaring out of one eye. "The lightningsh had set fire to the gash, and he blew right bang up."

"I don't believe it," Tommy said. "It is most ridiculous."

"Ridicilish!" Long Jem exclaimed, in no amiable tone. "What d'yer mean? D'yer mean to call me a liar?"

Long Jem rose to his feet with mischief in his one opened eye (the other he kept shut for obvious reasons), but Sam shot him over a chair, and sat on his head to keep him quiet, in the same style as refractory fallen horses are sometimes treated in the street.

"Let me ger up," Long Jem roared, in muffled tones.

"Not until you begs the company's parding." Sam said, jamming his elbows into Jem's ribs. "If you ain't quiet I'll persuade yer with a hinstrument known as a pocketknife."

"I beg everybodish pardons," Long Jem growled. "You're a nice fren' to sit on a chap's nut, as aches fit to split."

"And sarve you right," Sam said, releasing his captive and picking him up à la pantaloon. "Now then, jest you drop yer carcase inter that 'ere chair, and keep it quiet or else I shall have to treat you as my father did the walnut."

"Of course it's open to argeyment what he did," Long Jem said, groping about the table in an uncertain manner for his glass. "This is what I call —hic—conwiwial. Lesh have shome more whiskey."

"My father," replied Sam. "squeezed that 'ere walnut behind the door, and that's what I'll do with you, but—as Jem made a frantic grab at the bottle—I'm dashed if you have another drop tonight. Do you want to waller in your gore, you himage."

"I could waller in anythink." Long Jem said, with perfect truth. "My lud, I appealsh to you as a nobbleman and a genelman, with—hic— a 'art in your buzzum, am I drunksh?"

"Certainly not," Vansittart said, "but I think you have had sufficient until after the performance."

"Hear, hear, oncore!" Bellers-to-Mend, who was also slightly elevated, roared. Rool Brityannyer!"

"I think we had better be going," Lionel said, addressing the showman. "It is nearly nine o'clock, and unless we are sharp most of the people will have gone home."

"But look at Jem," Bellers-to-Mend cried, huskily. "I'll ax you as a uninterested party if he looks like workin' the greatest wonder of the age?"

"I'm all ri'," Jem replied. "You leave me alone. I knows what I'm a doin' of. Sam, your harm. For fo-o-rty years, my ole fren Sam, we climbed the—ch, d——"

"Wot now?" Sam roared, assisting Jem to his feet. "There never was sich a chap to tumble about."

"I've sot on some broken glass," Jem gasped.

"So you have," said Sam, as he proceeded to pick out the pieces. "Mister Thomas, you really must be more careful not to chuck tumblers about. This ere's a job for a sperienced dentist."

"Oh cuss it!" Long Jem groaned, as great tears of anguish ran in torrents from his eyes. "Mind how you pull 'em out, Sam."

"I'm as gentle as a monthly nuss," Sam replied. "How do you think I can get at the pieces if you wriggle in that manner?"

"I can't help it," Long Jem groaned, writhing like a tortured eel; "the hagony is summat hawful!"

The work was at last accomplished, and the party set out for the common, Sam and Bellers-to-Mend supporting Long Jem, who, under the influence of unlimited whiskey and sharp pangs of pain, staggered about, doubled up, and leapt into the air at frequent intervals.

Lionel and his friends followed up, keeping a respectful distance, for at times Mr. Bellers evinced a tendency to embrace them all round, especially whenever our hero made reference to old times.

"If you don't walk like a Christian," Sam suddenly exclaimed, seizing Long Jem by the throat, "I'll let you go your own way, and then you'll break your neck to a certainty."

"That's open to argyment." Long Jem replied, gloomily; "but I don't care if I do."

"Here's the show," murmured Bellers-to-Mend. "Put him inside, Sam, but mind you don't fall over the table, or you'll upset the whole arrangements."

Remarking that he would be careful to avoid the collision, Sam ran Long Jem into the tent, and tripping him up fell on the top of him.

"There, now you are all right," Sam said "and I'm sure you ought to feel very grateful to me."

"I ham," Long Jem growled, crawling from under Sam on all fours; "but it's open to argyment that you might ha' been a little less wicious."

"Bust your argyments!" Bellers-to-Mend roared. "Get behind the curtain and we'll begin at once. There are hundreds o' people waiting to come in."

"I'm all ri'," Long Jem cried, flourishing his arms. "Leremin, I'll astonish 'em."

Bellers-to-Mend did not hear this last remark. He was busily engaged in showing his visitors the decapitated head, and the principles on which it was made to talk, drink, smoke, laugh, show its teeth, and open and shut its eyes.

The head, made of a pliable composition, stood upon what looked like an ordinary kitchen table, the legs of which were screwed to the ground, and hollow. A tube inside the head passed down one of these fraudulent legs, and underground led to a false partition in the tent, behind which, of course, Long Jem was hidden, and astonished and horrified crowded audiences by speaking and breathing up the tube.

The motions and contortions of features were done by leaders communicating with the back of the tent in precisely the same style as the tube, and even as Tommy gazed upon the ghastly head it winked, and for the moment sent a queer sensation running through him.

"Now, gentlemen." said Bellers-to-Mend, "there is no time to lose. Take your seats."

As Bellers-to-Mend spoke he seized a huge drumstick, and hammered manfully at a gong, the sound of which brought a numerous concourse of people round the show, and it was soon full.

"This, ladies and gentlemen," said Bellers-to-Mend, mounting a chair, and pointing at the head in a solemn manner, "is the eighth wonder of the world. The head will smoke, drink, laugh, cry, and talk at the word of command."

"Can it sing?" a stout old gentleman asked.

"Can't it, just?" was the showman's reply. "Why,

THE VOICE OF IRISH MIKE, AS HE GREETED HIS OLD FRIEND, SEEMED TO TOMMY LIKE SOME HALF-REMEMBERED DREAM OF LONG AGO.

No. 36.

bless your 'art, some of the very best tanners as the world can produce have gone mad with henvy."

"Then," said the old gentleman, "I should like to hear a song."

"Not for a brown," the head observed, in a husky voice. "Five bub's the figger. Down with the dust, and name yer song."

"Dear me!" said the corpulent party, starting, and pushing up his spectacles, "this is very extraordinary. The natural voice is not very mellow."

"Meller!" growled the head; "wot d'yer mean by that? Get out, you bloated ole willin."

"I think, sir," Bellers-to-Mend said, a little nervously, "that you had better let me commence the performance in the usual way. You really mustn't put the head out of temper, or I cannot be answerable for the consequences."

"Go ahead, Bellers!" roared the head, and the old gentleman, leaping backwards, sent Tommy Codlings flying against Sam Scarecrow with such force that the long youth spun round like a teetotum.

"Bust it!" Sam growled, feeling his waistcoat tenderly. "O' course you must run agin somebody."

"I!" Tommy gasped, clasping his hands to the back of his head, which had come in violent contact with Sam's teeth. "It was not my fault."

"Sam!" Lionel called out.

"Yes, sir?"

"Have the goodness not to make so much noise."

"It's a wonder," Sam groaned, under his breath, that I'm able to speak at all. "There never was sich a one as Mister Codlings to chuck hisself about."

Mr. Bellers-to-Mend maintained a dignified attitude until silence was restored, and then, with a savage glare at the old gentleman, he resumed.

"What is your name?" he asked, turning to the head.

"That's my bizness," was the astonishing reply. "Give us summat to drink, or I don't answer another question."

"He is very playful to-night," Mr. Bellers-to-Mend said, turning a little pale. "Come now, tell the ladies and gentlemen what your name is, and where you came from."

Instead of a reply there came a peculiar sound from the other end of the tent, closely resembling the snore of a human being.

"Oh, dash it!" Bellers-to-Mend growled. "This is a pretty state o' things. Jem's gone to sleep, and I'm done like a dinner."

"I knowed you'd do it," he cried, turning furiously on the old gentleman. "Why couldn't yer wait until you were axed to speak. Take your penny you meddlin' old fool, and get out o' this tent."

"Hear, hear—ongcore!" Sam roared. "Turn him out."

"I dare you to touch me!" the stout one roared, flourishing an enormous umbrella. "You are a set of ruffianly vagabonds as—oh!"

This last ejaculation was caused by Bellers-to-Mend literally falling upon him in his wrath, and a yell of the first magnitude followed when the showman, almost beside himself with fury dealt his patron a violent blow on the nose with the drum stick.

"You villain!" gasped the afflicted one, as he stemmed a ruby torrent with his handkerchief. "You shall shuffer for this. If there is a law in the land I'll put it in force, and——"

"Here, come out of this," Bellers-to-Mend cried, in a kind of frantic shriek. "Now then, will you get out afore I does you a mischief?"

The old gentleman did get out, and performing a frenzied dance round the tent happened to kick the identical spot where Long Jem had fallen down, and was sleeping peacefully.

The stout party wore heavy boots, and the toe of one struck Long Jem on the head, and in an instant the acrobat was on his feet

"Who did that?" he yelled, rushing out from behind the screen. "Oh lor'! I'll swear it were a wile conspiracy agin my life."

"Hold your tongue, you hass and borned hidiot!" Bellers-to-Mend gasped in a whisper, barring the way. "Go back, and behave like a man. Don't you know where you are?"

"It ain't no fault o' mine if I don't," Long Jem growled. "Look at my 'ed."

"There sartainly air a bump on it," Bellers-to-Mend replied, as if he had made an important discovery.

"It's open to argyment who did it, but I'll soon find out," Long Jem howled, making a dash at the door.

"No, you don't," Bellers-to-Mend cried, catching Long Jem in his arms; "you don't move out o' this 'ere place if I knows it."

"And 'ere's another as backs up that 'ere resolootion," Sam said, moistening the palms of his hands. "Don't let him go, Bellers, or he'll pitch inter a p'liceman and get a month."

"Bellers," Long Jem said, with emotion almost amounting to tears, "I didn't think it of you. There air other heyes on us, and I knows my place, but if you don't let me go it will be Bellers-to-Mend in real earnest."

"I don't care," cried the perspiring showman. "Keep still, you heel, can't you?"

"No, and I won't," Long Jem roared, twisting himself about like a fresh-caught conger. "I warns you once."

"I don't care," Bellers-to-Mend roared. "I've got you, and I means to keep you. Oh Lord, this is awful. Clear the tent, young gentlemen."

Lionel, Vansittart, and Drummond hastened to comply with this very proper request, but the people were determined to see the fun out.

"Go it, long 'un," shouted a man of the costermonger style. "Give 'un the grip—that's the style. Hooray."

The next instant Vansittart was down on the fellow, and, having treated him to a gratuitous pyrotechnic display, shot him out into the open air, just as Long Jem and Bellers-to-Mend fell with a crash on the table.

The whole thing came down with a run, for, as we have observed, the legs were hollow and far from strong. The head was smashed to a pulp, and that belonging to Bellers-to-Mend seemed in a fair way of sharing the same fate, when the valiant Sam rushed upon Long Jem, and dragged him out of further mischief.

"He's mad drunk," Sam exclaimed, sitting on the acrobat's chest and checking a flow of profanity with a handful of sawdust. "I ain't hopen to swear as this won't end in spontanyeous combustedness. I say, somebody tie his feet, he's kicking like forty."

"Get orf my shest," Long Jem said, speaking with much difficulty through the sawdust. "Sham, your life won't be worth a nutshell arter this houtrage."

"All right, Jem," Sam replied, cheerfully, "I don't know of anybody as 'ud veep much for me, unless it's the girl as I intends to take for veal or for voe. Keep still, you warmint."

"What is to be done?" Vansittart said, turning to Lionel. "I think this has gone far enough."

"I am also of the same opinion," said Lionel, who was supporting Mr. Bellers-to-Mend. "Charlie, find a piece of cord, and tie his wrists and ankles."

"Mur—der," Long Jem roared, as Tommy added his weight to Sam's. "Oh! my ribs; they're bustin'."

"And think yerself lucky that it ain't no wus," Sam said, picking out about a quarter of a pound of damp saw-dust which Long Jem had discharged into his eyes." "Why, I'm ashamed o' you you young spider-legged orphan-spring of a wampire. That's right, Mister Drummond, make the knot firm."

"You're a tyin' up the flesh as well," Long Jem yelled, as great tears of anguish ran down his cheeks. "Mur-der—oh! my."

Charlie's task was soon accomplished, and the refractory acrobat was soon stowed away in a corner with a handkerchief tied round his mouth to keep him quiet.

"There," said Bellers-to-Mend, mopping his heated face, "it's all over now; and although it's 'ard to give the 'and when the 'art is riled, I'm ekal to the occasion, and if Long Jem will say that he's sorry, I'm hopen to forget and forgive heverythink."

"You have shown a very proper spirit," Vansittart said, patting the showman on the back; "and I am sure Jem has sufficiently recovered his senses to recognise the fact."

Long Jem rolled his eyes up till the whites were only visible, and gave vent to a deep-drawn groan of repentance.

"Will you be quiet if I untie your hands?" Charlie demanded.

Long Jem nodded his head and groaned again.

"Very well," said Charlie, taking out his pocket-knife; "but mind, no tricks, or it will be the worse for you."

"Stop a minute," Bellers-to-Mend said, holding up his hand. "I can hear somebody movin' about outside."

"See who it is, Tommy," Lionel said.

Tommy put his head outside the tent, and immediately saw great jagged flames rushing athwart the sky; and as a fearful numbing sensation filled his head, he recognised the unpleasant fact that his plump visage had got in the way of somebody's knuckles. "Oh! here, I say," he gasped, staggering back into the tent. "Look at this."

"Wot have you been and gone and done to yerself, sir?" Sam Scarecrow asked. "W'y, lor', there's a lump! Your nose is swellin' hawful."

"You need not tell me that," Tommy gasped, savagely. "I didn't do it myself, you idiot. It was some ferocious blackguard outside."

"Our costermonger friend, perhaps?" Vansittart said.

"Or the stout ole gent," Bellers-to-Mend suggested. "There was wenom in his ogles when I pitched him out."

"I don't know who it was," Tommy said; "but he had an awfully hard fist. I say, Li, are my eyes turning black?"

"Ripe sloes might turn red with shame," Lionel replied. "I say, old boy, you must apply the old remedy."

"What is that?"

"A piece of beefsteak," Lionel said. "But, first of all, let us see who this pugnacious prowler is."

Leaving Long Jem in the corner, they went out in a body, Tommy holding his nose, and groaning dismally; but there was nobody answering the description of the costermonger or the infuriated old gentleman about.

"It's just my luck," Tommy groaned. "If anybody hits me I never get a second shy at him, and, if I do, I get the worst of it."

"Never mind, old fellow," Charlie said, patting his fat friend on the back; "your turn will come some day, never fear. Now I will liberate Jem, who must be choking with repentance by this time. A parting glass, and then home."

"Agreed," said the others.

CHAPTER XXVIII.

MORE DREAMS — TOMMY PAYS MR. KRAMATOME ANOTHER VISIT—AWAY, AWAY, ANYWHERE BUT THERE!—A SENSATION—LIONEL IS ALARMED—OUT OF THE FRYING-PAN INTO THE FIRE—TOMMY MEETS HIS WIFE AGAIN—IRISH MIKE APPEARS ON THE SCENE—TOMMY UNDERGOES ALL THE HORRORS OF AN ANCIENT MODE OF EXECUTION.

WHEN Tommy Codlings woke up the next morning he knew it was late by the sun's rays, which were streaming into his room, and by the noise in the street.

"Why," he muttered, sitting up in bed, and yawning, "it must be nearly eleven o'clock. Oh, dear me! how my head aches; and yet I did not drink much. Dear me, what a size my nose is! Ah! I remember now. What a frightful prop it was, to be sure. If I ever go out with those fellows again, may I—— Halloo, who's that?"

It was Mr. Kramatome.

He stood on the other side of the door, holding the handle firmly in case of need, and inquired in a quivering voice how Tommy was.

"Oh, I'm all right," the fat youth replied, sniffing suspiciously. "What is the time, sir?"

"Half-past ten."

"Then I will get up," Tommy said.

"Are you there, Mr. Wilful?" Mr. Kramatome asked.

"There is nobody here but myself," Tommy replied. "You know as well as I do that this is not Wilful's bedroom."

Mr. Kramatome closed the door with a bang, and Tommy uttered an exclamation of surprise as he heard the key revolve in the lock.

"Now what is the meaning of this?" Tommy said aloud, as he jumped out of bed, with a force that made the window panes rattle. "I wonder what his little game is now?"

Mr. Kramatome's little game was to get downstairs as quickly as possible—a feat which he performed in an incredibly short space of time.

"Poor fellow," he muttered. "I thought Wilful was with him. I had a misgiving that something would happen to him, but I had no idea that he was so bad as to knock himself about."

He nearly fell over Lionel, who was coming in the opposite direction.

"Wilful," he said, holding up his hands; "I am surprised that you should have left Codlings alone."

"He is perfectly safe," Lionel said; "he was sleeping peacefully when I left him."

"But he is very much awake now," Mr. Kramatome replied. "Thinking that you were there I went up to his room, and he spoke to me like a bear with a sore head."

"I will go to him at once," Lionel said. "Should I ring please ask Lord Vansittart and Drummond to step up to me."

"I will," said Mr. Kramatome, and hurried away.

"There will be some fun before long," Lionel said, laughing, as he bounded up the stairs. "I wonder what Tommy will say when I tell him. Ha, ha, ha! This is almost as good as the larks we used to have at old Styngy's."

Tommy was kicking and thumping viciously at the door when Lionel came up.

"What now?" our hero exclaimed. "What on earth are you making that noise for?"

"Open the door, or I'll smash the panels," Tommy roared, "and if I can't do that I'll jump out of the window."

"Then jump clear of the spikes," said Lionel. "There is an awful row of them below. Mr. Kramatome has had them sharpened, and swears that he will impale the next posse of organ-grinders."

"It's my belief that he ought to be impaled himself," Tommy growled. "I wish he had been in Bulgaria a year ago."

"Upon my soul, your nature is changing from the amiable to the spiteful," Lionel said, as he opened the door.

"And isn't it enough to change anything?" Tommy said. "Look here, Li. Not five minutes ago old Kramatome came up here to ask how I was. When he found that I was alone he slammed and locked the door, and bolted himself."

"And no wonder," Lionel said, "after last night's performance. Put on your things, and come downstairs."

"What do you mean by last night's performance?" Tommy demanded, a little wrathfully. "I didn't black my own eyes, and as for Long Jem, I ——"

"A few days ago," Lionel mused aloud, "it was Irish Mike, and now it is Long Jem. What Long Jem are you talking about?"

"Why, that fellow who made such a fool of himself last night."

"I know somebody who made a fool of himself last night," Lionel said, sternly, as he looked at Tommy, "but his name is not Long Jem."

"Then it is his nickname."

"No, it is not."

"Well, dash it all, what is it?" Tommy roared.

"His name," Lionel said, as grave as a judge passing the extreme sentence of the law, "is Thomas Codlings, a young gentleman who, I regret to say, sometimes forgets himself. Tommy, let this be a warning to you, and never interfere with another fellow's sweetheart again."

"What are you talking about?" Tommy gasped, sinking into a chair. "I interfere with another fellow's gal. I—why, confound it, do you take me for an ass?"

"It is a matter of no moment what I think, or what I take you for just now," Lionel said; "but I repeat that, if you cannot go out without being the cause of so many disturbances, you had better stay at home, or go out alone."

"Li," Tommy cried, seizing our hero's arm; "don't humbug me, old boy. I can't bear it. Now, look here, about this Long Jem."

"I never knew but one man going by that name," Lionel replied, "and he was an acrobat."

"The self-same party," Tommy said.

"Ah! but that was years ago. He may be dead now for all I know," Lionel replied.

"Why, hang it, you were with him last night."

"I!" Lionel said laughing; "well, I like that. Who is humbugging now?"

"Do you mean to say," Tommy began, when Lionel took him up.

"I mean to say," our hero said, "that if you have got into your head that you saw Long Jem last night, you must have dreamt it—that's all."

Tommy's face was very pale as he opened his mouth, but no words came from it, for at that moment Sam Scarecrow opened the door, and thrust his head and shoulders into the room.

"How is Mister Codlings this morning?" Sam asked politely.

"You cut it," Tommy said, wrathfully. "Don't you see that I am conversing with your master?"

"I have heyes to see, and years to 'ear, sir," Sam replied, reproachfully; "and I begs your parding, but I didn't think as 'ow you would have done it."

"Done what?" Tommy roared, fairly beside himself.

"Wy, round on him as done you a sarvice," Sam retorted a little hotly. "Didn't I carry you hupstairs, and put you bed like a babby. Didn't I pitch inter that chap as fell foul on you when you wos the party as wos really to blame."

"This is another mystery," Tommy said, glaring stupidly, first at Lionel and then at Sam. "I cannot remember anything about it. I remember a fellow fetching me a prop at Wandsworth."

"You mean Hoxford-street," Sam said.

"I tell you it was at Wandsworth!" Tommy roared.

"And I ses as 'ow the fight took place in Hoxford-street," Sam retorted unblushingly, "jest agin the Circus. Why, lor' sir, yer must reckellect 'ow yer bullied the p'liceman when he wanted to put yer inter a cab."

"I don't believe it, Tommy gasped. " I can't, and I won't."

"What! is Tommy able to get up?" exclaimed the cheery voice of Lord Vansittart. "Aha! you got more than you expected last night, Codlings. That fellow had a long arm, and knew how to use it."

"I am getting more than I expected this morning," Tommy murmured, looking from one to the other in bewilderment. "What the deuce is the meaning of it? Dash it all! you fellows must be having a lark with me."

"That is very likely," Vansittart said, as he strode across the room, followed by Tommy. "I think you have been having a lark with us. By the way you must have spent a lump of money last night. The way you feed those waiters at the Holborn Restaurant was a sight once seen never to be forgotten."

"This is too much," Tommy gasped; "but now, I can settle that, come now. I had two £5 notes, a sovereign, and some loose change, and now—dash it all! there's nothing but a few coppers in my pockets."

"That's a clincher," Charlie Drummond said. "I did my best to prevent you from spending your money, but you would do it."

"I would do it, would I?" Tommy muttered, casting down his eyes. "So I didn't go to Wandsworth, I didn't see Long Jem, but got tight in Oxford-street, made a fool of myself, bullied a policeman, and flung my money about amongst a lot of sponging waiters. Very good. Is there anything that you have omitted out of last night's programme?"

A sad and determined look came over his face as he spoke, and could Lionel have but known its meaning he would have undeceived his jovial friends, and freely have given fifty pounds to have been able to do so.

In those few brief moments Tommy Codlings had made up his mind to run away.

He began to look upon himself as a nuisance to his friends, and inwardly vowed to trouble them no longer. If, he argued, that which they stated was true, he was the most extraordinary being on the face of the earth—one who never lived to behold realities, but passed his life in a series of dreams.

"All right, dear boys," he said cheerfully, and even smiling. "I expect this is one of my silly dreams. I know it must be so, because I know Li too well to think that he would let me run about with the idea that I was cranky, unless it was a fact."

Lionel's heart smote him as Tommy spoke, and he looked at Vansittart, and shrugged his shoulders, as much as to say, "You hear that, Van? Behold the picture of innocence. Poor old Tommy!"

"So you are really resigned at last?" said Charlie Drummond. "Well, I agree with you, Tommy; for, look here, why should a man bother himself about what he cannot help? Dreams are—— "

"I shall never have another," Tommy said. "Now, you fellows, get out, and let me dress. I shall be down in a few minutes."

"I can't make Tommy out this morning," Lionel whispered to Vansittart as they ran down the staircase. "I never saw him take it so cool before."

"Nor I," Vansittart returned. "Do you know, I believe that Tommy laughs in his sleeve at us. Falstaff, you know, told awful crammers to amuse Prince Henry; and who can say but that Tommy may be playing a capital part in pretending to take in these dreams?"

"If it is acting," said Charlie, "he could make his fortune on the stage any day. I never saw anything more real in all my life."

Mr. Kramatome was waiting for them at the bottom of the stairs.

"Well," said he, "how is our young friend this morning?"

"Much better," Lionel replied. "Indeed, I may say quite well."

"Are you sure?"

"I am quite sure, sir," Lionel said, "provided he is treated as before, and no mention is made of the past."

"This is very good news," said Mr. Kramatome, rubbing his hands gleefully, "and I cannot thank you too heartily."

"Don't mention it, sir," Lionel replied. "We were naturally anxious to see our friend well again. I think too many hours over his books turned his head."

"It may be," Mr. Kramatome said, thoughtfully; "and yet Codlings is not inclined to study even in his most serious moments."

The conversation here ceased on account of the sudden appearance of Tommy Codlings.

"Good m-morning," said Mr. Kramatome over Vansittart's shoulder.

"I should think it was almost afternoon," Tommy replied; "but I suppose I can have some breakfast?"

"Certainly," Mr. Kramatome said; "it has been kept nice and hot for you."

"Everything is made hot for me it seems," Tommy grumbled, as he sat down. "Ah! now I wonder what Li would say if he knew what was in my mind? But it is the best thing I can do. I begin to hate myself and everybody."

Poor Tommy had not much appetite, and pushing his plate away he went upstairs, and unlocking a drawer took what little ready money he had from a cash-box, and stowed it away carefully in his pockets.

"There will be enough to keep me alive until I can get something to do," he said. "I'll emigrate, and discover the source of the Nile, or do something big. Dash me if I don't!"

Tommy shook his head at himself in a very determined manner, and then, changing his shoes for a thick pair of boots, he crept downstairs as quietly as possible.

"I don't see why I should sneak out of the house," he muttered, stopping before Mr. Kramatome's study. "I may as well show myself, or perhaps one of the servants may prig the spoons, and swear I took them."

"Come in," Mr. Kramatome said, in answer to Tommy's knock, but looked very much inclined to say "get out" when he saw who his visitor was.

"I am going for a little walk," Tommy said, calmly. "It is a fine morning, and I think the air will do me good."

"Of course you will please yourself," Mr. Kramatome replied. "But remember you are far from strong, Codlings. Do not exert yourself."

"Thank you, I can take care of myself," Tommy said. "I want to write a line to Wilful. Will you oblige me with a sheet of paper and an envelope?"

"Shall I send for him?" Mr. Kramatome asked, looking suspiciously at Tommy.

"No," the fat youth said; "what I have to say is not of much consequence—therefore I do not wish to disturb him."

"Very good," said Mr. Kramatome, opening a handsome cabinet. "Sit down, Codlings, and help yourself."

The pen trembled in Tommy's hand as he wrote, and there were tears in his eyes as he flourished his name at the bottom of a short note; but he was firm again when he handed it over to Mr. Kramatome.

"And now, sir," said Tommy, putting out his hand, "I wish you a very good morning."

"He is worse, not better," Mr. Kramatome groaned, as he took the proffered hand. "What on earth does all this mean?"

Tommy overheard the last words, and, with the blood rushing into his cheeks, said—

"It means that I intend putting myself out of the reach of the infernal power you have exercised over me," he said, bringing his hand down on the table with a bang. "Ah, you may stare, Mr. Kramatome, for you know what I am saying is the truth.

Why couldn't you pick on a fellow with stronger nerves?"

"Oh Lord!" Mr. Kramatome gasped. "Dear me, this is very dreadful, and I am alone with him. Be calm, Codlings, I beg of you to be calm for—for my sake."

"Calm!" Tommy echoed. "I wonder that I keep my temper so well as I do. Some fellows would have shot you for less."

Mr. Kramatome gave a kind of spasmodic skip towards the bell-rope, but Tommy was down on him ere he could touch it.

"No, you don't," Tommy said, smiling grimly; "I have something to say, and I mean to say it—so you may as well sit down and listen comfortably."

"I will humour him," Mr. Kramatome thought, feeling every ounce of flesh upon his frame crawling.

"That's right," said Tommy, putting his back against the door. "Now, Mr. Kramatome, I ask you as a man and a gentleman, what you mean by it?"

"Mean by what?" Mr. Kramatome responded, faintly.

"Mean by what?" Tommy said, trying to sneer, but failing signally in the attempt. "Just as if you didn't know without my telling you."

"Oh, ah, of course," Mr. Kramatome said, doing his best to smile. "Ah, I think you mentioned it before. Well, you see, Codlings, you may not be aware of it, but mesmerism is a boon to thousands, and so I thought ——"

"That you would try it on me," Tommy interrupted. "Thank you for the information. Now, do you know what I am going to do?"

"Nothing rash I hope," Mr. Kramatome said, placing a hand as if by accident on a heavy ruler. "Remember, Codlings, if I have done anything it has been for your good."

"That be dashed," Tommy retorted, wrathfully. "Well, now, listen to this. I am going straight from here to a magistrate to summon you for a diabolical conspiracy. So once more I say good morning."

Tommy bounced out of the room, and Mr. Kramatome rushed to the bell-rope.

In a few seconds Lionel, Vansittart, and Charlie Drummond burst into the room, and found Mr. Kramatome still hard at work at the bell-rope.

"What in the name of goodness is the matter?" Lionel demanded. "Is the house on fire, or what?"

"The house is not on fire," Mr. Kramatome shrieked. "Codlings is the matter. That wretched youth is as mad as a March hare, and must be put under proper control at once."

"What has he done? Where is he?"

"Gone to a magistrate with some cock-and-bull story about me," Mr. Kramatome said, clutching at his scanty stock of hair. "He left a note for you. Perhaps that will throw some light on the matter."

Lionel burst the envelope, and started violently as his eyes fell on Tommy's handwriting.

"Van, Charlie," he cried, "listen to this. Confound it, what fools we have been! Tommy has bolted."

"Bolted!" Vansittart and Charlie cried in chorus.

"Aye," Lionel replied, turning pale. "Hear what he says. 'My dear Li,—When you get this I shall be away, and, unless by some strange accident, we shall never meet again. You don't know how it pains me to write these words, but as I am no use to anybody, and a misery to myself, I shall be better out of the way. Think of me kindly, and tell Van and Charlie to do the same. For my own part I shall never cease to think of you, and pray for your welfare with all my heart. Yours faithfully —Tommy.'"

"Great heavens!" Charlie said, sitting down with startling suddenness, "I did not think it would ever come to this."

Lord Vansittart said nothing, but bit his nails uneasily. Mr. Kramatome gasped like a fish out of

...... and Lionel stood like a statue staring at the fatal missive.

It slipped from his fingers, and as it fell fluttering to the floor he turned and left the room.

"Sam," he shouted, "come here—I want you directly."

"I'm a comin', sir," roared that faithful servant from the lower regions, and he ran up the stairs, wondering a little what his master could want at such an early hour in the day.

"Fetch my hat and coat."

"Yes, sir," Sam said, and then, with an anxious glance at Lionel's face—"ain't you well, sir?"

"I am very well," Lionel replied. "Ask no questions, but do as I tell you."

"There's summut hup," Sam said, as he departed. "I never seed master look like that 'ere afore. P'raps he and Kramatome have had a row, and the ole gentleman is a welterin' in his gore."

"Why don't you make haste, Sam?" Lionel cried, stamping his foot impatiently.

"Oh, bust it," Sam growled, "he's in a hawful temper. I'm a comin', sir."

Lionel had his hat and coat on when Vansittart and Drummond came out of Mr. Kramatome's room.

"Hallo, Li," said Vansittart, "you did not tell us that you were going out."

"Do you think I could stay here and Tommy away?" he said, with something very much like a tear running down his cheek. "Van, you can do as you like, of course, but I will not rest until I have found the dear boy again."

"I am with you," said Vansittart.

"And I," said Charlie. "Hang it, I feel as if I could knock my head against a wall."

"Never mind your own feelings—think of Tommy's," Lionel returned. "Now, Sam, brush yourself up, and look sharp about it, for I want you to come with me."

"I should like to ax one question," Sam said, hesitating.

"If you open your mouth to me again I will kick you downstairs," Lionel said. "Do you hear me?"

"Oh, I hear you, sir," Sam replied, and wisely fled, knowing that Lionel had a habit of keeping his word.

Mr. Kramatome offered no objection to our hero and his friends going in search of Tommy—indeed had he done so it would have been all the same, and like a sensible man he said nothing, beyond wishing the expedition all possible success.

Leaving them for a short time it is only right we should follow the footsteps of the unfortunate Tommy, who had left two good miles between himself and Mr. Kramatome's residence.

Shunning the wide and busy thoroughfares he dived down into a maze of narrow streets, smelling of horses, decayed vegetation, and fried fish.

He knew no more where he was than the man in the moon, and cared about as much, but suddenly he came to a full stop, and threw up his arms, as an expression of alarm sprang to his lips.

Tommy had good occasion for affright and astonishment, and damp and as limp as a wet rag he reeled against a wall, and stared at a tall gaunt woman and three of her "orphansprings," as Sam Scarecrow would have called the youngsters.

It was like a dreadful nightmare, when the legs seem as heavy as lead, the head as light as froth, and the hands forty times their natural size.

"Oh, dash it," Tommy gasped, turning as cold as one of Gatti's ices, "this must be another of my confounded dreams. Oh, lor', she is coming this way, and knows me."

The heroine of the tub, or in other words the washerwoman, recognised Tommy Codlings in an instant, and, having slapped the heads of her youngsters all round, smiled, and gave one of those peculiar corkscrew wriggles for which ladies of her class are so justly famed.

Tommy frowned as he kicked out spasmodically,

and the sudden motion brought back the power of his limbs.

He turned, and ran in a style he deemed himself quite incapable of, and this was the very worst thing he could do, for had he kept his ground the fair getter up of linen would have passed him with a curtsey, or at the worst lightened his pockets of a few shillings, but the moment Tommy's limbs were set in motion she gave chase, screaming to her cherished bairns to keep up, under a penalty of everlasting slappings.

It was truly a noble and exhilarating sight to see Tommy bounding along like some animated india-rubber ball, never stopping even for an instant to fetch his breath, but hatless, his hair flying in the wind, and his elbows pressed tight to his sides after the most approved professional style, he cleared the ground and his way of a good many people.

The first to come to grief was a blind beggar, who fell headlong into a confectioner's shop, and groped his way savagely amongst plates full of tarts, then a slim gentleman sat on a barrow full of cabbages, and a scissors' grinder found himself so mixed up with his machine that it was a mercy he did not grind himself so as to need the services of an undertaker.

Tommy felt, but heeded not these trifling collisions; he was desperate and did not care, because now he could hear the pattering of many feet behind him, and shouts arose that curdled his blood, and lent him new strength.

Rather than fall into that woman's hands again he would perish, or do something worthy of solitary confinement for life, and on he went, up one street, down another, across dingy squares, and at last to his consternation, found himself turning down a bye street, blocked at one end by a tall hoarding, and out of which there was no turning.

There was, however, a public-house, and Tommy made for it with all speed, determined on imploring the landlord's protection, and his hand was on the door when it was jerked open from the inside, and he fell into the arms of a tall wiry man, who threw his arms about him, and hugged him with the fondness of a bear.

"Let me go," Tommy gasped, "they are after me, and will murder me. Oh! my ribs."

"Shure an' it's him purty self, it is," said the man, as Tommy, more dead than alive, recognised in voice and form his old friend, Irish Mike. "Hooroo! an' it's meself that knew he'd come back some foine day."

"Mike," said Tommy, faintly, but glad, under any circumstances, to have found a protector, "get me away. Take me somewhere and hide me; there's a horrible woman running after me, and I would rather die a hundred deaths than she should find me."

"A woman, is it?" said Irish Mike, with a huge grin. "Ah! now, honey, what have you been afther? Bedad, it's more loike yourself to be afther the faymales."

"She swears that I am her husband," Tommy said, as well as he could speak, for want of breath; "but it can't be."

Mike handed his fat friend into the bar, and shutting the door, placed his back against it.

"I'm your friend," said he, "but moind it's meself that will niver intherfare between man and wife. Shure it's once that I did, and a purty batin' I got."

"Oh! lor'," Tommy gasped, "but I tell you that she isn't my wife."

"I'll swear he ran this way," exclaimed a voice, that made Tommy shudder like a jelly on a steamboat. "Ah! my dears, don't you cry, I'll be even with the beast when I catch him."

"Is that the crathur?" Irish Mike asked, looking over the blind.

"Yes," Tommy replied, squatting on the floor behind an empty barrel. "Look at her, and tell me if she looks the sort of woman I should take for a wife, and then the children—how is it possible that they can be mine?"

Perhaps the Irishman saw, in the lady's presence, some joke on the part of Tommy's companions, and determined to profit by it, and he winked in a solemn manner at the horrified plump youth, who was making strenuous efforts to squeeze himself through the counter.

"I see you don't believe me," Tommy groaned. "Oh Mike, on my honour, I don't know anything about the witch or her brats. If I do may I——"

"Hush, honey!" said Mike, with another glance over the blind. "It's meself that has hard you talk about a swateheart, but I never thought——"

The remainder was drowned by the landlord asking his barman what the row was about outside, a query satisfactorily answered by the appearance of the laundress and youngsters in the next compartment to that occupied by Irish Mike and Tommy.

"Now then, where is he?" demanded the irrepressible female, bringing her hand down heavily on the counter. "None of your tricks with me, for I won't have 'em. I'm a respectable, hard-working woman, and I'll have my rights as a Henglish-woman, or know the reason why."

"Where's who?" the landlord retorted angrily; and what do you want? If your game is a row you will find that two can play at it. Now then, cut it; you are drunk, and won't get served in this house."

"Drunk!" exclaimed the injured beauty. "Me drunk! Oh, you old willin! How dare you insinuate such a thing? I want my husband, and I'm told that he ran in here."

"Then somebody told you a lie," said the landlord. "There's nobody but a man who's been here this three hours, and a fat young chap."

"That's him," said the lady chuckling, and rubbing her hands gleefully.

"Which one?"

"The fat chap."

"Then," said the landlord, touching a spring which opened a door in the partition, "you'll find him there."

With all due deference to the renowned artist who is so ably illustrating this story we think he would have found it a work of some difficulty to have depicted the expression on Tommy's face as the gaunt female stalked into the compartment, dragging her children after her with as little ceremony as a clown handles a string of dummy sausages.

Would that we were gifted with the power of photographing in pen and ink, for we confess candidly any written description would fall short of the mark, and be a libel on Tommy's agonised features.

Let it suffice to say that he sat huddled up in a corner the very picture of abject misery, boiling rage, and the acme of fear, all combined.

"So here you are," said the lady, fixing a pair of stony eyes on him, "and a pretty dance you have led me."

"Dance," Tommy said, with a vague smile on his lips. "Go on, give us a jig."

"I'll jig you," said she, seizing him by the collar, and jerking him on his feet with such suddenness that every tooth rattled in his head. "You escaped me last time, but never agin if I know it."

"Not for Joe, if he knows it, not for Joseph," Tommy mumbled, evidently wool-gathering. "A capital song that. Sing the next verse. Let's be jolly."

"Shure now, an' what is the matter?" Irish Mike asked, scarcely knowing what to make of the proceedings. "Don't hurt him, marm."

"And pray who are you?" demanded the female, placing her arms akimbo, and thrusting her raspish-looking nose into Mike's face. "Mind your own business, and let mine alone. This man is my husband, and I can prove it by his own friends."

Irish Mike saw the drift at once, and calling the woman aside held a long conversation with her in whispers.

Tommy was still sitting in the corner, too frightened to move hand or foot.

"You won't get any more money in that quarter," Mike said, behind his hand, and bedad it's careful you must be that you don't carry mathers a little too far. Leave him to me."

"Not if I knows it," she replied. "I found him and I'll take him back."

"It's meself that intinds to do it," Mike replied. "I've known him and the young gintlemen ever since they were babbies. Perhaps, marm, afther your long run you would not object to a dhrop of the crathur to revive your spirits."

The laundress did not object, and the landlord a little conciliated by the peaceful turn of affairs served three glasses of whiskey, one of which Tommy disposed of by pouring it down his shirt front.

Irish Mike saw the accident, and not only provided another, but held the glass while Tommy swallowed its contents.

"Och, it's betther you feel now, lad," said the Irishman, slapping the plump one heartily on the back. "Bedad, the colour is coming back to your swate face already."

"Thank you," Tommy replied, coughing violently, "I—I—I do feel a little more like myself. Have—have you persuaded this good woman that she has made a mistake?"

"Hush, honey," Mike whispered in his ear, "not a word. Lave it to me, and it's meself that will pull you through."

Tommy had a grateful heart, and, with moistened eyes and quivering lips, he pressed the Irishman's hand, and was about to speak when there was a commotion outside.

"Bill," screamed the shrill voice of an unadulterated London boy, "make haste, here's a chap a goin' to bust a 'tater on his nose."

Tommy ran to the door, and, clapping his hands, cried—

"Long Jem—Jem, here, I say, come here."

The acrobat dashed through the crowd of urchins and seized Tommy by both hands.

"I'm 'artily glad to see you," he said, "though of course it's open to argyment whether in this dress ——"

"Never mind your dress," the delighted youth cried, glancing at the spangled tights. "Come in, I'm in such a mess."

"Wait a minute," Long Jem returned, "I must take care o' the 'taters or the kids will have 'em."

"No, no," Tommy cried, as a sudden fear fell upon him, "you must not go. Hang the potatoes I will give you twenty times their worth. Don't leave me, or she may do something desperate."

"She!" Long Jem gasped, thrusting his head through the door, and staring hard at Tommy's supposed wife. "Why, I say, it ain't for me to say anythink, but, young gentleman, to be in sich company! Oh my, what would your par say?"

"Don't say anything, or ask any questions," Tommy said, hurriedly, "but come in, and stick to me. That man is Irish Mike, and I know him well, that is he is a dream. Oh, dash it, what am I saying? Come in, and, if you wouldn't see me worse than murdered, take me away with you after you have had something to drink."

"Why don't you cut and run now?" Long Jem said, thrusting the door open with his foot. "Now's your time."

"Don't you see that she has got hold of the tails of my coat?" Tommy gasped.

"Well, I'm blessed," the acrobat muttered, as he pushed his way into the bar. "here's a tale for Bellers. Blowed if I can make it out. What a dramy it would make. Hact the first: wirtoo and williny. The son of a hairystocrat amid the scenes of wice. Hact the second: Long Jem to the rescoo. Tubloo and firevorks."

As the acrobat approached the counter the lady, who persisted in calling Tommy her husband, sniffed suspiciously, and Irish Mike glared at him in a manner that boded no good.

"I should like," Long Jem said, slowly, as he stirred a stiff glass of grog paid for by Tommy, "I should like a hixplination of this 'ere affair. It seems to me that there's a little plant on, and which I means to nip in the bud. I knows this genelman, and as he is a goin' away with me, the less said about the matter the better, I think, so let's be friends."

"Shure, now, who's this spalpeen?" Irish Mike exclaimed, appealing to the company generally. "The gintleman claimed my protection, and bedad he goes wid nobody but me."

"And, I say," screamed the laundress, "that I will take him home."

"I'm open to argyment with both of you," Long Jem, replied. "Let the gent choose for himself; come, now, I can't say no farrir than that."

"He ain't capable of chosin' for himself," the laundress blurted out. "He never was."

"I don't believe I am," Tommy groaned to himself. "Oh, lor', don't Irish Mike look savage? There'll be a fight, directly."

"Now, I tell you what it is," said the landlord, striding up. "I can't have this sort of thing here, and what is more I won't. If you want to quarrel, do it outside. Now, then, out you go."

And out they went, Tommy bent on bolting, but such a hope was blighted by his fair spouse pouncing on one arm, while her three children hung madly on the other. Irish Mike, with a howl that would have done credit to a Red Indian on the war-path, rushed forward and seized Tommy's left leg, and Long Jem collared the right.

Tommy yelled and kicked with all his might, but the louder he yelled, and the harder he kicked, the harder his persecutors tugged.

"Oh, dash it!" Tommy roared, "Oh, my legs and arms, they are coming out of the sockets. Murder!—help!—police!"

"I'll help you," the washerwoman shrieked. "Wait till I get you home."

Suddenly there was a turn of affairs. Long Jem, letting Tommy's leg go, gave Mike an awful left-hander, which sent him staggering into the road, then taking the laundress firmly by the waist he deposited her on a doorstep. and, flooring the juveniles with one sweep of his long leg, he threw Tommy over his shoulder, and sped away with the swiftness of a hare.

CHAPTER XXII.

ON THE TRACK—NO NEWS OF TOMMY—LIONEL BEGINS TO DESPAIR—SAM SCARECROW MAKES A RATHER UNPLEASANT DISCOVERY—OUR HERO IS MYSTIFIED—A FEW WORDS WITH AN OLD FOE.

PERHAPS, and we trust not, the reader has never been provided with the key of the street door, and left to roam about the silent thoroughfares of London from midnight to the dawn of day.

There is nothing more dismal, nothing more chilling, than the mighty metropolis, with its slumbering millions an hour after the doors of its theatres have been closed.

The dark phantom-like form of a policeman heavily booted, but cautious and cat-like of movement, glides round the corner out of some unexpected place, and flashing his bull's-eye on the weary pedestrian favours him with a scrutinising stare, and bids him a gruff good night as he turns away to resume his beat.

A waggon laden with vegetables comes lumbering along, awakening the echoes, and then, as the sound dies away, perchance the thoughful and despairing wanderer is regaled with the sight of half a dozen roistering fellows, homeward bound, holding each other up with all the affection of brotherhood, and yelling at the top of their voices; and, alas! he may find much food for reflection in the sight of some painted and bedizened creature in the form of a woman, sweeping the pavement with her ghastly finery, and screaming out such things that the very stones might blush with shame.

Let those who groan and wring their hands for reason of the heathen's ignorance look at home; let them take the trouble to spend but one night in the open streets of London, and they shall see and hear such things as will curdle their blood, and make them think with truth that a wondrously deep layer of sin and iniquity lies beneath the thin crust of civilisation and refinement.

If those whose pleasure or business takes them to the Edgware-road will take the trouble to linger for a moment at the top of Praed-street they will see a street rest protected by four posts and illuminated by a lamp.

These posts were occupied by four figures, dead beat and worn out, miserably cold, despite their thick warm overcoats, and complaining of a drizzling rain, which fell without intermission, finding its way into and through everything in a sneaky but determined fashion.

"This is pleasant," said Lionel, shuddering, as he sat swinging his legs on the post. "Hark, there goes Big Ben."

"Half-past one," Lord Vansittart groaned, jumping down. "Upon my life, this is fearful. I would not mind if we had only the shadow of a clue to work on. I begin to think that we shall return without Tommy after all."

"If I do," Lionel replied, "it will be against my will. No, Van, I have made up my mind to find him if I have to go barefooted. What is our misery to his? Poor old Tommy, so easily misled and imposed upon. I cannot bear to think of him."

"Well," Charlie Drummond chimed in, "we shall do no good by staying here. Come, let us go. Lionel, drop your walking-stick, and let us go in the direction the handle points."

"Not a bad idea," said Lionel, throwing up the cane. "See, it points up Praed-street, and if we follow it we shall come out by Kensington-gardens."

"Perhaps he has gone there for a night's lodging," Vansittart suggested. "You remember how Tommy once played at being a gipsy."

"Quite well," Lionel replied, smiling in spite of himself; "and a pretty muddle he made of it."

"Well, he may have taken it into his head to do it again," Vansittart said. "Who is that snoring?"

"It is Sam," Charlie replied. "Poor fellow! look at him, roosting as quietly as a barn-door fowl on that post."

"Wake him up," said Lionel, "or he will catch his death of cold."

Sam dispensed with anybody's services by throwing up his legs and falling on his back with a crash that startled the jaded steed of a passing night-cab into something like a gallop.

"Bust it!" Sam gasped, as he rose and rubbed his shoulder tenderly. "Blow me if I didn't dream as 'ow I fell down a mine miles deep."

"We must be moving again," Lionel said; "so pull yourself up. Stay, before we go on we will share what little whisky is left."

The flask was passed round and returned empty.

"Ah," said Sam, licking his lips, "that's wot I calls a reviver. There ain't a teetotaller as could stand agin a drop on sich a night as this. Blow me if I ain't wet through."

"So we are all for that matter," Lionel said. Now, lads, quick, march. Sam."

"Yessir."

"Make the best use of your wonderful eyes, and don't let so much as a black-beetle escape your notice," said Lionel.

"Hif I does, sir," Sam replied, emphatically, "tie me to the fust lamp-post, and leave me to perish."

Half an hour's weary tramp found them in Bayswater, and up to the railings skirting the park.

"Locked of course," said Lionel, trying a gate. "But locks, bolts, and bars, must fly asunder unless we can squeeze through. Sam, keep a sharp lookout for inquisitive policemen."

"Can't we manage to get over the top?" Vansittart said. "Up you go, Li, the height is nothing."

"But the spikes look ugly," Lionel replied. "Well, here goes. It's hard work climbing in a wet overcoat."

In almost less time than it takes to write it all were safe over the railings, and walking silently in the shadow of the dripping trees.

"I don't know which is the wust," Sam growled, as a thin stream of icy cold water ran down his neck. "A feller would be a hass to think of sleeping here."

"Hold your tongue, and attend to me," Lionel said. We must now disperse, and return to this spot in half an hour."

"That is if we are so lucky as to find it," Charlie said.

"It certainly is dubious," Lionel said, looking about him for some landmark. "Stay, we cannot miss each other if we go back to the road. Now, no more waste of time. I'll go west, Van had better take the north, Charlie, you go south, and Sam east."

"Au revoir, and good luck," Vansittart said, beating his hands on his shoulders. "Heavens, how wet my feet are, and the fellow swore that my boots were waterproof, and would stand anything."

"I feel like a hicicle," Sam said, as he moved away. "Oh, Mister Codlings, don't I wish somebody could conwince me this was a dream, and prove it. I'd give a quarter's salary with all my 'art."

Sam walked, and walked, slouching along, cursing the darkness as he stumbled over all kinds of things, but the climax of his misery was reached when he fell over an invisible wire rail, and stood on his head in a puddle of mud and water. What Sam said, as he staggered to his feet and shook himself like a retriever, is a matter of no moment, and cannot be here recorded; but we regret to say, that some very questionably adjectives were mixed up with his soliloquy.

"I shall be a pretty picter by daylight," he growled, "one as a hundataker may admire, p'raps. Hullo, wat's that?"

Something glided silently past him, and Sam's heart stood still.

"Oh! murder," he gasped, turning hot all over, "wot if it should be a ghost? But dash it, it can't be. Who's there?"

No reply was given to this query, but Sam thought he heard a rustling in front of him, and bounding forward, nearly fell into the arms of a man.

"Hullo," said Sam, "wat's your little game. Why couldn't you speak when I called out?"

The man evidently took Sam Scarecrow for a keeper, and muttered something to the effect that he was doing no harm.

"I orter know that woice," Sam mused; "consequently, I means to have a look at his face."

He had some matches in his inner coat pocket, and, after some little delay, he contrived to strike a light, but no sooner did he see the man's face than the match fell from his hand, and in a kind of shriek he yelled out—

"Oh! Lord, it's that willen, Grubbs."

Sam's first impulse was to run away, but on second thoughts he stood his ground and made a grab at his old foe's throat. They fell together on the wet grass, and with Sam's usual luck he managed to get undermost.

"So it is really you," Grubbe said, leaning on the long one's chest, and holding one hand over his mouth. "Curse you, do you think I could ever forget your ugly visage, and yet I have often longed to see it, that I may batter it out of all shape and form. Do you hear that?"

Sam did hear, and kicked frantically, but he was in the hands of a powerful man, and all his struggles were in vain.

"Ah! it's no use, my lad," Grubbe went on, "for I've got you tight. Many and many a time in my cell, or working like a slave in the quarries, I have longed for such a meeting as this, and wondered if my wish would ever be realised.

"As soon as I got my ticket of leave I came to London to hunt you and that whelp, Lionel Wilful, down."

Sam's indignation, on hearing his master called a whelp, was tremendous, and rage lent him a strength not his own; but Grubbe clutched his throat with fingers as powerful and relentless as a vice.

"Not yet," he hissed in Sam's ear; "I have not done with you yet. When I have done with you," he added, dropping his voice, "you will be of no use to anybody or anything except the worms, unless an undertaker conceives a fancy for you. I suppose you know what I am going to do, eh?"

Sam made no reply, for the simple reason that Grubbe would not let him speak; but he knew full well what the scoundrel meant.

"I am going to murder you," Grubbe went on, slowly and deliberately. "This little tickler," taking a huge clasp knife out of his pocket, and opening it with his teeth, "will do the job comfortably and silently. I suppose you would like to say a prayer before you die."

Sam nodded his head, and Grubbe laughed outright. "Then you won't do anything of the kind," he said with a brutal chuckle. "Ah! wouldn't you yell now if I only gave you the chance? Oh! this is glorious, and I must give myself the pleasure of looking at you a few times before I do the job. Squirm away, my fine fellow; make the best use of your limbs, for they will be still enough by-and-bye. I——" Grubbe ceased speaking, for a pair of strong arms were thrown around his neck, and in an instant Sam was free.

"What is this?" cried the well-known voice of Lionel. "Stand, whoever you are. Ah! would you?" He saw the gleam of the knife in the dim light, and dodged it as it descended.

"It's Grubbe, and he means murder," Sam gasped. "Don't go near him sir—he wery nigh did for me."

"Grubbe!" Lionel exclaimed as a momentary faintness bereft him of strength. "What new triumph of the devil's art can have cast the villain loose on society again?"

"Ha, ha, ha!" Grubbe laughed, retreating slowly into the darkness; "we shall meet again, never fear. Adieu for the present."

"What a fool I have been to let him slip through my fingers!" Lionel said. "Come on, Sam, we must track him down. Use your tongue as well as your feet, and bring up Van and Charlie."

They came running up with the hope in their hearts that Tommy had been found, but their faces fell when Lionel spoke.

"It is like looking for a needle in a bottle of hay," Vansittart said; "the fellow is far away by this time. Lionel, this vagabond is the bane of your life. What will you do?"

"Communicate at once with the police," our hero replied, "and make the murderous villain work the rest of his sentence, with such addition as he may be deemed worthy of."

"Oh! lor sir," Sam fairly blubbered as he leaned against a tree, "another minute and it would have

~~been~~ ll over with me. You should have seen his ~~neyes~~; they looked like sarpints in the dark. My 'art is that full, that I don't know how to thank you."

"Never mind, Sam," Lionel replied; "you would do the same for me. I don't know what made me go out of my track, but I did, and couldn't help myself. Dry your eyes, for there is too much water about the atmosphere already. Oh! that daylight would come!"

CHAPTER XXIII.

AN IMPORTANT CONFERENCE—TOMMY MAKES UP HIS MIND—LONG JEM FALLS—TOMMY BAFFLES HIS PURSUERS.

"THERE," said Long Jem setting Tommy down on the pavement; "I don't think there is much fear of our being followed here. Oh! lor, you are a weight certainly, and it's open to argyment whether you ain't the heaviest chap I ever seed of your age."

"I wish I could get thinner," Tommy moaned—I shouldn't suffer half so much. Jem, it was very kind of you to take me up, but I feel as if I had been rolled in a barrel down a mountain."

"Bust the joltin," said Jem, "wot would have been your fate? That 'ere woman meant wenom, and as for that Hirish party he looked all sorts of hevil things. But come along; if we stop, some o' them parties may find us, and then there'll be another jolly row."

"Wait a minute—only one," Tommy panted. "Ah! I feel better now. I'm ready. Where are you going to take me to?"

"Why, now I come to think of it," Long Jem said, scratching his head; "that's a question I can't wery well answer. You see since that bust up on Wandsworth Heath——"

"Then I did not dream it," Tommy ejaculated.

"Dream it," Long Jem repeated, shaking his head dolefully; "I wish you had. No, no sir, it air all true, and more, for the wery next night a crowd comes, headed by the furus old gentleman. He fust gives Bellers-to-Mend one in the wind, and horders his followers to go to vork, and didn't they go it? In five minutes there wasn't a square yard of canwas or a bit o' wood bigger than a lucifer match to be found anywheres."

"You must have sustained a great loss," Tommy said.

"It ain't the loss I complains of," Long Jem replied, "but Bellers is that wicious that I dare not look at him. He comes home last night rayther meller, and heaves a three-legged stool at me, but I ducked, and it went through the winder, and fell on the head of a stout old gent as was passin'."

"And then I suppose there was a row," said Tommy.

"That ain't the name for it," the acrobat replied; "hup comes the landlady with her husband and a few friends as were havin' a conwivial glass, and the way they vent on was hawful. They broke all the furniter, and then fell a top o' me and Bellers, and walloped us till we roared for mercy. I do assure you that I'm like a brown paper parcel steeped in winager. So you see me and Bellers are hangin out in a corfee shop till we starts for the country, which will be to-morrer or the next day at the latest."

"And you will take me with you," Tommy pleaded as they walked slowly along, "you don't know how miserable I am, especially now I find for certain that those I loved dearest on earth have deceived me."

"What! them as you was with t'other night?" Long Jem said, opening his eyes very wide.

"Yes," Tommy replied, mournfully, "I cannot tell you the story now, as it will take a long time to tell. Let me go with you, and I will not only give you what money I can, but make myself useful."

"It's open to argyment whether Bellers will like it," Long Jem said; "he's got a great opinion o' that 'ere Mister Wilful."

"So had I, until to-day," Tommy said, as tears started to his eyes; "but it is no use of thinking or talking about it. I am determined not to go back again, and, if you don't agree to my terms, somebody else will."

"There aint much room for argyment in that ere hobservation," Long Jem remarked. "Well, we'll hear wot Bellers ses, and, if he's agreeable, why, in course I am—for we rows in one boat, notwithstandin' the little tiffs we have occasionally."

Ten minutes' slow walking brought them to a dingy-looking house, over the door of which hung a cracked lamp, informing the public that refreshments and good clean beds could be procured within.

"Here we are," said Long Jem, pushing open a swinging door, and letting out a gust of heat, bearing the combined flavours of fried eggs, chops, steaks, bacon, and flabby pudding. "We lodges on the fust floor."

"Oh! on the first floor," Tommy said, a little dubiously, as he looked at the filthy staircase-walls, highly suggestive of stale cobwebs.

"Yes, come along," Long Jem replied, leading the way; "mind the fourth stair, there's a board out."

Tommy, following his conductor, groped his way up with a consciousness that the top railing of the balustrade was damp, and that there was a peculiar slipperiness about the stairs as if a colander of fat had been carried up and down for ages.

"Here we are," Long Jem cried, throwing open a door, minus a handle. "Bellers, behold!" Bellers-to-Mend raised his eyes, and smiled in a melancholy manner at Tommy, who, for the life of him, could not help thinking that a comb and brush were rather out of place on the tea-table, and that a tablecloth less stained with mustard would have added to the beauty of the apartment.

"You are welcome, sir," Bellers-to-Mend said, rising, and handing Tommy a chair; "you see us at our worst; in short, sir, we are down on our luck."

"I regret to hear it," Tommy replied. "Jem has told me something. We met in a peculiar manner, and after you have heard all you will think that I have come to a right conclusion."

"Name it, and I'll hear your story afterwards," Bellers-to-Mend said, rather shortly.

"It is that I wish to travel with you," Tommy blurted out. "I am sick and tired of my present life, and never intend going back to it any more."

Bellers-to-Mend was sitting on a three-legged stool, and after staring solemnly at Tommy for at least five seconds, he threw up his legs, clapped his hands, and burst into a loud roar of laughter.

"Why, you must be dreaming," he said, holding his sides, as he rocked to and fro.

"Dreaming," Tommy gasped, turning very pale at the bare idea; "I hope not."

"You must be," the showman said; "why, sir, do you know what sort of life we lead on the road?"

"Not from personal experience, although I have had my ups and downs," Tommy said—adding, after a pause, "that is to say, unless I have dreamed away a few years of my life."

"That's it, you may depend," Bellers-to-Mend returned; "why you aint no more cut out for a stroller than I am for a dook."

"That's open to argyment," Long Jem murmured, from behind a dense cloud of tobacco smoke.

"Bust your argyments," Bellers-to-Mend roared; "will you let me have my say out?"

"Go on, Long Jem replied, in an injured tone. "Go on, I'm the wictim of circumstances. Pitch inter me, I can stand it. Don't spare me on no account."

"You're enough to make a man bust with rage," Bellers-to-Mend roared, "wat with your argyments, your perwerse ways, and your fireworks, blowed if you aint almost worked us into the workhouse."

"I can bear it," Long Jem, moaned. "I was borned a horphan, and from my youth it were hever thus. I never missed——"

"He's going inter pothery, now," Bellers-to-Mend gasped, with a despairing look at Tommy, "Jem, far be it from my wishes to turn up wicious, especially afore a wisitor, but if you cut in when I'm speaking you'll have to argy on your back at the bottom of the stairs. Your father must have been a curiosity. I should like to have known him. Who was he? and what line did he take?"

"There's a considerable amount of mystery attached to that 'ere part o' my pedigree," Long Jem replied, with the air of a man who had accidentally swallowed a fish-bone; "but I have heard that my mother could argy agin any woman of her own hage and weight. Poor critter, she departed this life argying with the doctor about the number o' tendances."

"Well," Bellers-to-Mend said, turning to Tommy, "so you think you would like to travel with us. Well and good, but first listen to me, and then make up your mind."

"I will pay the greatest attention to you," Tommy said, "but let me tell you that I have made up my mind, and nothing will alter it."

"That's candid," said Bellers-to-Mend. "Vell, sir, I suppose it will be waste of breath to say much, but unless you have the constitution of a horse, unless you can put up with all kinds of weather, and sometimes go without grub for days at a stretch——"

Tommy started, and winced to such a degree that the showman hesitated.

"Ah!" said he, "I thought I should have you there, but it's a fact. Strollin' ain't bad when you have money, and things are prosperous, but I have told you that we are down on our luck, and p'raps may have to knock about for months."

"But listen to me," Tommy said, "I have four pounds, and——"

"I can't and won't think of it," Bellers said, holding up his hands; "no, no, sir, we can fight our own battles, but you are welcome to share what we have. Now I will hear how all this came about."

Tommy was not long telling his story, and the showman's face assumed a grave expression every time Lionel Wilful's name was mentioned.

"Bless him," Tommy said, with sudden emotion. "I know that he did not mean any harm; it is only his way, but I felt that reason was leaving me, and I could stand the distress of mind no longer."

"And what do you think he is thinking of now?" Bellers-to-Mend said, slapping his knees. "I'll be bound that he is sorry, and looking for you everywhere."

"That's open to argyment," Long Jem growled, and immediately apologised.

"Now, sir, I don't think you'll find a nap amiss," Bellers-to-Mend said, shaking his fist at Jem. Here's a rug and here's a pillow. Just you sleep on this 'ere determination of yours, and perhaps you'll think different when you wake up."

"I certainly am very weary," Tommy said, stretching himself out; "wake me in an hour's time. Now," thought he, "it may be mean of me, but I must not go to sleep. These men, in their good-heartedness, may send for Lionel, or devise some plan to get me back. It may be mean, but I must hear what they have to say."

"He's a stunner to snore," Bellers-to-Mend observed, after a pause of some ten minutes' dura-'ion. "Jem, this is a rum go."

"The rummest that I hever knowed," Long Jem said, thoughtfully. "The taters is gone, and sich cannot now be bought for money."

"Bust the taters!" Bellers-to-Mend gasped. "What a feller you are Jem! What's flukes to this young chap's troubles? I say, are you sure that he isn't shamming sleep?"

"No more than I am," Jem replied, bending over the apparently unconscious plump one's form. "He's as sound as a top."

"That's all right," Bellers-to-Mend replied, putting on his hat and coat with great caution. "Now, Jem, I rely on you to keep him here until I come back."

"Where are you a goin' to?" Jem demanded, with a flushed face.

"I'm going to find Mr. Wilful," the showman replied, "and tell him as how we've got his friend safe and sound."

Long Jem said something between his teeth which his companion did not hear, for he immediately left the room, and crept softly downstairs.

The instant the door had closed on him Tommy started to his feet with such a wild look on his face that Jem slunk into a corner, and looked about for some weapon to defend himself with in case of need.

"So," Tommy cried, "after all I have said, your friend would betray me."

"That's open to argyment," Jem said; "but wot if he do? ain't there me left?"

"I would rather die than be taken back," Tommy exclaimed, disregarding the acrobat's words. "Li says I am always dreaming, and that old scoundrel Kramatome swears that I am mad, and actually sent for a straight jacket. They said you were a dream. Are you one now?"

"That's a pint as can be only be argeyed one way," Jem replied. "I often wish as 'ow I was dream, or summat as good. No, sir; I'm as much alive as you are stout, and that is sayin' a good deal."

"Then I am off," Tommy said, making for the door. "Give my compliments to Mr. Bellers, and say that I am much obliged to him."

"You really mustn't be in sich a 'urry," Long Jem cried, barring the way. "You see I was left in charge of you, but——"

"I see what you want," Tommy sneered, taking out his purse.

"You've made a mistake this time," Jem said, with sudden dignity. "Put up yer money. I was about to observe that I knowed a party as 'ud be glad of a little tin to help him on to start a wan, but you've spiled it now. There's the door, you know your way downstairs."

"Jem," Tommy said, turning crimson. "if I've said or done anything to offend you believe me I am truly sorry."

"Don't mention it, sir," Jem said coldly, as he turned away and walked to the window. "I could have smuggled you away heasy enough or put you on the right track, but it ain't in me now. My pipe is out, and I haven't the 'art to say no more about the matter."

"Well, you will at least shake hands," Tommy said. "Let us part friends."

Long Jem turned suddenly round and, putting his hands on Tommy's shoulders, said—

"Bust it!" he said; "you ain't to blame. Now I come to think it did seem as if I wanted somethin'. I'll stand by you through thick and thin. Say the word, and I'll go anyvheres with you, and here's my hand on it."

In two minutes the room was empty, and Tommy had again baffled his pursuers.

CHAPTER XXIV.

A WORTHY PAIR—AN OLD CHARACTER IN A NEW PART.

THE big bell of the clock tower at Westminster had scarcely tolled the hour of ten when Lionel, tired and jaded, passed under the arch of Scotland-yard, and asked to see some gentleman in authority.

He was shown into a room, and sat for a few minutes thinking, with a sensation akin to awe, of

"GO AWAY!" ROARED MR. KRAMATOME. "KEEP THE GAME ALIVE!" SHOUTED LIONEL AND HIS CHUMS.

all the horrible mysteries talked of with the calmness of ordinary business within those walls.

Lionel expected to be confronted by an official man, bearded, heavily booted, and stalwart, but imagine his surprise on beholding a quiet old gentleman, who, taking his seat at the table, mildly inquired the visitor's business.

Lionel was not long in giving his statement, and the gentleman, without displaying the least surprise, horror, or emotion of any kind, rang a bell, and ordered certain books to be brought to him.

No such ticket-of-leave as Grubbe had reported himself in London; consequently the man was disobeying the law, or Lionel had made a great mistake.

"I could swear to him anywhere, and pick him out of a million," Lionel said; "so could my servant who was attacked."

The mild business-like old gentleman made a few notes, took Lionel's address, and told him to come on the following day.

"If he has not already left London," he said, "he cannot escape us; therefore we may have news for you. At the same time you might bring your servant up with you."

Lionel turned away from the office with anything but a light heart, and yet he seemed to breathe with more freedom in the street so full of noise and bustle.

"They take matters awfully cool," he muttered; "but it wouldn't do for them to show their feelings, even supposing they have any. I would give something handsome to find that villain Grubbe."

If Lionel had but known how close he was to the object of his thoughts this part of our story might have been told in a few strokes of the pen.

Our hero turned his face towards the Strand, and hailing a cab drove back to Mr Kramatome's, there to hear to his dismay that Mr. Bellers-to-Mend had called on the previous day, would leave no message, but promised to renew his visit that day.

"He has heard something of Tommy," Lionel said to Charlie. "Confound it, why could he not leave his message? Going to bed?"

"I must," Charlie yawned. "Give me four hours and I shall be ready again. What have you done with Sam?"

"He is asleep in the kitchen," Lionel replied. "I left him, poor fellow, snoring quite comfortably, with his head in the coal-scuttle and his feet in the fender. I think I will take a cup of black coffee, and try to get a nap myself."

"Do, my dear fellow," Drummond said; "you look fearfully tired. You must rest, or you will knock yourself up."

At the very time Lionel was sipping his coffee and smoking a cigarette the amiable Mr. Grubbe sat, biting his dirty finger nails, in a garret at the top of a house not a mile away from Rochester-row, in Westminster.

From his lofty situation he had a pleasing view of the roof and outer walls of Millbank prison, but, so far from this edifying sight arousing admiration in his breast, it caused him to feed more hungrily on his finger nails, and we regret to have to record that he swore roundly.

Ten years of almost maternal care, provided at an enormous cost by a considerate government, had not improved him in any way, but had turned him loose a greater blackguard, a more consummate villain than before.

Confinement had also brought the rough element of his nature to the surface, and we now find him a skulking, but cunning and savage old man.

"May a blight fall on him," he hissed, as he strode up and down the miserable apartment, "who stood between me and twenty thousand pounds! Who thwarted me when a boy, tormented me with his accursed practical jokes, and was the cause of my—my misfortune."

Another turn or two up the room, a few spiteful gnawings at his nails, and then he stopped and flung up his arms.

"Oh, that I had him here," he yelled—"here before me alone, bound and unarmed—I gloating over his misery, and torturing him before I sent him out of the world. Oh, how delicious! I can see it all. I can hear him begging for life, I see him writhe as I pinch and strike him, I ——"

"This is really very indiscreet of you. Don't you know that there are other people besides yourself in the house?"

Grubbe stopped, and allowing his arms to fall to his side he turned and looked at a head and shoulders thrust through the partly open door.

It was a very dirty head, and the shoulders were covered with a coat patched and greasy.

Presently the legs, arms, and body sidled into the room, and Mr. Styngy, ragged, grubby, and almost shoeless, stood like the very ghost of what had once been his respectable self.

He carried a mangy writing case under his arm, which like himself had seen better times, and clung to the remnant of a frock coat, as if desirous of sheltering its scratched and ill-used morocco face from the eyes of the world.

"My dear friend, you must have more command over yourself," Mr. Styngy said. "Think of the risk I run hiding you here. Were it known that you—ahem! never mind—why, sir, we should have the police down on us in five minutes, and all our plans would be for ever upset."

"Oh, it is all very well for you to lecture me," Grubbe said, savagely. "Think of what I have suffered. Did I round on you when, you know, you were as much in the swim as I?"

"Hush, hush," exclaimed Mr. Styngy, in a horrified whisper, and letting the dilapidated writing-case fall with a crash; "you forget yourself."

"I wish I could, sometimes," Grubbe snarled; "look at me and think what I was once. Curse me, if I dare face a looking-glass."

"There is no fear of your doing that here," Mr. Styngy replied, as he glanced round the miserably furnished room. "Now, my friend, you must be more reasonable; bury the past, look to the present, and hope for the future."

"That is very good advice," Grubbe growled, "but you do not know all yet. Sit down and listen to what I have to say?"

The Rev. Mr. Styngy sat down, with extreme caution, on a chair very shaky on its legs, and then, as his companion told him how and where he had met Lionel and Sam, Mr. Styngy's face turned all sorts of unnatural colours, and he breathed like a man being slowly suffocated.

"We must get way from here," he gasped. "What mad devil possessed you to do so rash a thing?"

"I would do it again," Grubbe replied, gnashing his teeth, "and I only regret that I allowed the ugly squinting cur to slip through my clutches. As for that whelp Wilful, I will kill him, or make his life a burden to him. I care not if I swing, for to go back from whence I came is worse than death."

"And yet," said Mr. Styngy, "it is but yesterday that you were so clear-headed and talking so reasonably, and now you have utterly ruined yourself and put me in jeopardy."

"Not so bad as that," the ticket-of-leave man said, with a coarse oath; "you talk of leaving here; I say no. If you want to avoid the police, put yourself under their very noses; run away, and the game is as good as over."

"Well," Mr. Styngy said, mopping his face with a highly ventilated handkerchief, "that may be all very well in its way, but verily I feel a kind of chill I never felt before. We must be very careful, my friend."

"Of course we must," Grubbe growled. "Leave me to take care of myself. If anything goes wrong I shall hear of it from Bill Belcher."

"And who is Bill Belcher?" Mr. Styngy demanded.

"A friend of mine,'" Mr. Grubbe replied, "who keeps a place where a man in trouble can lodge a few days."

"Oh!" Mr. Styngy ejaculated, dabbing away with his pocket-handkerchief; "I think I understand you, but——"

"Enough of this," Grubbe said, as a furious oath sprang to his lips. "Let us talk of something else. What have you been doing?"

Mr. Styngy growled, as he picked up and opened the writing-case.

"I have had an interview with Lady Waterbrush's secretary—a most agreeable young man I assure you—and if all goes well I shall, in vulgar parlance, land her ladyship to the tune of twenty pounds. I—ahem—have stated my unfortunate case clearly on five sheets of foolscap, and I have no fear that her ladyship, who, I am told, is a little queer about the upper story, and has already founded a home for stray cats, and another for orphan mice, will respond to my appeal."

"I hope she will," Mr. Grubbe said; "but of course that is not the only egg you have in the basket."

"I have a score at least," Mr. Styngy replied; "and ever. supposing half of them turn out bad, the other may turn out good birds. Hist, there is somebody coming upstairs."

CHAPTER XXV.

ON THE ROAD — THE BULL AND HORNS — MR. PIPPINDALE AND LONG JEM HAVE A CONVERSATION—TOMMY HAS AN ACCIDENT—A REHEARSAL AND ITS CONSEQUENCES.

"IT'S open to argyment whether you ain't knocked up."

These words, uttered by Long Jem, were addressed to Tommy Codlings, who sat on a mile-stone, swinging his weary legs, and yawning at the rate of twenty a minute. It was night, but moonlight and beautifully fine. A balmy breeze swept the landscape, wafting a thousand delicious perfumes from myriads of flowers with which hill and dale were studded. In a word, it was springtime, and Nature was rejoicing at having burst the bonds of cruel icy winter. It certainly was a lovely scene, but Tommy had no eyes for it, for his orbs were more often shut than open, and Long Jem had much to do to keep his fat companion from falling asleep.

"It won't do," said the acrobat; "once you goes orf, all the argyment in the world won't get you on your legs agin, so pull yourself up, sir, and let us get away. Five more miles will end our journey."

"Five miles!" Tommy groaned; "you might as well ask me to swim across the Atlantic."

"Now, why argy?" Jem said; "you've done twenty miles like a Briton, and it ain't in you to double up just at the moment when you ought to show the most pluck."

"That's right enough in its way," Tommy said, between a couple of yawns of such magnitude that it is a wonder he did not lay in a stock of lock-jaws; "but look at my boots, or rather what is left of them. I thought these boots would be easy to my feet, but I have found out my mistake."

"That's the way with most people as ain't used to padding the hoof," Jem replied; "thin soles is a mistake all the world over. Hullo, there! wake up." Jem caught Tommy, as he began to nod, and shaking him up, rather unceremoniously planted him on his feet in the middle of the road.

"Now, then, sir," Jem said; "let your motter be Nel desperatedum, and put your best foot forward."

"I wonder which is the best of the two," Tommy moaned, looking down ruefully as he hobbled along. "Let me hold your arm, or I shall go down flop."

For an hour and half they crawled along, and then Jem suddenly pulled up, and, pointing towards a light glimmering from a clump of poplars, said—

"That's the Bull and Horns, and in ten minutes we shall be in Drayton."

"Thank heaven," Tommy gasped, clutching at a gate-post for support. "Oh! shan't I sleep?"

"That's open to argyment," Jem said; "many's the time I've been too tired to get a wink, but anyways a pull through the sheets will do you good."

Stimulated with the thoughts of a supper in a good old country inn and an easy bed to follow, Tommy pushed on at Long Jem's side, and arrived in due time at the hospitable portal of the Bull and Horns.

The hostelry had been famed in its day, and the thatched gables had looked down upon many a gay and animated scene.

But where was the coach that had rattled so merrily along the road, its wheels adding music to the clattering hoofs of the four spanking greys? Where was the red-faced coachman, where the obliging guard who awoke the echoes far and wide for miles, as the horn, the pride of his heart, went to his lips.

All gone! The coach had long been broken up, the four greys fallen at the hands of the knackers, and guard and coachman had followed the way of all flesh, and the moon's beams fell upon their simple graves.

Nevertheless the Bull and Horns, in defiance of time and changes, stood, and preserved its old dignity.

The rooms, replete with massive beams and huge fireplaces, remained untouched; the original bar, with its shelves bearing armies of punchbowls, was there, and behind it stood a jolly host, and as buxom a hostess as any thoroughbred Englishman could wish to see.

Long Jem seemed to know his way about, and led the way to the kitchen, in which a huge log fire was burning quite unnecessarily, as there was no cooking going on, and the room was so hot that the windows were thrown open to allow the heat to escape.

There were several men talking over their beer, or lounging about, and they looked up as Long Jem and Tommy entered.

The fat youth took no notice of anybody, but throwing himself down in a corner, fell asleep, and began to snore with the persistence and noise of a litter of pigs.

A man rose up, and approaching Long Jem shook him warmly by the hand.

The stranger was tall and sallow, with long deep creases in his cheeks, and crow's feet under his eyes.

He wore a white hat, adorned with a narrow black hat-band, and a long ragged coat hanging down to his ankles.

"I'm 'artily glad to see you, Jem," said this individual. "What brings you this way?"

"Him," Long Jem replied, pointing at the slumbering youth, "and you. I promised as 'ow I would do you a good turn, Pippindale, and I'm a goin to do it."

Mr. Pippindale scratched his head thoughtfully, and then looked at Long Jem.

"I ain't good at riddles," he said, glancing rather unfavourably at Tommy, "and I don't wan't no fat boys, though I must own that he is a buster. I had a fine one myself once, but the public got tired of him, and shied nuts and horanges about to that extent that I was glad to get rid of him."

"Sit down," Jem said, "and hear wot I have to say, and then, p'raps you may alter your tune."

Mr. Pippindale ordered some beer, and then he and Jem settled themselves down in a retired part of the room, and held a long conversation, which seemed to end to the satisfaction of both, for they shook hands again with great fervour.

"Will you wake him, and introduce him?" Mr. Pippindale asked.

"Of course he will want his grub, and he can't eat it asleep," Long Jem replied; "but I don't think we will worry him about business to-night. He wants rest, poor chap. Lor', 'ow he do snore!"

"Never heerd such a one," Mr. Pippindale said; and then, placing his hands on Long Jem's shoulders, "I've had hard times; but, if the gent stumps up as you say he will, I'll buy Sam Slumper's rig-out, and make a fortin. Jem, I've a grateful 'art; and you shall be high stifler, and share the tin."

Long Jem shook his head.

"No," said he, after a pause; "I can't stay over to-morrer. I must go back to Bellers-to-Mend; but wot I am to say to him I know no more than that poker."

"Tell him you've been to see your sweetheart," Pippindale said, with the air of a man who had struck on some good idea.

"As if he would believe that!" Jem replied, contemptuously. "I must tell some fibs about his running away, and I going arter him. Lor', wot a world this is! Fancy a borned gent takin' up with sich as us."

"Sich as us!" Mr. Pippindale repeated indignantly. "Wot d'ye mean by that? Why, ain't we as good as them as walks about in fine toggery, and lives on the fat o' the land?"

"Of course that's open to argyment," Jem said, thoughtfully; "but even them as comes to see us despises us. Hush! he's wakin'."

A hot ember about the size of a walnut had playfully skipped out of the fire, and found its way down Tommy's neck, and he awoke, first rubbing his eyes, wondering what was the matter, and then giving vent to a prolonged yell of agony.

"What do you mean by it?" he said, glaring at Long Jem, and rubbing his back vigorously against the door-post.

"Mean by wot!" Long Jem gasped, thinking that his charge had gone mad in reality.

"Why, by touching me up with the hot poker," Tommy howled. "Wait till I get cool, and I will give you something to remember this."

"Upon the honour of a hacrobat, I never so much as touched you!" Long Jem declared.

"I'll take my Alfred David on that," Mr. Pippindale chimed in. "It was an accident."

"Accident be blowed!" Tommy growled. "My shirt is on fire. My eye, don't it smell!"

Mr. Pippindale seized a huge jug of water, and bore down on Tommy, and, twisting him over the back of a chair, poured about half a gallon of water over the suffering one's back.

"There now," said he, "don't you feel more comfortable?"

"I think it's put out," Tommy replied, screwing up his features, "but I know there must be an awful blister."

"Think yourself lucky that it aint wus," Mr. Pippindale said. "I knowed a chap as fell asleep agin a lime-kiln, and when he woke up there was nothin' left of him but his brass coat buttons and a pocket knife."

"I feel inclined to argy that pint," said Long Jem, "but supper fust and argyment arter. I feel as if I had swallered a hempty barrel and couldn't get rid of the hoops."

A round of cold beef, a loaf of bread, and a huge flagon of beer were brought in, and the three sat down with excellent appetites.

Tommy forgot his blister, Long Jem was too full to argue the extraordinary lime-kiln case, and Mr. Pippindale sat in his chair, staring pensively at nothing, and pondered deeply thereon.

They parted after a nightcap, in the form of a stiff glass of grog all round, and as Tommy crawled into bed he breathed a prayer of heartfelt thankfulness, and fell asleep to dream that he was back with his old friends, and that Mr. Kramatome had undertaken to walk on a tightrope stretched from West-

minster Abbey to Saint Paul's. Somehow or other it was himself that mounted the rope, and when half-way he discovered to his horror that it was on fire, and screaming for the fire brigade he screamed himself out of a deep but very troublous slumber.

It was daylight, and the sun was streaming brightly in at the window, and Tommy consulting his watch found that it wanted but a few minutes to seven o'clock.

"I'll get up, and take a walk before breakfast," he said, preparing to rise. "Ah, this is what I call peace—oh, lor'!"

This last ejaculation was caused by a stinging pain that ran through his back, causing great tears of anguish to start to his eyes.

"My back is red hot," Tommy groaned, falling back on the pillow. "Oh, dear! oh, dear! what a chap I am to get into a muddle!"

Tommy got out of bed with extreme caution, and dressed himself with such scrupulous care that it was nearly eight o'clock before he ventured to descend the stairs.

Long Jem and Mr. Pippindale were waiting for him, and the three went for a walk, which ended in Tommy parting with all his ready cash, and declaring that henceforth he would be a jolly stroller and astound the world with the wonderful contortions of his limbs.

Mr. Pippindale smiled as he slapped him on the back, and told him that he should take his first lesson that morning; and Slumper's booth and properties having been transferred for the consideration of three five pound notes, Tommy arranged himself in a suit of tights, much too long, but not half wide enough for him.

Mr. Pippindale stood ready with drum and pipes, while Long Jem, cranking up a rope, assisted Tommy up, and, giving him a balancing pole, instructed him in the art of tight-rope dancing.

"It's awfully shaky," Tommy panted, as he swayed on one side, and brought down the pole with an awful crack on Jem's head. "There, I knew how it would be. Why didn't you get out of the way?"

"Because I didn't see it a comin'," Jem gasped, staring vaguely at the performer. "Be a little more careful with that 'ere weapon; another one o' that sort 'ud settle me."

"How can I be careful?" Tommy roared, now in the middle of the rope. "I say, this sort of thing isn't in my line. Oh, I say, take me off, or I shall break my neck."

"Don't be afeard," Mr. Pippindale cried, encouragingly. "Walk to the hend, turn round on your toes, and come back. You're a doin of it splendidly for the the fust time."

"Am I?" Tommy gasped, swaying about like an expiring peg-top. "Why don't you take me down? Yah-h-h."

Long Jem made a rush at the fat one, but he was too late, for Tommy had broken his fall on Mr. Pippindale's white hat, and he, Tommy, and the drum came to earth with a mighty crash.

"Are you hurt?" Tommy exclaimed, as he scrambled to his feet.

"Busted, I think," the showman groaned from under the hat. "My head's driv inter my shoulders, and I heerd my backbone crack."

"That's open to argyment," said Long Jem, taking the dilapidated tile between his hands, and giving it a vigorous tug. "My heye, he must have fell a weight. You're a reglar fixter, Pippindale."

"I knows it," gasped the victim in muffled tones. "Go for a doctor, or I shall be stifled."

But Jem made another effort, and the hat came off with a sound something resembling a cork being removed from a bottle.

"Look at my nose," Mr. Pippindale gasped. "Oh, my years, they feel as if they had been 'arf biled, and then baked in a fierce hoven."

"They sartinly air a little red," Long Jem observed, regarding the showman's inflamed listeners with a critical eye. "Mr. Codlings, you must be a leetle more careful."

"Didn't I tell you what would happen?" Tommy groaned, pressing his hands to his stomach. "If I hadn't fallen on him I should have broken my neck."

"Get up agin, sir," Pippinpale said, desperately. "I'm a bachelor, and there aint a man I knows of as 'ud pay for a tombstone for me. Go ahead, and never mind my darned old carcase."

Tommy did go ahead, and, after numerous falls and astonishing feats with the balancing pole, he contrived to walk the length of the rope in safety, and Mr. Pippindale blew his lungs out of order on the pipes, and tortured the drum, while Long Jem looked on, clapping his hands, and shouting "hooroar!"

CHAPTER XXVI.

NEWS FOR LIONEL—SAM AND JOBLOT ON THE ROAD —THE STORM—A THUNDERBOLT AND A HAYSTACK ON FIRE—FOUND—JOY OF SAM.

"NO news of the fugitive, I suppose?"

These words, spoken by Lionel to Bellers-to-Mend, caused the showman to start out of a reverie.

"I've heerd nothin', sir," he replied, scratching his head in a perplexed manner, "but what licks me is the sudden disappearance of Long Jem. Dash me, if I can make it out, and for the fust time o' my life I'm done reg'lar brown. It's a Spinks, that's wot it is."

"Oh yes," Lionel said, "a mystery rivalling the Sphinx. Now, one thing is certain, Long Jem and Tommy are in company somewhere."

"That's evident," Bellers-to-Mend said, clenching his fist, and glaring savagely at the opposite wall. "I never thought as 'ow Jem would round on his old pal."

"Therefore," Lionel went on, "I do not despair, for they are bound to turn up one day."

"Onless they have gone on the contynent," Bellers-to-Mend suggested. "I'm afeard you'll have more trouble than you think. Jem is that artful when he likes that a fox might tuck his tail between his legs and blush for shame. If Jem and me ever do meet we'll have a reckonin' as can't be counted in figgers."

"Well," Lionel replied, rising, "his conduct, to say the least, is extraordinary. Good-day, Mr. Bellers. Will you call on me in the morning, or shall I look you up?"

"Just as you like, sir."

"Then come to Mr. Kramatome's not later than ten," said Lionel. "But should you receive the slightest clue telegraph at once."

"You may depend on me, sir," Bellers-to-Mend said, extending his hand. "Cheer up, sir, and don't let your sperrits go down, rayther swaller some to keep 'em up. That's my motter."

"No, thank you," Lionel said, laughing, "I find a cool head and a steady hand better for an emergency than an excited brain."

Lionel found his way downstairs, leaving Mr. Bellers-to-Mend to his own reflections, which were anything but of a pleasant nature.

Charlie Drummond and Lord Vansittart met Lionel a short distance from Mr. Kramatome's house, and our hero saw at a glance that something unusual had happened.

"Hallo, Charlie," he exclaimed, "you look rather wild about the eyes. What is in the wind now?"

Charlie Drummond, instead of replying, turned to Lord Vansittart, who moved his feet uneasily, and returned the look with compound interest.

"What on earth is the matter with you?" Lionel exclaimed. "Why don't you speak? Charlie, unless you tell me what is the matter, I shall forget myself and knock you down."

"Well then," Charlie gasped, "the very devil is the matter, Sam and Joblot have disappeared."

"What!" Lionel almost screamed.

"It is a fact," Vansittart chimed in. "This precious note was addressed to me. I will read it: 'My nobble lordship, I can't abear to see Mister Lionel looking so orfully quare, and as I knows wot prays on his mind I hev gone to find Mister Codlings myself. Not, my lud, that I means to coller him on my own imponsibility, but to bring back the noos of ware he is to be found. Your ludships obadient sarvint, SAM SCARECROW.—P.S. I have pressed Joblot into the sarvice, and he ses that he don't care if Mister Kramatome biles him over a slow fire.—P.S.S. Brake this gently to Mister Lionel, and tell him that arter I have found Mister Codlings he may kick me to his 'art's content.'"

"The fool!—the ass!—the idiot!" Lionel gasped, with marked emphasis on each epithet. "He must be mad to leave me at a time when I most want him."

"Sam is eccentric, but he is no fool," Vansittart said. "Give him a few days, and depend on it he will return with a satisfactory account of himself."

"I don't care if he does," Lionel replied savagely. "He had no right to disobey my orders, and I have a mind to discharge him for so doing."

"You will do nothing of the sort," Charlie said. "You would be like a fish out of water without Sam. I agree with Vansittart, and so will you when you get cooler."

"I will never forgive him for this," Lionel declared. "If he had asked my permission it would have been another thing, but to leave me in the lurch like this is too much of a joke."

"Come—come," said Vansittart, taking his friend's arm, "you are not talking like yourself. Have some lunch with us, and you will feel all the better for it."

"Lunch be hanged!" Lionel began, but the next instant the angry shadow had passed away from his face.

"You are both right," he said. "I ought to know Sam's character better than to distrust it for an instant. Ha, ha, ha! what will Kramatome say when he hears of Joblot's flight?"

"He knows all about it," Charlie replied; "and he is dancing about like a bear on hot irons. Don't go near him. It isn't safe; besides, I am getting hungry, and you can easily postpone the interview."

At the very moment that the three friends commenced strolling towards the Burlington, in Cork-street, Sam Scarecrow and Joblot sat stretching their legs outside an inn on the Romford road.

Before them on a table was about five pounds of cold roast pork, a huge loaf of bread, a jar of pickled onions, and a foaming pot of ale.

"Now," said Sam, looking at his melancholy companion, and sniffing suspiciously, "don't you pitch into that beer, and lose your 'ed; for there's lots to be done to-day. I've a wery lively recollection of wot whiskey did for you."

"Whiskers," Joblot replied feebly, "is only good for them as have strong constitootions; and mine won't stand it. Oh, lor'! Mister Scarecrow, I feel a kind of creepin' all down my back, and I a'most wish I hadn't come."

"You can go back if you like," Sam said; "but not a blessed bit o' that pork do you touch, nor a ha'penny do you get to help you on the road. There never was sich a chap as you."

"I can't help it," Joblot groaned; "I am so narvous."

"Narvous about wot?" Sam demanded savagely.

"I'm afeared that Mister Kramatome will send me to prison," the unhappy flunky replied, with tears in his eyes. "He is such a terrible man when he is angry."

"If you'll hact on my adwice," Sam returned, "you can make him afeared of you."

"I should like to know 'ow it is to be done," Joblot groaned.

"Well, we shan't be gone more than three days, at the most," Sam replied. "Well, o' course you must face him; and this is 'ow to do it. Walk bang inter his study, and catch him in the weskit as orften as will take his wind away, and when you have done that tell him that you've been and gone and thrown yourself on the parish in consequence o' shortness o' wittles, and that you've come back to show him how much stronger you are."

"I daren't do it," Joblot gasped. "It 'ud be as much as my life is worth."

"Pshaw!" Sam sneered. "If you had half my pluck, you would ha' doubled him up long ago. Bust old Kramatome! Let's have some grub. I'm as hempty as a drum."

Both attacked the good things before them, Sam keeping a wary eye on the beer, which he dispensed to his fellow traveller in moderate doses, and helped himself to such gulps that he gasped again every time he took his lips from the pewter.

"So," said Sam, leaning back on the bench, and ogling the clouds in a comfortable sort of way, "we air on the right track. The moment that tramp sed he had parsed a lean chap and one as fat as a prize pig I knowed 'em to be Long Jem and Mister Codlings. Drayton fair is to-morrer, and we shall drop down on 'em bootifully, but mind no roarin' when we see 'em, or they'll bolt again."

"I'll be wery careful," Joblot replied, half-asleep under the influence of unlimited pork and limited beer. "You'll stand by me in case of a fight, won't you?"

"You're big enough to take care of yourself," Sam retorted, wrathfully, "but I'll see that you aint killed outright."

Joblot jumped up, staring and affrighted.

"It won't come to anythink so bad as that, will it?" he almost howled.

"I don't know," said Sam, who took a great delight in frightening his companion. "Showmen air rum chaps when put out. I have been amongst 'em, so I ought to know."

Joblot got on his legs, and cast an anxious glance down the road leading to London.

"I think I'll go back," he gasped. "I aint a strong man, and any injury might be the death o' me."

"You'll go back when I go back," Sam said, seizing Joblot by the collar. "Say another word and I'll give you a taste o' somethin' you may hexpect, perwidin' Long Jem falls foul on you."

"Oh, lor'," Joblot roared, falling on his knees, "I never thought it would come to this. Don't hit me, Mister Scarecrow."

"Here, get up," Sam cried. "I won't hurt you if you are civil and obligin'. Git hup, you hass. Don't you see that heverybody is a grinnin' at you?"

Sam hauled his trembling companion to his feet, and having paid the score at the inn set out, with Joblot struggling painfully at his side.

It was pleasant country that they passed through, the sky was blue, and the sun shone beautifully, but soon dark and heavy clouds appeared in the south west, and the unmistakeable sound of distant thunder caused Sam to look up.

"There's goin to be a storm," he said, looking about him for the nearest shelter. "Dash it! I don't see a house nowhere; shan't we get jolly wet? Wot's the matter with you, Joblot? Blow me if you aint as green as a hoak in full bloom."

"I can't abear thunder and lightning," Joblot groaned; "it allus hupsets me, and makes me feel as if I had swallowed all the pills as Holloway ever made."

"I knowed a chap similar accordin," Sam replied. "He couldn't help it, poor chap, but it were that larfable to see him double up that I used almost to bust my sides. My heye, ain't it comin hup fast? Lor', there was a flash."

Joblot saw it, and he saw something else, that being a haystack, for which he made with all due speed, and dived into the loose stuff scattered about the ground.

"Well, I'm blowed," Sam gasped. "I had no idea he was so lively, he went through that like a 'arlequin, and there aint so much as his heels to be seen."

Sam sat down under a hedge, but a blinding streak, like some huge blue serpent of dazzling brightness, shot from the sky, and drove him out of that shelter.

"Hawful," Sam murmured, as a crash of thunder followed, shaking the very earth. "I have seen a good many things, but nothin' so bad as that."

As Sam uttered these words the clouds opened, and a comet seemed to shoot from them.

For a moment all was darkness again, but the next instant the atmosphere seemed ablaze with light as a deafening explosion took place, and Sam was twisted up and hurled to the other side of the road.

Dazed and bewildered he staggered to his feet, and was about to follow Joblot's example when he discovered that the haystack was on fire, and blazing merrily in spite of the drenching rain.

"If he wasn't struck he's frightened to death," Sam groaned. "Here, hi! I say, Joblot, get up, the stack is on fire."

One leg appeared from the hay and kicked spasmodically, and a sepulchral voice bade him go away, and leave the sufferer to die in peace.

"He is alive, and that's a comfort," Sam said, seizing the protruding leg, and tugging at it with all his might. "Come out, you fool, or you'll be burnt alive."

Showers of sparks and burning tufts of hay were falling in all directions, and Sam received a flaming halo on the crown of his hat, which he got rid of with some difficulty.

Joblot clung tenaciously to the tufts of grass until his coat-tails caught fire, and then he came out and danced about in the midst of the rain, thunder, and lightning, in a style that caused Sam to keep a respectful distance; he being under the impression that fright had turned the brain of Mr. Kramatome's devoted servant.

"Is it out?" Joblot roared.

"Yes, it's hout," Sam replied, "and a precious narrow escape you've had, and if it hadn't been for me you would ha' been a cinder."

"I feel very much like one—behind," Joblot groaned, pressing his hands to the spot which had passed through the fiery ordeal. "What was it? How did it happen?"

"It was a thunderbolt," Sam replied in a husky voice. "I seed it a comin', and summat lifted me orf my feet and chucked me bang agin that gate-post, and when I got up the stack was combusted, and that's all I know about it."

The storm passed over, but for hours the thunder rolled about in a grumbling style as if it longed to return, and Joblot, as every peal resounded, started, and seized Sam Scarecrow sometimes round the neck, sometimes by the arm, and finally sent him sprawling into the road by mixing his legs up strangely with his companions.

"If you lay hold of me agin," Sam growled, picking up his hat, and a few thorns out of his fingers, "I'll knock you down and jump on you. Blow me if I don't think you've got Saint Witusses dance. Keep still, can't you?"

"I wish I could," Joblot gasped, as another clap of thunder made him skip three feet into the air. "Ah, Mister Scarecrow, you don't know what I suffer."

"You needn't make other people suffer too," Sam growled. "Look at the knees of my trousers—they're cut through."

The unhappy cause of the accident stammered out an apology, and Sam, always ready to forgive, forgot everything but the mission on which they were bent.

Tired and worn out at last Sam sat down on the very milestone on which Tommy had rested his weary limbs, and Joblot, caring not a jot for the damp grass, threw himself down and fell asleep, to be roused by the vigorous application of a scarf-pin, plied by the ever energetic Sam.

"You'll ketch sich a cold that you'll sneeze your-self through everythink thinner than a nine-inch wall," Sam said. "Now then, hup you get, or I'll try wot heffect a penknife will have. There's the town, and we must find our way to it by back lanes, as Mister Codlings may drop on us afore we are aweer of it."

Joblot, stimulated into action, and smarting dread-fully, rose, and shaking himself like a drowsy retriever followed Sam across a footpath, and down a maze of lanes, until they, hiding behind a hedge, could see the open green on which a number of tents were pitched. Sam heard the beating of a drum, but his heart beat louder as Tommy, in all the glory of tights and spangles, emerged from a tent, arm in arm with Long Jem.

"There he is," Sam gasped, "don't he look lovely."

"He just do!" Joblot exclaimed in admiration; "I wish I was a hacrabat."

"Down you go," Sam cried in an agonised whisper as Tommy and Long Jem drew nearer. "Never mind the ditch, there ain't more than three feet of water in it. However, we've found him, and that's worth all the crown jewels."

Tommy and the acrobat passed on their way to the Bull and Horns unconscious that they were being so closely watched, and the moment they were out of sight Sam sprang to his feet and dragged Joblot half a mile before he could make out what the extraordinary and unexpected proceeding meant.

"I say," Joblot gasped out at last, "you're a pullin' my harm orf."

"Never mind your harm," Sam cried, wild with excitement; "come on, put three miles between him and us, and then I shall be satisfied."

"But I am so tired that I can hardly stand on my feet," Joblot pleaded. "Oh! lor, do rest jest a little while, please, only five minutes."

Sam made no reply, but produced the avenging scarf pin, and getting in the wake of Joblot charged him whenever he showed signs of flagging, and so they went on walking, running, and trotting, until the ancient church steeple of Drayton was no longer to be seen.

"There," said Sam, as he dropped himself down, "I can look Mister Lionel in the face now. We'll wait here until we can get a lift; and by all that is lucky, here comes a butcher's cart."

CHAPTER XXVII.

MR. STYNGY HAS AN IDEA—MRS. SCRUBBEM LETS THE CAT OUT OF THE BAG—MR. STYNGY HAS AN INTERVIEW WITH MR. KRAMATOME AND LIONEL —THE RESULT—MR. PHILO STYNGY ACTS AS GUIDE —THE CHEQUERS—A RETIRED LODGING—THE RE-VOLVING FLOOR.

AS the footsteps approached, sounding more dis-tinctly every moment on the stairs, Mr. Grubbe grasped the edge of the rickety table, and his face underwent a remarkable change in colour.

It was not white nor red, but a peculiar bilious green, such as may be seen on a fading cabbage in the full glare of the sunlight.

"Why don't you go to the door, and see who it is?" he gasped out.

Mr. Styngy did not move, but looked furtively at the half-open cupboard, as if some idea of hiding within it had entered his head.

"You coward!" Grubbe hissed, as he drew a huge clasp-knife from his pocket. "Hang it, I'll die game!"

The footsteps came nearer, and then an exceed-ingly unkempt head of hair, and anything but a clean face, was thrust into the room, as a shrill voice piped out—

"If you please, gentlemen, missus sent me up for the rent."

"Curse your mistress!" Grubbe exclaimed, but much relieved as he hid the knife. "Tell her that she will be paid this evening."

"If you please, sir," said the girl hesitating, "missus said as 'ow I was to wait for the money."

"Pay the wench and let her go," Grubbe said, turning to Mr. Styngy who was gazing thought-fully at the cracks in the ceiling. "Do you hear?"

"Yes, I hear," Mr. Styngy replied; "but as I have unfortunately been disappointed in the City, I——"

"Missus ses you are always being disappointed in the City, and that if you can't pay up reg'lar you had better go."

"Mrs. Scrubbem is an extremely impertinent woman," Mr. Styngy said, with a ghost of the old haughtiness in his voice; "she must wait."

"Oh, I must wait, must I?" shrieked out a voice that made Mr. Styngy jump like a pursued frog.

As these words were uttered a tall, fiery-faced woman pushed the miserable servant aside, and bounced into the room with awful suddenness.

"And what do you mean by that?" exclaimed the lady, placing her arms akimbo, and working herself into a passion. "Ah, you may look at me! I am not afraid of you!"

"My good woman," Mr. Styngy began, when Mrs. Scrubbem took him up like a feather before a whirlwind.

"I may be a widder left with five children," she exclaimed in the highest pitch her tongue could muster, "and I may have to stand at the wash-tub fourteen hours at a stretch, but I am not to be in-sulted by a parcel of wagabones who gets their livin' nobody knows how."

"Who insulted you?" Grubbe growled. "Hold your row, and be a little more reasonable."

"Pay what you owe and I'll be reasonable enough!" Mrs. Scrubbem exclaimed. "I can't live and eat and drink in other people's houses for nothing, and you shan't in mine. Why, if it hadn't been through a slice of luck all along o' Mister Wilful——"

Mr. Grubbe thundered out in such a voice that even Mrs. Scrubbem turned pale, and made a step towards the landing.

"Mister Wilful, him as lives with Mr. Krama-tome, and give me a couple o' sov'rins for havin' a lark with a fat young chap named Codlings, I might have been in the workus, and I might go there now for all you cared."

It was Mr. Styngy's turn to be surprised now.

Turning with the velocity of a teetotum he sat upon the window-sill, and stared at his landlady to such an extent that she thought he had gone mad.

"Codlings," he murmured, "not Thomas Cod-lings! Say that his Christain name is Thomas."

"Which it is," Mrs. Scrubbem returned. "What do you know about him?"

"He—he is the friend of my youth," Mr. Styngy replied, clapping his hands as in glee. "Oh, this is news, joyful news. Oh, Thomas, Thomas, how often have I longed to fold you in my arms! Oh, wayward youth, can it be true that I, who am now in—ahem!—needy circumstances, have found my former pupil."

"Stow this nonsense," Grubbe snarled. "Mrs. Scrubbem will tell you where to find him, and you must see him at once."

"I will," Mr. Styngy exclaimed, pumping up a few crocodile tears. "My good creature, you shall be paid in full, to say nothing of a handsome present

I intend to make you, in consideration of this most valuable information."

Mrs. Scrubbem was surprised, and somewhat humbled to find that her lodgers were at least of some consequence, and she readily gave Mr. Kramatome's address, which Mr. Styngy carefully noted down.

"I will call on Codlings at once," he said, carefully brushing a dilapidated and woe-begone hat. "Mrs. Scrubbem, I owe you a deep debt of gratitude."

"And so do I," said Grubbe, "for this young Wilful you speak of is the son of a lady I esteem, and I may say once admired. If I am not mistaken he was one of this young Codlings' schoolmates—"

"He was," Mr. Styngy said, "and many a time I ——"

"There, there," Grubbe interrupted, "Mrs. Scrubbem does not want to hear any more about him. She is a sensible, business-like woman, and wants her money."

"You've hit it exactly, sir," said Mrs. Scrubbem, a little more respectfully, and departed.

"This is splendid news," Grubbe said, softly, but with eyes flashing full of fiendish meaning.

"It is indeed," Mr. Styngy replied, calmly, "and if I am not mistaken I can make a market out of Codlings, who was always a warm-hearted and confiding boy."

"Curse Codlings," Grubbe said, surlily, "and what you can make out of him—I want revenge."

"And you shall have it," Mr. Styngy replied, "but we must be cautious. I will call at Mr. Kramatome's, where in all probability I shall see both Codlings and Wilful. Naturally they will be touched by my condition, and if I can only persuade Wilful to accompany me to ——"

"A place I know of," Grubbe chimed in, "and which I will tell you of presently, I shall have accomplished all I have to live for."

Mr. Styngy looked at his beloved friend, and shuddered.

"You will not do anything rash, I hope," he said, faintly.

Grubbe laughed outright in his face.

"What do you take me for?" he exclaimed. "Remember that whatever happens we row in the same boat. If you are chicken-hearted you can leave the business alone, but ——"

"I was merely suggesting that extreme caution is necessary," Mr. Styngy gasped. "My dear friend, I will stand by you."

"That is well," Grubbe said. "Now then go, and see what can be done. I shall be on thorns till you return."

Mr. Styngy was only too glad to get out of his amiable companion's sight, but so uncomfortable was he in his mind that he walked along like a man in a dream, running up against and jostling everybody and everything, from a costermonger's barrow to a lamp-post.

Violent indeed, and in some instances extremely rude, were the epithets poured upon his head, but Mr. Styngy heeded them not, even supposing he heard them, but kept the uneven tenour of his way until his fingers encircled the bell-handle of Mr. Kramatome's house.

"Dear me, how faint I feel," he murmured, as the sound of the bell reached his ears. "This is foolish—very, considering the circumstances. Ah! is Mr. Kramatome at home?"

"I'll see," the servant said, curtly, as she looked him up and down suspiciously. "I can take any message you like to him. Why didn't you ring the servants' bell?"

This query rather nettled Mr. Styngy, but he bottled his wrath, and smiled sweetly on the damsel.

"If you will take my card up to him," he said, "I have no doubt that he will see me."

The girl turned the paste-board over between her fingers, looked at the visitor, and then, with a half-frightened glance at the hats and coats in the hall, she closed the door with a bang in Mr. Styngy's face.

Mr. Kramatome was rather perplexed, for the girl had described the irate gentleman on the doorstep as a man in a threadbare coat, a greasy hat, and a shirt-front in much request of a washerwoman's services, but the learned examiner knew by experience that many men of talent and science utterly disregarded external appearance, and commanded the domestic to apologise for her rude behaviour and to show him up.

Mr. Styngy mounted the staircase with all the dignity he could muster, and as the appearance of comfort met his eyes he sighed heavily, and thought of Cheetham Hall and Tommy Codlings.

"My dear sir," Mr. Kramatome said, when his visitor was seated, "servants are the plague of my life, I assure you. Joblot, my footman, and a fellow with a squint, named Sam Scarecrow—Mr. Styngy, are you ill?"

"A mere passing faintness," Mr. Styngy replied, in a profuse perspiration. "The room is very warm."

"I do not find it so," Mr. Kramatome said, rising to open the window. "Now, sir, I am at your service. To what object may I attribute the honour of your visit?"

"You see before you," Mr. Styngy said, "a man who has seen better days."

"Oh!" ejaculated Mr. Kramatome, as his face lengthened, "really—ahem!—I have had so many calls on my purse lately that I am compelled to close it against all appeals."

Mr. Styngy had not come for assistance, and said so in such terms that Mr. Kramatome apologised.

"I took the liberty to call, in order that I might see two of my old pupils, now, I believe, in your charge. I allude to Lionel Wilful and Thomas Codlings."

"Codlings is not here," Mr. Kramatome replied. "The unfortunate lad has suffered for some time of a malady which has turned his brain, and but two days ago he fled from this house, and we can gather no tidings of his whereabouts."

"This news distresses me," said Mr. Styngy, burying his face in his handkerchief. "And Wilful?"

"Is in his room," said Mr. Kramatome. "Do not give way, my dear sir. Painful as your feelings may be there is yet hope."

Mr. Kramatome summoned a servant, and presently Lionel was ushered into the study.

Mr. Kramatome was rather surprised at the greeting our hero gave his old master. It was quiet and gentlemanly, but without the least warmth.

"Ah, Wilful, there is a change in me," Mr. Styngy said. "My days of prosperity are for ever gone I fear, but friends have come to the rescue. I am going to Australia, where I hope to bury the past, and look forward to a brighter future. I thought you would not be offended if I called to say good-bye."

Lionel was a little touched by this speech, and looking at Mr. Styngy compassionately said—

"I wish you well with all my heart, but how did you find me out?"

"I have seen you several times in the street," Mr. Styngy replied, "but I never liked to speak to you, for," looking at his clothing, "we are on a different footing now."

"I have known what adversity brings," Lionel said, looking at Mr. Styngy, who quailed before that honest glance; "but I am content to forget and forgive all."

"Even your bitterest enemy, Grubbe?" Mr. Styngy whispered. "I saw him this afternoon."

"Where?" Lionel exclaimed.

"Hush!" Mr. Styngy said. "I must speak to you alone. If you will come to my humble lodgings I can put you on the right track."

"I will go anywhere," Lionel said impetuously. "When and where shall I find you ?"

"I am always at home," Mr. Styngy whispered back. "I have a humble lodging in a locality known as the Chequers, in Smithfield, but as the place is rather difficult to find I will willingly accompany you."

"I shall be at liberty in a quarter of an hour," Lionel said.

Mr. Kramatome had not overheard the latter part of this conversation, having been summoned below, and he was infinitely surprised, on returning, to find that Lionel and Mr. Styngy were going out together.

"If you will follow I will lead the way," said Mr. Styngy.

"Why not have a cab ?" Lionel replied. "I will pay, and we shall reach your place all the quicker ; besides, we can talk as we go along."

"My young friend," Mr. Styngy replied, "I abhor cabs and cabmen, and I have vowed never to encourage one again. You can ride if you wish—I will walk."

"Oh, as you like," Lionel said, laughing. "I was thinking of you."

And Mr. Philo Styngy was thinking of himself too. His brain was in a whirl, and a fierce fire was consuming him.

Into what abyss was he drifting, and where would all this plotting and scheming end ? Perhaps, he thought, so sick and faint that he could scarcely stand, in a life-long imprisonment or the gallows.

He was a coward at heart, or he would have warned the lad, and brought the villainous convict to justice, and left himself to fate.

It was growing into night when Mr. Styngy turned from the main thoroughfare, and dived into a maze of courts and alleys so bewildering, so thronged with filthy children, foul-mouthed women, and men slouching about, that Lionel felt half inclined to turn back ; but whatever opinion he might have entertained of his guide's character, he had no suspicion that the oily, selfish, grasping villain was luring him on to destruction.

"This is a strange place," he said, coming up to Mr. Styngy's side ; "what on earth possessed you to pick out such a spot to live in ?"

"It is out-of-the-way and retired," Mr. Styngy replied. "There are no prying eyes here—a man might live and die and his next-door neighbour be none the wiser of his existence or exit."

"That I can readily believe," Lionel returned. "I thought I knew something of London but I find I am a mere babe in the wood. Is this the place ?"

"Yes," said Mr. Styngy, stopping to make sure himself, by glancing at the address given him by Grubbe. "Ground floor. Take no notice of anything or anybody. There are other lodgers in the house, and they are a little noisy at times."

"Live and learn," Lionel thought, as Mr. Styngy knocked at the door softly with his knuckles. "This will be something to tell Van and Charlie about."

The door was opened by a man with a patch over one eye, and a short black pipe stuck between his coarse lips.

"Come in," said this individual, without looking at Lionel. "Iv'e been a waitin' for you to come back, for there's only one key, and we can't very well halve it."

Mr. Styngy crossed the landing, and Lionel followed.

Suddenly the floor under his feet began to move, his feet reeled, and then, as a cry of terror burst from his lips, he felt himself going down—down—seemingly into the very bowels of the earth.

At last there was a crash, and he fell stunned and bleeding on a cold, damp slimy floor.

CHAPTER XXVIII.

SAM HAS A TURN UP WITH A BUTCHER—TWO ROUNDS AND A DAMP FINISH—SAM FALLS INTO SIN, AND STEALS A HORSE AND CART—ON THE ROAD—ARRESTED—THE BEADLE'S HOME—ESCAPE AND FLIGHT.

SAM'S eyes were not at fault.

A butcher's cart was coming down the road with a butcher within it, and, what was more, the butcher was very drunk.

Now, it is a strange fact that, when a butcher takes more of the potent than is good for his constitution, he invariably evinces a propensity to punch every head that comes in his way ; he is at once ferocious and bloodthirsty, raves, waves his arms, and finds his way to the police-station, accompanied by six or seven policemen, who treat him to the frog's march—that is to say, with his face downwards, and his legs and arms extended so as to render him absolutely powerless.

Horse, cart, and driver seemed to be actuated with the same desire.

The horse was doing its best to bolt ; the cart was wabbling about now on one wheel, and now on the other, and the butcher, holding the reins, lashed the poor beast, and encouraged it to a swift speed with shrill cries and innumerable curses.

"Here, hi! pull up, there," Sam roared ; "you'll break your neck, d'rectly."

"Don't care, if I do," hiccuped the champion of the cleaver, pulling up and glaring as ferociously as it is possible out of one eye. "Who are you to interfere with me I should like to know?"

"I'm nobody in particular," Sam replied. "Me and my mate want to get back to London as soon as possible, and I thought about axing you to give us a lift."

"I'll give you a lift," said the butcher, tumbling headlong out of the cart. "Hullo, why dash me if you don't squint like a Chinee bimage."

"Who said I didn't ?" Sam retorted, wrathfully. "Leave my heyes alone, will yer ?"

"Yesh, when I've done with 'em," the butcher roared ; "blow me if I don't knock 'em straight. I hates a man as squints."

"Keep orf," Sam roared, as the butcher commenced sparring. "Mind, I warns you, and don't want to take no mean adwantage, as you is that drunk that you can't stand."

"Come on," gasped the butcher, mistaking Joblot for Sam ; "I can see two of yer, but I knows there's only one."

"I ain't a fightin' man," Joblot gasped, retiring precipitately. "Mur—der."

"Here, I'll soon put a stop to this," Sam said, slipping out of his coat. "Come on you wampire?"

And the next instant the butcher was on his back, staring, with a placid countenance, at the bright blue sky.

"That's sobered you a bit, I think," Sam cried, dancing round his prostrate foe. "Sit hup and have a few more ; they'll bring you round quicker than all the sodery water in the world."

"I ran agin somethin'," the butcher said, feeling the bridge of his nose tenderly.

"Get hup, and I'll show you the way to run agin it once more," Sam said.

"So I will," roared the butcher, staggering to his feet, and rushing upon Sam with great fury.

Sam proved himself to be as merciful as he was powerful, and, waiting for his adversary, he merely tripped him up and sent him flying heels over head into a ditch.

"Now, Joblot," said Sam, jumping into the cart and taking the reins ; "we'll go to London in fine style. Come on, or I'm orf without yer."

"But I say," Joblot expostulated, "won't there be an awful row about this ?"

"Wery likely," Sam replied, calmly. "I've heerd that horse stealin' used to be a hangin' matter, and I ain't sure that the law is altered."

"Oh! lor," Joblot groaned. "I wish I was out o' this."

"You'll be nout of it presently," Sam said, savagely, as he gave the horse a flick. "Hopen your mouth agin, and I shoves yer inter the road."

For a few miles they rolled along in fine style, but suddenly to Sam's surprise, and no little alarm, the horse pulled up at the door of a public-house, and refused to move.

"Bust it, here's a go," gasped the youth with the squint eye, plying the whip vigorously. "Gee up, you warmint."

But the warmint obstinately refused to gee up, and the landlord, hearing the confusion, came out and stared mightily hard at the cart and its occupants.

"Hullo, wot's this?" cried Boniface. "Why dash me if that ain't Bill Savago's turn out. This 'ere's a case for the perlice."

Flight would have been easy, but Joblot was so completely doubled up with fright that he could not move hand or foot, and Sam could not find it in his heart to desert him at so critical a time.

"Pull yourself together, and cut and run," Sam gasped. "I'll cover your retreat."

"It ain't in me," Joblot moaned; "I couldn't run a hundred yards if you was to give me as many suvrins."

"This is a nice perdicament," Sam said.

"It air," the landlord said; "where did you get that ere cart?"

"We found it," Sam replied, and we was lookin' heverywheres for the howner."

"That won't do for me," the landlord returned. "Ere comes Mister Hevans—jest see if he'll believe that yarn."

Sam turned and beheld a burly man, arrayed in the full dress uniform of a beadle, sailing majestically down the road. "Come, I say, make a move," Sam gasped, damp with a sudden perspiration, as he bestowed a hearty kick on Joblot. "Bust me, if you ain't as bad as Punch after the performance. We can dodge the beadle."

"I could'nt dodge a beetle much more a beadle," Joblot whined. "Leave me to my fate."

"That be blowed," Sam said. "Well, I s'pose we must stay and make the best of it. I say, old red face, wot's the beadle got to do with this 'ere affair?"

"You'd better axe him," the landlord said, grinning all over his fat face. "Mr. Hevans is the perliceman."

"Then it's all over," Sam groaned; "we shall be collared and hauled afore the madgistrates, and remanded. Meanwhile, Mister Codlings will be—the Lord only knows where."

Evans, beadle and policeman, rolled into one, and, consequently, the terror of the village, strode up, and, after a brief consultation with the landlord, he, in a voice of thunder, called on Sam and Joblot to alight and surrender.

"All right," Sam said, rolling his helpless companion into the road, "you'll be sorry for this, my friend. There'll be a meetin' in Hyde Park about this 'ere tyranny. P'raps you don't know who I ham?"

"No, and I don't care," Mr. Evans said, producing a pair of handcuffs from his pocket. "Now, then, young feller, don't keep me waitin'."

Sam held out his hand, and the next instant he and Joblot were coupled together.

"Take care of the 'orse and trap until Savage turns up," the officer said, turning to the landlord. "I shall take these fellers 'ome till the mornin'."

"Mind they don't get away," Boniface said; "why not take 'em to the lock-up?"

"Because it's full o' tramps now," Mr. Evans replied. "Ah! I've had a busy time of it, but dooty must be done. Now then, my shavers, come along?"

"And this is wot you get for takin' care o' people's property," Sam said. "Come on, Joblot. Wait till I get afore them beaks, and see if I don't make 'em shake in their boots."

So saying Sam knocked his hat over his eyes with his disengaged hand, and, dragging Joblot after him, strode down the road with the air of an injured man.

Mr. Evans conducted our unfortunate friends to his house—a square, red-brick building, bearing the resemblance of a small Methodist chapel crushed down by some heavy weight.

Half a dozen squalling children hailed their parent, and a thin, consumptive woman appeared in the doorway, and held up her hands.

"More prisoners," she said. "Deary dear, there seems to be no end to 'em. What have the poor fellers been and gone and done?"

"That's no business o' yourn," Mr. Evans replied with questionable politeness. "Is tea ready?"

"It won't be long," said the little woman meekly, "no more than a quarter of an hour."

"Didn't I leave strict horders that it was to be ready at six o'clock?" Mr. Evans roared, hustling Sam and Joblot into the house. "Oh, you precious beauty!"

Mrs. Evans was not a beauty, and received the compliment with a heavy sigh as she commenced placing a small array of cups and saucers on the table.

"None o' your snivellin games," said the amiable beadle, visibly swelling with wrath; "they won't go down with me. I s'pose there's nothin' hextra for my tea."

"You left me with only a shilling this morning," his spouse replied, with a reproachful glance out of the corner of her eyes, "and every farthing went for the children's dinner. I have had nothing myself."

"And this is the effects of getting married," Mr. Evans exclaimed, waving his hands in the air. "I may be out mornin and night a-doin of my dooty, and wot do I meet with when I come home footsore and weary? Why, ugly looks, stale bread and butter, and wishy-washy tea. Bah!"

"Bah!" Sam echoed, and for the life of him he could not help it.

The sound of his voice roused Mr. Evans, who cast a withering look upon the prisoners.

"I'll put a stopper on you," he said, rising and placing his huge fist on the bridge of Joblot's nose. Come this way, and I'll show you where you are to sleep."

"You're a nice ole chap for a tea party, you air," Sam said. "If I was yer wife I'd pisen yer."

"Hold yer tongue, you wagabone!" roared the man in authority.

"You'll have to gag me fust, and that's agin the law," Sam said. "Lead on, you bloated willain. You've had your fling, but there's another day tomorrer, and may I be biled alive if I don't make yer smart for this."

Mr. Evans's reply to this threat was not a verbal one.

Lifting his foot he favoured Sam with a sounding kick, which shot that youth and Joblot out of the door into the back yard.

"Go it," Sam cried defiantly; "have another go. You'll get 'em back with composite hinterest."

The beadle unlocked a shed, and thrusting his prisoners in, pointed to a pitcher of water, and strode away.

"Aren't we to have any grub?" Sam yelled through the keyhole.

"Not a mossel," Mr. Evans replied. "Go to sleep, and think yourselves lucky that you're allowed to do that."

"Well," said Sam, as he and Joblot sat down on a heap of straw in the corner of the shed, "of all the blessed goes this is the blessedest. I say, wot defence can we make?"

"I'm sure I don't know," Joblot replied, blowing his nose in a red cotton handkercheaf. "Oh?

Mister Scarecrow, we are ruined, and it air all your fault."

"Drop that 'ere, and the sooner yer get out o' the water cart line the better I shall like it," Sam growled; "where's the good o' blubbering? Let us knock our heads together, and see if we can't save the beaks the trouble o' tryin' hus."

"Wot d'yer mean?" Joblot said, grasping at the faintest hope, as a drowning man will clutch at a straw.

"Why jest this?" Sam went on. "If we could only get these handcuffs orf, escape would be easy."

"But we can't get em off," Joblot groaned; "mine is bitin' inter the flesh like a wice."

"Now, listen to me," Sam whispered, "we must wait till arter dark, and then break the handcuffs if we can't get em orf." There's a loose brick in the wall, and that will do the business, but we mustn't be in a hurry. I wonder wot the time is now?"

"Not more than eight, I should think," said his companion in distress.

"Then we must keep still for a couple of hours at the least," Sam replied. "Country people believe that airly to bed and airly to rise is the proper thing, and there'll be precious few about after ten. I'm a goin' to have a nap, and you'd better foller soot, as the chimbley sweeper said to his boy."

"I shan't get a wink," Joblot groaned.

"Then you can wake me," Sam said, stretching himself out.

Sam immediately began to snore, and Joblot lay thinking dismally until he heard a church clock strike the hour of ten, and then he nudged the sleeper.

"Wot's the matter?" Sam said, sitting up and yawning. "It can't be time to get hup yet. Oh! lor, I forgot where I was."

"It's ten o'clock," Joblot said. "Hist, wot is that?"

"That busted beadle is lockin' his door, and is goin' to bed," Sam said; "now for it. Mind yer don't rasp that beak o' yourn agin the wall. It's awful dark."

Sam groped his way about until he found the loose brick, and extracting it, and the one under it, he warned Joblot to take care of his fingers.

"Now," said Sam, placing one of the bricks on the floor and pressing the other, "we puts the handcuffs over this ere, and I gives that bit as connects em a whack until we air free."

"Mind you hit straight?" Joblot said, trembling, as he obeyed.

"You might as well talk to a howl, and tell him to see in the day-time," Sam gasped. " I'll do my best to keep clear of your knuckles, but you must take yer chance."

Three smart blows, and the work was done, and Sam and Joblot rose and performed a joyful horn-pipe round each other, but their joy was short-lived, for the next instant a key turned in the lock, and the light of a stable lantern flooded the prison shed.

The prisoners started back as they beheld Mr. Evans and the butcher, whose eyes were bloodshot, and whose legs were still inclined to wander from each other.

CHAPTER XXIX.

LIONEL'S PRISON—GRUBBE UNFOLDS HIS PLANS.

FOR at least an hour Lionel lay inanimate, but conciousness returned, and raising himself on his elbow he looked around his dismal prison.

It was a fearsome place. Slimy water dripped from the roof, and now and then came the hurrying patter of savage sewer rats rushing in hordes of thousands in search of prey.

"Great Heavens!" Lionel murmured, "for what purpose have I been entrapped here? Oh, poor fool, that I have been, I see it all now. This is a plot between Grubbe and that sneaking hound, Styngy and I—I—I shall be murdered."

There are but few moments in the life of man when he feels what may be termed the essence of agony, and but one, when the awful thought checks the blood and stills the heart, when all earthly hope is gone.

Men lying condemned die a hundred deaths during those short fleeting hours prescribed by the law for repentance, and then in the end comes an un-natural calmness, and the rest is a dream.

Lionel, poor boy, saw everything in his mind's eye. The scenes of his past life rose before him. He saw himself a schoolboy, heard the ringing laughter of his companions, and then, like the shadow of a thundercloud, rose the form of his persecutor. What would he do? How would he act? One blow and all would be over, but Grubbe was cruel, and would torture, or perhaps starve him to death.

As this last thought flashed through his brain Lionel staggered to his feet and ran round the cellar, grasping at the walls, beating at them with his hands till blood spurted from his fingers' ends, and shouting hoarsely for help.

None came, and another hour passed slowly away.

He had thrown himself down again on the clammy floor when a sound attracted his attention, and looking up he saw the the trap-door open, and immediately after Grubbe, lantern in hand, was lowered by means of a rope, which was drawn up an instant after his feet had touched ground.

For a few seconds he neither spoke nor took the slightest notice of his prisoner, but having placed the lantern in the centre of the floor he turned and said—

"Lionel Wilful, I have waited patiently, and I am now rewarded."

"Rewarded!" said Lionel, drawing himself up as well as his aching bones would allow him. "I understand you. I am in your power. I need not say that this cowardly deed is yours. I need not say that you lured me here, in order that you might give vent to the spleen of your detestable nature. Say what you will, do what you will, there will be one great day of reckoning."

"It has come," Grubbe said, fiendishly. "I said it would. I swore that I would hunt you down. I prayed that I might live to see you as you are now, in my power, at my mercy, that I might beat, hack, and tear you at my own will and pleasure."

"Go on," Lionel cried, "I am compelled to listen."

"That is what delights me," Grubbe replied. "I could stand in this foul den night and day and feel happy with such a sight before me. Here is the lion tamed so completely, that, although he does not confess it, he trembles to the very core of his heart, and would beg on his knees for mercy if he thought for a moment it would be granted."

"You lie," Lionel exclaimed, springing forward. "Wretch, if you had the strength of twenty men— Oh, God, I am stabbed."

"Not altogether wrong," Grubbe said, coolly wiping the blood off a long knife, "but there is no harm done, youngster. If it is any consolation to you I do not mean to put you out of the way yet."

"If there is one spark of humanity in your nature," Lionel said, faintly stemming the flow of blood from his arm, " end this quickly, but, oh, that I had my strength, I would batter your false face beyond recognition."

"You are a little more unreasonable even than I am," Grubbe said, laughing hoarsely, "for I mean to keep yours before me in—ha! ha!—all its youthful beauty. I will tell you a little story. Listen."

"The scene opens at Heath House, Hampstead,' Grubbe said, marking each word with a movement of his forefinger; "and it is there where we first met, and it was there where you and that vile

"HERE, I SAY!" TOMMY YELLED, FAINT WITH FEAR, "LET ME OUT OF THIS."

squinting wretch, Scarecrow, openly insulted me before your aunt and your mother—a lady for whom I once entertained feelings of the greatest res ect, and I may say love."

"If I had to die ten thousand deaths," Lionel broke out, passionately, "I should lay down my life happy in the thought that she did not disgrace the memory of my father by uniting herself to one of the greatest scoundrels allowed to blight the earth."

"Thank you," Grubbe returned, smiling grimly, "you were always complimentary; but pray do not interrupt me, or I shall be under the painful necessity of stopping your mouth with a gag I have brought with me in case of emergency."

"Go on," Lionel said, "whatever you say or do matters but little to me now."

"Perhaps not," Grubbe replied, "but still I intend to have my say. Well, from the earliest moment we met we hated each other. I detested you as a school-boy because," here the villain thrust his sneering face close to Lionel's, "you were so frank, so generous, so open-hearted, and, curse you, you were so like your mother in features that I could have stabbed you willingly twenty times a day."

"God preserve my poor mother," Lionel thought, fervently, as tears started to his eyes.

"I had ruined her and you, when Sam Scarecrow foiled my plans, and I was sent away for twenty years," Grubbe went on; "but I did the canting dodge, and got the right side of the chaplain. There wasn't a man with a ticket on his arm that knew half so many texts by heart as I did; and the way I sang and prayed at chapel even moved the warders—fellows with hearts as hard as the granite we poor devils had to quarry. Ah! my lad, many a time as I have struck my pick deep into the earth, working until the perspiration has rained down into my eyes, I have seen you, as I see you now, and gone mad with the idea that I was hacking you, and not cold, senseless earth."

Lionel made no reply. Blood was oozing from the wound in his arm, and he felt weary and sick at heart.

"It was an artful dodge that brought you here," Grubbe said, "and you may make up your mind that you will never leave, for here you will die and be buried. Ha, ha! I never thought I should turn sexton. Listen, my noble-hearted young friend, food you may have in any quantity, such as biscuits and salt meat, but not one drop of water shall pass your lips. In a few days you will be a madman, and I will come and see you dance, and hear you rave."

"Oh! God," Lionel cried, clasping his hands, "what devil is this in human form?"

"Aye, devil indeed," Grubbe cried, beating his chest. "The fires of hell have consumed me, and nothing but revenge on you can quench them."

Lionel staggered to his feet and flung himself upon Grubbe, but the poor boy was too weak to stand any chance with the desperate villain, who, seizing him round the waist, flung him with stunning force against the wall, and left him moaning, blood-stained, and quivering on the floor.

CHAPTER XXX.

SAM AND JOBLOT ESCAPE—A LITTLE SCRIMMAGE—THE FLIGHT — BORROWING A FILE — JOBLOT'S APPREHENSIONS—MRS. SCRULBEM'S MAID TELLS THE TRUTH—THE MARCH TO BOLTER'S RENTS—THE CAPTURE—DOWNFALL OF MESSRS. STYNGY, GRUBBE, AND CO., AND RELEASE OF LIONEL WILFUL.

"OH, Lord!" Joblot gasped, and, falling down on his knees, held out his hands towards Mr. Evans.

"Git hup, you faint-'arted son of a milk-pail," Sam said, favouring his companion with such a kick that it fairly lifted him from the ground. "We are two to two, and it's a rum 'un to me if we can't get out o' this."

"But you know I can't fight," Joblot groaned.

"Try," said Sam, "or I leaves you to your fate."

This awful threat roused the unhappy footman to action, and before Mr. Evans could recover his astonishment at seeing his prisoners free he received a staggerer between the eyes that not only treated him to a gratuitous pyrotechnic display, but rolled him over on his back like a groggy skittle.

The lantern was dashed to the ground, and Joblot, pouncing upon it, dealt Savage, the butcher, an awful crunching blow on the head with it, and the man of beef, still shaky about the knees, fell headlong over the prostrate constable.

"Now's the time," Sam roared. "Use your legs, Joblot. Think as 'ow you're a runnin' of a race."

Joblot did run: fear lent him speed, and the worthy pair rushed down the road at the rate of ten good English miles an hour, and kept it up until they reached Intwood.

"We're safe now," Sam gasped, leaning against a door-post, and mopping his liberally-perspiring brows; "but, as there air sich things as telegraphs, we had better make the best of our time, and get to London."

"I shall never reach it, I'm sure," Joblot panted. "Oh, dear! oh, dear! 'ow bad I feel!"

"You can't feel wus nor me," Sam declared. "My heye, 'ow we did pelt along! Jobby, I gives yer credit. I wonder if we can find a hearly 'ouse for a liquor. I feels as dry as a sand-pit."

"And so do I," Joblot returned, lolling out his tongue. "I think a drink 'ud bring me round."

"Then we'll have it some'ow," Sam said; "but, I say, we can't go anywheres just yet."

"Wot's the matter now?" Joblot demanded.

"Why, haven't we each got a handcuff on?" Sam said. "Wot wouldn't I give for a file now!"

"There's a blacksmith's forge," Joblot said. "I wonder if we was to ask the man——"

"Don't talk like a hass." Sam interrupted. "Jest as if he wouldn't ax 'ow we come possessed o' these 'ere hornyments, and 'and us over to the fust bobby."

"The what are we to do?" Joblot whined dismally, as a new and hitherto unthought-of fear entered his mind.

"Why, help ourselves, to be sure," Sam said. "Necessity is the mother of inwention. In that 'ere forge is a broken winder. Well, the man ain't at work yet; so wot does we do but borrows a file, get rid o' these bracelets, and cut our sticks? Keep your heye open to see that nobody is comin', and I'll soon work the horacle."

Sam was as good as his word, and presently returned with his wrist free, and set to work to relieve Joblot of the suspicious embellishment.

"You see," said Sam, as they trudged along the road, "where there's a will there's a way. Ah! there's the smoke of London! Many's the time I've cussed it; but now I welcomes it as an ole friend."

The nearer they got to London the faster beat Joblot's heart. He was thinking of the probable reception Mr. Kramatome would accord him.

"He'll kick me from one end of the house to the other," groaned the unhappy flunky, "he'll put on his thick boots for the purpose, and shan't I suffer?"

"If I was you," Sam said, as they turned into the square, "he'd find that two could play at that game. Ah! here we are; keep up your pecker. Now then, here comes the milkman, and we can get down the airy."

"I feel hawful," Joblot said, pressing his hand to his waistcoat. "Hullo, what does this gal want?"

Sam turned and beheld a poor ragged girl, bonnetless, and, like the youth in the nursery rhyme, with one shoe off and one shoe on, running towards them, and hailing them breathlessly.

"I don't know her," Sam said, casting a suspicious glance at his companion; "Who is she?"

"I'm as much in the dark as you," Joblot declared, turning pale, nevertheless. "She must be mad."

"Oh! if you please, gentlemen," gasped the girl, as she came up, "wich is Mr. Crummytome's house?"

"This is the wery identical," Sam said, standing on the doorstep. "Wot d'yer want to know for?"

"Oh! don't ask me," the girl replied, pushing the hair out of her eyes. "I must see somebody, or he'll be murdered, if he aint already."

"Murdered!" Sam echoed, turning faint, and sitting down. "Who? Look 'ere, none o' your nonsense. I lives here, and if you play any of your tricks with me it will be all the worse for you."

"I aint agoin' for to go and play no tricks," the girl exclaimed. "Was there a gentleman o' th' name o' Wilful living here?"

"There was and is," said Sam, with sudden interest. "Wot do you want with him?"

"He aint here now, I know," the girl said, shaking her head; "he's been trapped by a couple o' willains, and I know where he is."

Sam jumped up and seized the girl by the throat, and shook her until her teeth rattled in her head.

"Wot's that you're tellin me?" he cried furiously. "Speak out or I'll throttle yer."

"You're a doin of it now," the unhappy damsel gasped. "Oh, don't hurt me sir, I'll tell you everythink."

"Make haste about it," Sam hissed between his set teeth. "Don't waste no words."

"I'm Mrs. Scrubbem's servant," the girl said, as soon as she could fetch her breath, and then she poured into Sam's ears the story of how Grubbe and Styngy had plotted against Lionel. "I listened at the keyhole," she said, in conclusion, "and I heerd him with the short hair say to the tall greasy-lookin chap, 'Bring him to No. 9, Bolter's Rents, in the Chequers, and if he ever gets out I'll swing for a fool.'"

"Why didn't you come afore?" Sam roared, agitated, and with a strong desire to clutch the girl's throat again.

"Because my missus wouldn't let me hout," the girl replied. "I told her, but she said it was no business o' mine nor hers; she wanted her rent, and didn't care about nothink else, but I got out o' the back winder this mornin, for I couldn't rest, knowing that the young gentleman was in trouble."

"And if we save him," cried Sam, "you shall never scrub a third-pair back agin, and, as for fine dresses you shall waller in silks and satings. Joblot, ring that 'ere bell, and if that don't wake him bust in the door, for hevery moment is of wital importance. This is Grubbe's work."

Tingle, tingle, ting, went the bell, and then Sam put the knocker to work in such a manner that every housemaid and milkman in the square came rushing up, and demanded what was the matter.

But the most anxious inquirer of all was Mr. Kramatome, who thrust his head out of the window, and roared like ten.

"Is Mr. Lionel in?" Sam cried, almost beside himself.

"No, you scoundrel!" Mr. Kramatome replied, ungraciously; "he went out yesterday with his old schoolmaster, and has not returned."

"Then come down, in God's name!" Sam said, sobbing. "P'raps he's being murdered this wery moment. Don't stand there staring like that, for it's true every word."

Mr. Kramatome banged down the window, struggled into his dressing gown, and came downstairs.

The hurry, confusion, and babel of voices that ensued as he opened the door, enabled Joblot to slip past his master unperceived, and for the present he was safe.

Every bell in the house was set ringing; and Lord Vansittart and Charlie Drummond were soon on the spot.

Almost in less time than it takes to tell it Sam, backed up by Lionel's friends, Mr. Kramatome, and a posse of police, pressed into the service from the nearest station, were on their way to the Chequers.

Sam was for running all the way, for every moment seemed an age to him, but the sergeant of the police would not hear of such a proceeding, and on reaching Bolter's Rents placed his men at different points, and, bidding Lionel's friends stand back, approached the door of No. 9 alone.

"Oh Lor'! why couldn't we make a rush, and get it over?" Sam groaned to Lord Vansittart. "That willain, Grubbe, will kill Mister Lionel the moment he sees the perlice, if he aint done it already."

"We must be ruled by those who are in the habit of handling such cases," Vansittart said, in a trembling voice. "Let us hope for the best, Sam. God grant that Lionel may be delivered to us safe and well."

"Amen," said Sam, Mr. Kramatome, and Charlie Drummond in a fervent chorus.

"Hush!" Charlie said, clutching at an iron rail, "there is the inspector's knock, and I can hear the bolts grating in their sockets."

The words had scarcely left his lips when there was the sound of scuffling, a call from a whistle rang out, and, in an instant, all was uproar.

Policemen hurried along in answer to the summons, truncheons rose in the air, a knife flashed, the sickening thud of human bodies falling followed, and then Grubbe, the Reverend Mr. Styngy, and their accomplice, Bill Belcher, lay securely handcuffed, huddled up, and cursing deeply, on the floor.

"Well caught," said the inspector, smiling, as he turned his face to the crowd at his back. "Now," stirring Grubbe up with his foot, "where is the gentleman?"

"Find him yourself," Grubbe howled, "and may all the curses——"

"Come, come," said the matter-of-fact inspector, "this sort of thing will do no good. If you won't tell me where he is, why, of course, we must find; but it will save trouble, you know—so out with it."

"My friend," said the Rev. Mr. Styngy, turning meekly to his companion in misfortune, "a kind answer turneth away wrath. I will tell him."

"I should like to have the pleasure of cutting your throat," Grubbe said, displaying every fang-like tooth in his head.

"Oh, this is not kind—this is not good. Mr. Policeman, you will find a spring in the wall behind that table—touch it, and behold, it will revolve, and in the cellar you will find our young friend. Ah, I always loved Wilful."

The inspector was not long in following Mr. Styngy's advice, and as the flooring gave way a well-known voice called faintly for help.

"Oh, Mister Lionel," Sam sobbed, as he flung himself down at his young master's side, "I will never leave you agin. Oh, what is this? There is blood on your clothes."

"It is nothing," Lionel said, smiling, as he pressed the faithful hand—"a flesh wound only. Ah, Vansittart and Charlie, I thought I should never see you again. To whom am I indebted for this timely rescue?"

"A gal," Sam said. "She's a waiting on Mr. Kramatome's doorstep now."

Lionel naturally demanded an explanation, which was given, and then kind and gentle hands bore him out of the horrible den to light and freedom.

A four-wheeled cab was procured for him and his friends, but Sam lingered.

"I must have a word to say to them gents," Sam said; "it will be a farewell wisit."

"Come away," Lionel said; "they will be dealt

with, and never trouble us again. I forbid you to return."

"Well, Sam muttered, as he mounted the box, a little dissatisfied, but overwhelmed with joy, "I never did see a hangel, but if there aint one in this 'ere cab I wish I may never be one—that's all. Drive on, cabby, and gently over the stones."

A few minutes later the prisoners were marched out, howled at, and stoned, even by the denizens of Bolter's Rents. Men, women, and children ran to catch a glimpse of their villainous features, and all day long an excited crowd begged to be allowed to see the trap so aptly laid for Lionel, and into which his foes had themselves fallen.

CHAPTER XXXI.

LONG JEM DISAPPEARS—TOMMY HAS A ROW WITH HIS MASTER—DRUMSTICK DISCIPLINE—A NIGHT IN THE WOODS—SOMETHING NICE FOR SUPPER— THE MYSTERIOUS FIGURE.

THREE days after the foregoing events Lionel had sufficiently recovered to undertake the journey in search of Tommy Codlings, and having lost sight of that young gentleman ourselves for some little period it is high time that we brought him before our readers again.

"I don't think the life of an acrobat will suit me," Tommy said a little dolefully, as he sat down on the big drum outside Mr. Pippindale's show. "I'm much too fat to do anything worth talking about with my legs and arms. Ah me, what a world this is!"

"It aint the world," said Mr. Pippindale, taking an extremely black short pipe from his mouth, "it's the people as is in it. I wonder who first thought of grumblin, which, I must say, is a little in your line."

"And wouldn't you grumble?" Tommy exclaimed. "I have as many bruises as there are spots on a leopard's skin."

"They are nateral to beginners," Mr. Pippindale returned with refreshing coolness. "When I fust took to the line I was more orfen on my head than on my feet, and the parformance was invoiluntary; but don't you despair, sir, you'll get on by-an-bye."

"The worst of it is I am always gettin off," Tommy growled; "but never mind, it is my own fault. I wonder what has become of Long Jem?"

"He wanished most mysteriously," Mr. Pippindale said, blowing away a cloud of smoke, "and never so much as said adoo to me."

"I can't make it out," Tommy said, rumpling his hair. "He is a peculiar character."

"He's one of a million, is Long Jem," said the showman admiringly, "and he knows wot's o'clock. It's my opinion that he's gone back to Bellers-to-Mend."

"There will be a precious row in that quarter," Tommy said, smiling, but becoming as suddenly grave. "Bellers-to-Mend may tell where I am, and let the cat out of the bag."

"What if he do?" Mr. Pippindale exclaimed, in utter defiance of all rules of courtesy. "You are old enough to know your own mind. It is my belief that if your friends get hold of you agin that they will shut you up in a 'sylum."

"I know old Kramatome would if he had his will," Tommy replied; "but Lionel was always such a good friend to me that I can hardly bring myself to believe that he would do any harm. Truly he drove me nearly out of my mind with his tricks."

"Of course he did," said Mr. Pippindale, winking mysteriously at his pupil; "and don't you think he had some hidden motive for so doing? Of course he don't know that you must come into a pile o' money one o' these days. Oh, no!"

"I don't want to quarrel with you," Tommy said, turning fiercely on the showman, "but if you ever attribute any mercenary motive to his conduct you and I will part company."

"The sooner the better," said Mr. Pippindale.

"What!" Tommy almost shrieked.

"The sooner the better," Mr. Pippindale repeated. "Get orf my drum."

"You are a scoundrel!" Tommy gasped.

"And you are a fat and good-for-nothing lubber," Mr. Pippindale repeated. "The money as I had of you won't pay for the grub you have devoured."

"I have been robbed!" Tommy yelled. "You are an ungrateful hound; but, mark me, you will rue this!"

"Get orf my drum," said the showman, grinning in the most exasperating manner, "or you'll bust it, and I don't want that to happen, for you can't pay for a new one."

"I will give you in charge for swindling me,' Tommy fumed; "you have cheated me out of twenty pounds, and now want to turn me adrift."

"Now, look 'ere," said Mr. Pippindale, rising and confronting his victim, "you talk of giving me in charge; you daren't do it."

"Why not?"

"Because it would bring your name afore the public," the showman replied. "Now, s'pose I hands you over to the perlice as a runaway loonatic, s'pose I haven't touched a farden o' your money, but am only taken care of it, because you can't take care of it yourself, what then?"

"I don't believe a word of it," Tommy said. "When I came to you, you hadn't a sixpence in the world to help yourself with. Long Jem told me so."

"Long Jem always was a liar," the showman said. "Now then, will you git orf my drum, or will you not?"

Tommy did get off, and, what is more, he picked up the drumstick and bestowed upon Mr. Pippindale's nose such a whack that it might have been heard a quarter of a mile off.

"You cold-hearted scoundrel," said Tommy, dancing round the showman; "you swindler of innocent lads. I'll precious soon teach you that, if I am fat and a little awkward, I am a match for you. Take that, and that, and that."

"Oh, lor'," Pippindale roared, "help, help, murder!"

"And now I am going," Tommy said, throwing down the drumstick; "I have only two pounds left, but I don't despair. I shall live to see you beg for your bread. I will find Long Jem, and he will make you smart. I will tell every man on the road of your conduct, and they will discard you as unworthy of the name of a stroller."

"Do your wust," Pippindale said, speaking with difficulty, for he was holding his injured nose. "I can make my case good, you fat, good-for-nothing hemblem of loonacy."

Tommy picked up the drumstick again, and flinging it at the head of the showman turned and walked away with as much dignity as the rotundity of his frame would allow.

He was very hot, and sat down under a tree to cool himself.

"I suppose this will be the last of all my ups and downs," he said. "What little money I have left will go fast enough, and then I shall be left to live, or rather starve on berries and roots. I wonder if the ravens will cover me up?"

Tommy sat for a long time ruminating, but he could hit on nothing definite.

"I might do well with a shooting gallery if I had sufficient money to buy one," he said. "I must do something. Coloured rock would melt in the sun this weather, and brown cakes are out of fashion, but I can't starve. Hang it, what shall I do?"

"Go back, go back, go back," exclaimed a voice in such tones, that Tommy started to his feet.

"Why. it's only a jackdaw in a cage after all," he said, smiling at his alarm. "Now, supposing that this should be a favourable omen. Ah, no, I must go on as I have begun. Confound it, that little row with Pippindale has made me quite hungry."

The village was close at hand, and Tommy walked through it, with a view of making a few necessary purchases wherewith to allay his increasing hunger.

"I won't be cast down," he muttered, "if I can get a piece of meat and a few vegetables, and borrow a boiler or something of the sort I'll spend a jolly night in the wood. A fig for to-morrow."

Tommy procured what he wanted, and set off in high glee to a secluded spot where there were no prying eyes to criticise his cooking.

"Now this would be jolly indeed," Tommy said, gathering some dry sticks for the fire, "if I had one or two jolly companions. This reminds me of playing the gipsy when I was a youngster. Hallo! what was that? I thought I heard something move in the bushes."

He turned, but could see nothing. It was getting dark, and the shadows cast by the flickering fire only added to the gloom.

"There is nothing like the country after all," Tommy muttered, throwing himself down on his back. "Fancy being in London on a hot sweltering day like this, nothing but bricks and mortar heated by the sun pouring down through an atmosphere as thick as peas-pudding. Confound it, there is that noise again! I suppose it is some old hare grubbing about."

Tommy got up to see how the good things in the cauldron were getting on, and simultaneously a long dark figure crept from a clump of bushes, and glided along the ground as silently and swiftly as a serpent.

It was the figure of a man, and by his side he trailed a long rope, and nearer and nearer he crept up to Tommy, who, all unconscious, stirred the cauldron, and smacked his lips as a savoury puff emanated therefrom.

Then from behind the bushes arose three heads, and Sam Scarecrow, for he it was, gathered up the rope with one arm, and tripped Tommy Codlings up with the other.

"Ah!" Tommy muttered, smacking his lips rapturously, "don't it smell jolly? Oh! won't I have a splendid supper? Hullo! why what——"

The rope was round him, and the fat youth was struggling in Sam Scarecrow's long and powerful arms.

"Mister Thomas," Sam gasped, as the heel of Tommy's boot barked his shin, "if you try that game on I shall have to trip you up, and sit on yer."

"Then let me go," Tommy cried furiously. "Do you hear? I'm dangerous. Leave hold of my arms, or I'll bite!"

"Tommy," said Lionel, stepping forward, "don't make an ass of yourself. We have had no end of trouble to find you, and, having done so, we mean to keep you. Come, give me your hand, and look up as you used to do."

"Look!" Tommy echoed. "I have suffered enough to make me look like an old man of ninety. I wonder my hair isn't grey. Don't think I'm going back to old Kramatome's; I'd rather jump into the river."

"Well, we will talk about that presently," Lionel replied. "Sam, turn Mr. Codlings round, and let him see who is here."

Tears started into poor Tommy's eyes as he recognised the familiar features of Lord Vansittart and Charlie Drummond.

"It does my heart good to see you," he said, stretching out his hands, and smiling; "and, Lionel, you know how I always loved and respected you; but I know this will end badly."

"It will, indeed, Tommy," Lionel replied, "if you persist in your obstinate conduct. We had some fun out of you over the dream trick, but we had no idea that you would take it so much to heart."

"Well, now I come to think of it, I must have been a fool," Tommy said. "Here, Sam, take off this rope. I give you my word of honour that I will not run away."

"Am I to do it?" Sam demanded, looking dubiously at his master.

"Certainly," Lionel replied, and in an instant Tommy was free.

"Now," said Lionel, "we will be your guests. What a cook you are—quite a chef, I declare!"

A happier party never sat down to a midnight picnic, and during the meal explanations were exchanged so much to Tommy's satisfaction that his fat face beamed with delight.

Then, in his turn, he narrated how he had been robbed by the treacherous Pippindale; and Lionel's face flushed with indignation.

"The heartless scoundrel!" said our hero. "We must find means to settle with him for this. Now, then, let us knock our heads together, and see what can be done."

"He has no money, for he gets drunk with every farthing he takes; but there is the show and a few other properties, all of which were bought with my money."

"Beggin' your pardon, sir," Sam said, "that 'ere show can be bust hup if you'll only say the word. I feel as if I should like to have a few words with the willain."

"You shall have your wish, Sam," Lionel said, rising. "Tommy will point out the show."

"And the exact place where he is snoring by this time like a grampus," Tommy said. "Come on; and don't forget the rope, Sam, as it may come in useful."

As Tommy had predicted, Mr. Pippindale was sleeping off the effects of some five-and-twenty glasses of hot gin and water; but his slumbers were far from easy.

Nightmare—the child of heavy suppers and excessive drinking—squatted on his chest, and Mr. Pippindale groaned and kicked in a spasmodic manner.

"My heye, aint he a goin' it!" Sam chuckled, stooping down, and feeling about the booth. "I can feel the top of his 'ed, sir. Shall I give him a buster?"

"You may give him a tap sufficiently hard to wake him," Lionel replied.

"Werry good, sir," Sam returned, making a running noose in the rope. "Naterally the warmint will come out, and then I'll lasso him."

All unconscious of his impending fate Mr. Pippindale slept on. He was dreaming that Tommy, three times his ordinary size, had returned, and was throttling him, when the figure disappeared, and a shower of sparks rained down before his eyes, and huge flashes of jagged light lit up the booth.

"Wot was it?" gasped the showman, sitting bolt upright, and feeling the top of his cranium. "Were it a thunderbolt or were it wolcanic disruption? Oh, cuss it, there's another in the small of my back."

As Mr. Pippindale invariably went to bed in his clothes the trouble of dressing was saved, and he staggered out into the open air, expecting to see some extraordinary phenomenon.

Something extraordinary did take place. A handkerchief was clapped over his eyes, a rope was bound tightly round his arms, and, before he knew exactly what had happened, he was thrust with a mighty crash head first into the big drum.

Then followed the sound of things being ruthlessly kicked about, the rending and tearing of canvas, and all was still.

Some gipsies found him in the morning just as the avengers had left him—a sorry sight, and the show a perfect wreck.

CHAPTER XXXII.

THE TRIAL—MR. STYNGY APPEALS FOR MERCY—
SAM IN THE WITNESS-BOX—THE SENTENCE—A
SCENE IN COURT.

COMMOTION and confusion reigned at the Old Bailey. Lawyers and their clerks bustled in and out of the court with piles of books and bags full of briefs and documentary evidence. Barristers lounged about, chatting carelessly, and within a few yards five-and-forty prisoners awaited an earthly tribunal.

The judge arrived and took his seat; then all was silence.

A rattling of keys, the creaking of a heavy door, and the prisoners were brought up in batches.

There was the murderer, with the sullen dogged look in his eyes; the burglar who cracked the jeweller's shop so neatly, knowing full well that he would crack nothing but granite for years to come; there was the haggard woman, pale and shrinking, standing there with the blood of her child, born of sin and misery, upon her hands; there was the gaunt lad with the cunning face and leering mouth, nodding jauntily to some brother thief in the gallery; and last, but not least, two men were put into the dock, charged with conspiring to take the life of one Lionel Wilful.

Both knew that nothing short of a miracle could save them from ending their days in a convict prison, but Grubbe was defiant, and laughed hoarsely as the clerk of arraigns called on him to plead.

"I will plead not guilty," he said, "not because I know that I have any chance of escape, but I may as well see the whelp once more."

"How say you, Philo Styngy, are you guilty or not guilty?" demanded the clerk.

"My lord and gentlemen of the jury," said Mr. Styngy, with a cringing bow, "it is not for me to stand here in defiance of the mass of evidence that will be brought against my unfortunate self, but —"

"You must plead one way or the other," said the clerk. "Are you guilty or not guilty?"

Mr. Styngy looked down on the floor, up at the ceiling, cast a hurried glance at the anxious spectators, and then, as great scalding tears rushed from his eyes, he stretched out his hands, and made a frantic appeal for mercy.

"I swear I had no thought of shedding blood," he exclaimed. "Why should I bear malice against the lad? He was my pupil once, and I loved him with the affection of a father."

"I will hear anything you may have to say in extenuation," the judge said, "but you must plead, or the trial must proceed in the ordinary course."

"Then I plead guilty to conspiring to extort money, but as to the charge of attempted murder I emphatically declare that I am innocent."

The counsel for the prosecution here rose, and opened the case in the stereotyped style.

Placing the facts before the jury he commented on the enormity of the crime with which the prisoners were charged, and, having settled it to everybody's satisfaction that they deserved the greatest punishment short of hanging, he struck the table a blow with his brief, and called Sam Scarecrow.

Sam stepped into the witness-box, and having squinted most hideously at every body, folded his arms, and proceeded to answer the questions put to him.

"You are, I believe," said the counsel for the prosecution, "servant to Mr. Lionel Wilful."

"Wich I am," Sam replied, "and I'd like to say a few words about that young gentleman as is——"

"You must confine yourself to answering the questions," the judge interrupted.

"Wery good, my lord," Sam replied, "but my blood biles when I think wot that young gentleman have put hup with from that ere willain in the dock!"

"Your indignation is perfectly just," said the counsel with a glance at the jury; "but, as his lordship observes, it is out of place here. Do you remember the night of the fourteenth of April?"

"I shall never forget it," Sam replied.

"What took place then?"

"We was in Kensington-gardens, a lookin' for Mister Thomas Codlings, as runned away in consequence of too many dreams."

"Too many what?" demanded the judge, dipping his pen in the ink.

"Mister Codlings had sich a pile o' dreams, my lord," Sam replied, "that he never knowed when he was awake. In fac', he orften believed hisself to be somebody else."

"I never heard of such an extraordinary case," said the judge, pushing up his spectacles. "Witness, you may proceed."

"I was lookin' for Mister Codlings," Sam went on, "when I pitches over somethin', and the next hinstant I hears a growl. I gets up and strikes a light, and then I sees Grubbe."

"The prisoner on your right," suggested the counsel.

"That's him, the willain!" Sam replied. "Well, my lord, and gentlemen all, I were that taken back that I dropped the light, and then Grubbe rushes on me, and gets me down."

"What followed then?"

"He drawed a knife," Sam said, amid an impressive silence, "and said as how he meant to murder me, but Mr. Wilful come hup at that wery moment, and I was saved from an airly grave."

"And you have no doubt of the identity of your assailant?"

"Doubt about his wot?" Sam demanded.

"You are satisfied that the prisoner Grubbe was the man," said the counsel, hiding a smile behind his hand.

"Now is that likely?" Sam urged. "Jest as if I couldn't pick him out of a million. I hown that my eyes ain't all as could be wished, but they never deceived me yet, and never will."

"Answer the question in a straightforward manner!" thundered the judge. "Was Grubbe the man who attacked you, or was he not?"

"I'm on my hoath," said Sam, "and he were."

"That is all I have to ask you, Mr. Scarecrow," the counsel said, taking his seat.

"Have you any questions to ask the prisoner?" said the clerk of arraigns, rising and addressing Grubbe.

"None," was the sullen reply. "I only regret that I was fool enough not to settle him when I had the chance."

A murmur of indignation ran round the court; the ushers made a din by roaring for silence, and Sam vanished.

Lionel was called next, and as each fact of the prisoners' villany was brought to light the excitement became intense, and the officials had all their work to do to maintain order.

At last the case was over, the jury found both prisoners guilty on all counts, and the usual question was put to them demanding why the sentence of the law should not be passed upon them, when Grubbe, turning to the Reverend Philo Styngy, and extending his hand, said—

"I don't suppose we shall ever have the chance of speaking to each other again, but what is the use of snivelling? You were as deep in the mud as I was in the mire, but if you think I have wronged you I am sorry. Give me your hand, man."

A warder interposed his burly form between the prisoners, muttering that it couldn't be done, as it was against the rules.

"My lord," Grubbe said, turning to the judge, "I have nothing to say; but you will, I'm sure, grant me this last favour. It is the only one I shall ever have the power of asking. This man and I have been friends for years. You will let me grasp his hand for the last time."

"I have no objection to that," the judge replied. "Stand aside, warder."

The man did as bidden, and Grubbe instantly threw himself upon Mr. Styngy, and bore him to the ground with a crash that shook the court-house to its foundations.

"You white-livered hound," Grubbe hissed, clutching Mr. Styngy's throat in a vice-like grip, "you hypocritical whining dog, I have longed to hold you like this. Ah, the strength of twenty men cannot save you. They will send me to drudge out my life? No, they shall hang me like a dog, and you shall be the cause."

Four powerful warders flung themselves upon the desperate man, and with their united strength strove to tear him away. Grubbe clung to his victim, who, with lolling tongue and eyes starting from his head, shrieked for help and mercy, until the walls echoed with his hideous cries.

CHAPTER XXXII.

DR. ERASMUS TEUFELSHOF.

A RAPID stir and rustle of garments, a tumultuous murmur of voices, replaced the silence which had hitherto marked the deep interest of the spectators; but simultaneously several warders, who had been looking for something of this kind, flung themselves upon the prostrate forms of the prisoners.

They were not surprised at Grubbe's act of violence, but they were at the quiet way in which he allowed himself to be dragged apart from Styngy. One of them turned him over on his back, and then the set frown on his face changed to a look of alarm as he whispered hurriedly to his mate—

"Pass the word for the doctor, George. "He's broke a vessel."

Grubbe's features were of a deadly leaden hue. His lower jaw had dropped, and from one corner of his mouth a thin red stream was trickling.

"This one's the same," replied the second warder, as he raised the Rev. Philo Styngy. "They've cheated the judge, Bill, after all."

The intelligence was quietly passed up to the bench, the motionless forms were carried into the robing-room, and laid on a table gently and reverently, for the dread hand of death invests the meanest beggar or the greatest criminal with a majesty which all must feel.

There happened to be some half dozen doctors present who were to give evidence as to the sanity of a gentleman recently deceased, whose will was not exactly according to the ideas of his relatives, and who, therefore, dutifully desired to have the defunct testator proved mad, and the will set aside.

The doctors were all great men, who glorified the regions of Savile-row, Cavendish-square, and Harley-street, and whose profession had so permeated their very apparel that the creak of their boots or the sheen of their spotless shirt fronts would convey relief and comfort to a patient.

Their opinions were soon given. They were unanimous upon the first point—viz., that both Grubbe and Styngy were dead. Upon the second—viz., the cause of death—they were also agreed, mirabile dictu! and it was comfortably settled that the Rev. Philo Styngy had died from the rupture of a blood-vessel in the brain, and that Grubbe perished from failure of the heart's action, induced by great excitement.

The authorities were a little puzzled at first. It was rather an out-of-the-way case to deal with. The prisoners had been found guilty, but sentence had not been passed, and, according to the strict letter of the law, they were not convicts.

An inquest was held at once, as the coroner happened to be sitting, and that official being anxious to spare the pockets of the ratepayers—except, of course, where his own fees were concerned—did not think it necessary to order a post-mortem examination.

There was no mystery about the case; so he and the jury were satisfied with very little evidence Then came the question of burial.

A warm dispute would, no doubt, have taken place between the gaol officials and the parish officers as to who should *not* have this trouble and expense—for it costs something to inter even a pauper criminal—had not a little, high-shouldered, long-haired man stepped forth, and made a request to the coroner.

He was shabby and dirty, but his English was only tinged with a very slight German accent.

He gave his name as Erasmus Teufelshof, doctor in medicine of the University of Gottingen. He had known the deceased men when they and he were studying in Germany, and out of respect for the memory of those old days he would stretch his slender means, and give them something better than a pauper's funeral if the hochwohlgeboren coroner would allow him.

The coroner replied, in effect, that his sentiments did him credit, and, if he could satisfy the officials of his respectability, and if there was nothing in the existing law which forbade it, he would be permitted to do as he pleased.

His references were quite satisfactory—that is, he gave the coroner's officer a sovereign, and as there was no particular statute against such a contingency, the bodies of Grubbe and Styngy were handed over to him, and there was an end to them as far as the law was concerned.

Dr. Erasmus Teufelshof was ready for them in his little ramshackle cottage, situated at the bottom of a lane midway between Anerly and South Norwood, and in which he lived with a housekeeper, older, dirtier, and shabbier than himself.

At the rear of the German doctor's cottage was an outhouse, lit from the top by a large skylight, and entered through a door singularly massive, and well protected by bars and bolts for such a place, and into this the shells containing the bodies were carried.

Its furniture was simple but peculiar. In the centre was a long low table, covered with zinc, and with a narrow gutter running round the upper edges.

A strong deep shelf was fitted to the wall, and on it was an endless variety of chemical and surgical apparatus, notably, a powerful Smee battery and a Rhumkorff coil.

At that end of the shed farthest from the door was a copper with a furnace beneath, and attached to the copper by a pipe was a coffin-shaped stone trough of very large capacity.

Dr. Teufelshof's proceedings when he found himself alone with the bodies were not altogether such as one might have expected from a man who, at considerable trouble and expense to himself, procured all that was mortal of two dear friends, for the purpose of interring them in sacred soil.

He first removed the lids of the shells, and then by an exertion of strength which seemed supernatural in one so small and decrepid, lifted the bodies on to the table.

Then, with a pair of long keen scissors, he cut off every particle of clothing until they lay there gaunt and hideous, naked as the day they came into the world.

Then, with a rapid practised hand, Doctor Teufelshof felt the cold limbs, bending the joints, lifting the heavy heads, and letting them fall with a dull thud upon the metallic covering of the table.

"Himmel!" he ejaculated, with a chuckle of satisfaction, "I was right. The rigor mortis has not set in. I shall succeed. But to work—to work!"

With a noiseless dexterity and rapidity that was more like the operation of some well-oiled piece of machinery, the German began his mysterious task.

The lifeless bodies he first carefully washed with

warm water, in which he had dissolved a quantity of some white powder, and then with the scissors previously employed he cut away as close as possible all the hair from the back of the heads.

This done, and done so quickly that it seemed the work of a magician, he bound round the necks, wrists, and ankles of each a length of fine copper wire, thus locking them together in death more tightly than ever they had been in life.

Then the huge battery was taken from its place on the shelf, placed in position on the table, and its terminal wires carefully connected with the wires uniting the corpses.

That done the German doctor paused for the first time and looked musingly at the ghastly objects stretched before him.

"Ach!" he ejaculated, "if I had only those great English doctors here now how could I make their wise heads to wag when I told them what I have it in my mind to do! Verdammte schwein-koppen! they laugh at me because I am little and shabby, and smell of snuff. They have said that these men are dead, they have sworn it in their court of justice. The law has struck them off its record—they exist no longer. They are mine then. Behold how Erasmus Teufelshof gives both law and doctors the lie!"

And with a touch of his hand the German doctor completed the circuit, and sent the turning point of electricity tingling through the dull nerves and stagnant blood of the corpses.

CHAPTER XXXIII.

CONCLUSION.

A MOMENT'S suspense and eager watching and then Erasmus Teufelshof threw up his arms, and uttered a wild cry of delight.

"Mein Gott!" he shrieked, dancing round the table like a madman. "They live, and to me, the poor, despised little doctor, will be given the credit of the greatest discovery of the age. Ha! See, their limbs quiver—their eyes open. They live—they live! Ha, ha, ha!"

* * * * * *

Sam Scarecrow sat swinging his legs on a stile, guarding a pleasant footpath across a field of golden wheat.

It was a beautiful balmy day late in summer, a haze lingered over the distant hills, a river like a truant silver thread twined its way through town, hamlet, and village, laughing joyously as it hurried on to the ocean.

Sam had no eyes for the lovely scene stretched out before him, his resplendent orbs being concentrated on a pair of hazel-brown eyes, belonging to a very neat and pretty girl, whose coquettish little head was adorned with a most aggravating straw hat bound with blue ribbons.

Sam's arm was round this young lady's taper waist, and he sighed dismally as she laughed at something he whispered in her ear.

"Don't larf at me, Mary," said the long youth, as his face suddenly fell. "It cuts me to the 'art."

"I can't help it," the blushing little beauty replied. "You are so funny. Now, Sam, don't be ridiculous."

"Aint I to have a kiss?" Sam groaned. "Just one—only one."

"Not one," said Mary, releasing herself from the ardent youth's embrace, and skipping lightly down from the stile. "What do you think Mr. Wilful would say?"

"Why," Sam replied, "he would say that I made a very good chice. I'll tell you wot, Mary, we'll go to him and ax him when it will be convenient for us to get married."

"Oh, indeed!" said Mary. "You forget that I have not yet given my consent."

"Wot!" Sam yelled, narrowly escaping breaking his neck by falling backwards over the stile. "Didn't you say——"

"Oh, I say a great many things that I don't mean," Mary interrupted.

"But didn't you promise me—come now?" Sam gasped.

"Promises like pie crusts are made to be broken."

Sam opened his eyes very wide, and then shut them so close that it was a wonder he ever got them open again.

Drawing a large cotton handkerchief from his pocket he waved it frantically in the air, and then covering his face with it wept so copiously and with such gusto that the crows within an area of half a mile made themselves scarce.

"Alas!" roared Sam, "it were ever thus. Mary, fare thee well, you will never see me agin. I knows where there is a deep water-butt, and I can't swim."

"What nonsense!" Mary said, shaking her dress like a petulant child. "I am sure there are hundreds of better-looking gals than I am who would be glad of you, Sam."

"There aint," bellowed the lanky one. "I never could get a sweetheart afore—dash it, I don't mean that. I mean I could never get one I could like 'arf so well as you. Oh, my poor 'art, it's bustin'."

"I am very sorry to see you take on like this," Mary returned, pouting, while something suspiciously like a couple of tears stood in her bright eyes. "I am afraid that I shouldn't make you a good wife."

"'Ow do you know till you try?" Sam roared. "Only say yes, and you will make me the happiest man alive; reject me, and never more shall this poor 'art suffer. I means it, Mary—I does indeed."

Mary was drawing closer to him by imperceptible degrees.

"I'm sure I would make you happy if I could," she said, applying her apron to her eyes, "but I am not worthy of you, you who are so good and noble."

"I aint 'arf so nobble as you," Sam said, looking out from behind the handkerchief. "Which way is it to be, Mary—heverlasting ji or despair?"

There is a language of the eyes more speaking than that performed by the lips, and Sam with a bound and a skip caught Mary once more round the waist, and imprinted a sounding kiss on her lips.

As they walked along, now so cosy and happy, their faces were turned towards Heath-house.

The windows, framed with honeysuckle and jessamine, were wide open, to admit the glorious sunlight and pure air that make the heart leap with gladness and quicken the pulse.

A strain of music suddenly burst on the air, and Sam and Mary stopped to listen for a moment to that plaintive, beautiful, and heart-stirring strain of "Home, Sweet Home."

Mrs. Wilful was at the piano, and Lionel stood leaning lovingly over her shoulder.

There were other figures in the prettily-furnished room. Charlie Drummond, Lord Vansittart, and our old friend, Tommy Codlings, a trifle fatter than of yore, and, if possible, a little more rosy.

The last chords struck, and Mrs. Wilful rose from the piano, and, smoothing her beloved boy's hair with her fair hands, said—

"Lionel, we must never part again."

"Never, if we can help it, mother," Lionel replied; "but it is not for us to foretell the future. We can only hope for the best; and God grant we may all live in peace, happiness, and contentment!"

"Amen!" said Lord Vansittart fervently; and Charlie's eyes glistened as he looked at the happy pair.

Tommy did not say anything, for the simple reason that he was asleep; but presently he awoke with a start, and murmured something about luncheon.

"You have another hour to fast yet, Tommy," Lionel said, laughing; "so make yourself as comfortable as you can in the meantime. Hullo! who are these coming up the garden? Sam Scarecrow and Mary, I declare!"

"Sam looks as if he has eaten something to disagree with him; and Mary is as red as a poppy," said Lord Vansittart. "I wonder what is the matter?"

"I think I can guess," Charlie Drummond replied. "Hush! They are coming this way."

The loving couple entered the house, and presently a servant appeared with a message to the effect that Sam desired to speak to Lionel at his earliest convenience.

"Send him up at once," said Lionel; and presently Sam made his appearance, rather weak about the knees, but with a fixed determination on his face.

"What is the matter, Sam?" Lionel demanded; and as the long youth rolled up his eyes, and rumpled his hair, Mrs. Wilful leant over her music.

"I have come, sir," Sam began—"that is, which I've orften wished to say; but—Oh, lor! dash it! I beg pardon, marm, and gentlemen all."

"Go on, Sam," said Lionel. "Take your own time. You don't look very well. Sit down."

"It ain't for the likes o' me to sit down in your presence," Sam said. "No, sir, I'd rather stand. And, if you please, sir, me and Mary have made up our minds."

"I'm all abroad at present," Lionel said, but really guessing the truth. "What have you made up your minds about?"

"Why, you see, sir," replied Sam, "I ses to Mary, and Mary ses to me, wich you will understand, sir, as you well know, and may probably be aware on, that, howsomdever, we was sort of sweethearts when Mary was at old Growlagain's; and so, arter a long time, and Mary now being in your service, and I, as will never leave you unless you kick me hout of

the house, have come to the conclusion to get married."

"Oh, indeed!" said Lionel. "Sam, I can speak for my mother as well as for myself. You are a good fellow, and, if Mary is willing, we have no objection to offer. Indeed, we have talked of the probability of your marrying Mary before."

Sam looked at his young master, then at his mistress; he strove to speak, but no sound came from his lips, and, with a bellow, he turned, and fairly ran out of the room.

"Stop—stop!" Lionel cried. "Sam, stop, or I shall be very angry with you. I want to speak to you."

"My 'art is so full, sir," Sam said, sitting down on the landing, "that, I believe, if I had stopped in that room another instant I should have busted right orf."

"I trust that such a calamity will never take place," Lionel said. "Tell Mary that her mistress wishes to see her alone in the drawing-room."

Happiness reigned at Heath House that day: reunions of friends are always pleasant, but what joy must have been felt by those who had passed through so much trouble, patient, hoping, never really fearing but that Providence in the end would bring about a most right and just triumph over sin and wickedness!

Fain would we linger, but the thread of our story has spun out; yet we cannot turn away without a few parting words.

We have been boys again with Lionel and his chums—we have rejoiced and sorrowed with our hero.

We have laughed at Sam Scarecrow's eccentricities, and at Tommy Codlings' scrapes, and in our heart of hearts we live again in the past, and clasp the shadowy hands of those characters whom we now leave.

END OF PART III.

www.ingramcontent.com/pod-product-compliance
Lightning Source LLC
Chambersburg PA
CBHW081157170626
46813CB00009B/3224